THE TIME OF
THE HUNTER'S MOON

by the same author

MISTRESS OF MELLYN
KIRKLAND REVELS
BRIDE OF PENDORRIC
THE LEGEND OF THE SEVENTH VIRGIN
MENFREYA
THE KING OF THE CASTLE
THE QUEEN'S CONFESSION
THE SHIVERING SANDS
THE SECRET WOMAN
THE SHADOW OF THE LYNX
ON THE NIGHT OF THE SEVENTH MOON
THE CURSE OF THE KINGS
THE HOUSE OF A THOUSAND LANTERNS
LORD OF THE FAR ISLAND
THE PRIDE OF THE PEACOCK
THE DEVIL ON HORSEBACK
MY ENEMY THE QUEEN
THE SPRING OF THE TIGER
THE MASK OF THE ENCHANTRESS
THE JUDAS KISS
THE DEMON LOVER

VICTORIA HOLT

*

The Time of the Hunter's Moon

BOOK CLUB ASSOCIATES LONDON

This edition published 1984 by
Book Club Associates
by arrangement with William Collins Sons & Co Ltd

Printed in Great Britain by
Richard Clay (The Chaucer Press) Ltd,
Bungay, Suffolk

CONTENTS

The Forest Fantasy	7
The Abbey	68
Marcia	108
A Summer Interlude	154
Rooks' Rest	168
The Ruby Earring	196
In the Devil's Den	226
Midsummer Moon	256
A Visitor in the Country	302
The Alarming Discovery	323
The Meeting in the Mountains	358
Revelation	376

The Forest Fantasy

---*---

I was nineteen when what I came to think of as the Forest Fantasy occurred. Looking back it used to seem mystic, like something which happened in a dream. Indeed there were many times when I almost convinced myself that it had not happened outside my imagination. Yet from an early age I had been a realist, a practical person, not given overmuch to dreaming; but at that time I was inexperienced, not really out of the schoolroom and only in the last stages of my prolonged girlhood.

It happened one late October afternoon in woods in Switzerland not far from the German border. I was in my last year at one of the most exclusive schools in Europe to which Aunt Patty had decided I must go to 'finish me off' as she put it.

'Two years should do it,' she said. 'It's not so much what it does for you, but what people believe it to have done. If parents know that one of us went through the polishing process at Schaffenbrucken they will be determined to send their girls to us.'

Aunt Patty was the proprietress of a school for girls, and the plan was that when I was ready I should join in the enterprise. Consequently I must have the very best of qualifications to fit me for the task and the additional polish was intended to make me irresistible bait for those parents who wanted their daughters to share in the reflected glow which came from that glory which was Schaffenbrucken.

'Snobbery,' said Aunt Patty. 'Sheer unadulterated snobbery. But who are we to complain if it helps to keep Patience Grant's exclusive Academy for Young Ladies a profitable concern?'

Aunt Patty was rather like a barrel to look at, being short

7

and very plump. 'I like my food,' she used to say, 'so why shouldn't I enjoy it. I believe it to be the bounden duty of everyone on Earth to enjoy the good things which the Lord has bestowed on us, and when roast beef and chocolate pudding were invented they were made to be eaten.'

The food was very good at Patience Grant's Academy for Young Ladies – very different I believed from that which was served in many similar establishments.

Aunt Patty was unmarried 'for the simple reason,' she would say, 'that nobody ever asked me. Whether I should have accepted is another matter but, as the problem never presented itself, neither I nor anyone else need be concerned with it.'

She enlarged on the subject to me. 'I was on the shelf from the nursery,' she said. 'I was the perennial wallflower of the ball. Mind you, I could climb a tree in those days before I was so incommoded by avoirdupois, and if any boy dared pull my pigtails he had to move fast to avoid battle, from which, my dear Cordelia, I invariably emerged the victor.'

I could believe it, and I often thought how stupid men were because none of them had had the good sense to ask Aunt Patty to marry him. She would have made an excellent wife; as it was she made me an excellent mother.

My parents were missionaries in Africa. They were dedicated – saints, they were called; but like so many saints they were so concerned with bringing good into the world at large that they did not seem to care so very much for the problems of their small daughter. I can only vaguely remember them – for I was just seven years old when I was sent home to England – looking at me sometimes, faces shining with zeal and virtue, as though they were not quite sure who I was. I wondered later how in their lives of good deeds they had ever found the time or inclination to beget me.

However – it must have been to their immense relief – it was decided that life in the African jungle was no place for a child. I should be sent home, and to whom should I be sent but to my father's sister Patience.

8

I was taken home by someone from the mission who was travelling back for a short stay. The long journey seems very vague to me but what I shall always remember was the rotund figure of Aunt Patty waiting for me when I disembarked. Her hat caught my attention first of all for it was a glorious affair with a blue feather perched on the top. Aunt Patty had a weakness for hats which almost rivalled that of food. Sometimes she even wore them indoors. And there she was – her eyes magnified behind pebble glasses, her face like a full moon shining with soap and water and *joie de vivre* under that magnificent hat with the feather wobbling as she took me to her enormous lavender-scented bosom.

'Well, here you are,' she said. 'Alan's girl . . . come home.'

And in those first moments she convinced me that I had.

It must have been about two years after my arrival when my father died of dysentery, and my mother a few weeks later of the same disease.

Aunt Patty showed me the paragraphs in the religious papers. 'They gave their lives in God's service,' it was said.

I am afraid I did not grieve very much. I had forgotten their existence and only remembered them very rarely. I was completely absorbed in the life of Grantley Manor, the old Elizabethan house which Aunt Patty had bought with what she called her patrimony two years before I was born.

We had great conversations – she and I. She never seemed to hold anything back. Afterwards I often reflected that most people seem to have secrets in their lives. It was never like that with Aunt Patty. Words flowed from her and there was never any restraint.

'When I was away at school,' she said, 'I had lots of fun but never enough to eat. They watered down the broth. Soup, they called it on Monday. That wasn't bad. A little weaker on Tuesday, getting so feeble on Wednesday that I used to wonder how much longer it could totter on before it was revealed as plain H_2O. The bread always seemed stale. I think that school made me into the gourmand I am for I vowed when I left it I would indulge and indulge. If I had a

9

school, I said to myself, it should be different. Then when I came into money I said, "Why not?" "It's a gamble," said old Lucas. He was the solicitor. "What of it?" I said. "I like a gamble." And the more he was against it the more I was for it. I am a little like that. Tell me "No, you can't" and as sure as I'm sitting here I'll soon be saying, "Oh yes you can." So I found the Manor . . . going cheap with things having to be done to it. Just the place for a school. I called it Grantley Manor. Grant, you see. A little bit of the old snobbery creeping in. Miss Grant of Grantley. Well, you would think she had been living there all through the centuries, wouldn't you? And you wouldn't ask; you'd just think it. Good for the girls that is. I planned to make Patience Grant's Academy into the most exclusive establishment in the country, like that place Schaffenbrucken in Switzerland.'

That was the first time I had heard of Schaffenbrucken.

She explained to me. 'It is all very carefully thought out. Schaffenbrucken selects its pupils with care so that it is not easy to get in. "I'm afraid we have no room for your Amelia, Madame Smith. Try again next term. Who knows you might be lucky. We are full up now and have a waiting list." A waiting list! That is the most magic phrase in the vocabulary of a school proprietress. It is what we all hope to achieve . . . people fighting to thrust their daughters into your school, not as the case usually is with your trying to wheedle them into doing so.'

'Schaffenbrucken is expensive,' she said on another occasion, 'but I think it is worth every penny. You can learn French and German from the people who speak it as it should be spoken because it's their own language; you can learn how to dance and curtsey and walk round a room with a book balanced on your head. Yes, you say. You can learn that at thousands of schools. True, but you won't be seen as you will be if you have the Schaffenbrucken glow on you.'

Her conversation was always punctuated by laughter.

'So it is a little Schaffenbrucken bloom for you, my dear,' she said. 'Then you will come back here and when we let it be known where you have been, mothers will be fighting to

10

send their daughters to us. "Miss Cordelia Grant is in charge of deportment. She was at Schaffenbrucken, you know." Oh, my dear, we shall be telling them we have a waiting list of young ladies clamouring to be coached in the social niceties by Miss Cordelia Grant of Schaffenbrucken fame.'

'One day,' she said, 'this school will be yours Cordelia.'

I knew she meant when she died and I could not imagine a world without her. She was the centre of my life with her shining face, her spurts of laughter, her racy conversation, her excessive appetite and her hats.

And when I was seventeen she said it was time I went to Schaffenbrucken.

*   *   *

Once again I was put in the charge of travellers – this time three ladies who were going to Switzerland. At Basle I should be met by someone from the school who would conduct me the rest of the way. The journey was interesting and I recalled the long voyage home from Africa. This was very different. I was older now; I knew where I was going; and I lacked that fearful apprehension of a very small girl on a journey to the unknown.

The ladies who conducted me across Europe were determined to look after me and it was with some relief, I imagined, that they handed me over to Fräulein Mainz who taught German at Schaffenbrucken. She was a middle-aged woman, rather colourless, who was glad to hear that I had learned a little German. She told me my accent was atrocious but that would be rectified; and she refused to speak anything but her native tongue for the rest of the journey.

She talked about the glories of Schaffenbrucken and how fortunate I was to be chosen to join this very select group of young ladies. It was the old Schaffenbrucken story and I thought Fräulein Mainz the most humourless person I had ever met. I suppose I was comparing her with Aunt Patty.

Schaffenbrucken itself was not impressive. The setting

11

was, though. We were a mile or so from the town and surrounded by woods and mountains. Madame de Guérin, French-Swiss, was a middle-aged lady of quiet authority with what I can only call a 'presence'. I could see how important she was to the Schaffenbrucken legend. She did not have a great deal to do with us girls. We were left to the care of the mistresses. There was dancing, drama, French, German, and what they called social awareness. We were meant to emerge from Schaffenbrucken fit to enter into the highest society.

I soon settled into the life and found the girls interesting. They were of various nationalities and naturally I became friendly with the English. Two girls shared a room and it was always arranged that nationalities should be mixed. I had a German girl for my first year and a French one for the second. It was a good idea, for it did help us to perfect our languages.

Discipline was not strict. We were not exactly children. Girls usually came between sixteen and seventeen and stayed until nineteen or twenty. We were not there to be fundamentally educated but each of us must be formed into a *femme comme il faut* as Madame de Guérin said. It was more important to dance well and converse gracefully than to have a knowledge of literature and mathematics. Most of the girls would go straight from Schaffenbrucken to their debut into society. There were one or two of them like myself who were destined for something different. Most of them were pleasant and looked upon their stay at Schaffenbrucken as an essential part of their upbringing – ephemeral but to be enjoyed as much as possible while it lasted.

Although life in the various classrooms was easy going there was a certain strict surveillance kept on us and I was sure that if any girl came near to being involved in a scandal she would be sent packing at once, for there would always be some ambitious parent eager to put a daughter into the vacant place.

I went home for Christmas and summer holidays, and Aunt Patty and I would have a hilarious time discussing Schaffenbrucken.

12

'*We* must do that,' Aunt Patty would say. 'I tell you that when you come home from Schaffenbrucken we'll have the finest finishing school in the country. We'll make Daisy Hetherington green with envy.'

That was the first time I heard Daisy Hetherington's name. I asked idly who she was and received the information that she had a school in Devonshire which was almost as good as Daisy thought it was, and that was saying a good deal.

I wished I'd asked more later. But naturally then it did not occur to me that it might be important.

I came to what was to be my last term at Schaffenbrucken. It was late October – wonderful weather for the time of year. We got a lot of sun at Schaffenbrucken and that made the summer seem to last a long time. It would be so hot in the day and suddenly, as soon as the sun disappeared, one would realize what time of year it was. Then we would huddle round the common-room fire and talk.

My best friends at that time were Monique Delorme, who shared my room, and an English girl Lydia Markham and her room-mate Frieda Schmidt. The four of us were always together. We talked constantly and used to make excursions into the town together. Sometimes we would walk and if the wagonette was going into town, a few of us would go in that. We took walks in the woods, which was allowed in parties of six – or at least four. There was a certain amount of freedom and we did not feel in the least restricted.

Lydia said that being at Schaffenbrucken was like being in a railway station waiting for the train that would carry you to a place where you would be a properly grown-up person. I knew what she meant. This was merely a stopping place in our lives – a stepping stone to some other place.

We talked about ourselves. Monique was the daughter of a noble house and would be whisked almost immediately into a suitable marriage. Frieda's father had made his fortune out of pottery and was a businessman of many interests: Lydia belonged to a banking family. I was a little

13

older and as I should be leaving at Christmas felt very much the senior.

We noticed Elsa almost as soon as she joined the establishment. She was a small pretty girl with fair curly hair and blue eyes; she was vivacious and had a certain elfin look. She was unlike any of the other servants and she was engaged on short notice because one of the maids had eloped with a man from the town and Madame de Guérin must have thought she would give Elsa a trial until the end of the term.

I was sure that if Madame de Guérin had really known Elsa she would not have allowed her to stay even until the end of the term. She was not at all respectful and did not seem to be in the least in awe of Schaffenbrucken or anyone in it. She had an air of camaraderie which implied that she was one of us. Some of the girls resented it: my own intimate quartette was rather amused by it; perhaps that was why she was always turning up in our rooms.

She would come in sometimes when the four of us were together and somehow sidle herself into the conversation.

She liked to hear about our homes and asked a good many questions. 'Oh, I'd like to go to England,' she said. 'Or France . . . or Germany . . .' She would lure us to talk and she looked so pleased to hear about our backgrounds that we couldn't help going along with her.

She herself had come down in the world, she said. She was not really a serving maid. Oh no! She had thought she was set for a comfortable future. Her father had been, well . . . not exactly rich, but not wanting anything. She was to have been launched into society. 'Not like you young ladies, of course, but in a more modest way. Then my father died. Hey Presto!' She waved her arms and raised her eyes to the ceiling. 'That was the end of little Elsa's glory. No money. Elsa on her own. There was nothing for me to do but work. And what could I do? What had I been trained for?'

'Not as a housemaid,' said Monique with good French logic.

At which we all laughed, including Elsa.

14

We couldn't help liking her and we used to encourage her to come and talk to us. She was amusing and very knowledgeable about the legends of the German forests where she said she had spent her early childhood before her father brought her to England, where she had lived for a while before coming to Switzerland.

'I like to think of all those trolls hiding underground,' she said. 'Used to make my flesh creep. There were nice stories too about knights in armour coming along and carrying off maidens to Valhalla . . . or somewhere.'

'That was where they went when they died,' I reminded her.

'Well, to some nice place where there was feasting and banquets.'

She took to joining us most afternoons.

'What would Madame de Guérin say if she knew?' asked Lydia.

'We'd probably be expelled,' added Monique.

'What luck for all those on the waiting list. Four at one go.'

Elsa would sit on the edge of a chair laughing at us.

'Tell me about your father's *château*,' she would say to Monique.

And Monique told her about the formality of her home and how she was more or less betrothed to Henri de la Creseuse, who owned the estate adjoining her father's.

Then Frieda told of her stern father who would certainly find a baron at least for her to marry. Lydia spoke of her two brothers who would be bankers like her father.

'Tell me about Cordelia,' said Elsa.

'Cordelia is the luckiest of the lot,' cried Lydia. 'She has the most wonderful aunt who lets her do just what she likes. I love to hear about Aunt Patty. I am sure she'll never try to make Cordelia marry some baron or old man because he has a title and money. Cordelia will marry just whom she pleases.'

'And she'll be rich in her own right. She'll have that lovely old manor house. It'll all be yours one day, Cordelia, and you won't have to marry someone to get it.'

15

'I shan't want it because it means Aunt Patty would have to die first.'

'But it will all be yours one day. You'll be rich and independent.'

Elsa wanted to know about Grantley Manor and I gave a glowing description. I wondered if I exaggerated a little, stressing the splendours of Grantley. I certainly did not in describing the eccentric charm of Aunt Patty. No one could really do her justice. But how happy I was talking of her and how the others envied me, coming as they did from sterner and more conventional homes.

'I reckon,' said Elsa one day, 'you'll all be married very soon.'

'Heaven forbid,' said Lydia. 'I want to enjoy myself first.'

'Have you ever been to Pilcher's Peak?' asked Elsa.

'I've heard of it,' said Frieda.

'It's only two miles from here.'

'Is it worth seeing?' I asked.

'Oh yes. It's in the forest; a strange rock. There's a story about it. I always liked those stories.'

'What story?'

'If you go there on certain times you can see your future lover . . . or husband.'

We laughed.

Monique said: 'I've no particular desire to see Henri de la Creseuse just now. Time enough when I leave.'

'Ah,' said Elsa, 'but it may be the fates have decided he is not meant for you.'

'And the man who is will appear at this place? What is this Pilcher's Peak?'

'I'll tell you the story. Years and years ago they used to take lovers caught in adultery to Pilcher's Peak, make them climb to the top and then throw them down. They always took them there on the night of the full moon. So many died that their blood made the ground fertile and the trees grew round the Peak and made the forest.'

'And this is the place we ought to visit?'

'Cordelia is in her last term. She won't have many

16

opportunities, and she ought to see it while she can. Tomorrow night it will be full moon and it's the Hunter's Moon too. That's a good time.'

'Hunter's Moon?' echoed Monique.

'The one that follows the Harvest Moon. It is one of the best and it is the time of the hunting season. It comes in October.'

'Is it really October?' asked Frieda. 'It seems so warm.'

'It was cold last night,' said Lydia, shivering in memory.

'In the day it is lovely,' I said. 'We ought to make the most of it. It's odd to think I shall not be coming back.'

'Shall you mind?' asked Monique.

'I shall miss you all.'

'And you will be with that wonderful aunt,' said Frieda enviously.

'And you'll be rich,' said Elsa, 'and independent too, for you will own that school and the wonderful old manor house.'

'No, no. Not for years. I'd have it when Aunt Patty dies and I'd never want that.'

Elsa nodded. 'Well,' she said, 'if you don't want to go to Pilcher's Peak I'll tell some of the others.'

'Why don't we go?' said Lydia. 'Is it tomorrow . . . the full moon?'

'We could take the wagonette.'

'We could say we wanted to see some of the wild flowers in the forest.'

'Do you think we should be permitted? Wild flowers are scarcely a topic for the drawing rooms of the élite. And what wild flowers are there at this time of the year?'

'We could think of something else,' said Lydia.

Nobody could, however, and the harder we thought the more enticing a trip to Pilcher's Peak became.

'I know,' said Elsa at length, 'you are going into the town to select a pair of gloves for Cordelia's aunt. She was so impressed by those Cordelia came home with and of course they can't make such gloves . . . so chic, so right . . . anywhere but in Switzerland. That will seem very plausible to Madame. Then the wagonette instead of going into the

17

town turns off and goes into the forest. It is only two miles. You could ask for extended time as you wish to call into the pâtisserie for a cup of coffee and one of those cream gateaux which can only be found in Switzerland. I am sure permission would be granted, and that will give you time to go to the forest and sit under the lovers' oak tree.'

'What perfidy!' I cried. 'What if Madame de Guérin knew that you were corrupting us? You'd be turned out to wander in the snowy mountains.'

Elsa put the palms of her hands together as though in prayer. 'I beg you do not betray me. It is only a joke. I wish to put a little romance into your lives.'

I laughed with the others. 'Well, why shouldn't we go? Tell us what we do, Elsa?'

'You sit under the oak. You can't fail to see it. It's there below the Peak. You just sit there and talk together . . . just naturally, you know. Then if you are lucky, your future husband will appear.'

'One between four of us!' cried Monique.

'Perhaps more . . . who can say? But if one comes that is enough to show you there is something in our legend, eh?'

'It's ridiculous,' said Frieda.

'It will be somewhere to go,' added Monique.

'Our last little outing before winter comes,' said Lydia.

'Who knows? It may start tomorrow.'

'Then too late for Cordelia,' Lydia reminded us. 'Oh, Cordelia, do persuade Aunt Patty to let you stay another year.'

'Two is really enough to put the polish on. I must be positively gleaming already.'

We laughed awhile and we decided that on the following afternoon we would go to Pilcher's Peak.

*   *   *

It was a clear afternoon when we set out. The sun made it as warm as spring and we were in high spirits as the wagonette turned off from the road to the town and took us up to the forest. The air was clear and crisp and the snow sparkled on the distant mountain-tops. I could smell the pungency of

18

the pines which made up most of the forest, but there were among the evergreens some oaks, and it was one of these which we had to look for.

We asked the driver about Pilcher's Peak and he told us we couldn't miss it. He'd show us when we turned the bend. We would see it then rising high above the ravine.

The scenery was superb. In the distance we saw mountain slopes, some of them wooded near the valleys, the vegetation growing more sparse further up.

'I wonder which of us will see him?' whispered Lydia.

'None,' responded Frieda.

Monique laughed. 'It won't be me because I am already bespoke.'

We all laughed.

'I think Elsa makes up half the things she says,' I added.

'Do you believe that about her coming down in the world?'

'I don't know,' I said thoughtfully. 'There is something about Elsa. She's different. It could be true. On the other hand she might have made it up.'

'Like the visions of Pilcher's Peak,' said Frieda. 'She's going to laugh at us when we get back.'

The sound of horses' hoofs was soothing as we rocked happily to and fro. I should miss these outings when I left. But it would be wonderful of course to be home with Aunt Patty.

'There's the Peak,' said the wagoner, pointing with his whip.

We all looked. It was impressive from this spot. It looked like a wrinkled old face . . . brown, creased and malevolent.

'I wonder if it's meant to be Pilcher?' said Monique. 'And who was Pilcher anyway?'

'We'll have to ask Elsa,' I said. 'She seems to be a mine of information on such matters.'

We were in the forest now. The wagon drew up and our driver said: 'I'll wait here. Now you young ladies take that path. It leads straight up to the base of the rock. There's a big oak tree at the bottom called Pilcher's Oak.'

19

'That's what we want,' said Monique.

'Less than half a mile.' He looked at his watch. 'I'll be ready to take you back say in an hour and a half. Orders is that you're not to be late.'

'Thank you,' we said and we set off over the uneven ground towards the great rock.

'There must have been a violent volcanic eruption here,' I commented. 'So Pilcher's was formed and much much later the oak tree grew. Seeds dropped by a bird, I daresay. Most of them are pines round here. Don't they smell delicious!'

We had almost reached the oak growing close to the rock. 'This must be it,' said Lydia, throwing herself down and stretching out on the grass. 'This smell makes me feel sleepy.'

'That lovely redolent odour,' I said, sniffing eagerly. 'Yes, there is something soporific about it.'

'What now we're here?' asked Frieda.

'Sit down . . . and wait and see.'

'I think it's foolish,' said Frieda.

'Well, it's an outing. Somewhere to go. Let's pretend we are shopping for gloves for my Aunt Patty. I do want to get her some before I leave.'

'Stop talking about leaving,' said Lydia. 'I don't like it.'

Frieda yawned.

'Yes,' I said, 'I certainly feel like that too.'

I stretched myself out on the grass and the others did the same. We lay there, propping up our heads with our hands and gazing up through the branches of the oak tree.

'I wonder what it was like when they threw people over,' I went on. 'Just imagine being taken up to the top, knowing you were going to be thrown over . . . or perhaps asked to jump. Perhaps some fell on this spot.'

'You make me feel creepy,' said Lydia.

'I suggest,' put in Frieda, 'that we go back to the wagonette and go into the town after all.'

'Those little cakes with the coloured cream are delicious,' said Monique.

'Would there be time?' asked Frieda.

20

'No,' said Lydia.

'Be quiet,' I commanded. 'Give it a chance.'

We were all silent and just then he came through the trees.

He was tall and very fair. I noticed his eyes immediately. They were piercing blue, and there was something unusual about them; they seemed as though they were looking beyond us into places which we could not see . . . or perhaps I imagined that afterwards. His clothes were dark and that accentuated his fairness. They were elegantly cut but not exactly in the height of fashion. His coat had a velvet collar and silver buttons, and his hat was black, tall, and shiny.

We were all silent as he approached – awe-struck, I suppose, devoid for the moment of our Schaffenbrucken polish.

'Good afternoon,' he said in English. He bowed. Then he went on: 'I heard your laughter and I had an irresistible urge to see you.'

Still we said nothing and he went on: 'Tell me, you are from the school, are you not?'

I said: 'Yes, we are.'

'On an excursion to Pilcher's Peak?'

'We were resting before we went back,' I told him, as the others seemed to remain tongue-tied.

'It's an interesting spot,' he went on. 'Do you object to my talking to you for a moment?'

'Of course not.' We all spoke together. So the others had recovered from their shock.

He sat down a little distance from us and surveyed his long legs.

'You are English,' he said, looking at me.

'Yes . . . I and Miss Markham. This is Mademoiselle Delorme and Fräulein Schmidt.'

'A cosmopolitan group,' he commented. 'Yours is the school for the young ladies of Europe. Am I right?'

'Yes, that is it.'

'Tell me why did you take this excursion to Pilcher's Peak today? Is it not rather a summer outing?'

21

'We thought we'd like to see it,' I said, 'and I probably shan't have an opportunity again. I'm leaving at the end of the year.'

He raised his eyebrows. 'Is that so? And the other young ladies?'

'We shall have another year, I expect,' said Monique.

'And then you return to France?'

'Yes.'

'You are all so young . . . so merry,' he said. 'It was very pleasant to hear your laughter. I was drawn towards it. I felt for a moment that I must join you. I must share your spontaneity.'

'We didn't realize that we were so alluring,' I said, and everybody laughed.

He looked about him. 'What a pleasant afternoon! There is a stillness in the air, do you feel it?'

'Yes, I think I do,' said Lydia.

He looked up at the sky. 'Indian summer,' he said quietly. 'You will all go to your various homes for Christmas, will you not?'

'It is one of the holidays we all go home for. That and the summer. Easter, Whitsun and the rest, well . . .'

'The journey is too far,' he finished for me. 'And your families will welcome you,' he went on. 'They will have balls and banquets for you and you will all marry and live happy ever after, which is the fate which should await all beautiful young ladies.'

'And doesn't always . . . or often,' said Monique.

'We have a cynic here. Tell me,' his eyes were on me. 'Do you believe that?'

'I think life is what you make it,' I was quoting Aunt Patty. 'What is intolerable to some is comfort to others. It is the way in which one looks upon it.'

'They certainly teach you something at that school.'

'That's what my aunt always says.'

'You have no parents.' It was a statement rather than a question.

'No, they died in Africa. My aunt has always looked after me.'

22

'She's a marvellous person,' said Monique. 'She runs a school. She's just about as different from Madame de Guérin as anyone could be. Cordelia is the lucky one. She's going to work with her aunt and share the school, which will be hers one day. Can you imagine Cordelia as a headmistress!'

He was smiling directly at me. 'I can imagine Cordelia's being anything she wishes to be. So she is a lady of substance, is she?'

'If you ask me she is the luckiest of the lot of us,' said Monique.

He continued to look at me steadily. 'Yes,' he said, 'I think Cordelia can be very lucky indeed.'

'Why do you say "can be"?' asked Frieda.

'Because it will depend on her herself. Is she cautious? Does she hesitate or does she grasp opportunities when they are presented to her?'

The girls looked at each other and at me.

'I'd say she would,' said Monique.

'Time will tell,' he replied.

He had a strange delivery, which was a little archaic. Perhaps that was because he was speaking English which might not have been his native tongue although he was very fluent. I fancied I caught a trace of a German accent.

'We always have to wait for time to tell us,' said Frieda rather pettishly.

'What do you wish then, young lady? To take a glimpse into the future?'

'That would be fun,' said Monique. 'There was a fortune teller in the town. Madame de Guérin put that out of bounds . . . but I believe some of them went.'

'It can be very absorbing,' he said.

'You mean . . . to look into the future?' That was Monique and he leaned forward and took her hand. She gave a little squeal. 'Oh . . . can you tell the future then?'

'Tell the future? Who can tell the future? Though sometimes there are visions . . .'

We were all subdued now. I felt my heart beating wildly.

There was something very extraordinary about this encounter.

'You, Mademoiselle,' he said, gazing at Monique, 'you will laugh through life. You will go back to your family *château*.' He dropped her hand and closed his eyes. 'It is in the heart of the country. There are vineyards surrounding it. The pepper pot towers reach to the sky. Your father is a man who makes arrangements worthy of his family. He is a proud man. Will you marry as he wishes, Mademoiselle?'

Monique looked a little shaken.

'I suppose I shall marry Henri . . . I quite like him really.'

'And your father would never allow it to be otherwise. And you, Fräulein, are you as docile as your friend?'

'It's hard to say,' said Frieda in her matter-of-fact way. 'I sometimes think I shall do what I please and then when I'm home . . . it's different.'

He smiled at her. 'You do not deceive yourself and that is a great asset in life. You will always know which way you are going and why – although it is not always the path which you would choose.'

Then he turned to Lydia. 'Ah, Miss,' he said, 'what is your fortune?'

'Heaven knows,' said Lydia. 'I imagine my father will be more concerned with my brothers. They're a good bit older than I and they always think boys are more important.'

'You will have a good life,' he said.

Lydia laughed. 'It's almost as though you are telling our fortunes.'

'Your fortunes are for you to make,' he replied. 'I only have certain . . . what shall I say . . . sensitivities.'

'It's Cordelia's turn,' said Monique.

'Cordelia's turn?' he said.

'You haven't told her anything yet . . . about what's going to happen.'

'I have said,' he replied mildly, 'that that will depend on Cordelia.'

'But haven't you anything to tell her?'

24

'No,' he said. 'Cordelia will know . . . when the time comes.'

There was a deep silence. I was very much aware of the quietness of the forest and looming over us the grotesque formation of rock, which one's imagination could easily twist into menacing shapes.

It was Monique who spoke. 'It's rather uncanny here,' she said and shivered.

Suddenly a sound broke the silence. It was the rather melodious call of the wagoner. His voice seemed to hit the mountain and echo through the forest.

'We should have started back ten minutes ago,' said Frieda. 'We'll have to hurry.'

We all jumped to our feet.

'Goodbye,' we said to the stranger.

Then we started down the path. After a few seconds I looked back. He had disappeared.

*   *   *

We were late back but nothing was said and no one asked to see the gloves which we were supposed to have bought in the town.

Elsa came to our room after supper. It was that half hour before prayers which was followed by our retiring for the night.

'Well,' she said, 'did you see anything?' Her eyes glistened with curiosity.

'There was . . . something,' admitted Frieda.

'Some *thing* . . .'

'Well, a man,' added Monique.

'The more I think of him,' added Lydia, 'the more strange he seemed.'

'Do tell,' cried Elsa. 'Do tell.'

'Well, we were sitting there . . .'

'Lying there,' said Frieda who liked details to be exact.

'Stretched out under the tree,' went on Lydia impatiently, 'when he was suddenly there.'

'You mean he appeared?'

'You could call it that.'

25

'What was he like?'

'Handsome. Different . . .'

'Go on. Go on . . .'

We were all silent trying to remember exactly what he had looked like.

'What's the matter with you all?' demanded Elsa.

'Well, it was rather strange when you come to think about it,' said Monique. 'Did it strike you that he seemed to know something about us all. He described the *château* with the vines and towers.'

Frieda said: 'Many *châteaux* in France have their vineyards and almost all have pepper pot towers.'

'Yes,' said Monique. 'And yet . . .'

'I think he was most interested in Cordelia,' announced Lydia.

'Why should you think that?' I demanded. 'He didn't tell me anything.'

'It was the way he looked at you.'

'You're not telling *me* anything,' complained Elsa. 'I sent you there, don't forget. I've a right to know.'

'I'll tell you what happened,' said Frieda. 'We were silly enough to go to the forest when we might have gone into the town and had some of those delicious cream cakes . . . and because we'd been so silly we tried to make something happen. All that did was that a man came up, said he liked to hear us laugh and talk for a while.'

'Trust Frieda to get it all neatly tied up,' said Lydia. 'But I can't help thinking that there was more to it than that.'

'I reckon he's a future husband for one of you,' said Elsa. 'That's how the story goes.'

'If you believe that why didn't you go and meet yours,' I asked.

'How could I get away. I'm watched. They'd suspect me of shirking my duties.'

'Rest assured,' said Frieda, 'that those suspicions will soon be confirmed.'

Elsa laughed with us.

She at least was delighted with the excursion.

*   *   *

26

All through November we were making plans to go home. For me it was a time tinged with sadness. I was going to hate saying goodbye to them all; but on the other hand I was looking forward to going home. Monique, Frieda and Lydia all said we must keep in touch. Lydia lived in London but her family had a country house in Essex where she spent most of her holidays, so we should not be so very far away from each other.

For a few days after that encounter in the forest we talked a great deal about what we called our Pilcher's Peak adventure. We had very quickly transformed it into an uncanny experience and we endowed the stranger with all sorts of peculiarities. He had had piercing eyes which shone with an unearthly light, according to Monique. She exaggerated what he had told her and was beginning to believe he had given her an accurate and minute description of her father's *château*. Lydia said he had sent shivers down her spine and she was sure he had not been human.

'Nonsense,' said Frieda, 'he was taking a walk in the woods when he felt like a little conversation with a group of giggling girls.'

I wasn't sure what I thought and, although I was aware that the encounter was being considerably embellished, it had made a deep impression on me.

Term ended at the end of the first week in December. As most of us had to travel long distances Madame de Guérin always liked us to get on our way before the snows came too heavily and made the roads impassable.

There were seven English girls who would be travelling on the same route. Fräulein Mainz saw us all onto the train and when we reached Calais it had been arranged for one of the travel agents to see us onto the boat. At Dover our families would be waiting for us.

I had made the journey several times before, but this was to be the last time, and that made it different.

We had a compartment to ourselves and, as we had done the journey before, it was only the younger ones who exclaimed at the grandeur of the mountain scenery and remained at the windows while we travelled through the majestic Swiss countryside. The older ones had grown blasé – myself and Lydia among them.

The journey seemed endless; we talked; we read; we played games and we dozed.

Most of them were half asleep and I was gazing idly out at the scenery when I saw a man. He was passing along the corridor. He looked in at our compartment as he went. I gasped. He appeared to glance at me but I was not sure that he recognized me. He was gone in a matter of seconds.

I turned to Lydia who was seated next to me, asleep. I jumped up and made my way along the corridor. There was no sign of him.

I went back to my seat and nudged Lydia.

'I . . . I saw him,' I said.

'Saw what?'

'The man . . . the man in the forest . . .'

'You're dreaming,' said Lydia.

'No. I was sure. He was gone in a flash.'

'Why didn't you speak to him?'

'He was gone too quickly. I went after him but he had disappeared.'

'You were dreaming,' said Lydia and closed her eyes.

I was very shaken. Could it have been an apparition? It was over so quickly. He had been there . . . and then he was gone. He must have moved along that corridor very quickly. Had it really been the man himself or had I dreamed it?

Perhaps Lydia was right.

I looked out for him during the rest of the journey to Calais but he was not there.

The train had been delayed because of the snowdrifts and we were eight hours late reaching Calais. It meant that we had to take the night ferry and it must have been about two o'clock in the morning when we embarked.

Lydia was not feeling well; she was cold, she said, and felt a little sick. She had found a spot below where she could wrap herself up and lie down.

I felt the need for fresh air and said I would go on deck. I was given a rug and found a chair. True it was cold but I felt

28

snug beneath my rug and I was sure Lydia would have been wiser to have come up with me rather than stay in the airless part of the ship.

There was a faint crescent moon, and myriads of stars were visible in the clear night sky. I could hear the voices of the crew not far off and I enjoyed the rocking of the ship, gentle as yet, but there was no wind and I did not anticipate a rough crossing.

I was thinking of the future. It would always be fun with Aunt Patty. I could imagine long cosy evenings by her sitting-room fire while she drank hot chocolate and nibbled macaroons for which she had a special fancy. We would laugh over the day's events. There would always be something to laugh about. Oh, I was looking forward to it.

I closed my eyes. I was rather sleepy. The journey had been tiring and there had been a great deal of fuss getting into the ship. I must not sleep deeply for I should have to find my way back to Lydia before the ship docked.

I was aware of a faint movement at my side. I opened my eyes. A chair had been moved silently and now, with its occupant, it was beside me.

'Do you mind if I sit with you?'

My heart started to beat furiously. The same voice. The same air of being not quite of this world. It was the man of the forest.

I was too startled to speak for a moment.

He said: 'I will be quiet if you wish to sleep.'

'Oh no . . . no . . . It is . . . isn't it?'

'We met before,' he said.

'You . . . you were on the train?'

'Yes, I was on the train.'

'I saw you pass the window.'

'Yes.'

'Are you going to England?'

It was a foolish question. Where else could he be going since he was on the Channel steamer?

'Yes,' he said. 'I trust I shall see you while I am there.'

'Oh yes. That would be pleasant. You must call on us.

29

It's Grantley Manor, Canterton, Sussex. Not far from Lewes. It's quite easy to find.'

'I'll remember that,' he said. 'You will see me.'

'Are you going home?'

'Yes,' he answered.

I waited but he did not tell me where. There was about him an aloofness, something which warned me not to ask questions.

'You will be looking forward to your meeting with your aunt.'

'Very much.'

'She seems a very indulgent lady.'

'Indulgent? Yes, I suppose so. She is warm-hearted and loving and I don't think she ever felt any malice towards anyone. She has wit and says amusing things but she is never hurtful . . . unless anyone hurts her or hers, then she would respond with gusto. She is a wonderful human being.'

'Your devotion to her is apparent.'

'She was a mother to me when I needed one.'

'A rare person clearly.'

There was a short silence and then he said: 'Tell me about yourself.'

'You don't want to talk very much about *yourself*,' I commented.

'That will come. Now it is your turn.'

It was like a command and I found myself talking of my early life, remembering things which I thought until this moment I had forgotten. I remembered incidents from Africa, the hours in the mission hall which had seemed endless, the singing of hymns, prayers, always prayers, little black babies playing in the dust, the multi-coloured beads which jangled at their necks and waists, strange insects which looked like sticks and seemed as sinister as the snakes which slithered through the grass and of which one had to be very careful.

But mostly I talked about Aunt Patty and the Manor and the school itself and how much I was looking forward to being a part of it.

30

'You are fully qualified,' he said.

'Oh yes, Aunt Patty saw to that. I have studied a number of subjects and then of course I went to Schaffenbrucken to be finished off, as Aunt Patty puts it.'

'A very expensive school. Aunt Patty must be a rich woman to be able to send her niece there.'

'I think she looked upon it as a good investment.'

'Tell me about the Manor,' he said.

So I talked, describing it room by room and the grounds which surrounded it. There were twenty acres. 'We have a paddock and stables and playing fields, you see.'

'It sounds commodious.'

'It has a high reputation. Aunt Patty is always trying to increase it.'

'I like your Aunt Patty.'

'No one could help doing that.'

'Loyal Miss Cordelia.'

He lay back and closed his eyes. I thought it was an intimation that he did not want to talk for a while. So I did the same.

The rocking of the boat was soothing, and as I was really very tired and it was the middle of the night, I went into a light doze. I awoke suddenly to the sounds of activity about me. I could just catch a glimpse of the coastline ahead.

I turned to look at my companion. There was no one there. His chair and his rug were gone.

I stood up and looked about me. There were not many people on deck, and certainly no sign of him.

I went down to find Lydia.

*　　　*　　　*

Aunt Patty was at the docks waiting to greet me, looking rounder than I remembered and her hat was splendid – ruchings of blue ribbon and a bow as wide as herself.

I was clasped to her fondly and was able to introduce Lydia who couldn't resist saying: 'She is just as you said she was.'

'Been telling tales about me in school, eh?' said Aunt Patty.

31

'All she told us was lovely,' said Lydia. 'She made us all want to come to your school.'

I was hastily introduced to the woman who had come for Lydia. I gathered she was a sort of housekeeper, and I again rejoiced in Aunt Patty who had come herself to meet me.

Aunt Patty and I settled into the train, talking all the time.

I did look round for the stranger but he was nowhere to be seen. There were so many people about and it would have been something of a miracle if I had been able to see him. I wondered where he was going.

At the Canterton station, which was little more than a halt, we were met by the fly and whisked home in a very short time. I was moved as always by the first sight of Grantley Manor after an absence. Red-bricked, lattice-windowed, it looked gracious rather than grand, but most of all it looked like home.

'Dear old place,' I said.

'So you feel like that about it, do you?'

'But of course. I remember the first time I saw it . . . but by then I knew everything was going to be all right because I had met you.'

'Bless you, child. But believe me, bricks and mortar don't make a home. You'll find a home where you find the people who make home for you.'

'As you did, dear Aunt Patty. The girls love hearing about you . . . the macaroons and the hats and everything. They always call you Aunt Patty as though you are theirs too. I feel I want to say, "Here, stop it. She's mine." '

It was lovely to step into the hall, to smell the beeswax and turpentine which always clung about the furniture mingling with the smell of cooking which came from the other side of the screens.

'It's a queer time to arrive. It's just past noon. Do you feel tired?'

'Not really. Only excited to be here.'

'You'll be tired later. Best to have a rest this afternoon. Then I want to talk to you.'

32

'Of course. This is the great occasion. I have said good-bye to Schaffenbrucken.'

'I'm glad you went there, Cordelia. It will be a blessing.'

'It will bring them streaming in.'

She gave a little cough and said: 'You'll miss all the girls though, won't you, and the mountains and everything.'

'I missed you most of all, Aunt Patty.'

'Go on with you,' she said, but she was deeply moved.

If I had not been a little bemused by the man whom I called the Stranger, I might have noticed there was a change in Aunt Patty. It was hardly perceptible, but then I knew her so well. I might have asked myself if she was a trifle less exuberant than usual.

I did get a hint though from Violet Barker – Aunt Patty's housekeeper, companion and devoted friend who had been with Aunt Patty when I first arrived all those years ago. She was rather angular and lean – the complete opposite of Aunt Patty. They suited each other perfectly. Violet had nothing to do with the teaching of pupils but she did manage the household with expertise and was a very important part of the establishment.

Violet looked at me so cautiously that I thought Aunt Patty must have talked with such earnestness of Schaffenbrucken polish that Violet was trying to discern it.

Then she said quite suddenly: 'It's the roof. It would have to be done within the next two years they say. And that's not all. The west wall wants propping up. It's been a wet winter so far. It's given your aunt concern. Did she say?'

'No. Well, I have just got home.'

Violet nodded and pressed her lips tightly together. I might have guessed that something was very wrong.

It was after dinner at about half past eight when Aunt Patty and I were in her sitting room with Violet when she told me.

I gasped and couldn't believe I was hearing correctly when she said, 'Cordelia. I've sold the Manor.'

'Aunt Patty! What do you mean?'

'I should have warned you. Led up to it. Things have not

33

been too flourishing for the last three years.'

'Oh, Aunt Patty.'

'Dear child, don't look so tragic. I am sure it is going to be all for the best. I'm sorry I have to confront you with a *fait accompli*. But there was no help for it, was there, Vi? We talked it over and over and this offer came along. The house needs a fortune spent on it. Times haven't been so good for some years. I've had some bad debts.'

I guessed that. I knew of at least three pupils whose parents hardly ever paid the fees. 'Bright girls all of them,' Aunt Patty used to say. 'A credit to the school.' Times were hard. No watered-down soup for Grantley. I had often wondered how she managed at the fees she charged, but as she had never mentioned the matter to me I had supposed that all was well.

'What are we going to do?' I asked.

Aunt Patty burst into laughter. 'We are going to cast aside our troubles and enjoy life. That's right, eh Violet?'

'So you say, Patty.'

'Yes,' said Aunt Patty, 'the fact of the matter is, dear, that I have been thinking for some time that I should retire and I should have done it long ago but for . . .' She looked at me and I said: 'But for me. You were keeping it for me.'

'I thought it would be a future for you. I thought I'd retire and just be an adviser when I was wanted or something like that. It was the idea behind Schaffenbrucken.'

'And you sent me to that expensive school when you were already in financial difficulties.'

'I was looking ahead. The trouble is things have gone a bit too far. There would have been the enormous expenditure on repairs. It would have been crippling. Well, not exactly but it would have made the alternative impossible. So . . . the opportunity came and I decided to sell.'

'Will it be a school?'

'No. Some millionaire who wants to restore the place and be a lord of the manor.'

'Aunt Patty, what about us?'

34

'All arranged, dear. Most satisfactorily. We have an enchanting house in Moldenbury . . . near Notthingham. It's a lovely village right in the heart of the country. It's not as big as Grantley of course and I can only take Mary Ann with me. I hope the rest of the staff will stay on to serve the new owners of Grantley. The parents have all had their notices. We are closing down at the end of the Spring term. It is all settled.'

'And this house – where is it? Moldenbury?'

'We are negotiating for it. It will pass into our hands shortly. Everything is arranged to our mutual satisfaction. We shall have enough to live on in a simple way perhaps but adequate for our needs and we shall give ourselves up to life in the country, following all sorts of pursuits which we never had time for before. We shall adjust happily, as I keep telling Violet.'

I glanced at Violet. She was not quite as optimistic as my aunt, but optimism was not one of Violet's qualities.

'Dear Aunt Patty,' I said. 'You should have told me before. You shouldn't have let me go on at that place. It must have been ridiculously costly.'

'Having put my hand to the plough I was not going to spoil the ship for a ha'p'orth of tar, and if a job is worth doing it is worth doing properly. I can't think of any more maxims but I am sure they abound to support me. I have done the right thing by you, Cordelia. Schaffenbrucken will never be wasted. I'll tell you more later on. I'll show you the books and how things are going. Also I've got to talk to you about our new home. We'll go and see it one day before the start of next term. You'll love it. It's the dearest little village and I have already made the acquaintance of the rector who seems a very charming gentleman with a wife who is overflowing with welcome for us. I think we are going to find it very amusing.'

'And different,' said Violet sombrely.

'Change is always stimulating,' said Aunt Patty. 'I think we have been moving along in the same groove for too long. A new life, Cordelia. A challenge. We shall be

35

working for the good of our new village . . . Fêtes, bazaars, committees, feuds. I can see we are going to have an interesting time.'

She believed it. That was the wonderful thing about Aunt Patty. She saw everything as amusing, exciting and challenging and she had always been able to convince me, if she was not managing to do the same with Violet. But then Aunt Patty and I always said that Violet enjoyed adversity.

I went to bed rather bemused. There were hundreds of questions to be asked. The future was a little hazy at the moment.

$$* \qquad * \qquad *$$

During the next day I learned more from Aunt Patty. The school had been, as she said, ticking over, for some little time. Perhaps her fees were not high enough; she had, she was told by her financial advisers, overspent on food and fuel, and the amount of those costly items was out of proportion to receipts.

'I didn't want to make it into a Dothegirls Hall such as Mr Dickens wrote about in his wonderful book. I didn't want that at all. I wanted my school to be . . . just as I wanted it, and if it can't be that, then I'd rather there was no school. So that is how it is going to be, Cordelia. I can't say I'm sorry myself. I wanted to pass it on to you, but there is no point in passing on a concern which would have tottered into bankruptcy. No, cut your losses, said I. And that is what I am doing. In our new home we'll all have a rest for a while and we'll plan what we are going to do next.'

She made it all sound like a new and exciting adventure on which we were embarking and I caught her enthusiasm.

In the afternoon when classes were in progress I went for a walk. I left about two o'clock intending to be back before it was dark, which would be soon after four. School would be breaking up in the next week or so and after that only one more term. There would be the bustle of departure; the mistresses would be arranging journeys for the girls, seeing them to trains, just as it had been at Schaffenbrucken. I supposed many of the teachers were anxious, wonder-

36

ing about their new posts and certain that they would not find many employers as easy-going as Aunt Patty had been.

I detected an air of melancholy over the house. Both pupils and mistresses had appreciated the atmosphere of Grantley Manor.

Without Aunt Patty at my side to stress how wonderful everything was going to be, I too felt the depression. I tried to imagine what my future would be. I couldn't just live all my life in a country village even though Aunt Patty would be with me. Somehow I did not think Aunt Patty believed I could either. I had caught her almost speculative gaze on me, rather secretive as though she had something up her sleeve which she was going to produce to the wonderment of all who perceived it.

I always enjoyed my first walk after returning to Grantley. I usually went into the little town of Canterton, looked into the shops and stopped for a chat with the people I knew. It was always a pleasure. Today it seemed different. I did not feel the same urge to talk to people. I wondered how much they knew about Aunt Patty's move and I couldn't really talk about something of which I knew so little as yet.

I passed the woods and noticed that there were plenty of berries on the holly this year. The girls would be picking it very soon now, for the last week of term would be given over to Christmas jollity. They had already decorated the Christmas tree in the common room and put the presents they had bought for each other under it. Then there would be a concert and carol singing in the chapel. The last time . . . What a sad phrase that was.

A pale winter sun momentarily showed itself between the clouds. There was a chill in the air but it was mildish for the time of year.

There were not many people about. I had not met anyone since I had left the Manor. I glanced towards the wood and wondered whether the girls would find much mistletoe this year. They usually had to hunt for it, which made it seem precious, and made a great show of fixing it in those places where they could be caught and kissed – if

37

there were any males about who might be tempted to do so.

I hesitated by the woods. Then as I was deciding that I would skirt them and go as far as the town without actually going in, I heard a footstep behind me. I felt a rush of emotion and told myself afterwards that I knew who it was going to be before I turned round.

'Why?' I cried. 'You . . . here?'

'Yes,' he said with a smile. 'You told me you lived in Canterton so I thought I would have a look at it.'

'Are you . . . staying here?'

'Briefly,' he replied.

'On your way to . . . ?'

'Somewhere else. I thought I would call to see you while I was here, but before doing so I was hoping to meet you so that I could ask if it would be correct for me to call. I passed the Manor. It is a fine old place.'

'You should have come in.'

'First of all I wanted to find out whether your aunt would receive me.'

'But of course she would be delighted to receive you.'

'After all,' he went on, 'we have not been formally introduced.'

'We have met four times, if you count the time on the train.'

'Yes,' he said slowly, 'I feel we are old friends. Your welcome home was very warm I gather.'

'Aunt Patty is such a darling.'

'She is clearly devoted to you.'

'Yes.'

'So it was the happiest of homecomings?'

I hesitated.

'Not?' he asked.

I was silent for a few seconds and he looked at me with some concern. Then he said: 'Shall we walk through the forest? I think it rather beautiful at this time of the year. The trees without their leaves are so beautiful, don't you think? Look at the pattern that one makes against the sky.'

'Yes, I have always thought so. More beautiful in winter even than in summer. This is hardly what you call a forest.

It's more of a wood . . . just clumps of trees which don't extend for more than a quarter of a mile.'

'Nevertheless let us walk among the beautiful trees and you can tell me why your homecoming was not as usual.'

Still I hesitated and he looked at me with a slightly reproachful air. 'You can trust me,' he said. 'I will keep your secrets. Come, tell me what worries you.'

'It was all so different from what I expected. Aunt Patty had not given me a hint.'

'No hint?'

'That everything was not . . . as it should be. She . . . she has sold Grantley Manor.'

'Sold that beautiful house! What of the flourishing establishment?'

'Apparently it did not flourish. I was astounded. I suppose one takes these things for granted. There was no reason why I shouldn't. Aunt Patty had never as much as hinted that we were becoming poorer.'

There seemed to be a sudden chill in the forest.

He had stopped in his walk and looked at me tenderly. 'My poor child,' he said.

'Oh, it isn't so bad. We're not going to starve. Aunt Patty thinks it is all to the good. But then everything that happens seems to her all to the good.'

'Tell me about it . . . if you wish to.'

'I don't know why I am talking to you like this . . . except that you seem so interested. You just seem to appear, first in the forest, then on the ship and now . . . You are rather mysterious, you know.'

He laughed. 'That makes it all the easier for you to talk to me.'

'Yes, I suppose it does. I was going to avoid going into the town because I didn't want to talk to people there who have known us for years.'

'Well, tell me instead.'

So I told him that Aunt Patty had had to sell the Manor because it was too expensive to keep up, and that we were going to a small house in another part of the country.

'What shall you do?'

'I don't know . . . We have this little house somewhere in the Midlands, I believe. I really haven't heard much about it yet. Aunt Patty makes it seem . . . not so bad, but I can see that Violet – that's her very special friend who lives with us – is very disturbed.'

'I can imagine so. What a terrible blow for you! My deepest sympathy. You seemed so merry when I saw you with your friends in the forest, and I fancied they were all a little envious of you.'

We walked across the stunted grass and the wintry sun glinted through the bare branches of the trees. The smell of damp earth and foliage was in the air and I couldn't help feeling that something significant would happen because he was with me.

I said: 'We have talked about me. Tell me about yourself.'

'You won't find that very interesting.'

'Oh, but I shall. You have such a way of . . . appearing. It is quite intriguing, really. The way you came upon us in the forest . . .'

'I was taking a walk.'

'It seemed so strange that you should be there, and then in the train and on the boat . . . and now here.'

'I am here because I saw it was on my route and I thought I would drop in to see you.'

'On your route to where?'

'To my home.'

'So you live in England.'

'I have a place in Switzerland. I suppose I would say my home is in England.'

'And you are on your way to it now. Why, I don't even know your name.'

'Was it never mentioned?'

'No. In the forest . . .'

'I was just a passer-by then, wasn't I? It would not have been *comme il faut* to exchange cards.'

'Then on the boat . . . you were just there.'

'You were rather sleepy, I think.'

'Let's end the mystery. What is your name?'

He hesitated and I fancied that he did not want to tell me. There must surely be some reason why. He certainly was an enigma.

Then he said suddenly: 'It is Edward Compton.'

'Oh . . . then you *are* English. I wondered whether you were entirely. Where is your home?'

He said: 'It is Compton Manor.'

'Oh . . . is it far from here?'

'Yes. In Suffolk. In a little village you will never have heard of.'

'What village?'

'Croston.'

'No. I have never heard of it. Is it far from Bury St Edmunds?'

'Well . . . that would be the nearest town.'

'And you are on your way there now?'

'Yes, when I leave here.'

'Are you staying in Canterton for a while then?'

'I thought I would . . .'

'For how long?'

He looked at me intently and said: 'That depends . . .'

I felt myself flush a little. It depended on me, he was implying. The girls had said that I was the one in whom he was interested, and I had instinctively known this from our first meeting in the forest.

'You must be staying at the Three Feathers. It is small but has a good reputation for being comfortable. I hope you will find it so.'

'I am comfortable,' he said.

'You must come to meet Aunt Patty.'

'That would be my pleasure.'

'I should be getting back now. It grows dark so early.'

'I'll walk with you to the Manor.'

We left the wood and took to the road. The Manor was before us. It looked beautiful in the already fading light.

'I can see you admire it,' I said.

'It is sad that you have to let it go,' he answered.

'I haven't really got used to the idea but, as Aunt Patty says, it isn't bricks and mortar that make a home. We

41

shouldn't be happy there worrying all the time because we couldn't afford it, and she says that renovations would have to be done soon or it would be falling about our heads.'

'How frustrating.'

I stopped and smiled at him.

'I'll leave you here, unless you would like to come in with me now.'

'N . . . no. I think it better not. Next time perhaps.'

'Tomorrow. You might call for tea. Four o'clock. Aunt Patty makes rather a ritual of tea. She does of all meals. Come just before four.'

'Thank you,' he said.

Then he took my hand and bowed.

I ran into the house without looking back. I was excited. There was something about him which was so intriguing. At last I knew his name. Edward Compton of Compton Manor. I imagined it . . . redbrick essentially Tudor rather like our own Manor. No wonder he was interested in Grantley and genuinely shocked because we were having to sell. He would understand what it meant parting with a fine old house which had been one's home for a long time.

Tomorrow I would see him again. I would write to all the girls and tell them about this exciting meeting. There hadn't been time on the boat to tell Lydia that I had seen him again there. I doubt whether she would have listened much. We had been so intent on disembarking and meeting those who had come to fetch us.

Perhaps in time there might be more to tell her. I was very fascinated by the mysterious stranger.

*   *   *

When I returned to the house Aunt Patty was in a state of excitement.

'I have just had confirmation from Daisy Hetherington who is coming to see us. She is arriving at the end of the week on her way to her brother's for Christmas. She will stay a couple of nights.'

I had heard her mention Daisy Hetherington many times and always in tones of great respect. Daisy Hetherington owned one of the most exclusive schools in England. Aunt Patty couldn't stop talking about her.

'Aunt Patty,' I cut in. 'The most extraordinary thing has happened. There was a man whom I met at Schaffenbruck-cn and he happens to be in Canterton. I've asked him to tea tomorrow. That will be all right, won't it?'

'But of course, dear. A man, you say?' She clearly had her mind on Daisy Hetherington. 'That will be nice,' she continued absently. 'I've told them to get the tapestry room ready for Daisy. I really think it is the nicest room in the house.'

'It certainly has lovely views . . . but they all have.'

'She'll want to hear about the move. She always likes to know everything that's going on in the scholastic world. Perhaps that is why she is so successful.'

'Aunt Patty, you sound just the tiniest bit envious, which is unlike you.'

'Not me, my dear. I wouldn't change places with Daisy Hetherington for Colby Abbey Academy itself. No, I'm content. Glad to give up. It was time. There is only one regret and that is you. I'll confess I wanted to hand on a fine and flourishing business to you . . .' Her eyes began to twinkle. 'But you never know what is waiting to turn up. Cordelia, I think it will be a little quiet for you in that country village of ours. You've been to Schaffenbrucken and you're fully qualified. You see Daisy Hetherington's Colby Abbey Academy for Young Ladies – to give it its full title – has a reputation which we never had. Colby is synonymous with Schaffenbrucken . . . or almost. I was just wondering . . .'

'Aunt Patty, did you ask Daisy Hetherington to stay here or did she ask to come?'

'Well, I know how much she hates staying at inns. I said it was scarcely out of her way and she might as well stay here for a couple of nights. I have a few pieces she might find useful. There's that roll top desk and some of the girls' desks too and books. She was quite interested and she would like to meet you. I have told her *so* much about you.'

I knew her well. I could see those rather mischievous

43

lights in her eyes when she was planning something.

'Are you asking her to find a place for me in her school?'

'Well, not exactly asking her. And in any case it would be for you to decide. It is something you will have to think about carefully, Cordelia. How will you like country life? I mean village life centred round the church. It is all right for old birds like Violet and me, but for a young girl who has been educated with a view to using that education . . . ? Well, as I said it will be for you to decide. If Daisy likes you . . . I know she will like your qualifications. Daisy is a good woman . . . a little stern . . . a little aloof and very, very dignified . . . in fact the opposite of your old Aunt P, but a shrewd business woman, one who knows where she is going. You'll see for yourself. If she took you in, after a while you might have a very good position there. I was thinking of a partnership. Money? Well, I'm not destitute and I'll be comfortable enough with what I have and what I'll get for Grantley. It's a very good price. Colby Abbey breaks up for Christmas a week before we do . . so I've asked her here. It's not a bad idea that she should come when the girls are breaking up for Christmas. Then she won't be able to criticize our methods of teaching which I am sure she would. You'll admire her. She possesses those qualities which I lack.'

'I shall certainly not admire her for that.'

'Oh, you will. I wasn't the right type to run a successful school, Cordelia. Let's face it. None of the girls is in the least in awe of me.'

'They love you.'

'There are times when respect is more important. I can see my mistakes . . . looking back. Nothing very clever about that, I suppose. But at least I'll admit to them and there is a certain wisdom in that. My plan is this, Cordelia. You have a choice . . . that is, if Daisy goes along with us, which I intend she shall. If she offers you a post in her school, and if in five or six years time you have wormed your way in and poor Daisy isn't getting younger and I have a little capital on the side . . . see what I mean? That is why Daisy's visit is so important. And here are you, fresh from

44

Schaffenbrucken. I happen to know she hasn't anyone there with that special brand of polish on them. If she likes you – and I can't see how she could fail to – there's a chance. And, Cordelia my dear, I want you to think very hard about taking it. It was the one thing which made all this acceptable to me and I can see that if it works as I plan, everything that has happened is going to be a blessing in disguise.'

'Aunt Patty, you are an old schemer. Just suppose she liked me and agreed to take me . . . I shouldn't be with you.'

'My love, that little house will be waiting for you. School holidays will be our red letter days. Dear old Vi will give an extra polish to the brass – she has a fetish about that brass of hers – I shall be in a whirl of excitement. Just imagine the rejoining in the house, "Cordelia is coming home". This time next year I can see it all so clearly. We'll all go to the carol service in the church. The rector is such a nice man. In fact it is a very friendly place.'

'Oh, Aunt Patty,' I said. 'I was so looking forward to being with you. After all, in three years I have seen very little of you.'

'You will see more of me when you are in Devon. Not just Christmas and summer. There is a station about three miles from the house and we'll have the little dog cart. I'll come to meet you. Oh, I am so looking forward to it. And if you were at a school like Colby Abbey, where believe me the nobility send their daughters, you'd be getting into the right genre . . . if you know what I mean. We had a knight or two, but let me tell you, Daisy Hetherington has earls' daughters and the odd duke's.'

We were laughing as it was always so easy to do with Aunt Patty. She had the unique gift of making any situation amusing and tolerable.

My thoughts were in disorder. I had wanted to teach; in fact I had felt I had a special vocation for it; it was what I had been brought up to expect for years, but I did feel this situation was too much for me to take in all at once: the removal from Grantley; the prospect of a new home with

45

Aunt Patty and Violet, and then to be presented with the possibility of a career in my chosen profession with a hope of my own school at the end of it! But in the forefront of my thoughts was Edward Compton, the man who had a habit of appearing mysteriously in my life and was at last taking on what I thought of as a natural image.

Before, he had been like a fantasy, nameless, and I could not fit him into a home. Now I knew. He was Edward Compton of Compton Manor and he was coming to tea with us tomorrow afternoon. Sitting with Aunt Patty and Violet he would shed that aura of make-believe, and I wanted him to do that.

He excited me. He was so handsome with those beautifully chiselled features and that exciting look of another age, which had fallen from him a little in the wood. When he had said his name – with the slightest hesitation so that it had seemed as though he was unwilling to give it – he had become like a normal human being. I wondered why he had been a little reluctant to tell me. Perhaps he knew that coming upon us in the forest, and again on me on deck, he had created an aura of mystery and he wanted to cling to it.

I laughed. I was looking forward to seeing him more than I would care to admit to Aunt Patty; and he dominated my thoughts even to the extent of the coming of Daisy Hetherington and the effect this might have on my future.

* * *

My disappointment was so bitter next day when Edward Compton did not appear that I realized how deeply I had allowed my feelings to become involved.

Aunt Patty and Violet were ready and waiting for him. I had expected he would arrive a little before four o'clock as tea was served at that hour, but when at four thirty he had not appeared, Aunt Patty said we should start without him. And this we did.

I was listening all the time for his arrival and gave rather absent-minded answers to Aunt Patty and Violet who talked continuously about Daisy Hetherington's visit.

46

'Perhaps,' said Aunt Patty, 'he was called away suddenly.'

'He could have sent a message,' said Violet.

'Perhaps he did and it went to the wrong place.'

'Who could mistake Grantley Manor?'

'All sorts of things could happen,' said Aunt Patty. 'He could have had an accident on the road coming here.'

'Shouldn't we have heard?' I asked.

'Not necessarily,' replied Aunt Patty.

'Perhaps he changed his mind about coming,' suggested Violet.'

'He asked for the invitation,' I said. 'It was only yesterday.'

'Men!' said Violet, speaking from vast ignorance. 'They can act very funny at times. It could be anything . . . You never know with men.'

'There'll be an explanation,' said Aunt Patty, spreading her meringue with strawberry jam and giving herself up to the ecstatic enjoyment of it. 'I tell you what,' she said when she had finished it, 'we could send Jim to the Three Feathers. They'd know if there had been an accident.'

Jim was the stable man who looked after the carriage and our horses.

'Do you think it looks as though we're too interested?' asked Violet.

'My dear Vi, we *are* interested.'

'Yes, but him being a *man* . . .'

'Men have mishaps as well as women, Violet, and it seems a funny thing to me that he didn't come when he said he would.'

They talked a little about Edward Compton and I explained how, with a party of girls, I had met him in the forest and afterwards by a strange coincidence he had been on the Channel boat. Then he happened to be here.

'Oh, I reckon he was called away suddenly,' said Aunt Patty. 'He left a message to be delivered but you know what they are at the Three Feathers. Pleasant . . . but they can be forgetful. Do you remember, Vi, when one of the parents wanted to stay for a night and we booked her in and

47

Mrs White forgot to make a note of it. We had to put her up at the school.'

'I remember that well,' said Violet. 'And she liked it so much she stayed an extra day and night and wanted to come again.'

'So you see,' said Aunt Patty and went on to talk of the preparations for Daisy Hetherington's visit.

It was an hour later when Jim returned from the Three Feathers. No Mr Compton had been staying there. All they had at the moment were two elderly ladies.

That seemed very strange. Hadn't he said he was staying at the Three Feathers . . . or had I imagined that he must be?

I was not sure. When he had told me his name I had begun to feel that mysterious air retreating. Now it was back again.

There was something odd about this stranger from the forest.

*　　　*　　　*

There was no message from Edward Compton and I went to bed mystified and disappointed, for he had, after all, expressed a wish to call. I was sure something unexpected had happened.

I spent a disturbed night of jumbled dreams in which he figured mixed up with Daisy Hetherington. In one near nightmare I dreamed that I was at Colby Abbey Academy, which was some great menacing Gothic castle, and I was searching for Edward Compton. When I found him he was a monster – half man, half woman, himself and Daisy Hetherington; and I was trying to escape.

I sat up in bed breathless and I guessed I had been shouting in my sleep.

I lay still trying to quieten my mind.

Such a lot seemed to have happened in a short time that it was small wonder I had disturbed dreams. As for Edward Compton if he had decided he did not want to visit us and had not the courtesy to let us know, so much for him. But I did not believe that was the case. What had been so striking

48

about him had been that air of almost old-world chivalry.

It was all rather mysterious. I should probably find the solution soon. Perhaps a message would be on its way to me now.

When I went down, breakfast was over and the girls were on their way to their various classes. Lessons were always a little perfunctory at such a time with break-up so near and the Christmas spirit everywhere.

During the morning I went into the town. Miss Stoker, the owner of the little linen draper's shop, was in the street inspecting her display of doilies and tablecloths laid out with branches of holly here and there designed to catch Christmas shoppers.

She greeted me with pleasure and said how upset she was because we were leaving. 'The place won't be the same without the school,' she said. 'It's been here so long. Mind you, when we heard it was to be a school . . . that was years ago . . . there was some of us that wasn't too pleased. But then Miss Grant . . . she was a great favourite . . . and all the girls. It did you good to see them coming into the town. I tell you it won't be the same.'

'We shall miss you all,' I said.

'Times change, I always say. Nothing stands still for long.'

'Not many people in the town just now,' I said.

'No. Well, who'd be here at this time of the year?'

'You'd notice strangers, wouldn't you?'

I looked at her expectantly. Miss Stoker had the reputation of knowing everything that went on in the town.

'The Misses Brewer are at the Feathers again. They were here last year. They like to break the journey on the way to visit their cousins where they go for Christmas every year. They know they can trust the Feathers. And they're glad of them there. Not much custom about in winter. Tom Carew was saying to me that there's a tidy trade for spring, summer and autumn but the winter it's as dead as a doornail.'

'And so the Misses Brewer are the only guests just now.'

'Yes . . . and lucky to have them.'

49

That was double confirmation. If anyone else was staying there, Miss Stoker would know.

All the same, when I escaped from her I went into the Three Feathers and wished the Carews the compliments of the season. They made me welcome and insisted that I drink a glass of cider.

'We were struck all of a heap when we heard Miss Grant had sold the Manor,' said Mrs Carew. 'Real shock, wasn't it, Tom?'

Tom said: 'My word, yes. All shook up and no mistake.'

'It had to be,' I replied and they sighed.

I asked how business was.

'Stumbling on,' said Tom. 'We've got two guests . . . the Misses Brewer. They've been here before.'

'Yes, I heard from Miss Stoker. And they are the only two?'

'Yes, the only two.'

I couldn't be more sure than that.

'Your Jim seemed to think we might have a friend of yours . . .'

'We just thought he might be coming here. A Mr Compton.'

'Perhaps he'll come later on. We could give him a really nice room if he was to.'

I came out of the Three Feathers very disconsolate. I wandered through the town and then I remembered the Nag's Head. It was scarcely an hotel, rather a small inn, but they did have a room or two which they let now and then.

I went into the Nag's Head and saw Joe Brackett whom I knew slightly. He welcomed me and said how sorry he was that I was leaving. I came straight to the point and asked him if a Mr Compton had taken a room with him.

He shook his head. 'Not here, Miss Grant. Perhaps at the Feathers . . .'

'No,' I said, 'he didn't stay there either.'

'Are you sure he's staying in this town? I can't think where else he could be unless it's Mrs Shovell's. She lets a room now and then . . . just bed and breakfast. But she's laid up this last week . . . one of her turns.'

50

I said goodbye and made my way back to the Manor. Perhaps there would be a message, I thought.

But there was no message.

In the afternoon I helped the girls decorate the common room and late that afternoon Daisy Hetherington arrived.

* * *

I was definitely impressed by Daisy Hetherington. She was a spare angular woman, very tall. She must have been five feet ten inches in her stockinged feet. I myself was tall but I felt almost dwarfed beside her. She had very clear ice-blue eyes and white hair, elegantly dressed. Her pallor and classic features gave her a look of having been carved out of stone. There was something stony about her, but there was an air of nobility. She would be a model headmistress, I knew at once, because she would inspire immediate awe and a great deal of respect. She would demand the best and those about her would give it because they knew she would accept nothing less. She would give perfection and want it in return.

The only thing which did not fit was her name. Daisy suggested a modest little flower hidden among the grass. She should have had a queenly name: Elizabeth, Alexandra, Eleanor or Victoria.

No one could have been less like Aunt Patty, who seemed to become more rotund, more easy-going, and more frivolously lovable in her presence.

Aunt Patty had sent one of the maids to my room to tell me that Miss Hetherington had arrived and they were in the sitting room before going in to dinner. Would I join them there?

I went down. I remember I was wearing a blue velvet dress with a white jabot at the neck. I had dressed my thick straight chestnut-tinged hair high on my head to give me further height and, I hoped, dignity. I felt that, in the presence of Miss Hetherington, I should need all the self-esteem I could muster. I looked at myself in the mirror. I was not by any means good-looking. My light brown eyes

51

were a little too far apart; my mouth too wide; my forehead too high to be fashionable; my nose, as Monique used to say, was 'enquiring', which meant it had a slight tilt at the tip which added a touch of humour to an otherwise rather serious face. I had wondered why Edward Compton had appeared to be more interested in me when Monique was very pretty and Lydia quite attractive. Frieda was a little severe but she had a directness which was appealing. I shared the freshness of youth but I certainly was not the most attractive of the four. It seemed odd that Edward Compton should have selected me. Unless, of course, our meetings had been by chance. The one in the forest was and so was the one on the boat, but he had taken the trouble to come to Canterton and that must have been to see me. Then why had he made the arrangement to come to tea and then failed to do so?

There was only one explanation. We had met in the forest and he had forgotten all about me until he saw me on the boat. He was passing through and had stopped off at Canterton. Then he remembered I lived there. We met by chance and perhaps I had forced him to accept the invitation, by making it so that it would be impolite to refuse. In any case he had thought better of coming and had slipped quietly away.

I must stop thinking of him. It was far more important to make a good impression on Daisy Hetherington.

I went down.

Aunt Patty was looking delighted. She sprang up and coming to me put her arm through mine.

'Here's Cordelia. Daisy, this is my niece, Cordelia Grant. Cordelia, Miss Hetherington, who owns one of the finest scholastic establishments in the country.'

She took my hand in hers, which was surprisingly warm. I had expected it to be cold . . . as stone.

'I am delighted to meet you,' I said.

'It is a pleasure to make your acquaintance,' she replied. 'Your aunt has been telling me so much about you.'

'Come and sit down,' said Aunt Patty. 'Dinner will be

52

served in about ten minutes. Isn't it fun to have Miss Hetherington with us!'

She was smiling at me, almost winking. Fun seemed a strange word to use in connection with Miss Hetherington – except that, with Aunt Patty, all life fitted into that category.

I sat down, very much aware of the piercing blue eyes on me searchingly and I felt every detail of my appearance was being noted and that everything said would be weighed up and used in evidence for or against me.

'As you know, Cordelia has just returned from Schaffenbrucken,' said Aunt Patty.

'Yes, so I understand.'

'Two years she was there. Few people stay longer.'

'Two or three years is the usual span,' said Daisy. 'It must have been a most exhilarating experience.'

I said that it was.

'You must tell Miss Hetherington about it,' said Aunt Patty.

She was sitting in her chair smiling and nodding. Her pride in me was a little embarrassing, and I felt I must do my best to deserve it.

So I talked of Schaffenbrucken – the daily pattern, the classes, the social activities . . . everything I could think of about the school until Violet coughed timidly and said we should go in to dinner.

Over the fish, Daisy Hetherington brought up the subject round which she had been skirting until this moment.

'My dear Patience,' she said, 'I hope you are doing the wise thing in giving up.'

'No doubt of it,' said Aunt Patty cheerfully. 'My lawyers and the bank all think it's right . . . and they are rarely wrong.'

'So it is as bad as that!'

'As good as that,' retorted Aunt Patty. 'There comes a time when a woman wants to break away. The time for me is now. We want a peaceful life . . . all of us, and that is what we are going to get. Violet has been working far too

53

hard. She's going to keep bees, aren't you, Violet?'

'I always had a feeling for bees,' said Violet, 'ever since my cousin Jeremy was all but stung to death when he got in the way of the queen bee.'

Aunt Patty burst out laughing. 'She had a grudge against her cousin Jeremy.'

'No such thing, Patty. It served him right though. He was always interfering. My mother used to say "Let a bee be and he'll let you be."'

'Bee-keeping may be an interesting hobby,' put in Daisy, 'but if you are looking for profit . . .'

'All we are looking for is some lovely honey,' said Aunt Patty. 'It is delicious in the comb.'

I knew Aunt Patty. She was deliberately making the conversations frivolously light; she was most anxious that Daisy Hetherington should not guess what a serious purpose she had.

'We are all looking forward to the simple life,' she went on. 'Violet, Cordelia and I.'

Daisy Hetherington had turned her eyes on me. I could almost feel them probing into my mind. 'Shall you not find it rather restricting, Miss Grant? At your age, after your education, and your sojourn at Schaffenbrucken . . . it seems rather a waste.'

'Schaffenbrucken is never a waste,' put in Aunt Patty. 'It stays with you all your life. I always regret *I* never went, don't you, Daisy?'

'I consider it to be the ideal finish to an education,' said Daisy. 'That . . . and other establishments like it.'

'For instance Colby Abbey Academy for Young Ladies,' said Aunt Patty rather mischievously. 'Oh, a great reputation! But in our hearts we know that nothing . . . simply nothing . . . compares with Schaffenbrucken.'

'All the more reason why your niece should not stultify in the country.'

'It is for Cordelia to choose what she will do. She was really brought up to teach, weren't you, Cordelia?'

I said yes, that was so.

Daisy turned to me. 'You have a vocation, I daresay.'

54

'I like the idea of being with young people. I always thought that was how it would be.'

'Of course, of course,' said Daisy. 'I should like to look round a little while I'm here, Patience.'

'But of course. This is the last week you know. It is all Christmas festivities. Not so much of the school curriculum now as Christmas jollities . . . and as it will be the last Christmas . . .'

'What are your girls going to do when you close . . . end of next term isn't it?'

'I daresay some of the parents will consider Colby Abbey if I let them know you are a friend of mine. They like connections. Many parents were very interested to hear that Cordelia was at Schaffenbrucken. They thought, of course, she was going to teach here.'

'Yes, yes,' said Daisy, and even she could not hide the speculation in her eyes.

I was being considered and strangely enough I was intrigued by it. In a way I was attracted by Daisy Hetherington. She challenged me. I knew that she was a woman whom I could admire. She would be hard; I could not imagine her ever being governed by sentiment, but she would be just and appreciative of good work – indeed, I could not imagine her tolerating any other sort.

I thought of long days in the country . . . doing nothing in particular; listening to Violet on beekeeping, partaking in village fêtes, holding stalls at bazaars, sharing jokes with Aunt Patty . . . and what else? Going on like that until I married. Whom would I marry? The vicar's son if he had one. But vicars almost always seemed to have daughters. The doctor's son? No. In spite of the fact that I should have a home with Aunt Patty, I wanted something more. Aunt Patty herself was the first to understand this. We should not want to spoil our precious relationship by boredom. She thought I should go out into the world and had made it clear to me that she saw through Daisy Hetherington a way to start about it.

Daisy told us about Colby Abbey Academy for Young Ladies and as she talked she seemed to lose her granite

55

look; a faint colour came into her cheeks; her blue eyes softened; it was clear that the very centre of her life was the school.

'We have the most unusual setting. The school is part of the old Abbey. It gives us such a rare atmosphere. I think settings are so important. Parents are quite impressed when they see the school for the first time.'

'I thought it was a little spooky when I saw it,' said Aunt Patty. 'Violet had nightmares in that room you put her in.'

'It was due to the cheese I'd eaten for supper,' said Violet. 'Cheese does that to me.'

'People can imagine anything anywhere,' said Daisy, closing the subject. She turned to me. 'As I was saying, a most interesting setting. So much of the old Abbey was destroyed during the Dissolution, but quite a large part remains . . . the refectory buildings and the Chapter House. In the sixteenth century the house we now occupy was restored by one of the Verringers, and they built the Hall at the same time using some of the stones from the Abbey. It's the home of the Verringer family who own the Abbey and most of the land for miles round. They are very rich and influential landowners. I have two of the girls with me . . . so convenient for them and good for the school at the same time. I should not expect Jason Verringer to send them anywhere else. Yes, a most unusual setting.'

'It sounds very interesting,' I said. 'I suppose the ruins of the Abbey are all around you.'

'Yes. People come to see them, they are written about, and that brings the school to people's notice. I should like to buy the place but Jason Verringer wouldn't allow that. Naturally, I suppose. The Abbey lands have been in the family since Henry the Eighth gave them to them when the Abbey was partially destroyed.'

'I'm glad I was able to own Grantley,' said Aunt Patty.

'How fortunate that you were!' retorted Daisy tersely. 'It has stood you in good stead when the school failed.'

'Oh, I wouldn't say failed,' said Aunt Patty. 'It is just that we have decided to part company.'

'Oh I know . . . on the advice of your lawyer and banker.

56

Very wise, I am sure. But sad. Yet perhaps for you the quiet country life will have its charm.'

'I intend that it shall,' said Aunt Patty. 'We all do, don't we Cordelia . . . Violet? Vi dear, you're dreaming. You can hear those bees buzzing, I'm sure. I can see you with one of those things they wear over their heads to prevent them getting stung, going out to tell the bees all the local gossip. Did you know, Daisy, that you have to tell the bees . . . or it's unlucky or even worse. They don't like it. They fly away in high dudgeon and they may be so incensed that they plant a few stings first. Did you know they leave their stings behind in the flesh when they sting and it kills them. What a lesson to us all. Never give way to anger.'

Daisy said to me: 'I am sure that after your training and your session at Schaffenbrucken you will feel you want to use your qualifications.'

'Yes,' I replied. 'I think I might feel that.'

Then she went on talking almost directly to me of Colby Abbey Academy, of the number of teachers she had, of the subjects which were taught, how she was concentrating on older girls. 'Most of ours leave at seventeen. Some have actually gone on to Schaffenbrucken or some place on the Continent. Why do people always think they have to go abroad to learn the social graces? Surely we in this country are the best exponents of them in the world. I want to make people realize that, and I have been thinking of adding some extra training for older girls . . . say eighteen or nineteen . . . dancing, conversation . . . debates.'

'Oh yes, we had that sort of thing at Schaffenbrucken.'

She nodded. 'We already have a dancing master and a singing master. Some of the girls have excellent voices. Mademoiselle Dupont and Fräulein Kutcher teach French and German and are very adequate. One must have the natives of the respective countries.'

I listened attentively. She had inspired me with a desire to see the Abbey school.

It seemed disloyal to Aunt Patty to want to get away from home, but I really did believe I should not want to be there all the time, and coming home for holidays would be wonderful. I could almost hear the humming of Violet's bees and see Aunt Patty wearing an enormous hat sitting under one of the trees at a white table on which were laid out cakes, meringues and strawberry jam. Pleasant . . . homely . . . comfortable, but I could not stop thinking of that Abbey school with the ghostly ruins nearby and the mansion, the home of the all-powerful Verringers, a few miles away.

I was still thinking of it when I retired and I had not been in my room more than five minutes when Aunt Patty came in. She threw herself in the armchair puffing slightly with exertion and merriment.

'I think she's hooked,' she said. 'I think she is going to make an offer. She always makes quick decisions. Prides herself on it. I could see that Schaffenbrucken was turning the scales.'

'I was rather intrigued.'

'I could see it. She'll make you an offer. I think you ought to take it. If you don't like it and she tries to ride roughshod over you, you can walk out at once. But she won't. Give her a fair day's work and she'll look after you. I know her well. But as I say, if anything should go wrong, Vi and I will be waiting for you. You know that.'

'You always made things very easy for me,' I said emotionally. 'I'll never forget arriving at the dock and seeing you there in that hat with the blue feather.'

Aunt Patty wiped her eyes. There were sentimental tears but tears of laughter too. 'Oh, that hat. I still have it somewhere. I reckon the feather's a bit mangey. I could put a new feather on it. Why not?'

'Oh Aunt Patty,' I said, 'if Daisy Hetherington does offer me a post . . . and I take it . . . it isn't because I don't want to be with you.'

'Of course it's not. You've got to have a life of your own and it's not for the young to bury themselves with the old. Vi and I have our interests. Your life is just beginning. It's right for you to step out into the world, and as I said, play your cards rightly and one of these days . . . who knows? She doesn't own that place, you see. Just a lease on it, I

58

suppose. She must have got that from those Verringers she's always talking about. She's comfortable enough there. I'd like you to go in with Daisy. I have a great respect for her really. At the best it could lead to big things and at the least it could be valuable experience.'

We embraced. She tiptoed out looking happily conspiratorial; and I went to bed and slept well after my previous night's distorted dreams.

*　　　*　　　*

The next day I had a long talk with Daisy Hetherington, and the outcome was that if I would care to join her school at the beginning of the Summer term she would be pleased to have me. I should work out a curriculum similar to that which had been followed at Schaffenbrucken and in addition to taking debating and conversation classes I should exercise the girls in deportment and teach them English.

It seemed an interesting project and as she had already whetted my curiosity with descriptions of the school which was part of an abbey, I was very inclined to accept.

However as I was concerned about Aunt Patty and I knew she was urging me to go for my own good rather than her pleasure, I did hesitate.

'I must have your reply immediately after Christmas,' said Daisy, and it was left at that.

Aunt Patty was delighted. 'The right approach,' she said. 'Not too eager. Well, Daisy will depart immediately after the carol concert. She is staying for that, just for the pleasure of telling us how much more accomplished are the carol singers of Colby Abbey Academy for Young Ladies.'

In due course Daisy left with gracious thanks for our hospitality and with the command that my reply must be with her before the first of January.

Then it was time for the girls to leave. We said sad farewells to them all. Otherwise Christmas was much as it had always been. There was the traditional goose and Christmas pudding and many of our neighbours joined us during the two days. The local fiddler came in and we danced in the hall. But everyone was aware that it was the

59

last time and that must mean a certain amount of sadness.

I was glad when it was over, and then I had to make my decision, which I suppose I had already done. I wrote to Daisy Hetherington accepting her offer and telling her that I should be prepared to start at the beginning of the Spring term.

There was packing to do and the new house to visit. It was pleasant – quite charming in fact, but of course rather insignificant compared with the Manor.

I had heard nothing from Edward Compton. I was surprised and hurt for I had expected some explanation. It seemed so extraordinary. Sometimes I began to think I had imagined the whole thing. When I looked back I realized that apart from the encounter with the other three girls, I had been alone when I saw him – on the train, on the boat, and in the woods. I could in some moments convince myself that I had imagined those meetings. After all there was something about him which was different from other people.

I realized then that I knew little of men. A lot of girls would have been far more experienced long ago. I suppose it was due to being at school so long. Young men had just not come into my life. Monique had met her Henri whom she knew she was going to marry. Frieda might not have met any more men than I had. Lydia had brothers and they had friends whom they sometimes brought home. She had talked of them when she came back after holidays at home. But I had lived in a society dominated by women. There was, of course, the vicar's new curate. He was in his twenties and shy; there was the doctor's son who was at Cambridge. Neither was very romantic. That was it. Edward Compton was definitely romantic. He had stirred new interests in me. Perhaps because he had showed rather clearly that he liked me . . . preferred me. One must be gratified to be so preferred among three far from unattractive girls.

Yes, I was bitterly disappointed. It had begun so romantically . . . and then to peter out!

Perhaps that was one of the reasons why I was reaching

60

out for adventure. I wanted to take a challenge, to start in new territory.

I certainly should when I went to the Colby Abbey Academy.

When Aunt Patty had shown me the new house at Moldenbury, I had expressed a greater enthusiasm than I had really felt – just to please her. We had explored the rather large garden and decided where Aunt Patty should have her summer house and Violet her bees, which should be my room and how it should be furnished.

On the way home we had to wait at the London terminal for catching the train to Canterton and, while I was there, I saw a notice which mentioned trains to Bury St Edmunds.

I think the idea started to grow in my mind then.

*　　　*　　　*

I knew I was going to do it, although I was not quite sure how I should act when I got there.

Perhaps I shouldn't seek him out. Perhaps I just wanted to assure myself that he had really existed and that I had not been dreaming and imagined the whole adventure.

The farther I grew from the affair the more mystic it seemed. He was unlike anyone I had ever known before. He was very good looking, with those sculptured features – rather like Daisy Hetherington's, but there was no doubt in my mind that she was a real person! Seeing him in the forest with my three friends had been real enough, but had I begun to imagine certain things about him? It was probably due to Elsa's talk about the mysticism of the forest legends that sometimes in my thoughts made him seem part of them. Could I have imagined that I saw him in the train, on the boat and here in Canterton? Had I imagined the whole thing? No. It was ridiculous. I was no dreamer. I was a very practical young woman. It was a little alarming to think that one could imagine certain happenings so that one was not completely convinced that they had actually happened.

I wanted to shake myself. That was why when I saw that notice about Bury St Edmunds I had the idea of going on a voyage of discovery. I had mentioned Bury St Edmunds –

61

as the only town I knew in Suffolk – and he had said yes . . . his home was near there.

Croston. That was the name he had mentioned. The little town near Bury St Edmunds. Suppose I went there and found Compton Manor. I should not call of course. I could hardly do that. But I should convince myself that he was a rather ill-mannered young man and I was a sensible young woman who did not go off into flights of fancy and then wonder whether they were real or not.

Then the opportunity presented itself.

It was between terms. The negotiations for the house were completed. Aunt Patty would leave Grantley at the beginning of April. I should then be on my way to Colby Abbey school.

A great deal of activity was in progress. Aunt Patty enjoyed this. There was so much furniture and effects to be disposed of and she was having certain alterations made to the new house so that there was continual coming and going. Violet was harassed and said she didn't know whether she was on her head or her heels, but Aunt Patty flourished.

She had to go to Moldenbury to see the architect and decided that while she was in London, where it was necessary to change trains, she would stay a few days and make some purchases and see about the sale of the school equipment which remained at Grantley; then she would go on to Moldenbury. It was decided that I should accompany her.

When we were in London I said I should like to stay a little longer as I had some shopping to do for myself and it was arranged that I should stay at Smiths, the small and comfortable family hotel which Aunt Patty always used when she came to London and where they knew her well, while she went on to Moldenbury. When she came back to London we could return to Grantley together.

Thus I found myself alone and I knew that if ever I was going to make that tour of investigation I must do so now.

I left early in the morning and as the train carried me to

62

Bury St Edmunds I asked myself whether I was being impulsive in what I was doing. What if I came face to face with him? What would be my excuse for seeking him out? He had come to Canterton, hadn't he? Yes, but this was different. He had shown quite clearly that he did not want to continue the acquaintance . . . friendship . . . or whatever it was. It was not very good manners to seek him out therefore.

No. But I had no intention of calling at Compton Manor if I found it. I would go into a nearby inn and ask discreet questions. If the people of Suffolk were as fond of a gossip as those of Sussex, I might find out what I wanted to know, which was, I assured myself, merely to find out whether there had ever been a man called Edward Compton, so that I could rid myself of this absurd notion that I had been suffering from some sort of hallucination.

It was a bright cold morning – rather bracing – and as the train carried me along I grew more and more excited. We were in on good time and I was elated when, asking how I could find my way to Croston, I was told there was a branch line with a service every three hours, and if I hurried I could just catch the next train.

I did so and congratulated myself as we puffed along through the pleasant but flat countryside.

Croston was nothing more than a halt. I saw a man who might have been a railway official and I approached him. He was oldish with a grey beard and rheumy eyes. He looked at me with curiosity, and it struck me that he did not see many strangers.

'Is Compton Manor near here?' I asked.

He looked at me oddly and then nodded. Again my spirits rose.

'What do you want with the Manor?' he asked me.

'I . . . er . . . wanted to go that way.'

'Oh, I see.' He scratched his head. 'Take the footpath. It'll take you into Croston. Then through the street and bear to the right.'

It was working out very easily.

Croston was one short street of a few thatched cottages,

63

a village shop, a church and an inn. I bore to the right and walked on.

I had not gone very far when I saw an old signpost. Half of it was broken away. I looked at it closely. 'Compton Manor,' I read.

But which way? It must be up the lane for the only other way was where I had come from. I started up the lane and turning a bend I saw a mansion.

Then I gasped in horror. This could not be the place. And yet there was the signpost . . .

I approached. It was nothing more than a shell. The stone walls were blackened. I went through an opening in those scorched walls and noticed that there were weeds growing among the grass where once there had been rooms. Then the fire was not recent.

This could not be Compton Manor. It must be farther on.

I left the blackened ruin behind me and found the road. There was nothing before me but open fields, and because of the flatness of the land, I could see for miles ahead and there was certainly no house there.

I sat down on the grass verge. I was baffled. Seeking to solve the mystery. I had plunged farther into it.

There was nothing to do but retrace my steps to the station. There would be about two hours to wait for the next train to Bury St Edmunds.

Slowly I walked into the town. My journey had been fruitless. I came to the church. It was very ancient – Norman I guessed. There were very few people about. I had been rather silly to come.

I went into the church. It had a beautiful stained glass window – rather impressive for such a small church. I approached the altar. Then I was looking at the brass plaque engraved on which were the words 'In memory of Sir Gervaise Compton, Baronet of Compton Manor'. I looked about me and saw that there were other memorials to the Compton family.

While I stood there I heard a step behind me. A man was coming into the church carrying a pile of hassocks.

'Good morning,' he said, 'or rather afternoon.'

'Good afternoon,' I replied.

'Taking a look at our church?'

'Yes. It's very interesting.'

'Not many visitors come. Though it is one of the oldest in the country.'

'I thought it must be.'

'Are you interested in architecture, Madam?'

'I know very little about it.'

He looked disappointed and I guessed he had wanted to give me a lecture on Norman versus Gothic. He must be a church warden or verger or something connected with the church.

I said: 'I have been looking at that burned-out house along the road. Could that be Compton Manor?'

'Oh yes, Madam. That was Compton.'

'When was the fire?'

'Oh, it must have been nigh on twenty years ago.'

'Twenty years ago!'

'Terrible tragedy. It started in the kitchens. The shell of the place is left. I wonder they don't rebuild or something. The walls are still sturdy. They were built to last a thousand years. There's been talk about it but nobody ever does anything.'

'And the Compton family?'

'It was the end of them . . . they died in the fire. A boy and a girl. Tragic it was. People still talk of it. Then there was Sir Edward and Lady Compton. They died too. In fact the whole family was wiped out. It was a big tragedy for this place, for the Comptons *were* Croston at that time. It's never been the same since. No big family to take the girls into service and take care of the interests of the village . . .'

I was scarcely listening. I was saying to myself: How could he have been Edward Compton of Compton Manor? They are all dead.

'They recovered most of the bodies. They're all buried in the churchyard here . . . in the special Compton grounds. I remember the funeral. We often talk of it. "Croston's day

65

of mourning" I call it. Are you interested in the family, Madam?'

'Well, I saw the house . . . and it is a terribly sad story.'

'Yes. They were Croston all right. Look round this church. You see they've left signs everywhere. That's their pew in the front there. No one's used it since. I'll show you the graves if you'd like to step out.'

I followed him out to the graves. I was shivering slightly.

He said: 'Chill wind springing up. We get some rough winds here. It can be pretty biting when they blow from the east.'

He wended his way through the tombstones and we came to a secluded corner. We were in a well-tended patch where several rose trees and laurels had been planted. It must look very pretty in summer.

Then he said: 'That's Sir Edward. You can see the date. Yes, it is just over twenty years. All these graves . . . victims of the fire. That's Lady Compton and that's little Edward and Edwina his sister. Poor little mites. They never had a life. It makes you wonder, doesn't it. He was two years old and Edwina was five. They come into the world and then are taken away. It makes you wonder . . . If they could look down and see what might have been . . .'

'It's very kind of you to show me,' I said.

'A pleasure. We don't get many interested. But I could see you were.'

'Yes,' I said, 'and thank you very much.'

I wanted to be alone. I wanted to think. This was the last thing I had expected to find.

I was glad of the long journey back during which I could ponder on what I had seen and try to grasp what it could possibly mean; but when I reached London I was no nearer solving the mystery.

Could it really be that the man I had seen was a spectre . . . a ghost from the past?

That theory would explain many things. Yet I could not accept it. One thing was certain – there was no Edward Compton of Compton Manor. There had not been for more than twenty years!

66

Then who was the strange man who had made such an impression on me, who had looked at me – yes, I would confess it now – with admiration, and with something which indicated to me that we could have a closer relationship and that was what he was hoping for.

How could I have imagined the whole conception? He had been in the forest. Was it possible that in that forest which Lydia always said was a little spooky – the same word which Aunt Patty had used about the Abbey school – strange things could happen?

I must forget the incident. I could not allow it to go on occupying my thoughts. It was one of life's strange experiences. They did happen from time to time. I had read of them and there was no explanation.

I was sure I should be wise to try to put the entire matter out of my mind.

That was impossible. When I shut my eyes I could see that tombstone. Sir Edward Compton . . . and that of the little boy, another Edward.

It was mysterious . . . rather frightening.

Oh yes. I must certainly try to put it out of my mind.

The Abbey

*

It was a lovely spring day when I arrived at Colby Abbey station. I had been enchanted by the countryside which I had glimpsed through the windows of the train – lush green meadows and wooded hills and the rich red soil of Devonshire with the occasional glimpse of the sea.

The sun was warm although there was a slight nip in the air as though to remind me that summer had not yet come. I had said goodbye to Aunt Patty and Violet with much laughter, a few tears and constant reminders that we should all be together in the summer vacation. It was exhilarating as starting a new life must always be, and I was extremely fortunate in having Aunt Patty. Her last injunction had been: 'If Madam Hetherington doesn't treat you with the right respect, you know what to do. But I think she'll behave herself. She knows that you are not exactly hers to command like some of those poor girls who have to toe the line or wonder where their next meal's coming from.'

'You've always been a bulwark in my life,' I told her.

'I hope that's not meant to be taken too literally, dear. I know I'm overfond of good food, but bulwark . . . no, I don't like the sound of that.'

That was how we parted. The last I saw of her from the train window, for she and Violet had come to London to see me off, was a smile though I knew the tears were not far off.

So here I was arrived at last, and as I stepped out of the train a man in smart livery came towards me and asked if my name was Miss Grant, for if so, he had come to drive me to Colby Abbey Academy where I was expected.

'The trap's in the yard, Miss. Be this your bag? 'Tis just a step or two . . . nothing more.'

I went through the barrier with him and there was what he called the trap – a rather smart two-wheeled vehicle drawn by a grey horse.

He took my bags and stowed them away.

'Reckon, Miss,' he said, 'you'll be comfortable up with me.'

'Thank you,' I said when he helped me up.

'It be a nice day for coming, Miss,' he said. He had a black beard and dark curly hair – a stocky, middle-aged man, who spoke with that burr with which in time I should become familiar.

He was inclined to be talkative. As he whipped up the horse he said: 'The young ladies 'ull be coming next Tuesday. It'll give you time to settle in, Miss. Bit different when they'm all here, eh? Some of 'em stays at school this time of year though. It's only at Christmas and summer we have a full turn-out. Too far for some to go home, you do see?'

'Yes,' I said.

'Do 'ee know Devon at all, Miss?'

'No, I'm afraid I don't.'

'You've got a real treat in store. God's own country. A little bit of heaven itself.'

'I'm glad to hear that.'

'It be true, Miss. Sir Francis Drake, now. He were a Devon man. Saved England from them Spaniards, they do say. It were a long time ago though. Glorious Devon they call it. Devonshire cream and cider . . . They do make songs about it.'

'Yes, I have heard some of them.'

'You'll see the big house in a minute. The Abbey's a good three miles on.'

'Is that the home of the Verringers?'

'Yes, that be the Hall. Look, there's the graveyard by the church.'

Just at that moment a bell began to toll.

'There be the funeral today. Funny time to arrive, Miss, if 'ee don't mind me saying so. Her ladyship going out like and you coming in.'

69

His beard shook. He seemed to find that rather amusing.

'Whose funeral did you say it was?'

'Lady Verringer's.'

'Oh . . . was she an elderly lady?'

'No. She'm Sir Jason's wife. Poor lady. Not much of a life. Been invalid for ten years or more. Fell from her horse. They don't have much luck . . . them Verringers. They do be cursed, I reckon, like folks say.'

'Oh?'

'Well, it goes back . . . right a long way. And the Abbey and all that. There's stories about them. There'm folks as think it was either Abbey or Verringers and it ought to have been the Abbey.'

'It sounds mysterious.'

'Oh, it goes back a long way.'

We had turned into a lane so narrow that the bushes from the hedges brushed the sides of the trap. Suddenly my driver pulled up. A carriage was coming towards us.

The driver of the carriage had pulled up too. He had no alternative and the two men were glaring at each other.

'You'll have to back, Emmet,' said the driver of the carriage.

My driver – Emmet apparently – remained stubbornly stationary. 'You've less far to go back, Tom Craddock,' he said.

'I b'ain't going back,' said Tom Craddock. 'Look out, Nat Emmet, I've got Squire here.'

I heard a voice shout: 'What in God's name is going on here?' A face looked out of a window and I caught a glimpse of dark hair and angry dark eyes.

' 'Tis Nat Emmet, Sir Jason. He be bringing the new young lady to the school and he's blocking the road.'

'Get back at once, Emmet,' cried the imperious voice and the face disappeared.

'Yes, sir. Yes, Sir Jason. That's just what I be doing . . .'

'Be sharp about it.'

Emmet got down and we started to move back, and finally reached the wide road.

70

The carriage came out at a sharp pace and the driver gave Nat Emmet a victorious grin as it went past. I tried to catch a glimpse of the man inside the carriage but he was out of sight.

The funeral bell started to toll once more.

'He's just come from burying his wife,' said Emmet.

'So that's Sir Jason himself. He seemed a bit choleric.'

'What's that, Miss?'

'He seems a bit quick-tempered.'

'Oh, Squire don't like anything to get in his way . . . like his poor lady. There's some as say she was in his way. But I'm talking out of turn. But there's things folks don't keep quiet. And why should they?'

We went quickly through the lane.

'Don't want to meet no others,' said Emmet. 'Not that I'd go back a second time . . . except for Squire and we're not likely to meet him again, are we?'

We trotted along while he made observations which did not interest me greatly because my thoughts were with the Squire and the lady who had been in his way and for whom the dismal bell was tolling.

'If you look when we turn this bend, Miss, you'll be getting your first view of the Abbey,' Emmet told me.

Then I was alert . . . waiting.

It lay ahead of me, grand, imposing, tragic, a shell encasing past glory. I could see the sun glinting through the great arches which were open to the sky.

'That be it,' said Emmet, pointing with his whip. 'It be quite a sight, b'ain't it? In spite of being nothing but an old ruin . . . 'cept the part that ain't. Well, folks seem to think a lot of our Abbey. Wouldn't let it be touched. It was a good thing they did their bit of building in days gone by.'

I was speechless with a kind of wonder. It was indeed a magnificent sight. Away to the hills the trees were in bud; the sun glinted on a brook which was wending its way across a meadow.

'Look over to the right of the tower, Miss, and you'll see the fish ponds. That's where the monks used to catch their supper.'

71

'It's wonderful. I had not imagined anything quite so . . . impressive.'

'There's folks as won't go near the place after dark. Miss Hetherington her don't like us to say it, but it be true. She thinks it will frighten the young ladies so they'll ask to be took away. But I tell you there's some as say they can hear bells at certain times of night . . . and monks chanting.'

'One could quite believe that.'

'You're seeing it in sunlight, Miss. You want to see it by the light of the moon . . . or better still when there's just a few stars to light the way.'

'I daresay I shall,' I said.

We were getting nearer.

'It be comfortable enough in the school, Miss. You'd hardly know where you was to. Miss Hetherington, her's done wonders. Just like a school it is inside . . . and when you hear all them young ladies laughing together, well, you forget all about them long dead monks.'

The trap had drawn up in a courtyard. Emmet jumped down and helped me down.

'I'll see to your bags, Miss,' he said.

I was facing a door in a greystone wall. Emmet pulled the bell and the door was immediately opened by a girl in uniform.

'Come in, Miss Grant. It be Miss Grant, b'ain't it? Miss Hetherington said as you was to be took right up to her the moment you arrive. She's just having tea.'

I was in a large hall with a vaulted ceiling. It looked like a monastery; there was a coldness in the air which I noticed after the warmth of the sun outside.

'Did you have a good journey, Miss?' asked the girl. 'It seems the train was on time.'

'Very good, thank you.'

'The other mistresses haven't come yet. They'll be here tomorrow, but it's when all the young ladies are here . . . that's when we know it.' She turned to me and raising her eyes to the ceiling jerked her chin upwards.

'This way, Miss. Look out. These staircases can be dangerous. If you slip on the narrow bit . . . particularly

72

coming down, you can come a cropper. Hang on to this rope. Supposed to be a banister. This is how the monks had it, so we have to have it that way too.'

'It's an ancient building.'

'Built up from parts of the ruins, Miss. We're always hearing about it . . . how we ought to appreciate it and all that 'cause the monks had it that way. Myself, I'd rather a nice wood banister.'

We had come to a long corridor. It had a vaulted ceiling like that in the hall, and there were rooms leading from it.

'This way, Miss.' The girl tapped on a door and a voice which I recognized immediately as that of Daisy Hetherington called: 'Come in.'

'Ah, there you are.'

She had risen. She was taller than I remembered; and here within these walls she looked more than ever as though she had been carved out of stone.

'It is so nice to see you. You must be tired from your journey. Grace, bring another cup and some more hot water. First you will have some tea – it is quite freshly made – and then you shall see your quarters. I trust you have had a good journey. You are very much on time.'

'The train was exactly on time.'

'Take off your coat. That's right. And sit down. I am pleased to see you, Cordelia. I shall, however, call you Miss Grant, except when we are on our own. I don't want there to be any differences.'

'No, of course not.'

'I daresay you were impressed by the Abbey.'

'Very. Although I have seen little so far, just the first impression. And that is truly staggering.'

'I know the effect it has. We, who live in the midst of these ancient stones, I'm afraid are apt to forget all they stand for.'

'It is certainly a wonderful setting.'

'I think so. It makes us different. I think living in such a place gives the girls an understanding of the past. We have always done very well with history. Ah, here is the hot

73

water. Let me pour out for you. Do you take cream or sugar?'

'Neither, thank you.'

'You are not like your aunt. She always shocks me by the amount of sugar she takes in her tea.'

'She loves all sweet things.'

'To her cost.'

'She is happy as she is and manages to make all those about her the same.'

'Ah, Patience. Well, here you are. I shall myself show you round after tea . . . before it gets dark. I enjoy showing people round for the first time. I gloat over it. It really is unique, I am sure. It is wonderful what those Elizabethan builders managed to raise up out of the ruins. We should call ourself the Phoenix, I always say.'

'What part of the monastery is this?'

'It's the Chapter House and Monks' Dorter and the Lay Brothers' Dorter and their library, kitchens and infirmary. This part was left almost untouched when the despoilers came in. It was the towers and the chapels which were so badly desecrated.'

'So this is almost as it was when it was built, I suppose.'

'Yes, in the mid 1100s. The monks built it with their own hands. Think of the activity which must have gone on. They had to bring the stone here you know . . . and then build. Of course, it was a labour of love. You can feel that . . . particularly in the nave and the aisles . . . even though they are open to the sky.'

'I am so looking forward to seeing it all.'

'I knew you would be. I sensed that you would have a feeling for it. Some people have, some haven't.'

She passed me a plate of thin bread and butter.

'I am glad you were able to come before the others arrive tomorrow . . . or most of them. Mademoiselle Dupont and Fräulein Kutcher are here. They stay for the shorter holidays and go to their homes twice a year. It is expensive travelling back and forth to the Continent. They are good, both of them. Jeannette Dupont finds discipline difficult, but the girls are fond of her and if her teaching is not quite

74

orthodox she gets results. Fräulein Kutcher is completely different. An excellent teacher, and she has a certain dignity which is necessary when teaching girls. They have to respect you, you know. I hope you will find you have that quality. You will soon discover. I took a bit of a risk, you know . . . as you have never taught before.'

'If you are not pleased with me, you must say so immediately. Aunt Patty would be rather pleased, I think. She would like me to be with them.'

'I should hate to see you stultify in a country village after your education. No. I have never failed in my judgement yet, and I don't expect to now. Do you ride?'

'I did quite a lot at Grantley.'

'Good. We have a riding master who comes in three times a week to teach the girls. They go out in parties, but I like to have a mistress with them. You can use the horses in your spare time, if you like. We are rather isolated and you would have to walk everywhere if you didn't ride. The town is three miles from here . . . such as it is. The Hall is just beyond.'

'I passed that on my way here.'

'Oh yes. There's a funeral today. Poor Lady Verringer passed away. A happy release, some say. Fiona and Eugenie will have been at the funeral. I suppose we shall have to allow them to wear black instead of their school uniforms for some months. It's so tiresome. I wouldn't allow it for anyone else. But they being who they are . . . and so close to the school . . . I don't see how I can do anything else.'

'I suppose it was their mother who has died. I saw their father.'

'No. Not the mother. Their aunt. And you saw Sir Jason?'

'Yes, in his carriage. We met it in the lane.'

'He would have been coming from the funeral. He is the girls' uncle. He and Lady Verringer had no children. A sadness for them, I knew. Fiona and Eugenie are Sir Jason's wards – his brother's children. They lost both their parents when they were quite young. Their home has always been the Hall . . . even when their parents were

75

alive. Their father was a younger brother of Sir Jason. It was not, of course, like having children of their own and there is no direct heir. The Verringers have been at the Hall since it was built in the mid 1500s. The whole of the Abbey lands came into their possession after the Dissolution of the Monasteries.'

'I see. I quite thought the girls were his.'

'They have been with me for three years. They came when Fiona was fourteen. She is the elder, though not by much. There is just about eighteen months between her and Eugenie. Yes, she must have been fourteen because she is seventeen now . . . but soon to be eighteen, so Eugenie will be turned sixteen.'

'The girls are mostly round about that age, are they?'

'From fourteen to eighteen. Very much like Schaffen-brucken, I imagine.'

'Yes, very much so.'

'I aim to turn out girls who will be fit to mingle in the highest society. That, I think, is important. Now to get down to practical matters. You will be taking English. That will consist of literature, of course. The girls study the classics with you. And I want you to concentrate on their social education. Conversation . . . debates on current affairs. We have a dancing master . . . ballroom dancing, you know. He comes three times a week, but there will be dancing practice every day and you and perhaps one of the others will be in charge of that. Then there is music. Mr Maurice Crowe gives lessons to the whole school once a week, but he teaches pianoforte and violin to those who want it. We concentrate on music and the arts generally. We have an art mistress in Eileen Eccles. She may be arriving tonight. I have had a word with her. You and she can arrange to put on a play for the school. We have done that before and it is a great success. Parents like to see their children act. Last time we were allowed to do it at the Hall. They have a very fine ball-room which is ideal for the purpose.'

'It sounds very interesting.'

'I am sure you will find it so. Now for sleeping arrangements. The rooms are necessarily small; they were once the sleeping quarters of the Lay Brothers and we are not allowed to tamper with anything structurally, though Sir Jason has allowed one or two concessions to fit in with the school. For instance, we have partitioned one room as it was twice as large as the others, and made two bedrooms of it. It is not easy to accommodate so many people. One large dormitory would have been more normal. As it is we have two girls in each room and, as they are more or less in sections, I have put one mistress in charge of four bedrooms, which means eight girls. Your room is next to your four. You make sure that they are in their rooms every night, that they rise when the bell rings, and that they conduct themselves in an orderly manner.'

'A sort of house mistress.'

'Exactly, except that we are all under one roof and the other sections are not far away. The girls you will have are on the whole pleasant malleable creatures. Gwendoline Grey shares with Jane Everton. Gwendoline is the daughter of a professor and Jane's father is a manufacturer in the Midlands. Not the same class as Gwendoline but plenty of money. I mix my girls carefully. Jane will learn from Gwendoline and perhaps Gwendoline a little from Jane. In the next room is the Honourable Charlotte Mackay. Her father is Lord Blandore, and she is with Patricia Cartwright, from a banking family. Caroline Sangton's father is a city importer and she is with Teresa Hurst. By the way Teresa spends most of her holidays at school. Her father grows something in Rhodesia . . . tobacco, I think. Sometimes we can pack her off to her mother's cousins, but not always, and I fancy they get out of having the child when they can.'

'Poor Teresa,' I said.

'Yes indeed. And I am also giving you the Verringer girls. They are in one of your rooms. So that is your little family as I call it. I am sure you will find everything goes smoothly. Now have you finished your tea? Then I will take you to your room myself. Your bags will be there and if you are not too tired and would like to look round I will show

77

you. Perhaps you would like to freshen up after your journey? If you will come now we'll go to your room and you can wash and change if you like and hang up your things. Then I will show you round the Abbey.'

'Thank you. That will be very interesting.'

'Come then.'

I followed her over the stone-flagged floors, up staircases rather like the one I had seen – treacherously narrow where it reached the post and wider at the other end, with its rope banister.

At length we came to the bedrooms. Mine was small with thick stone walls which made it seem cold, and the window was long and narrow. There was a bed in it, a cupboard, a chair and a table.

'You are thinking it is a little spartan,' said Daisy. 'Mine is the same. Remember this is an abbey and I impress on the girls that we are privileged to be here. Now I will show you where we wash. I have been allowed to divide this into cubicles . . . a great concession, I do assure you. The Lay Brothers would have washed in this trough which ran along the whole length of this section. However, you will find this more in keeping with modern times. I have put mirrors in too. Now you have seen your quarters and the rooms of the girls who will be in your charge. Shall I send for you in half an hour? One of the maids will bring you to my study and then we can go on our tour of exploration.'

I washed, changed my travelling clothes and hung up my things in the cupboard. I was rather unsure of my feelings. I was excited by everything I had seen and I felt that I understood Daisy Hetherington, respected her and would get along moderately well with her. On the other hand, although I found my surroundings of immense interest there were moments when I was repelled by them. Perhaps it was because the past was too close; it intruded. What could one expect within the actual walls of an abbey!

I was ready and waiting when the summons came. I was imagining telling Aunt Patty all about it when we were together in the summer. That cheered me considerably.

78

I was conducted to the presence of my employer.

'Ah!' Her cool blue eyes surveyed me and I gathered she approved of my white blouse and navy blue skirt. 'Here you are. Now I will take you first over our own establishment. If there is time I will give you some idea of the surroundings, but these you will discover in more detail later. I have a picture here of the Abbey as it was before the Dissolution. It wasn't drawn until the beginning of this century, but it is a good job of reconstruction and it wasn't so difficult with the outline there, as you might say. Only the slightest degree of imagination was necessary. Our monks were Cistercians and so the Abbey is built in that style. You see it is constructed on either side of a stream which runs into the fishponds. They in their turn go into the river. We are about eight miles from the sea. There are three fishponds, one flowing into another. There are some good fish in there too. Emmet and some of the others fish there frequently and much of our Friday fish comes from the ponds. I think it is a very important tradition. Here you can see the nave and the transept. That is the chapel of six altars. There is the Chapter House and the Gate House and the Great Hall . . . the Abbot's House, the refectory, the store house and buttery. You'll find everything on the plan. And here *we* are. Now . . . shall we go?'

We came out into the fresh air. It seemed warm outside. Daisy talked as we went along. It was a fascinating tour and I found I could not take in all I had to see; but what I was deeply aware of was the brooding atmosphere of the Abbey – and particularly that part which was roofless. It seemed uncanny to walk over those stone flags, past great pillars which seemed meaningless since they were supporting walls and arches which were now a ruin, and through which I could see the sky. I understood how imaginative people fancied they heard the sound of bells and the chanting of monks when dusk fell. I had yet to see the place without the bright sunshine. I could believe it was very eerie in the dusk and for the first time I wondered whether Daisy Hetherington had been wise in taking part of the old Abbey for her school. Wouldn't it have been better in some

79

fresh open country or facing the sea somewhere along the South Coast.

But of course it did make the school unique, and that was what Daisy was striving for.

'You are silent, Cordelia,' she said. 'I understand. You are overcome. It is the effect it has on all sensitive people.'

'The girls . . . how do they feel about all this antiquity?'

'Frivolous creatures most of them . . . unaware of it.'

'And the mistresses?'

'Oh, I think some of them are surprised when they first come. But it grows on them. They realize that they are privileged.'

I was silent. I touched the rough stone wall and looked through the Norman arch to the sky. Daisy Hetherington patted my arm. 'Come along in,' she said. 'We dine at seven thirty.'

Dinner was served in the Lay Brothers' Refectory which must have been more or less the same as it was seven centuries before with its vaulted ceiling and long narrow slits of windows.

Daisy presided at the head of the table looking like an abbess herself. The food was excellent. 'All home-grown,' she told me. 'It is one of the features of the place. We have plenty of space. The old kitchen gardens for instance, and we make good use of them. I have two gardeners working full time, and Emmet helps out. So do the other stable boys.'

I could see that this was a very large establishment. It made Grantley Manor seem almost amateur in comparison.

At dinner I was introduced to Mademoiselle Jeannette Dupont, Fräulein Irma Kutcher and Eileen Eccles, the art mistress, who had arrived. I was able to talk both in French and German which delighted not only those I talked to but Daisy herself who, although she herself did not venture beyond English, liked to stress the fact that I was fluent in both languages.

Jeannette Dupont was in her mid twenties, I imagined, and rather pretty. Irma Kutcher wasn't much older but

80

appeared to be, as she was rather stern-looking, and I was sure took her post very seriously.

Eileen Eccles was the typical art mistress with rather untidy hair and expressive dark eyes; she wore a loose dress of mingling shades of brown with a faint touch of scarlet and she looked every inch the artist.

We talked of school matters, and I had the feeling that I should not find it too difficult to fit into Daisy's establishment. She herself did most of the talking and it was all about the school and the idiosyncracies of certain pupils. I felt I was getting a real grasp of everything.

When dinner was over we went into Daisy's study and there the conversation continued in the same vein until she said she was sure I was tired and would like to retire.

'The rest of the mistresses will be arriving tomorrow or the next day. And on Tuesday all the girls who have been home will be coming back.'

Mademoiselle asked if the Verringer sisters would be returning on Tuesday.

'Of course,' said Daisy. 'Why not?'

'I 'ave thought,' said Mademoiselle, 'that there is this death in the family . . . and they stay at home to mourn.'

'Sir Jason wouldn't want that. They'll be better off at school. They'll be joining us on Tuesday. Charlotte Mackay will be with them. She has been spending the holiday at the Hall. It must have been rather awkward to have her there at such a time. However, I believe the families know each other. Now, I am sure Miss Grant is very tired. Miss Eccles, perhaps you would take Miss Grant to her room. I am sure she will soon find her way around but just at first it can be confusing.'

Miss Eccles rose and led the way.

When we were on the staircase, she turned to me and said: 'Daisy can be a little overpowering at times. It's not so bad when there are more of us.'

I didn't answer that but merely smiled and she went on: 'This place takes a bit of getting used to. I can't tell you the number of times I nearly packed up and went home during

81

my first term. But I stuck it out, and in a funny sort of way it grows on you. I think I'd be rather sad to leave now.'

'Mademoiselle and Fräulein seem very pleasant.'

'They're all right. So is Daisy in her way. All you have to do is keep on the right side of her and remember that, like God, she knows all, sees all and is always right.'

'Sounds simple but faintly alarming.'

'Keep everything in order and she's all right. Have you taught before? Oh no, I remember you've just come from Schaffenbrucken. I ought not to forget that. Daisy's told us about a dozen times already.'

'They make such a fuss about that place.'

'It is the *Ne plus ultra.*'

I laughed.

'At least in Daisy's eyes,' she went on. 'You're teaching social graces, I believe.'

'Yes, I have to work out how I am going to do that.'

'Just walk in the steps of Schaffenbrucken and you can't go wrong.'

'It must be gratifying to teach art when you find talent.'

'We haven't a Rubens or a Leonardo among us, I'm afraid. At least, if there are, we haven't at the moment discovered them. If they can produce a recognizable landscape I'm happy enough. Perhaps I'm not being quite fair. There are actually two girls who have a little talent. Here you are. This is where you sleep. You've got the important Verringers under your wing. I think that's because Daisy feels they might imbibe a little Schaffenbrucken even while they're sleeping. There! It's a little chilly. It always is. You could easily imagine you were a monk. Daisy likes us to follow the monastic ways as much as possible. Don't worry. They haven't laid out your hair shirt. You just forget you're in an abbey and get a good night's sleep. I'll see you in the morning. Good night.'

I said good night. I liked her. She amused me and it was comforting to know that I had pleasant companions like those I had met on this night.

I brushed my hair and undressed quickly. On the table there was a mirror and I guessed that was one of the

82

modern concessions which Daisy liked to stress. I felt the bed. It was narrow as befitted my cell-like room, but it seemed comfortable.

I got into bed and pulled the sheets up round me. It was difficult to get to sleep. The day had been too exciting and my surroundings were so unusual. I lay with the sheets up to my chin thinking about it all and wondering about – and yes, looking forward to – the future.

I wanted most of all to make the acquaintance of the girls.

As the time passed I seemed to grow more and more wide awake. It is always difficult to sleep in new places and when one is in an ancient abbey, full of the impressions of another age, it is only natural that one should be wakeful. I turned to the wall and stared at it. There was enough light coming through the narrow window to show me the marks on the grey stone, and I wondered how many monks had lain staring at the walls during long nights of meditation and prayer.

Then suddenly I was alert. I had heard a faint sound and it was not far away – a quick intake of breath and then a suppressed sob.

I sat up in bed listening. Silence and then . . . yes. There it was again. Someone not very far away from me was crying and trying to stifle the sound.

I got out of bed, felt for my slippers and put on my dressing gown. The sound was coming from the room on my right . . . one of the rooms of which I was to be in charge.

I went into the corridor, my slippers making a faint sound on the flagged stone.

'Who's there?' I said quietly.

I heard the quick intake of breath. There was no answer.

'Is anything wrong? Just answer me.'

'N . . . no,' said a frightened voice.

I had located the room and I pushed open the door. In the dim light I saw two beds and in one of them a girl was sitting up. As my eyes grew accustomed to the gloom I saw

83

that she had long fair hair and wide startled eyes, and must be about sixteen or seventeen years old.

'What's wrong?' I said. 'I'm the new mistress.'

She nodded and her teeth started to chatter.

'It's nothing . . . nothing,' she began.

'It must be something,' I said. I went to her bed and sat down on it. 'You're unhappy about something, aren't you?' She regarded me solemnly with those wide scared eyes. 'You needn't be afraid of me,' I went on. 'I know what it is to be homesick. That's it, isn't it? I went away to school . . . in Switzerland actually . . . when I was your age.'

'D . . . did you?' she stammered.

'Yes, so you see, I know all about it.'

'I'm not homesick . . . because you can't be sick about what isn't, can you?'

I was remembering. 'I think I know who you are. You're Teresa Hurst, and you've been staying at the school during the holiday.'

She seemed relieved that I knew so much.

'Yes,' she said. 'And you're Miss Grant. I knew you were coming.'

'I'm to be in charge of this section.'

'It won't be so bad when the others come. It's rather frightening at night when it's all so quiet.'

'There's nothing to be frightened of really. Your parents are in Africa, aren't they?'

She nodded. 'Rhodesia,' she added.

'I know what it feels like, because funnily enough my parents were in Africa too. They were missionaries and they couldn't have me with them so I was sent home to my Aunt Patty.'

'I was sent to my mother's cousins.'

'What a coincidence! So we were both in the same boat. I hated the thought of coming to England and leaving my parents. I was scared. Then I came to my Aunt Patty and that was lovely.'

'My cousins don't really want me. They always make excuses at holiday times. The children have measles, or

84

they are going away . . . and so I stay at school. I think I'd really rather. It's just at night . . .'

'I shall be here now and the girls will be coming on Tuesday.'

'Yes, that makes it better. Did you mind going home to your Aunt Patty?'

'I loved it. She is the best aunt anybody ever had, and I've still got her.'

'That must be lovely.'

'Yes, it is. Anyway I'm here now. I'm sleeping close to you. If you are frightened, just come and tell me. Will that be all right?'

'Yes, that will be lovely.'

'I'll say goodnight then. Are you all right now?'

'Yes. I'll know you're there. It's only that sometimes the girls laugh at me. They think I'm a bit of a baby.'

'I'm sure you're not that.'

'You see they go to their homes and they never want to come back to school. They love the holidays. I dread them. It makes a difference.'

'Yes, I know. But you'll be all right. You and I will be friends, and you'll know I'm here to help you.'

'I think it's *funny* that your parents were in Africa too.'

'Yes, quite extraordinary, isn't it? Clearly we were meant to be friends.'

'I'm glad,' she said.

'I'll tuck you in. Do you think you could go to sleep now?'

'Yes, I think so, and I won't mind if I think I see . . . shadows. I'll know I can come to you. You did mean that, didn't you?'

'I did. But I don't think you'll be coming because everything is going to be all right. Good night, Teresa.'

'Good night, Miss Grant.'

I went back to my room. Poor lonely child! I was glad I had heard her and had been able to give her a little comfort. I would look out for her in the days ahead and make sure she was not bullied.

I took some time to get warm enough for sleep but I think

85

that little encounter had soothed me as well as Teresa Hurst and finally I did sleep. I had wild dreams though. I dreamed that I was riding through the nave in a carriage and I was aware of the mighty buttresses on either side of the carriage and the blue sky overhead. Suddenly another carriage was blocking the way and I saw a man emerge from it. He looked in at my window at me and shouted: 'Go back. You are in my way.' It was a wild dark face; then it changed suddenly and it was that of Edward Compton.

I awoke uneasily and for a moment wondered where I was.

Only a dream, I told myself. I did dream more than I used to. It was ever since I had met the stranger in the forest.

*   *   *

I awoke, sat up in bed and looked at the bare stone walls and sparse furnishings, and a feeling of excitement swept over me.

I washed and dressed. I took a look into Teresa Hurst's room. Her bed was neatly made and she was not there. I wondered if I was late.

I found my way down to the room in which we had dined on the previous evening. Daisy was seated at the table and Mademoiselle Dupont and Fräulein Kutcher were with her.

'Good morning,' said Daisy. 'I trust you slept well.'

I thanked her and told her that I had.

I acknowledged the greetings of the others and Daisy signed for me to be seated.

'In between terms we breakfast between seven thirty and eight thirty,' she said. 'In term it is seven thirty, and two of the mistresses supervise in the main dining room where the girls eat. After that it is prayers in the hall and we usually have a little talk – not more than five minutes – given by one of us. Something uplifting . . . a sort of text for the day. We take it in turns. Lessons start at nine. Do help yourself from the sideboard. We are rather unceremonious at breakfast.'

86

While I was helping myself to cold York ham and coffee, Eileen Eccles came in.

I sat at the table and we talked of the school – or mainly Daisy did; the rest of us listened. As the newcomer, many of her remarks were addressed to me.

'The mistresses should all be here by Monday morning. Then we shall be ready for the girls. There will be a meeting of us all in my study on Monday afternoon and then we'll run through the term's work. I daresay you will want to have something prepared which we can discuss . . . and to explore the place of course.' She smiled round the company. 'I am sure you will find many who will want to tell you anything you want to know.'

Eileen Eccles said: 'I shall go into the town this morning. There are one or two things I want to get. I'm short of paper and brushes. Would you care to come with me? It'll give you a chance to look at the town.'

'Thank you,' I said. 'I should like that.'

'You do ride, don't you? It's the only way we can go in.'

I replied: 'Yes, and thank you.'

Daisy smiled her approval.

It was a beautiful morning. Eileen took me to the stables and pointed out a little bay mare. 'You'll like her,' she said. 'She's got spirit and yet she's easy to handle.' She herself took a grey horse. We're old friends,' she said, patting his flank, and he stamped his foot as though expressing agreement with her.

Soon we were on our way to the town.

'It's not far,' she said, 'which is a mercy. The horses are a godsend. They give us a chance to get well away from the school now and then. Thank goodness that the management of a horse is one of the necessary accomplishments of well-brought-up young ladies.'

We rode past the fishponds glinting in the early morning sunshine. I looked round at the ruins and thought once more how magnificent they were – far less eerie in the early morning light.

'You'll get used to them,' said Eileen. 'I scarcely notice them now. At first I used to glance over my shoulder

87

expecting some black-robed figure to leap out on me. That was before I discovered that their habits were white – which somehow would make them even more ghostly – by moonlight at least, don't you think?'

'I think one would be scared to encounter them, whatever colour they wore!'

'Don't worry. They're all dead and gone, and in any case if their spirits lingered on I am sure they would approve of Daisy. It is people like the Verringers who would have to be on their guard.'

'Well, I suppose if the Verringers hadn't taken the place some other family would.'

'Not the point, my dear Miss Grant. The Verringers *did*.'

We came out into a lane and I was struck by the lush beauty all around me. Green grass, red earth, horsechestnuts and wild cherry in bloom, and the sudden burst of a song from a sedge-warbler near the fishponds.

I said: 'I met Teresa Hurst last night. Poor child. She seems lonely. I understood how she felt. I might have been in a similar position.' Then I was telling her about Aunt Patty.

'Mind you,' said Eileen, 'Teresa does lack spirit. She rather allows herself to be weighed down by her misfortunes instead of putting up a fight.'

'I shall see more of her. I had a little talk with her last night. I think we got on quite well.'

Eileen nodded. 'She draws quite well and unlike some of them she does know the difference between olive green and Prussian blue.'

She turned into a field, tapped her horse's flank and we cantered forward. 'Short cut,' she said, over her shoulder.

Then I was looking down on the town.

'Pretty isn't it, in sunlight,' said Eileen. 'Typical Devon small town. But some of the shops are quite adequate and it's better than nothing. They have a very good inn. Drake's Drum. I thought we'd meet there. I shall be at least an hour making my purchases. A bit boring for you to trail round with me and I like to be alone when I buy. You could explore a bit outside the town. The country's pretty. Or leave your horse in Drake's yard. In any case let's meet there in an hour, shall we? Then we'll have a glass of cider. They're famous for it.'

I said that would suit me very well.

I thought I would ride through the town, turn into the country for a look round and then explore the town afterwards. It was very small and I did not think I should need more than half an hour just to look round at first.

She showed me the inn with its coloured sign showing Sir Francis with his drum; and she rode into the yard, and I went on.

As the town was little more than a main street I was soon into the country lanes. They were beautiful, narrow and twisting so that they presented an element of excitement leading one to wonder what the next turn would reveal.

I must have ridden for some twenty minutes when I thought it was time I turned back to the town. I had come through so many narrow winding lanes and I had not thought very much about the direction in which I was going, for it did not occur to me that it might be difficult to find my way back. I turned my little mare and we ambled along for five minutes or so before we came to a cross roads. I didn't remember seeing it before and there was no signpost. I tried to work out which of the four roads I should take.

While I hesitated I saw a rider coming along one of the roads – a man on a grey horse – and I decided I must ask him the way when he came up.

He had seen me and was riding towards me. As he pulled up I noticed something familiar about his face and I knew at once who he was, for although I had only caught a brief glimpse of him, when he had put his head out of the carriage window, it was one of those faces when once seen would not easily be forgotten.

I thought with mingled annoyance and excitement: the great Sir Jason himself.

He swept off his hat as he approached.

'You are lost,' he said almost triumphantly.

'I was going to ask you the way back to Colby.'

'The town, the Hall or the Abbey?'

'The town. Can you direct me?'

'More than that. I happen to be on my way there myself. I shall escort you.'

'That is very good of you.'

'Nonsense. It is good of you to allow me to.'

He was surveying me rather boldly in a manner which made me feel uncomfortable. This is a little different, I thought, from the choleric passenger in the carriage.

'Thank you. It is not far, I am sure. I can't think how I lost my way.'

'It is easy enough to lose one's way. These roads twist so much that you are turned and turned around until you don't know which direction you are facing. It's a very pleasant morning, don't you think?'

'Very.'

'Doubly so now.'

I did not answer.

'I will introduce myself,' he said. 'I'm Jason Verringer of the Hall.'

'I know,' I replied.

'Then we are old acquaintances for I know who you are, too. We met before. In a lane. You were sitting up with Emmet. Is that so?'

'Yes, and you angrily commanded us to retreat.'

'That was before I saw you.'

I tried to move my horse forward, which was a silly thing to do as he was showing me the way and in any case he was immediately beside me, but I did find his manner disturbing.

'Had I known Emmet was driving the very accomplished new schoolmistress to the Academy, I should have ordered my driver to go back.'

'It is of no importance,' I said.

'It is of the utmost importance. It was our first encounter, and I must tell you how delighted I am to meet you. I have heard so much about you from Miss Hetherington.'

90

'Oh, does she discuss her staff with you?'

'My dear young lady, when such a prize falls into her hands she discusses her with everyone. I gather you have all the graces bestowed on you by some foreign establishment.'

'I am sure you are exaggerating.'

'Not in the least. I am so pleased to discover that a lady of almost divine qualifications has one little human weakness. She lost her way.'

'I have many weaknesses, I do assure you.'

'That pleases me. I shall hope to discover them.'

'That is hardly likely. This is not the way I came.'

'No. I don't suppose it is. What do you think of the countryside. This is good rich land . . . the richest in England, some say. It has served us well through the centuries.'

'And no doubt will go on doing so.'

'No doubt. You will be meeting my wards . . . my two nieces in fact. They attend the Academy. It is gratifying to know that they will be taught by someone with such talents.'

I felt irritated because I knew he was mocking me with his constant references to my education.

I said: 'I trust you will be satisfied. I look forward to meeting them. I understand from Miss Hetherington that they will be coming to school on Tuesday.'

'That is the arrangement.'

'It must be pleasant for them to be at school so near their home.'

He lifted his shoulders.

'You may have heard that we have just had a bereavement in the family.'

'Yes, I am sorry. The funeral was yesterday – the day when I arrived.'

'That was strange, wasn't it?'

'Strange?'

'That I should have been coming from my late wife's funeral when our carriages met.'

'I would hardly call it strange. They just happened to be

91

in the same spot at the same time. These lanes are very narrow. Vehicles meeting like that must be quite a common occurrence.'

'Not as often as you would think,' he said. 'I suppose we don't get a great deal of traffic. I do apologize for ordering your carriage to go back.'

'Please forget it. It's of no importance.'

'You thought me a little . . . arrogant?'

'I understand that you must have been very upset on such an occasion.'

'Then we are friends?'

'Well . . . hardly that . . .' I looked ahead. 'It seems rather a long way back to the town.'

'You did stray rather far.'

'Why, it is nearly a quarter to eleven. I am meeting Miss Eccles at the Drake's Drum at eleven.'

'The Drake's Drum is a very good hostelry. It does good business on market days.'

'How far are we from the town?'

'You'll be there by eleven.'

'Is it as far as that?'

He raised his eyebrows deprecatingly and nodded.

There was something about the smile which played about his lips which disturbed me. I wished I had tried to find the way myself. I was sure that he had taken me round a long way.

'I shall hope to see more of you, Miss er . . .'

'Grant.'

'Yes, Miss Grant. I hope you will visit the Hall sometimes. We have a concert now and then to which Miss Hetherington comes and allows some of her staff and even pupils to attend. There are occasions when I am invited to the school, so I am sure we shall face opportunities of meeting.'

I was silent for a few moments. Then I said: 'Are you sure this is the road?'

'I assure you that it is.'

We rode on in silence for some time and then with great relief I saw the town ahead of us.

92

I spurred my horse and we galloped along together until we reached the outskirts of the town.

'You see,' he said, 'I have delivered you safely. I believe you thought at one time that I was leading you astray.'

'I thought it was a long way back.'

'For me the time flew.'

'I know where I am now. Thank you for your help.'

'It was the greatest pleasure.'

He remained by my side until we reached the Drake's Drum. Eileen Eccles was already there. She had come out into the porch where she had obviously been looking anxiously for me.

'I lost my way,' I said.

Jason Verringer took off his hat and bowed to us. Then he rode off.

I said to Eileen: 'I met him when I was wondering which road to take and he showed me the way back. Where shall I put my horse?'

'I'll show you.'

She led me to the yard and then we went back into the inn parlour.

'He has soon discovered you,' she said.

'I was lost. He appeared by chance and offered to show me the way back. It did seem a very long way.'

'I daresay he saw to that. Come into the parlour. I'll order some cider for you. I was beginning to get a little worried.'

'So was I. I thought I was never going to get back. I wasn't sure of the way but I believe I could have found it myself as easily.'

'So you were escorted by the mourning widower.'

'He didn't seem to be mourning particularly.'

'Rejoicing more likely from what I hear.'

The cider came. It was cool and refreshing.

'They're noted for it in this part of the world,' said Eileen. 'So you haven't seen anything of the town. Not that there's much to see.'

'Did you find what you wanted?'

93

'Not exactly what I wanted but what I can make do with. This will help us along for a while. There won't be any time for looking round now. We have to start back as soon as you've finished your cider.'

'I wish now that I had stayed in the town.'

'He would have discovered you sooner or later. He has a reputation, you know, for assessing the females within his range.'

'Oh . . . but he is in mourning at the moment. Only yesterday his wife was buried.'

'I am sure he was scarcely beating his breast, tearing his sackcloth and scattering his ashes.'

'Far from it.'

'At least he's honest. He probably feels like killing the fatted calf. No, that's the wrong analogy. He's rejoicing anyway . . .'

'Was it as bad as that?'

'There's a tremendous amount of gossip about him. That's one thing the Verringers have always done. Provided the neighbourhood with plenty to talk about. The story is that he married that wife of his . . . arranged marriage . . . because she brought some big estate with her. But she had an accident in the hunting field, not long after the marriage, which crippled her and that meant that there was no Verringer heir – and as there have been Verringer heirs from 1500 and something, ever since the Verringers took over the Abbey lands, that was a matter which could bring no delight to the family. Sir Jason would end the direct line because his younger brother, father of the two girls, died. Would the estates go to a female? Horror throughout the land! And yet, what short of murder could give Sir Jason another chance?'

'Murder!'

'Not a word to be lightly bandied about among ordinary folk. But Verringers? Who shall say? In any case the lady dutifully died and, as you arrived, the bell was tolling for her.'

'You make it sound very macabre.'

'I am told that any adjective may be applied to the

94

Verringers and often is. Well, the lady died and there are rumours around . . .'

'I thought she was ill for a long time.'

'Crippled. Useless for reproduction purposes. But not an illness which is going to prove fatal, you understand. Then Marcia Martindale appears on the scene, gives birth to an infant, and Lady Verringer dies.'

'This is all becoming very involved.'

'You are going to live here so you will have to learn something of the local inhabitants; and the most colourful, exciting, dramatic – one might say melodramatic – are the Verringers. With Jason there have always been . . . women. It is a family trait and, with an incapacitated wife, what can anyone expect of such a virile lusty gentleman? There's a house not far from the Abbey. It's called Rooks' Rest – presumably because it is surrounded by elms in which rooks choose to make their nests. It's a small house, Queen Anne and elegant. One of the Verringer aunts lived there for years. Then she died and the place was vacant for a few months. It must have been about eighteen months ago when Marcia Martindale was installed there – strikingly handsome and undoubtedly pregnant. Sir Jason set her up there, and there she has remained. It is rather blatant but, when you are in the position of Sir Jason, you don't have to worry about local reaction. He is after all the powerful overlord, owning all the property and the houses people live in. Such people cannot pass too much judgement on these little peccadilloes. They may be sniggered at, always behind a concealing hand, and little more than a shrugging of the shoulders, and raising of eyes to heaven is permitted.'

'Nevertheless a great deal of scandal does seem to be circulating about that man.'

'My dear Miss Grant . . . may I call you Cordelia? Miss Grant is rather formal and we shall be seeing a lot of each other.'

'Please do . . . Eileen.'

'That's settled. What was I saying? Oh . . . little Miranda. Nobody doubts who her progenitor is. It's all so blatantly obvious, and Sir Jason would scorn to cover up any of his actions because he would construe that as weakness. He is the law around here. The rumour is that he has one child and could get more. Who knows, the next might be the longed-for boy. The stage is set. And what happens? Lady Verringer dies.'

'It sounds diabolical. How did she die?'

'I believe it was an overdose of laudanum. She suffered pain and used to take it. That's the story. You came in at the end of the act to hear the bell tolling for the departed lady. Now the curtain will rise again . . . on what?'

'You do make it sound like a melodrama.'

'Believe me, Cordelia. What did I tell you? Where that man is there will be melodrama. Now I have acquainted you with our greatest scandal, and what is more to the point, you have finished your cider. It is time we left.'

We paid for the cider, complimented the landlord on his brew, and came out into the sunshine.

*　　　*　　　*

Over the weekend the mistresses began to arrive as Daisy had said they would.

There was Miss Evans who taught geography; Miss Barston who specialized in needlework stressing embroidery and *gros point*; and Miss Parker who instructed the girls in physical exercises. Mathematics was taught by a man, James Fairley, who like the dancing, riding and music masters did not live in – as Daisy thought it was quite unsuitable for men to live under the same roof as the girls. She was sure the parents would not like it.

'Not,' commented Eileen, 'that they could not get up to certain tricks without necessarily sleeping under the monastic roof. But it is the look of the thing that counts.'

I found my fellow teachers all inclined to be pleasant and I was sure that I was going to get along very well with them.

It was the advent of the girls for which I was eagerly waiting.

On Monday they began to arrive – many on the morning

train and others in the afternoon. The atmosphere of the place was immediately changed. The Abbey became a school. There were excited voices, reunion of friends, frenzied talk about what they had done during the holidays.

On Monday evening at seven o'clock they were all gathered for what Daisy called Assembly in the hall which had been the Lay Brothers' infirmary. I looked eagerly along the lines of faces. The eldest must have been eighteen; the youngest fourteen. I felt a little uneasy on account of my own youth rather than my inexperience. I wondered how many of those young women would feel about being instructed by someone not very much older than themselves.

However, I was determined to be dignified and maintain discipline at all costs, for I did know from my experience at Schaffenbrucken that once that slipped there could be trouble.

There was a dais at the end of the hall and on this sat Miss Hetherington with her staff ranged round her. She addressed the girls briefly, welcoming them back to what she hoped would be a productive term.

'We have to welcome a newcomer to our ranks. Miss Grant. We are delighted to have her with us, and I am sure you will greatly profit from what she has to teach you. She herself has lately come from Schaffenbrucken in Switzerland of which you will all have heard.'

I saw one girl whisper to another behind her hand and the other suppressed a giggle. The whisperer was a tall girl with sandy hair worn in a plait round her head. I sensed something aggressive about her, and I felt that if ever she came within my orbit I might be called upon to do battle with her.

'Now, girls,' went on Daisy, 'we shall all go to supper and afterwards you will retire quietly to your rooms. Many of you are in the same ones as last term, but there have been changes. You will see from the notice on the board. Dismiss now.'

We ate together – the mistresses at one table, the girls at

97

another. Miss Parker said grace and I learned that she was responsible for religious instruction.

After supper we went to our rooms. I was glad of this because I wanted to make the acquaintance of the girls who had been allotted to my care.

I noticed that the Verringer girls were not there and remembered that they were among those who were returning on Tuesday.

As I went into my room there was a hushed silence. I knew the girls were in their rooms listening and I thought it would be a good idea to visit them and have a little talk with each of them. I recalled what Daisy had told me about them. I knew Teresa Hurst of course and that she was sharing with Caroline Sangton. I didn't expect trouble from Teresa. She and I had become good friends since our first encounter and I was aware that she was already growing fond of me. She had told me a little about the girls in my section. Caroline Sangton, who shared with her, was the daughter of a city businessman and rather looked down on by the others led by Charlotte Mackay, because they had heard there was something derogatory about being in 'trade'. Caroline was a stolid girl apparently, who didn't much care what the others thought, and she and Teresa got along quite well together without actually becoming great friends.

Most of the girls were crazy about horses and waiting impatiently for riding times – especially Charlotte Mackay who was the best horse-woman of them all. Teresa did not say, but I guessed, that she herself was not so eager and was, in fact, a little scared of the horses.

I went first to Teresa who introduced me to Caroline with an air of pride because she already knew me. I was pleased to see how relaxed she was in my company. If all the girls were as easy to understand as Teresa, my task would present few difficulties.

'We're glad you've come, Miss Grant,' said Caroline. 'Teresa was telling me all about you, and my father is very pleased that we are going to have social training.'

'I am sure you will profit from it, Caroline,' I said in my

98

best schoolteacher manner. 'You'll keep your room tidy and there must not be talking after "lights out". I have explained that to Teresa.'

'Oh yes, Miss Grant.'

'Well, good night, Caroline, and good night, Teresa. I am sure you are glad to have your room-mate back.'

'Yes thank you, Miss Grant,' said Teresa smiling shyly at me.

I was sure I had an ally in Teresa.

The next visit was not quite so harmonious, and I was a little dismayed to find that the whisperer I had noticed was one of my girls – in fact she was the Honourable Charlotte Mackay, tall, rather gawky, though she might grow into gracefulness, sandy haired with a quantity of freckles and scanty eyebrows and lashes. Her companion was Patricia Cartright, the banker's daughter. Patricia was small and dark and I guessed would not be a trouble-maker on her own but might well respond to Charlotte Mackay's influence.

Neither of the girls was in bed. Patricia Cartwright was seated at the dressing-table brushing her hair; Charlotte Mackay was sprawling on her bed fully dressed.

She did not rise when I entered, though Patricia stood up rather shame-facedly.

'Hello,' I said. 'Charlotte Mackay and Patricia Cartwright. I am looking in to see you all before we retire. I am sure we shall get along very well together if you keep your rooms tidy and remember that there must be no talking after "lights out".'

'Mademoiselle never complained,' said Charlotte Mackay. So I gathered Mademoiselle Dupont had occupied my room last term.

'Then I am sure I shall have no need to either.'

Charlotte and Patricia exchanged covert glances – a habit which irritated me as it implied a suggestion of conspiracy between them against me.

'Good night,' I said firmly.

'Oh Miss er . . .' began Charlotte.

I felt I should have told her to stand up when addressing

99

me, but was unsure whether it would have been wise at this stage to insist on that. The last thing I must show was uncertainty, but I did not want to begin by declaring war on this girl whose manner betrayed a certain bellicose attitude towards authority.

'Yes, Charlotte?'

'Last term I shared with Eugenie Verringer.'

'Oh, I see. This term she is with her sister.'

'We wanted to be together this term. We planned to be together.'

'I am sure you will get along very happily with Patricia.'

'Patricia was with Fiona.'

'Well, it will be a little different this time.'

'Miss Grant, *I* want to be with Eugenie and Patricia wants to be with Fiona.'

I looked from one to the other. Patricia did not meet my eyes and I knew she was being forced into this by Charlotte Mackay.

'I can't see any reason why we should be changed,' went on Charlotte.

'Miss Hetherington doubtless can.'

'You're in charge, Miss Grant. It is for you to say. It's nothing to do with Miss Hetherington.'

I was angry. I knew that she was baiting me as some young people did when they thought they had a weakling to deal with. I could understand why Teresa was uneasy when she talked about Charlotte. I had no doubt that Charlotte was a bully – and I would not have bullying while I was in charge.

'Will you please stand up or sit up properly when addressing me. It is impolite to loll on your bed like that.'

'Not how they do in Schaffenbrucken,' said Charlotte with a sly smile.

I went to her, seized her by the arm and forced her to sit up. She was so taken by surprise that she did so.

'Now,' I said. 'I want you to understand. We shall get along well together while you behave correctly and in such a manner becoming to a young lady. You will occupy the rooms which Miss Hetherington has assigned to you, unless

100

it is her wish to make changes. Do you understand? Good night and remember no talking after "lights out".'

With a feeling that I had won the first skirmish I went out and into the room occupied by Gwendoline Grey and Jane Everton. They were sitting up in bed and had evidently been listening. Their eyes were round with wonder.

'Gwendoline. Jane,' I said. 'Tell me which is which. Ah. I see. I am looking in to make everyone's acquaintance as we shall all be together for this term. I am sure everything will be comfortable if you remember the simple rules. Well, good night, girls.'

'Good night, Miss Grant,' they said.

Pleasant girls, both of them, I thought; but I was still uneasy after my encounter with the Honourable Charlotte.

I went to my room and to bed. It was nine o'clock, the time ordained by Miss Hetherington for 'lights out'.

I lay waiting. I quite expected to hear the sound of voices from Charlotte's room. To my surprise there was silence; but I had an idea that the war was not yet won.

*   *   *

The next morning the Verringer girls arrived. Miss Hetherington sent for me to meet them in her study. I thought this was a little unwise and it surprised me that Daisy should have done it, for it must have made the girls feel that they were of special importance.

'Ah, Miss Grant,' said Daisy as I entered, 'here are Fiona and Eugenie Verringer. They have just arrived.'

Fiona came forward and took my hand. She was a tall pretty girl with flaxen hair and hazel eyes; she had a pleasant smile and I liked her, which surprised me as I was expecting the worst from a connection of Jason Verringer.

'Good morning, Miss Grant,' said Fiona.

'Good morning,' I replied. 'I am pleased to meet you at last, Fiona.'

'And Eugenie,' said Daisy.

I felt a quiver of alarm. She was so like him. She had very dark hair and large lively dark brown eyes. Her olive skin had the smoothness of youth and her face was long; she

101

reminded me of a spirited young pony. There was something rebellious about her; it was in her springy dark hair, her wide eyes and her firm chin. She might have been his daughter rather than his niece.

'How do you do, Eugenie?' I said.

'How do you do, Miss Grant?'

Both of the girls were dressed in black. Fiona's became her fair hair. Eugenie needed brilliant colours.

'They are joining us late,' said Daisy, 'because of the unhappy event which took place at the Hall.'

'Oh yes,' I said, looking at both girls. 'I'm sorry.'

'There's no need to be sorry, Miss Grant,' said Eugenie. 'It was what is called a happy release.'

'Death is always sad,' I said.

Daisy frowned. She did not like the conversation to stray from the conventional.

'Well, my dears,' she said, 'you may go to your rooms. There is a little change this term. You are together.'

'Together!' cried Eugenie. 'The last time I was with Charlotte Mackay.'

'Yes, I know. This term you are with Fiona.'

'I don't want to be with Fiona, Miss Hetherington.'

'Oh come, my dear, that's not very polite, is it?'

Fiona looked slightly disconcerted but Eugenie went on: 'Oh, please, Miss Hetherington. Charlotte and I *understand* each other.'

'It is arranged, dear,' said Daisy coolly, but there was a glint in her eyes which should have been obvious to Eugenie.

Eugenie, however, was fearless, and she was not afraid to speak out. 'Well, it is not the law of the Medes and Persians, is it?'

Daisy smiled very coldly. 'I can see, dear, that you have been paying attention to Miss Parker's lessons. She will be gratified. However, you will remain with your sister this term. Now go to your rooms and Miss Grant is going to stay here with me as I have something to say to her.'

The girls went. I thought, That is the way to treat Miss Eugenie. Victory for Daisy.

102

When the door shut on the girls Daisy raised her eyebrows.

'There is always trouble with Eugenie,' she said. 'Fiona is such a good girl. You will have to be firm with Eugenie and Charlotte Mackay. Did you have any trouble last night?'

'A little. Charlotte was rather truculent.'

'The Mackays are. It's a title of only two generations. The family has never really grown accustomed to being members of the nobility and have to remind people of it at every turn. I should have thought by now they would have got used to it. What happened?'

'It was this matter of sharing with Eugenie Verringer.'

'They are two troublemakers. Last term they shared. Mademoiselle was quite incapable of keeping order. That is why I have taken her away from that section.'

'And given it to me . . . a newcomer!'

'I thought you would be able to deal with it, Cordelia, after all your training at Schaffenbrucken.'

'That has a lot to answer for.'

'Of course it has. It is the reason why you are here. I am confident that you will know how to deal with these recalcitrant girls. Mademoiselle was hopeless. She always is at discipline. Her classes are often in complete disorder, but she is a pretty creature and gentle and the girls are really fond of her. They would never let the troublemakers go too far against Mademoiselle. It will be necessary to take a very firm hand with Mesdames Eugenie and Charlotte. Let them see that you are in complete command and you will subdue them. They are like animals really. You know how they have to be trained. Unfortunately Eugenie is a Verringer and as you know all this belongs to the Verringer estate. What with that and Charlotte's father's title, we have two opinionated rebels on our hands. But you will deal with them. Stand firm and never let them get the upper hand.'

'Have I your permission to take what action I feel necessary?'

'Yes. Do what would have been done at Schaffenbrucken.'

103

'I don't remember any such situation arising there. Girls there were not wildly excited about titles and estates. Most of them came from families who had them for generations so they were commonplace.'

Daisy flinched a little and then murmured: 'Of course. Of course. Do what you think best.'

'Very well then. I shall be firm and demand discipline.'

'Splendid,' said Daisy.

*   *   *

In the common room – which Daisy insisted was called the calefactory – where the staff congregated before dinner (called supper during term) everyone welcomed me and told me how everything was conducted.

It was Eileen who explained to me about Daisy's determination that we should never forget we were in an abbey, and that was why instead of having a common room we had a calefactory.

'You may if you wish refer to it as the calefactorium. Either term is permissible. It is the apartment which was used by the monks when they wanted to get a little warmth. Poor things, they must have been frozen half the time. Underneath were the flues which gave it a little heat . . . hence the name. You can imagine them all hastening here when they had a few moments in which to relax, just as we do. There you see history repeating itself.'

'I'll remember,' I said.

The others talked about lessons and pupils and I was able to have a word with Mademoiselle Dupont.

'Oh,' she cried, throwing her hands into the air. 'I am 'appy because I am no longer with those naughty girls. Charlotte Mackay . . . Eugenie Verringer . . . they talk and laugh . . . and I believe 'ave feasts in their bedrooms. The others join them. I hear them laughing and whispering . . . And I pull the bedclothes over my ears and I do not hear them.'

'You mean you allowed them to do that!'

'Oh, Mees Grant, it is the only way. Charlotte . . . she is

104

the one who will say what is to be . . . and Eugenie . . . she is another.'

'If that is allowed to go on, they'll be managing the whole section.'

'It is so, alas,' said Mademoiselle sadly.

Her expression was one of condolence but she could not hide her pleasure in having escaped.

I was very uneasy, but at the same time I couldn't help a slight feeling of exhilaration. Perhaps I liked a battle. Aunt Patty had always said I did, although I had never had the occasion to face one with her and Violet. But once or twice over some domestic trouble my fighting spirit had shown itself. 'Determination to win is a good friend providing you use it only when necessary,' Aunt Patty had said. 'But don't forget such good friends can become enemies, like fire for instance.'

I did remember; and I was going to teach those girls a lesson other than those they would learn in the classrooms.

The routine did not change – assembly, prayers, supper; and then dismiss.

There was a hubbub in the washing cubicles and after that retirement to rooms and 'lights out'.

I had decided to make it a rule that I visited the girls last thing and said good night to them making sure that they were all where they should be and ready for slumber.

I knew there was something wrong when I entered Teresa's room for she looked unhappy – and I guessed it was on my account. Caroline looked very meek lying in her bed; and I said good night to both girls.

Gwendoline Grey and Jane Everton were also in their beds and although they lay quietly, almost demure, they had an air of waiting.

I went into Charlotte's room where I knew I should find trouble, and how right I was! Charlotte was in one bed, Eugenie in the other.

I said in a voice which could be heard in all the other bedrooms: 'Eugenie, get out of that bed at once and go back to your own.'

Eugenie shot up in bed and I was aware of her angry dark

105

eyes glaring at me. 'This is my bed, Miss Grant. It was my bed last term.'

'But not this,' I said. 'Get up at once.'

Charlotte was looking at Eugenie urging her to rebellion.

'Where is Patricia?' I said. I looked into the next room. She was in one bed, Fiona in the other. They both looked alarmed.

I said: 'Get out of that bed, Patricia.'

She did so at once.

'Put on your slippers and dressing-gown.'

She obeyed meekly.

I went with her into the next room. 'Now, Eugenie, get out of Patricia's bed and go back to your own.'

'Mademoiselle . . .' began Charlotte.

'This is no concern of Mademoiselle's. She is no longer in charge. I am and I will be obeyed.'

'You are not really grown-up yourself.'

'Don't be insolent. Did you hear me, Eugenie?'

She looked at Charlotte and without meeting my eyes muttered: 'I'm not going.'

I felt inclined to pull her out by force. If Charlotte came to her aid, the two of them might overcome me; and in any case violence was out of the question.

I remembered something Teresa had said. They were crazy about horseriding – and in particular Charlotte.

'I think you are,' I said. 'I am going to start from now and the longer you remain in that bed the longer will be your detention. We are studying *Macbeth* this term and for the number of minutes you stay in that bed you will be detained and learn that number of lines from the play. The detention will take place during riding lessons, so that any disobedient girl will not join the others.'

Charlotte shot up in bed.

'You can't do that,' she said.

'I can assure you I can.'

'Miss Hetherington . . .'

'Miss Hetherington has given me permission to take what action I consider necessary. We are starting from

106

now. If you do not get out immediately, Eugenie, you and Charlotte will begin your detention during tomorrow's riding time.'

This was important. I could feel the tension. I had to be firm now or lose the battle. I wondered what Daisy would say about curtailing lessons for which the girls' parents paid highly.

I stood looking at them.

Charlotte's love of horses won the day.

She looked sullenly at Eugenie and said: 'You'd better go . . . for now . . .'

Eugenie got out of bed. The curtailing of riding would be as much a tragedy for her as it was for Charlotte.

As she dashed past me, I said: 'For now . . . and the rest of the term . . . if you want to enjoy your riding. Now Patricia, get into your bed, and let me hear no more talking. Good night, girls.'

In the next room Eugenie was lying with her face to the wall and Fiona gave me an apologetic look as she returned my good night.

I went back to my bed. Victory. But I was trembling.

Marcia

*

I was rather surprised that I had won so easily for when I made my rounds after there was no more trouble. The girls were in their right beds and although Charlotte ignored me and Eugenie was a trifle sullen, I found the others quite charming; and Teresa made it clear that she was my slave.

I knew that Charlotte taunted her with being a toady and that Eugenie showed her clearly that she despised her, but oddly Teresa – no doubt because she felt she was sure of my support – had developed a little more boldness and seemed to be able to deal with their taunts.

I found lessons stimulating. I had a subject very dear to my heart – English literature – and it was very interesting for me to read my favourite Jane Austen and the Shakespeare plays with closer attention than I had given them before, to read them with the girls, to dissect them, and search for hidden meanings. I had four classes a week on this subject and therefore took all the girls in the school at some time, which meant that Charlotte and Eugenie were in two of the classes. Charlotte refused to work, and Eugenie – who was a year or so younger and very much under her influence – tried not to, but I was amused to discover that she had a genuine love of literature and could not entirely suppress her interest. Teresa was there trying very hard to please me. I was really enjoying it.

The social classes were less successful, I imagined. We discussed all sorts of subjects and the girls had to learn how to walk and act gracefully – just as we had at Schaffenbrucken. It was all rather amusing.

I enjoyed the sessions in the calefactory. Sometimes Daisy joined us there. We were more free and easy when she was not present, of course. I learned that the Hon.

Charlotte – as she was ironically referred to – was considered to be a universal *bête noire*. 'Clogs to clogs,' said Miss Parker who prided herself on her frank speaking. 'I should be very pleased to see the Hon. Charlotte in hers.'

Teresa was a mouse, they said. A silly timid little thing.

I defended her and pointed out that it was due to her background.

Eugenie was a terror, was Miss Parker's comment. 'She's a Verringer and that is about the worst tag you could fit onto anyone. Fiona's a nice little thing, however.'

Matt Greenway, the riding master, who happened to be present on that occasion, added that it was difficult to believe they both came out of the same stable.

'Quite different in looks and character,' said Eileen Eccles. 'It's amazing. And they talk about heredity. To me, it's environment that counts.'

'Presumably their environment was the same,' I pointed out. 'They were both brought up at the Hall apparently.'

'Well, they say the mother was gentle and meek. Rather like Fiona, I imagine. As for Eugenie, she's got the Verringer devil in her.'

I enjoyed those gossipy sessions and they helped me a great deal in getting to know the girls and that was a tremendous asset when dealing with them. Eileen Eccles was perhaps more interested in people than the others and she provided a great deal of information.

'We shall be stuck with Teresa again this coming summer, I gather,' she said. 'Her relations have written to say they'll be away for several months.'

'Poor child,' I said. 'It must be boring for her being here all alone for the summer.'

'I suppose it's too much to expect the parents to get her out of Rhodesia. No sooner would she be there than she would have to start back. I'm sorry for the girl. I am really.'

I had Teresa on my mind quite a bit. When I came out of class she would often be hanging about offering to carry my books for me. I had seen the supercilious looks of Charlotte but Teresa did not seem to care, thought I gathered that in the past she had been afraid of Charlotte.

Then there was the gossip about the Verringer girls.

'Eugenie,' said Mademoiselle throwing up her hands in horror. 'She is one naughty little girl.'

Fräulein Kutcher expressed the opinion that there was too much homage paid to the Verringers. It set them apart.

'I think there is something in that,' said Eileen Eccles.

Matt Greenway said: 'Eugenie will be a real horse-woman.' As though that made up for her failings in other directions.

'They'll be very rich . . . those two girls,' said Eileen.

'It is not good for them to know this,' put in Mademoiselle.

'But they do know it,' insisted Eileen, 'and it seems to have gone to Miss Eugenie's head.'

'How rich are they?' I asked.

'Infinitely,' replied Eileen with a laugh. 'I did hear something about uncle's liking to get his hands on the money.'

'Uncle? You mean Sir Jason?'

'I do indeed, my dear, if you must give him his rightful title.'

'Is he not rich then?'

'As Midas . . . or Croesus if you prefer. But you know money has that effect on some people. The more they have, the more they want. Ever since the King favoured them and bestowed on them the Abbey lands, they have been piling it up. So have our two little heiresses. They divide the brother's fortune when they come of age or marry, and I believe if Fiona dies it all goes to Eugenie, and if Eugenie should visit that bourn from which no traveller returns, then Fiona takes all.'

'Yes,' I said. 'I do agree that it is a mistake for young people to know that they are rich. Though Fiona seems a very pleasant modest young girl.'

'It is because you are making comparisons. Most people compared with Eugenie would seem pleasant and modest.'

We all laughed.

'Oh, I am sure Fiona is,' I said.

Yes, the days were passing pleasantly. I found that I

110

could do what was expected of me and Daisy was pleased with the contribution I made to the school. She was sure my classes were getting more and more like Schaffenbrucken every day.

I very much enjoyed the riding sessions. The enthusiasm of Matt Greenway had communicated itself to the girls and most of them had that natural affinity young girls have for the horse.

Whenever we set out for rides I was always prepared for a pleasant time. Even the Hon. Charlotte seemed tolerable on a horse; it was as though at last she had found something for which she had more consideration than she had for herself. She adored her horse; and Eugenie was almost as fanatical about hers. It was interesting, I pointed out in the calefactory, how much more human Hon. Charlotte became when she was on horseback.

Very often two of us went with the girls. Daisy thought that was better than one so that there was someone in authority at the head and rear of the party.

The exercise was pleasant and I suppose I did this about twice a week, for the girls rode every day. Then Daisy had given me permission to take a horse whenever I wanted one, provided it was not during the girls' riding time. So it was a very happy arrangement.

I wrote to Aunt Patty that I was settling in and enjoying my work. I would tell her everything in detail when I arrived home for the summer holidays.

*   *   *

When I had a free hour or so between lessons, I made a habit of taking out the horse which I usually rode, and exploring the countryside. I liked walking but naturally one could only go a certain distance on foot, and riding gave me far more scope.

When I walked I liked to do so within the Abbey precincts and I could never do this without experiencing that uncanny feeling that I was stepping back into the past. The atmosphere was overwhelming even in the brightest sunlight and I would find myself fancying I heard footsteps

111

following me on the flags. Once I thought I heard chanting. But I convinced myself it was the whistling of the wind. There were times when I was drawn to the ruins by an irresistible urge to be there; at such times I believe I really expected to see some manifestation of the past.

Eileen Eccles, who had made several drawings of parts of the ruins, said she felt the same. In some of her pictures she had sketched in white-clad figures. 'I just found myself putting them in,' she said. 'It was as though they belonged.'

I thought that rather strange, for she was a very prosaic person on the whole.

But it was true that no one, however matter-of-fact, could live close to such antiquity and not be affected by it.

Eileen often took her classes out to parts of the Abbey and it was not unusual to come across them seated at some vantage point, sketch books in hands.

Miss Hetherington wanted the girls to have a real appreciation of their surroundings, for it was just that environment which set the Academy apart from other schools.

On this particular occasion I had no class until three thirty, and as the midday meal was over at two, I had an hour and a half in which to take a ride.

It was a lovely day. We were in the middle of June and I could scarcely believe I had been so long at the school. I really felt as though I had known it for a long time. I could look back on the last weeks with satisfaction. I could do my work adequately. My English classes were as successful as I could hope for; I had one or two girls who showed great interest and to my amazement Eugenie Verringer was one of them. The Hon. Charlotte continued to be troublesome and to annoy me in a hundred ways – whispering during classes, urging others to disobedience, tormenting Teresa Hurst – in fact generally making a nuisance of herself; and she had her cronies besides Eugenie. But these were minor irritations and the inevitable lot of anyone who taught. The teacher must sometimes expect to be a target, especially if she was not very much older than the pupils.

I had evidently found the right way to keep just ahead of Charlotte and I was thankful for her devotion to horses

112

which gave me a weapon to use against her. She would always fall short of doing something which would deprive her of one moment with her beloved horse.

These were my thoughts as I rode out on that June afternoon. I reminded myself – as I often did – of how I had been lost on my first venture and as there must be no repetition of that, I always noted well the way I came. There might not be anyone to show me the way this time. Not that Sir Jason had been much help on that other occasion. I had confirmed my suspicions, since I had been riding round a little on my own, and I knew now that he had taken me a very long way round on my way back to the town.

Why, I wondered? He had known I was anxious to get back. Because he was perverse? Because he knew that I was anxious? Because he wanted me to feel lost and dependent on him? He was not really a pleasant man, and I hoped that I should not have to see him often. It was a pity that the school was so near the Hall.

I turned away from the town taking a road which I had not taken before, making a special note of the landscape as I passed so that I should know my way back. I passed a tree with its bare branches standing out starkly among others which were in full leaf. It must have been struck by lightning or blasted in some way. It was dead. But how beautiful it was! Strange, in a way it looked ghostly, eerie, menacing even with its bare branches lifted to the sky.

It was a good landmark.

I went up a lane and came to a house. I noticed the tall elms about it and looking up I saw the rooks' nests high in the trees.

Something someone had said flashed into my mind. I had heard of this place.

And there was the house – simple but beautiful – clearly built at the time when architecture was at its most elegant – uncluttered, with long windows symmetrically placed on its brickwork, very plain so that the door with its fluted Doric type columns and glass fanlight seemed particularly handsome. The house was shut in by intricate ironwork which

113

looked like lace and made a perfect frame for this charming residence.

I couldn't help pausing to admire and as I was about to ride on, the door opened and a woman came out. She was holding a child by the hand.

'Good afternoon,' she called. 'You can't go any further. It's a cul-de-sac.'

'Oh thank you,' I replied. 'I was exploring and I paused to admire your house.'

'It is rather pleasant, isn't it?'

'Very.'

She was coming towards the railing.

'You are from the school, aren't you?'

'Yes. How did you know?'

'Well, I've seen most of them, but you are new.'

'I came at the beginning of the term.'

'Then you must be Miss Grant.'

'Yes, I am.'

'One hears quite a lot in a place like this,' she said. 'How are you liking the school?'

She was up to the fence now. She was strikingly handsome in her dress of lilac-coloured muslin. Tall, willowy, she carried herself with an almost studied grace. Her abundant reddish brown hair was piled high on her head; her eyes were enormous, light brown, heavily lashed.

The child surveyed me with interest in her bright dark eyes.

'This is Miranda,' said the woman.

'Hello, Miranda,' I said.

Miranda continued to regard me with an unblinking stare.

'Would you like to come in? I'd show you the house. It's quite interesting.'

'I'm afraid I haven't time. I have a class at three thirty.'

'Perhaps another time. I'm Marcia Martindale.'

Marcia Martindale! Sir Jason's mistress. Then the child was his. I felt myself recoil a little. I hoped she did not notice. I felt an immense pity for her. It must be most unpleasant to be a woman in her position. She would have

114

placed herself in it, of course, but in what circumstances? My dislike for Sir Jason Verringer increased in that moment. What sort of man could he be to bring his mistress so near to his home and blatantly set her up in her own establishment with their child?

'Thank you,' I heard myself say. 'Another time . . .'

'I'd be so glad to see you at Rooks' Rest.'

I looked up at the tall elms. 'Do the birds disturb you with their cawing?'

'One gets used to it. It wouldn't be the same without them.'

'It is a beautiful house. It looks cool . . . and aloof, as it were . . . almost modern when compared with the Abbey and the Tudor Hall.'

'It is very comfortable and I am fond of it.'

'You have lived in it for a long time, I suppose?'

'No. I came here just before Miranda was born. We're on the Verringer estate, you know. Well, most of the land about here is.'

'Yes,' I said coolly.

'Do come again. I like to hear about the school. Come when you have time. Have a cup of tea or a glass of something . . . whatever you fancy. I hear that you are doing well at the school.'

'Oh, where did you hear that?'

'One hears . . .' She turned to the child. 'I don't think we are going to persuade her to come in, Miranda,' she said.

Miranda continued to regard me stolidly.

'She seems very interested in me at least,' I said.

'Miranda is interested in everything about her and particularly people. Do promise to come and see me. I love to see people and I see so few.'

'Thank you. I will. I'll wait until I have a free afternoon. That doesn't happen often but it does come round now and then.'

'Do please do that.'

'Goodbye,' I said.

She stood waving to me, raising the child's arm and urging her to do the same.

115

I came quickly out of the lane past the dead tree which was raising its arms to the sky, despairingly it now seemed to me.

What a friendly woman! I thought. She is really beautiful. How could she so demean herself? *His* mistress . . . bearing his child . . . perhaps in the hope that because she could bring about such an achievement, when he was free he would marry her. Well, he was free now.

My revulsion against him was increasing every minute. He was arrogant, I knew. Could it really be that he was a murderer. He appeared to believe he had a right to take what he wanted no matter what he did to others who were in his way.

Thinking of that woman I felt very depressed. I wished I had not let my afternoon's relaxation take me past Rooks' Rest.

*　　*　　*

June was almost over and at the end of July we should break up for the holidays. I was very much looking forward to seeing Aunt Patty and how she had settled into her new home, although of course she wrote often and told me the details of her new friendships and the frolics and mishaps which for her turned out to be hilarious adventures.

That afternoon I had a free session and was to take the girls on their ride. Miss Barston was to accompany me. I would rather have had Eileen Eccles or Miss Parker because Miss Barston was not the best of riders and was, I fancied, more nervous on a horse than she should be.

On another occasion she had made excuses so I was not surprised when Daisy called me to her study just as we were about to leave.

'Miss Barston says she has a great deal of preparation to do if she is to get the samplers ready for next lesson. She was planning to do it this afternoon. None of the others has any spare time.'

'That's all right,' I said. 'I can manage. It is the older girls

116

and most of them are good riders.'

Daisy looked relieved. 'I am so glad you add this accomplishment to your others.'

'The riding sessions are very enjoyable,' I said.

And that was how we came to set out that afternoon with only one mistress in charge – myself.

There were ten girls. Teresa was there. I knew that she would be riding close to me. She had never lost her nervousness but seemed to feel that I was a sort of talisman or lucky charm, and when she was close to me she lost much of that tension which conveyed itself to the horse – and that could mean trouble.

Charlotte was there with the two Verringer girls.

We trotted through the lanes in good order, Charlotte keeping up the rear with Fiona and Eugenie. I often had a niggling fear that when Charlotte was of the party she would attempt to show her superiority in some way and cause trouble. She was quite capable of urging some of them, who did not have her skill, to take risks. I had warned her of this with the only threat which would work with her. Unless her behaviour was beyond reproach she would find she was not riding so often.

Teresa trotted along beside me, a little uneasy as she would always be on a horse, but the improvement in her was amazing. In time she would lose her nervousness, I assured myself.

We were talking about the trees and the plants, a subject in which Teresa was very interested and in which she certainly excelled; and she was delighted when she could tell me the names of plants of which I had never heard.

Ahead of us I could see the Hall. It was a most imposing house built in the Tudor style but seeming of an earlier age, because instead of the customary red brick it was in the grey stone of the Abbey. Much of the stone had been taken from the Abbey which gave it its distinction. I could see the broad low arch flanked on either side by tall octagonal towers. Many gables and turrets caught the eye – all dominated by the tall Gate House.

As we came close to it, suddenly a light carriage appeared on the road. It was drawn by two magnificent grey horses and was pelting along at a dangerous speed. It appeared to be coming straight for us. I called to the girls to slow down and draw in to the side of the road.

The carriage was close. I heard Teresa cry out and then her horse was off. It bolted right in front of the carriage and across the road to the Hall.

I spurred up my horse and galloped after her.

'Don't be frightened, Teresa,' I shouted . . .

She wouldn't hear me, of course.

I reached her just as she was thrown out of the saddle onto the grass in front of the Hall. I dismounted and ran to her. She lay still and was very pale.

'Teresa . . .' I cried. 'Oh, Teresa . . .'

To my immense relief she opened her eyes and looked at me. I thanked God she was alive.

The carriage was close by and a man jumped out of the driver's seat and ran towards us.

It was Jason Verringer.

My greatest emotion then was anger. 'So it was you,' I cried. 'You're mad . . . This child . . .'

He took no notice of me but knelt and bent over Teresa.

'Here,' he said. 'You've taken a toss. We all do that at some time. Anything broken? Let's see if you can stand up.'

Teresa shrank from him. 'Miss Grant,' she whispered.

I said: 'It's all right, Teresa. I'm here to take care of you. You don't appear to be badly hurt. Let's see if you can stand.'

Jason Verringer helped her to get up. It was clear that she could stand without pain.

'I don't think there are any bones broken,' he said. 'I'll get the doctor to have a look at her right away. Now I'm going to carry you in,' he said to Teresa.

She looked at me appealingly.

'I'll be with you,' I said. 'Don't be afraid, Teresa. I'm going to stay with you.'

I remembered then that I was in charge of the whole

118

party. I saw the girls on their horses, watching, appalled by what had happened.

My horse was quietly nibbling the grass. I could not see Teresa's.

I went over to the girls.

I said: 'You've seen what happened to Teresa. They are going to send for a doctor. I don't think she is badly hurt. I want you all to go back to the school and tell Miss Hetherington what has happened.' I looked at Charlotte. I went on: 'Charlotte, I am putting you in charge.'

There was a faint flush on her cheeks and I saw her head shoot up and the look of pride on her face.

'You are a good horse-woman and you are in the lead. Look after everyone. Make sure they keep with you.' I had cast my eyes over the party and made sure that they were all there. 'Get the girls back as soon as you can and tell Miss Hetherington that Teresa is at the Hall and that I shall stay with her until she is fit to ride back. Is that understood?'

'Yes, Miss Grant,' said Charlotte earnestly.

'Now go,' I said. 'All follow Charlotte and do as she says. There is nothing to be afraid of. Teresa is not badly hurt.'

I watched them ride off. Then I turned towards the Hall.

My fear was rapidly turning to anger. He had done this. He was the one who had thoughtlessly driven out at such a fast and furious pace. He had startled the horses and Teresa had been unable to control hers. And I was in charge!

I walked hastily into the Hall, through the door over which was an ornate coat of arms carved into the stone. I was in a vast hall with a vaulted ceiling. Weapons adorned the walls and a family tree was carved over the fireplace. Several people stood in the hall and they all looked scared.

'The little girl is in the blue bedroom, Miss,' said a man who was clearly an important person in his own right – a butler or major-domo I imagined. 'The doctor has already been sent for and Sir Jason says would you be so good as to go up there as soon as possible. One of the maids will take you.'

I nodded and followed a girl up the carved staircase, the

119

posts of which were decorated with Tudor roses and fleurs-de-lys.

In a bedroom with blue curtains and touches of the same colour throughout the room, Teresa lay on a bed. Her relief at the sight of me was obvious.

Jason Verringer turned as I entered.

'The doctor should be here within half an hour. I have told him he is urgently needed. I am sure she is not badly hurt, but it is wise to have a doctor in such cases. No bones are broken evidently. There may be a little shock, concussion . . .'

'Stay here, Miss Grant,' said Teresa.

'Of course I will.'

'Miss Grant will stay here as long as you do,' said Jason Verringer in a gentle voice which seemed somehow incongruous coming from him.

I could not look at him. I was so angry. This was his fault. He had no right to be driving at such speed through narrow lanes.

He brought a chair so that I could sit down by the bed.

'Miss Grant,' whispered Teresa. 'What of the others? Where are they?'

'They've gone back to school. I put Charlotte in charge. She's the best horse-woman. She'll manage.'

'I don't want to ride again . . . ever. I never did. I was so frightened.'

'Don't worry about it now. Just lie quietly.'

One of the maids came.

She said: 'It's hot sweet tea. Mrs Keel says it do be the best thing times like these.'

'It can't do any harm,' said Jason Verringer.

'Could you drink it, Teresa?' I asked.

She hesitated. I put my arm about her and lifted her up. She sipped it and a little colour came back into her cheeks.

The minutes ticked by and it seemed more like an hour before the doctor came.

'You had better stay here while he examines her, Miss Grant,' said Jason Verringer, and he went out leaving me with Teresa and the doctor.

120

The examination revealed that Teresa was badly bruised but that no bones were broken. She had had a lucky escape. She was terribly shaken though. I noticed how her hands trembled.

The doctor said: 'You lie there and you'll soon be all right. You're best in bed.'

I followed him out of the room. Jason Verringer was in the corridor waiting.

'Well?' he said.

'She's all right,' said the doctor. 'But very shocked. She's a nervous girl, isn't she?'

'Yes,' I said, 'she is.'

'There might be a touch of concussion. I think it very likely. She should not be moved for a day or so. Well, not today in any case.'

'There's no problem about that,' said Jason Verringer. 'She can stay here.'

'That would be wisest,' said the doctor looking at me.

'I think she would be happier if we could get her back to the school,' I said. 'It's not very far.'

'That's quite unnecessary,' put in Jason Verringer. 'She'll be perfectly all right here. She shouldn't be moved, should she, doctor?'

The doctor hesitated.

'Should she?' repeated Jason Verringer.

'I'd rather she wasn't,' said the doctor.

I frowned.

'The girl doesn't want to be separated from Miss Grant,' said Jason Verringer. He smiled. 'There is no reason why she should be. The Hall is big enough to accommodate both the girl and Miss Grant.'

The doctor smiled apologetically at me. I must have conveyed my repulsion at staying in the Hall. 'I wouldn't want her upset in her present state,' he said. 'Sir Jason's solution seems the best in the circumstances.'

I felt very upset. The relief that Teresa was not badly hurt had no sooner come than this further problem presented itself. I knew I could not leave Teresa. On the other

121

hand I loathed the thought of spending a night under this roof.

The less anxious I felt about Teresa the more angry I was with Jason Verringer. He had been the cause of the accident, and now he was more or less telling the doctor what he must say.

I had a notion that the idea of my spending a night under his roof was amusing him, and that he was as eager that it should happen as I was that it should not.

I heard myself say in a voice which I hoped was steady: 'Miss Hetherington will have to be informed.'

'She will know of the accident by now. I will send over to her immediately and tell her what the doctor says. Thank you so much, doctor. There is nothing else we can do, I suppose?'

'I will send up some liniment.' He looked at me. 'Apply it once . . . and once only. It is too strong to use often. It should help the bruises. Then I will send some medicine to soothe her. If she has concussion that might not be immediately obvious. Don't let her get excited. She should be herself in a week . . . or less, providing there are not unforeseen consequences.'

Jason Verringer went off with the doctor and I went back to Teresa. She was greatly relieved to see me and I assured her that everything was going to be all right.

Teresa closed her eyes and seemed to sleep, and it must have been half an hour later when a maid arrived to tell me that Miss Hetherington was below. I went down to the hall with all speed.

On the way down I glanced through a window and saw the school carriage with Emmet in the driving seat.

Daisy Hetherington was seated at a table with Jason Verringer beside her.

'Here is the excellent Miss Grant,' said Jason.

'Oh, Cordelia,' said Daisy, forgetting ceremony at such a moment. 'The child is not harmed, I believe.'

'She is sleeping now. I think it is mainly shock.'

'That this should have happened to one of our girls!'

'These things will happen when drivers take their car-

122

riages along the road at such speed as to frighten everyone nearby.'

Daisy looked faintly shocked and a little alarmed.

'I know that accidents will happen,' she murmured.

My anger was hard to suppress. Because *he* had done this we had to shrug it aside, pretend it was a natural everyday happening. He gave me a kind of triumphant smirk.

Daisy went on as though I had not spoken. 'Sir Jason tells me that the doctor says she should not be moved tonight.'

'He did say that.'

'It was good of you, Sir Jason, to send for the doctor so promptly and to offer hospitality.'

'The least I could do,' said Jason Verringer.

'Indeed yes,' I began angrily even though Daisy was present and was reminding me that we had to be affable to our rich and powerful landlord.

Daisy said quickly: 'Teresa must stay here for the night and as she is such a highly excitable girl and you, my dear, are the only one who can soothe her . . . well, Sir Jason has most kindly invited you to stay here too.'

I felt trapped. 'That would be –' I began.

'The ideal arrangement,' he interrupted. 'I am sure Teresa will be happy enough to rest in peace if she knows you are at hand.'

'Well, thank you so much, Sir Jason.' Daisy had turned to me. 'I will have certain things you will both need sent over. Now I think I must go. But I know I can leave Teresa safely in your hands, Cordelia. I must get back and make sure things settle to normal. They are in a state of excitement.'

'Charlotte Mackay brought the girls back safely, I hope,' I said.

'Oh yes, and clearly enjoyed her moment of authority. I haven't seen Charlotte so contented before. She was quite polite and very docile. You did the best possible in the circumstances. Now I will send the things over and, on receiving a message tomorrow, Emmet will drive the carriage over and bring you back.'

So it was settled.

123

Jason Verringer and I accompanied Daisy to her carriage.

'There is nothing to fret about,' he said to her. 'The girl is just shocked and I can see Miss Grant is a most sensible young lady.'

I knew that Daisy was trying to hide a certain uneasiness and I guessed that she was no more happy about leaving me at the Hall than I was to stay. However, we were in this unfortunate situation and Daisy could see no diplomatic way out. Tactful relations with Sir Jason were necessary to the well-being of the school and the school was all important to Daisy.

'I will send Emmet over with what you need,' were her parting words, and I stood disconsolately looking after her carriage.

Jason Verringer turned to smile at me.

'I am looking forward to the pleasure of dining with you, Miss Grant,' he said.

'There is no need to stand on ceremony, Sir Jason. If something can be sent up to Teresa's room for both of us, we shall be very satisfied.'

'But I should be most *dis*satisfied. You are an honoured guest and I want you to know it.'

'I don't feel in the least honoured. This is something which should never have happened.'

'You make it very clear that you blame me.'

'How could you drive as you did! You should have known that you could frighten the horses. They are only girls . . . not very practised some of them. It was thoughtless . . . more than that, it was . . . criminal.'

'You are hard on me. I was thoughtless, I admit. I have driven those greys several times a week and have never before encountered a party of schoolgirls hack-riding through the lanes. Perhaps I could say if I wanted to answer your recriminations that they should not have been on that stretch of road. But I won't go into that because I have no desire to displease you.'

'You may say exactly what you wish. The girls always ride through the lanes. What is different about that one?'

124

'It happens to be the one which leads to my house.'

'You mean it is your private property.'

'Dear Miss Grant, you are a newcomer to Colby, otherwise you would know that most of the land hereabouts is my property.'

'Does that mean that none of us has any right to be here?'

'It means that you are here by my permission and if I wish I could close any of the roads.'

'Why do you not? Then at least we should know where we might ride and walk in safety.'

'Let us go in. I have told them to prepare a room for you. It is one of our best rooms and fairly near the blue room.'

I felt suddenly alarmed. There was something satanic about him. He looked complacent too and I did not care for the boldness of his expression. It was as though he was making plans and was very confident of their success.

'Thank you,' I said coldly, 'but I should prefer to stay in Teresa's room.'

'We can't allow that.'

'I'm afraid I could not allow anything else.'

'There is only one bed in the blue room.'

'It is a very large one. I am sure Teresa would be happier if I shared it.'

'I have asked them to prepare a room for you.'

'Then it will be ready for your next guest.'

'I see,' he said, 'that you are determined to have things the way you want them.'

'I am here to look after Teresa and that is what I intend to do. She has had a terrible shock thanks to . . .'

He looked at me reproachfully and I went on: 'I would not want her to wake up in the night and wonder where she was. She might be alarmed. After all, there could be unpleasant after-effects of this fall. I should be with her.'

'Teresa is very lucky. She has such a delightful and faithful watchdog.'

'We shall be very comfortable, and thank you for allowing us to use your blue room.'

'It is the least I can do.'

'Yes,' I said coolly.

125

He was smiling as we went in.

'You will of course dine with me,' he said almost humbly.

'It is kind of you but I think I should be with Teresa.'

'Teresa will need rest. When the sedative arrives the doctor wants her to take that right away.'

'I would not leave Teresa.'

He bowed his head.

I went up to Teresa. She was very drowsy. 'I'm so glad you're here, Miss Grant,' she said.

'I am going to stay with you, Teresa. There is room for us both in this bed. It's a huge one, isn't it? A little different from those at school.'

She smiled faintly and contentedly and closed her eyes.

Very soon Jason Verringer was at the door.

'The doctor has sent these,' he said. 'Here is the liniment. And this is the medicine. He has sent a note to say that she should be given this after you have applied the liniment. Then she should sleep through the night. That is what she needs more than anything.'

'Thank you,' I said, and I went with him to the door.

'When she is asleep ring the bell,' he said. 'I will send someone up to bring you down. It will not be a ceremonious meal – just a quiet little tête-à-tête.'

'Thank you, but no. I do not think Teresa should be left.'

I went back to Teresa and applied the liniment to the bruises. I thought how lucky she had been and my anger welled up once more.

'You will sleep here, won't you, Miss Grant?' pleaded Teresa.

'I certainly shall.'

'I wouldn't like to be here on my own. I keep thinking of it. I heard the horses pounding along . . . and I knew old Cherry Ripe didn't like it . . . she didn't like me either. I knew she was going to bolt and I shouldn't be able to hold her.'

'Stop thinking of it. It's over now.'

'Yes, and you're here and I'm never, never going to ride a horse again.'

'We'll see how you feel about that later on.'

126

'I don't need to wait till later on. I know now.'

'Now, Teresa, you're getting excited. You're not supposed to. Let's get this liniment done. What a smell! Rather nice though, really. Does it smart? Well, that means it's doing you good. The doctor says it is very effective. You'll be all colours of the rainbow in a day or so.'

I corked up the bottle and put it down. 'Now you are going to have this dose and it will make you sleep and you'll forget all about it. All you need to remember is that I am here and if you want anything you only have to tell me.'

'Oh, I'm glad you're here. Is Miss Hetherington cross with me?'

'Of course not. She's as concerned as everyone else is.'

'Charlotte will sneer now, won't she?'

'Charlotte behaved quite well really. She took the girls back. I am sure she wouldn't want you to be hurt.'

'Then why is she always trying to hurt me?'

'She doesn't really mean to hurt, only to deliver little pinpricks.'

'I don't mind about her nearly so much as I used to. It was different when you came. It was because you were in Africa too, and then you came home to Aunt Patty. I wish I had Aunt Patty.'

There was a discreet knock on the door. It was a maid with a case which she said had just been sent from the school. I opened it. In it was a note from Daisy saying that here were some things which she thought we might need. There were my night-clothes and those of Teresa and I was astonished to see that she had sent one of my dresses – my best blue silk.

I wanted to give Teresa her sedative, so I asked if she would care for me to help her into her nightgown as she would be more comfortable in that than in her undergarments. She had discarded her riding habit when examined by the doctor and it now lay over a chair. So I helped her undress and put on her nightgown. Then I said: 'Drink this and then I think you are going to feel very sleepy.'

She did. She went on talking for a little while in a

127

desultory way, her voice growing more and more drowsy. The sedative was beginning to work.

'Teresa,' I said gently, and there was no answer.

She looked very young and vulnerable lying there and I thought how sad it was that her parents were so far away and that the distant relatives in England did not want to be bothered with her. I wondered if her mother and father longed to have her with them; and my thoughts went once more to Aunt Patty and all I would have to tell her when I saw her again.

There was a gentle tap on the door. I crept to it and opened it. Jason Verringer was standing there with a middle-aged woman.

'How is Teresa?' he asked.

'Sleeping. The sedative worked quickly.'

'The doctor said it would. This is Mrs Keel my very worthy housekeeper. She will sit with Teresa while we dine and if Teresa should awaken she will come for you immediately.'

He was smiling at me with just a hint of triumph. I hesitated. I did not see how I could refuse. Mrs Keel was smiling at me. 'You can trust me,' she said. 'I'm used to looking after people.'

There was no help for it. I had given way limply because I could not refuse before his housekeeper. It would be insulting to her to suggest that she was incapable of looking after Teresa – who was asleep in any case. So I should have to dine with him after all. I had to admit secretly that I was not as averse to the prospect as I had pretended to be. I did find a certain pleasure in letting him know that I was not by any means attracted by him, because I was sure he was trying to impress me. From what I had heard of his reputation he was considered – or considered himself – irresistible to women. It would be amusing and rather stimulating to let him see that here was one who was quite immune to his masculine charms.

'It is good of you,' I said to Mrs Keel. 'She is a sensitive girl . . . and if she should awake . . .'

'She is not likely to,' said Jason Verringer. 'And if by any chance she does, Mrs Keel will immediately fetch you. So that is arranged. Mrs Keel will come up in half an hour. If you are ready then we can go straight in to dinner.'

Short of putting myself in the awkward position of explaining that I knew of his reputation and did not consider him a suitable companion, I could see no way out; and the only possible action was to accept graciously and get away as quickly as I could.

So I inclined my head in acknowledgement of the arrangements, thanked Mrs Keel and said I would be ready in half an hour.

I changed into the blue silk and felt a certain pleasure because Daisy had sent that one which was my most becoming.

I brushed my hair until it shone. There was a faint and rare colour in my cheeks which brightened my eyes. Really, I thought. I am quite looking forward to this just for the pleasure of bringing home to him the fact that all women are not as impressed with him as he believes them to be.

Mrs Keel tapped gently at the door. She came in and we stood side by side looking down on Teresa.

'She is sleeping deeply,' I whispered.

Mrs Keel nodded. 'I'll call you at once if she wakes.'

'Thank you,' I said.

One of the maids was waiting outside to take me down, and I was conducted to a small room with a door which opened onto a courtyard. He was already there waiting for me, looking very satisfied.

'I thought we would eat in here,' he said, 'and then, if you have no objection, afterwards we could take coffee and port or brandy or something in the courtyard. It is pleasant out there on summer evenings. I often sit out there if I have a guest.'

'That sounds very agreeable.'

'You must be hungry, Miss Grant.'

'I think the events of the day are enough to rob anyone of appetite.'

'When you see our excellent duckling you will change your mind. I am sure you will appreciate our cook. I am

129

very fortunate. I have good servants. It is the result of careful selection . . . and training. You eat well at that exclusive establishment for young ladies, I believe.'

'Yes. Miss Hetherington insists on that. Much of the produce comes from the Abbey gardens.'

'Carrying on the old monastic traditions. Ah, traditions, Miss Grant. How they rule the lives of people like us. Do sit down. There . . . opposite me so that I can see you. I always enjoy these intimate dinner parties more than those in the great hall. This, of course, is only big enough for four at the most, but two is more suitable.'

It was a charming room, oak-panelled with a painted ceiling on which fat cupids disported on fleecy clouds while an angel looked benignly on.

He saw me looking at it.

'It provides quite a celestial atmosphere, don't you think?'

I looked at him and the thought struck me that he was like Lucifer shut out of heaven. That seemed ridiculous and fanciful and far from the point. I was sure he would never allow himself to be shut out of any place he wanted to be in.

'Yes,' I said. 'It does. Although what cupids are doing up in the clouds, I am not sure.'

'Looking for an unwary heart to pierce with the arrows of love.'

'They would need a very sure aim if they planned to strike someone on earth . . . even if the clouds are low-lying.'

'You have a practical mind, Miss Grant, and I like that. Ah, here comes the soup. I trust it will be to your liking.'

A discreet manservant was carrying in a tureen from which he served us. Then he produced a bottle of wine and poured it into the glasses.

'I hope also that you will approve of the wine,' said Jason Verringer. 'I chose it specially. It is of a vintage year . . . one of the best of the century.'

'You should not take such pains on my account,' I

replied. 'I am not a connoisseur and cannot really appreciate it.'

'Didn't they teach appreciation of good wine at that very select school in Switzerland? I am surprised. You should have gone to that one in France . . . I forget its name. I am sure the knowledge of wine would have come into their curriculum.'

He tasted the wine and raised his eyes to the ceiling with an expression of mock ecstasy.

'Very fine,' he said. 'Your health, Miss Grant, and that of the girl upstairs.'

I drank with him.

'And to us,' he added. 'You . . . myself . . . and our growing friendship which has begun in rather dramatic circumstances.'

I took another sip and put down my glass.

He went on: 'You must admit that all three occasions of our meeting have been unusual. First a hold-up in a narrow lane; then you are lost and I come to your rescue; and now this affair of the runaway horse, which has led to our being here together.'

'Perhaps you are the sort of person to whom dramatic things happen.'

He considered that. 'I suppose something dramatic happens to most people now and then in their lifetimes. What of you?'

I was silent. My thoughts had gone back to that meeting in the forest and my uncanny – as it now seemed – encounters with a man who, according to a tombstone in Suffolk, had been long since dead. Strangely enough, this man, whose most outstanding quality was his vitality and firm grip on life, was reminding me more vividly of my strange experience than I had been for some time now.

He leaned forward. 'I seem to have awakened memories.'

He had a way of penetrating my thoughts which I found disconcerting.

'As I was involved in those events which you call dramatic, I suppose you would say I had experienced them too.

131

Drama, like everything else, is in the mind of those who take part in it. I don't think I see those incidents – apart from what happened to Teresa – as dramatic.'

'Do have some more soup.'

'No, thanks. It was delicious, but I am too concerned about Teresa to give your food the attention it deserves.'

'Perhaps at some later time you will make up for your neglect.'

I laughed and he signed for the butler to bring in the duckling.

He asked about his nieces and how I thought the Academy was benefiting them. Out of loyalty to Daisy, I assured him that the benefits were great.

'Fiona is a quiet girl,' he said. 'She takes after her mother. But quiet people are sometimes deceptive. Out of your vast experience you will know that.'

'I have learned that we know very little about anybody. There are always surprises in the human character. People say so and so acted out of character. That is not really so. They have acted according to some part of their character which they have not hitherto shown to the world.'

'That's true. So we can expect Fiona one day to surprise us all.'

'Perhaps.'

'Eugenie not so, because nothing she did would surprise me very much. Would it you, Miss Grant?'

'Eugenie is a girl whose character is as yet unformed. She is ready to be influenced. She is – rather unfortunately – by a girl named Charlotte Mackay.'

'I know her. She has been here for holidays. I also know her father.'

'Charlotte is very anxious that no one should forget she is an Honourable when it would be so much more becoming if she sought to conceal the fact.'

'Do you approve of concealment, Miss Grant?'

'In certain circumstances.'

He nodded slowly and attempted to fill my glass. I put my hand over it to prevent his doing so for I was sure he would have filled it even though I declined.

132

'You are very abstemious.'

'Shall we say unused to drinking a great deal.'

'A little afraid that those excellent wits might become a little befuddled?'

'I shall make sure that they do not.'

He filled his own glass.

'Tell me about your home,' he said.

'Are you really interested?'

'Very.'

'There is very little of interest. My parents died. They were missionaries in Africa.'

'Do you share their piety?'

'I'm afraid not.'

'One would have thought that parents who were missionaries would have produced offspring eager to carry on the good work.'

'On the contrary. My parents believed ardently in what they did. Although I was very young when I left them, I realized that. It was goodness in a way. They suffered hardship. In fact they died for their beliefs in the end, you might say. I suppose that is the supreme sacrifice. Then I came home to a beloved aunt and I saw a different sort of goodness. If I were able to emulate the goodness of one or the other I would choose that of my aunt.'

'Your voice changes when you speak of her. You are very fond of this aunt.'

I nodded. There were tears in my eyes and I was ashamed of them. Disliking him as I did, he yet had the power to play on my emotions. I was not sure what it was – the words he used, the inflections of his voice, the expression in his eyes. Oddly enough I felt there was something rather sad about him, which was absurd. He was arrogant in the extreme, seeing himself more than life size, the master of many, and wanting to prove himself to be the master of all.

'I was sent to live with her,' I continued, 'and that was the best thing that ever happened to me . . . or ever will, I imagine.'

He lifted his glass and said: 'I will make a prophecy.

133

Things as good are going to happen to you. Tell me about your aunt.'

'She ran a school. It didn't pay. I was going to work with her. But she had to sell up so I came here.'

'Where is she now?'

'In a little house in the country. She has a friend who lives with her. I shall go to her as soon as school breaks up.'

He nodded. 'It seems to me, Miss Grant,' he said, 'that you are a very fortunate young lady. You have been to that place in Switzerland when your aunt was more affluent – or did your parents leave you well provided for?'

'Everything they had went into their mission. It was my aunt who sent me to the school. She could ill afford it, I am sure, but she insisted on my going and she kept me there. And that . . . made it easy for me to come here.'

'Miss Hetherington talks of little else but your talents and the Schaffenbruckenization of her school.'

I laughed and he laughed with me.

'There is a soufflé. You must eat up every scrap, otherwise there will be rebellion in the kitchens.'

'Dare anyone rebel against you?'

'No,' he answered. 'It would be a private rebellion. In any case they know I should never be guilty of such a heinous offence as to reject their excellent handiwork. It is you who will receive their condemnation.'

'Then I will do my best to avoid it.'

'I am sure you would always do your best.'

The soufflé was indeed delicious and I had to admit that I had had an excellent meal – very different from the plain, though very good, fare we had at the Abbey.

He talked about the school, the history of the Abbey and how it came into his family soon after the Dissolution.

'My ancestor had performed some service to the King . . . somewhere abroad I believe, and for services rendered was allowed to buy the Abbey lands – and what remained of the Abbey itself – for a pittance. I think it was two hundred pounds . . . although perhaps that was not such a pittance in those days. He built the Hall and set himself up as a nobleman. He prospered, but people in the surrounding country never took kindly to the family. They looked upon us as usurpers. The Abbey had always done so much for the poor. There was always a meal for wanderers and a place to sleep. When the abbeys went, the roads were full of beggars, and robbery increased. So you see, the Verringers were a poor exchange for the monks.'

'I wonder they didn't try to surpass them.'

'You mean judging from the actions of this scion of the old race. Well, they were so busy setting themselves up as lords of the neighbourhood, and that didn't necessarily involve becoming its benefactors. There are some rogues among us. I must show you the portrait galleries. Our villainies are written on our faces and I think take precedence over the virtues. But you shall see and judge for yourself.'

We had finished the soufflé and I said: 'I think perhaps I should make sure that Teresa is all right.'

'And mortally offend Mrs Keel! She is zealously guarding the girl. If you went up now she would suspect you didn't trust her. Come into the courtyard. It is quite pleasant out there when it gets dark and the candles are lighted. They are in niches cut into the stone. We don't get many nights when we can sit in the courtyard, so we do like to make the most of them.'

I had risen and he was beside me. He took the crook of my elbow in his hand and led me through the door.

There was a white table in the courtyard and two chairs beside it on which cushions had been placed.

The air was still and silent and I felt an excitement grip me. I thought about school. Supper would be over and the girls would soon be settled for the night. I should be on my rounds if I were there and wondering whether Charlotte or Eugenie would make some difficulty.

'We will have coffee if you would like it and perhaps a little port . . .'

'Coffee please, no more wine.'

'There must be something you would like. Brandy?'

'Coffee will be enough for me, thanks.'

We sat down and the drinks were brought out.

135

'Now,' he said, 'we shall not be disturbed.'

'I was unaware of being disturbed before.'

'We live surrounded by servants,' he said. 'One is inclined to forget that they are a race of detectives. One should be wary of them.'

'If one has something to hide perhaps?'

'Who has not something to hide? Even excellent young ladies from Schaffenbrucken may have their secrets.'

I was silent and he poured out wine for himself.

'I wish you would try a little,' he said. 'It is . . .'

'Vintage port, I am sure.'

'We are proud of our cellars, my butler and I.'

'And I am sure you have much in them of which to be proud.'

'And we like others to share in our treasures. Come, just a little.'

I smiled and he half filled my glass.

'Now we can both drink to each other.'

'We have done that already.'

'We can't have too much good fortune. To us, Miss Grant . . . Cordelia. You are looking aloof. Do you not care for me to use your Christian name?'

'I think it is rather . . . unnecessary.'

'I think it is a most suitable name. You are Cordelia from the top of your head to the tips of your toes. I could not imagine you as anything but Cordelia and even without your permission I am going to use it. Do you not find the air of Devon delightful?'

'Yes.'

'I am always glad that our Abbey was a Devon one. It might have been in the bleak, bleak north. They have some fine ones up there. Fountains, Rievaulx . . . and others.'

'I have heard of them.'

'I don't think any of them surpasses ours . . . or even equals it. But perhaps that is what is called pride of possession. We are a ruin, are we not . . . as they are, but we are also a young ladies' Academy. Who can compare with that?'

'It seems a strange place for a school.'

'In the midst of all that antiquity. What better place for young people to learn about the past?'

'That is what Miss Hetherington always says.'

'She is a fine woman. I admire her. I am glad she has her school here. It is so convenient for my wards, and without it I should not be sitting here enjoying one of the most delightful evenings of my life.'

I laughed lightly. 'You are a master of hyperbole.'

He leaned forward and said earnestly: 'I mean it.'

'Then,' I retorted, 'you cannot have had a very exciting life.'

He paused for a while. Then he said; 'The darkness is beginning to descend. We won't light the candles yet. Look. The stars are beginning to come out. Why do people say the stars are coming out, when they are there all the time?'

'Because they only accept what they see.'

'Not discerning like you, Cordelia. You and I do not have to have everything made blatantly obvious, do we?'

'To what are you referring?'

'To life,' he said. 'You will not judge me from what you are told by others, will you?'

'It is not for me to judge.'

'Perhaps I put that wrongly. You will not assess my character from the gossip you may hear.'

'I will repeat that it is not for me to judge.'

'But you do . . . without thinking you are. You hear something about a person and if it is not contradicted, you believe that against him or her.'

'What are you telling me?'

'That I know there is a great deal of scandal circulating about me. I don't want you to believe it all. At least I want you to understand how it came about.'

'Why should it affect me?'

'Because after tonight you are going to be my friend, are you not?'

'Friendship is not put on like a hat or coat. It develops . . . it grows . . . It is something that has to be proved.'

'It will develop,' he said. 'It will be proved.'

137

I was silent for a while.

'I daresay,' he went on, 'I have done a good many things during my life of which you would not approve. I would like you to understand a little about my family. Do you know we are said to have descended from the Devil?'

I laughed.

'Ah,' he went on. 'You think that is very likely, don't you?'

'On the contrary. I think it is very unlikely.'

'Satan takes on many forms. He doesn't have to be a spirit you know, with cloven feet.'

'Tell me how the Devil became one of your ancestors.'

'Very well. It was the third generation of Verringers. The old Queen had died and Scottish James was on the throne. Do you know it has been the curse of our family that we cannot get male heirs? I know it is a bit of an obsession with many families who can't. But it was our particular problem, and in those days when a family was new to the nobility it had to be built up on a firm foundation. You see, even now I have no son to follow me; and my brother had two daughters. They like the direct line and the family name to be there because it belongs and not because one of the daughters has obliged her husband to take it. Well, this particular Verringer of Colby Hall could only get a daughter and she was the plainest creature ever to be seen in Devonshire . . . so plain that, in spite of her fortune, no husband could be found for her. Now she must get a child, and to do that she must marry and the husband must keep the sacred name of Verringer. Time went on. She was thirty years old and did not grow any more attractive with the passing of the years. Her father was desperate, and one day he sent a band of his servants, armed, to hide in the woods and to bring home to him any traveller who was moderately handsome, in good health and looked as though he might be capable of begetting children.'

'You are making this up.'

'I'll swear that it is one of my family's legends. Do you want to hear what happened?'

I nodded.

138

'Well, in time they brought back a young man. He had been riding alone through the forest. He was handsome, vigorous and most attractive in appearance. Only because there had been so many of them and he was alone had they been able to overpower him. When my ancestor saw him he was overjoyed. So was his ugly daughter. "Marry my daughter," said the father, "and you shall have lands and possessions." "I have lands and possessions, and no wish to marry your daughter," said the young man. The father was very angry and ordered him to be put into one of the dungeons – yes, we have a few. They are used for cold storage now. They were to keep him there until he agreed. But the weeks passed and the young man would not agree. No one came to rescue him. My ancestor would not allow him to be starved or tortured because he wanted to produce a perfect child, and since the young man could not be bribed with possessions it seemed as though the plan would founder. But the Verringers have always been noted for their tenacity. The prisoner was brought up from the dungeons and put into one of the best bedrooms. There were fires in the room and he was supplied with the best food and plenty of wine. The Verringers have always kept good cellars. My ancestor realized that it had been a mistake to put the young man into the dungeon. Soft living is much more conducive to seduction. And one night, when the young man had partaken very well of the good things which the wily Verringer had had sent to his table, a potent aphrodisiac was tipped into his wine. He was very sleepy and when he had retired to his bed, the daughter was slipped beside him. During the night she conceived a child.'

'Are you telling me this to show what enterprising men the Verringers are?'

'Partly, but more than that. Listen to the sequel. Strangely enough when the young man knew that the girl was pregnant through his endeavours, he agreed to marry her and there was great rejoicing throughout the Hall. In due course she produced a child – a boy, strong, healthy and as handsome as his father. Strange things began to happen then. Fire was seen over the child's cradle, but

139

there was no fire there in truth. The child laughed as no newly born baby had ever laughed before; and he grasped everything which came within his reach. They wanted a grand christening, and the chapel was prepared for this. But on the day before this was to take place, the young man went to his father-in-law and said: "There must be no Christian ceremony. You do not know who I am. You thought you were playing with me, but in truth it was I who was playing with you. I was aware of your plans; I allowed myself to be caught and brought here so that I might give my seed to your family. Do you guess who I am?"

'The story is that my ancestor fell to his knees in terror for he was unable to look into the face of the young man, for when he did so it was as bright as the sun and nearly blinded him.

' "I am Lucifer, son of the morning," said the young man. "I have been cast out of Heaven. I am ambitious. I wanted to excel God himself. You are ambitious. You would make yourself powerful beyond all others. You tried to use me to achieve this end. So I have given you a son. Lucifer. And every man-child of your clan in the generations to come will have me in him." And that is the way the Verringers are indeed spawn of the Devil.'

'You tell the story very well indeed,' I said. 'I felt I was really there. I could see that young man and the dénouement.'

'Does it excuse us?'

'Certainly not.'

'I thought that if we had the devil in our blood we could be allowed a little licence.'

'I suppose there are legends like that attached to most families who can trace their line back so far. I believe something like it was said of the Angevin line of the royal family from which so many of our kings came.'

'The story has been passed down through the generations.'

'And no doubt you all thought you had to live up to it.'

'We did not have to work very hard to do so, it appears.

140

But I wanted you to understand that when we do behave badly it is not entirely our own fault.'

What was he telling me? That he was capable of a ruthless act? Murder? I could not shut out of my mind the thought of that unwanted wife lying on her pillows, the bottle containing the fatal dose of laudanum in her husband's hands. Had he administered it?

'You are pensive,' he said. 'You are thinking that you do not accept my excuses.'

'You are right,' I answered. 'I do not.'

He sighed. 'I knew you wouldn't, but I did want to explain. What a heavenly night! There is a scent of flowers in the air and you look very beautiful sitting there, Cordelia.'

'It is because it is almost dark.'

'You have always looked beautiful to me in strong sunlight.'

'I think it is time for me to say good night and thank you for a very good meal.'

'Not yet,' he said. 'This is such a lovely night. How still it is! Not a breath of wind. It is rarely like this and a shame not to take advantage of it. You dismiss my fantasy. But many people have fantasies in their lives. Have you?'

I was silent. He sent my mind back again to that Suffolk churchyard, and before I could stop myself I was saying: 'Something strange happened to me . . . once.'

'Yes?' He was leaning forward eagerly.

'I haven't talked about it much, not even to my aunt.'

'Tell me.'

'It seems so absurd. It happened when we were at Schaffenbrucken. There were four of us and we had heard that if we sat under a tree . . . a certain tree . . . in the forest at a certain time . . . it had to be something to do with the full moon, and this was the time of the Hunter's Moon which was supposed to be especially good . . . Well, we heard that if we sat under this oak, we might see the man we were going to marry. You know how foolish girls can be.'

'I don't think it is foolish. I think it would show a very

141

lethargic and incurious mind not to want to see one's future partner.'

'Well, we went and there was a man . . .'

'Tall, dark and handsome.'

'Tall, *fair* and handsome actually. And he seemed strange, remote, perhaps that was because of the story. We talked to him for a while and then went back to school.'

'Is that all?'

'No, I saw him again. It was on the train coming home to England . . . just in a flash he was there and he was gone. Then he was on the boat coming to England. I was on deck, half asleep, it was night, you see, and then . . . suddenly it seemed, he was there beside me. We talked, and I suppose I was rather drowsy for when I opened my eyes he was gone.'

'Went up in a puff of smoke?'

'No . . . just gone . . . in a natural sort of way. I saw him again near Grantley Manor where we used to live. He talked to me and I discovered his name. He said he would visit us but he did not come. Then . . . and this is what is really odd; I went to the place where he said he lived and I discovered the house. It had been burned down more than twenty years before. I saw his name on a tombstone. He had been dead for more than twenty years. Don't you think that is as strange as your family's trafficking with the Devil?'

'I didn't . . . until you got to the visit to the place where he was supposed to live. That is very strange, I grant you. The rest is easy. He came to the forest by chance. You endowed him with all the noble and somewhat supernatural qualities because you were young and impressionable and believed in the legend. He was impressed by you, which does not surprise me in the least. He saw you on the journey. He sat beside you and talked and then his conscience smote him. He had a wife and six children waiting for him at home. So he slipped away unobtrusively. Then he couldn't resist the temptation to see you again, so he waylaid you. He was to visit you and your aunt, and then

142

his better feelings triumphed once more and he went home to his family.'

I laughed. 'It sounds plausible in a way, but it doesn't explain the name on the tombstone.'

'He chose a name at random, not wanting to give you his own for fear some whisper of his adventures reached the ears of his beloved and faithful wife who was waiting for him. Now if I accept your encounter with the mystic stranger, you must accept my Satanic ancestor.'

'I don't know why I am telling you this. I have never told anyone before.'

'It's the night . . . a night for confidences. Do you feel that? The darker it gets, the more clearly I can see into your mind . . . and you into mine.'

'But what explanation could there be?'

'You talked to a ghost . . . or a man who was acting as one. People do strange things, you know.'

'I am sure there is a logical explanation to your story . . . and to mine.'

'Perhaps we shall find the answer to yours. Mine is a little too far back to prove except that our deeds are living evidence of our progenitor's existence.'

I found myself laughing. The port is very heavy, I thought, and I was aware of a pleasant lassitude and the certain knowledge that I did not want the night to end just yet.

He said, as though he read my thoughts: 'I am very happy tonight. I want this to go on and on. I am not often happy like this, you know, Cordelia.'

'I have always thought that true happiness came through service to others.'

'I see the missionary forebears peeping out.'

'I know it sounds sententious, but I am certain it is true. The happiest person I have ever known is my aunt, and when I come to think of it she is always unconsciously doing something for someone else's benefit.'

'I want to meet her.'

'I doubt you ever will.'

'I shall, of course,' he said, 'for you and I are going to be . . . friends.'

143

'Do you think so? I have a feeling that this is an isolated occasion. We are sitting here in the darkness with the stars above and the smell of flowers in the air and it is having an effect on us. We are talking too much . . . too freely . . . Perhaps tomorrow we shall regret what we have said tonight.'

'I shall regret nothing. Life has been smooth for you, Cordelia, once you were rid of your missionaries. The fairy godmother aunt provided you with your dress so that you could go to the ball; she turned the pumpkin into the coach and the rats into horses. Cinderella Cordelia is going to the ball. She is just meeting the Prince and he is not an elusive spirit who is nothing but a name on a tombstone. You know that, don't you, Cordelia?'

'Your metaphors are taking such a wild turn that they are waking me up and reminding me that it is time I said good night.'

'You see,' he persisted, 'there was no fairy godmother for me. Mine was a harsh childhood. All the time one had to excel. There was no tenderness . . . ever. It was tutors who had to get results. There was always correction . . . physical mostly. I was in a prison . . . like the handsome young man who turned out to be the Devil. I was wild, adventurous, wicked often, always seeking for something. I don't know what. But I think I am beginning to. Then I went to Oxford and lived riotously because I thought that was the answer. I was married . . . very young . . . to the suitable young girl who was as ignorant of life as I was. I had my duty to perform, which was the same as that of my ugly ancestress. I had to produce the boy. My brother had married young. He had the two girls, as you know. For myself there was nothing, and my wife had a riding accident three months after our marriage and was incapable of bearing children after that. I am not going to say that I was miserable, but frustrated, always . . . dissatisfied. She died. We buried her the day you came here.'

'I know,' I said gently. 'You were coming from the funeral.'

'I had to get away. I couldn't stand any more of it. Then I saw you in the lane.'

144

'And forced me to retreat,' I said lightly.

'I caught a glimpse of you as we went past. You looked wonderful, different from anyone I had ever known, like some heroine from the past riding in that carriage.'

'Boadicea?' I suggested lightly.

'I wanted to know you from that moment. And then when I found you lost . . .'

'You took me for a long ride round the town.'

'I had to talk to you for as long as possible. And now . . . this . . .'

I thought then of the handsome woman and the child I had seen in the garden of Rooks' Rest, and I said: 'I believe I have met a friend of yours.'

'Oh?'

'Mrs Marcia Martindale. She has a beautiful little girl.'

He was silent and I thought: I should not have said that. I am getting careless, not thinking before I speak. How could I have ever told him about the stranger in the forest? What is happening to me?

I was startled suddenly as a black shape flashed over my head. It was eerie and I had the sudden feeling that in this ancient home there must be ghosts who could not rest, spirits of those who had met violent ends. Perhaps his wife . . .

'What was that?' I cried out.

'It was only a bat. They are flying low tonight.'

I shivered.

'Innocent little creatures,' he went on. 'Why do they inspire people with fear?'

'It is because they get into one's hair and are said to be verminous.'

'They wouldn't hurt you if you didn't hurt them. Oh . . . here he is again. It must be the same one. You're looking really alarmed. I think you believe they are messengers from the Devil. You do, don't you? You think I have summoned them up to do my bidding.'

'I know them for bats,' I said. 'But that doesn't mean I like them.'

145

I was saying to myself: I must go in, but there was something in me pleading for a little longer. I wanted to stay out in this magic night and learn more about this man, for he was revealing a great deal about himself. I had thought of him as brash and arrogant. He was; but there was something else about him – a sadness, even a vulnerability, something which touched me in a way.

And then . . . suddenly we were no longer alone. She came into the courtyard. She was dressed in a riding habit and was bareheaded; her beautiful reddish hair was caught up in a kind of snood.

I recognized her at once.

'Jason!' she cried in a strangled voice which conveyed sadness, despair and acute melancholy.

He rose to his feet. I could see that he was very angry.

'What are you doing here?' he demanded.

She flinched and stood back a little, her very white hands on which she wore several rings were crossed over her breast, which heaved with emotion.

She said: 'I heard there was an accident. I thought it might be you, Jason. I have been frantic with anxiety.'

She looked magnificent and yet she managed to be pathetic at the same time. I believed I was looking at the one-time cherished mistress who could no longer please as she once had, was aware of it, and heart-broken because of it.

He said in a low voice: 'I must introduce you to Miss Grant who is from the girls' academy.'

'We have already met,' I said. 'And you must excuse me. I must go to see Teresa.' I looked straight at Marcia Martindale who seemed to express anguish, sorrow and despair all at the same time. 'One of our girls had a fall from her horse. That is why I am here. She is asleep in this house and I am here to look after her.'

I saw the look of relief on the woman's face. It was certainly the most expressive face I had ever seen. Her feelings were there for everyone to see.

'I trust . . .' she began.

146

'Oh, it is nothing much,' I said quickly. 'The doctor was afraid of concussion and it was thought better to keep her here overnight. Mrs Keel is watching over her until I go up. Well, good night and thank you, Sir Jason, for your hospitality.'

I hurried out of the courtyard and went into the house, trying to find my way to the blue room. My exhilaration of a short time ago had sunk to depression.

What had happened to me in the courtyard? There had been some enchantment about the night. It was the darkness, the food, the wine . . . his personality, my inexperience perhaps . . . his conversation which I found stimulating. I must have been completely bemused to imagine for a moment that he was not the man I knew him to be from all that I had heard about him.

He now had to face the mistress whom he had deserted for an evening's adventure with someone who was new to him.

It was just what I would expect of him!

She had shattered something, that woman. It was just as well, for she had brought me back to reality. I hoped I had not been too indiscreet and tried to remember what I had said. How had he managed to carry me along with him? I had almost begun to like him.

I saw a maid on the stairs and asked her to show me the blue room, which she did.

Mrs Keel rose from her chair as I entered.

'She's fast asleep. Hasn't stirred the whole time,' she said. 'Are you staying here now?'

'Yes,' I said. 'I shall sleep on one side of the bed. It's big enough. I shan't disturb her and if she wakes I shall be there.'

'That's right,' said Mrs Keel. 'Well, I'll say good night.'

She shut the door quietly. I still felt bemused. It was the food and wine, I told myself. It had nothing to do with him.

There was a key in the door.

I turned it, locking myself in with Teresa.

I felt secure then. Tomorrow if Teresa was well enough –

147

and I knew she would be – we would go back to the school and I, no less than Teresa, would have to forget about our little adventure.

* * *

I lay beside Teresa, but sleep was elusive. I felt stimulated and excited and was wondering what Sir Jason and Marcia Martindale were saying to each other down there. I could imagine the recriminations. I should like her to know that there was no need for her to lose any sleep on my account. I was not the sort to be taken in by a plausible philanderer. Yet while I was talking to him – although I had been wary and believed that I could see through him with the utmost ease – I had to admit that I had been a trifle fascinated. He was blasé, ruthless, what would be called 'a man of the world', and I realized – and so did he – that I had had little experience of such people. There had been no doubt that he was stressing his interest in me. But innocent as I might be, I was fully aware that a man like Jason Verringer would be *interested* in that certain way in many women at the same time.

How foolish I had been to think – just for a short while – that he had a special feeling for me. What struck me as so very strange was that I should have told him about my adventure with the man in the forest when I had not even talked to Aunt Patty about that. It had been because we had been sitting there while it grew darker and darker and the bats flew overhead. If it had been broad daylight, I should never have talked as I did.

Well, it was over. It had come to an abrupt ending with the dramatic appearance of his mistress.

Forget the man, said my common sense. Go to sleep.

I closed my eyes and tried. I had locked the door because I had a suspicion that he might come into the bedroom perhaps on a pretext of explaining Marcia Martindale's sudden appearance. But Teresa was here . . . a sleeping chaperone. The door was locked and she lay beside me in her sedated sleep.

At last I dozed.

148

When I awoke it was dark. I could not remember where I was for some moments, then memory came flooding back.

'Teresa!' I said softly.

'Yes, Miss Grant.'

'So you're awake.' I sensed her anxiety and I went on: 'You're not badly hurt, Teresa. You're going to be walking round normally in a day or two.'

'I know.'

'Well then, just try to go to sleep. It's the middle of the night. There's nothing to worry about. We shall stay here until the morning and then Emmet will come to collect us.'

She said: 'I wish it wasn't summer.'

'Why ever not! Why, it's the best time of the year. Think of the lovely sunshine, the walks, the picnics, the holidays . . .'

I stopped. How foolish of me, how tactless.

There was a brief silence and I went on: 'Teresa, what shall you do during the summer holidays?'

'I shall stay at school.' Her voice sounded utterly dreary. 'I suppose Miss Hetherington will have to let me, but it is a nuisance for her. I'm the only one.'

A sudden impulse came to me and I said: 'Teresa, suppose . . . just suppose . . . it were possible for me to take you home with me for the holidays.'

'Miss Grant!'

'Well, I suppose I could. Aunt Patty would be all right . . . and Violet. I'd have to get Miss Hetherington's permission.'

'Oh, Miss Grant . . . I'd see Aunt Patty and Violet's bees. Oh, Miss Grant. I want to come . . . so much.'

I stared into the darkness. Perhaps I should have thought about it more carefully before mentioning it. But, poor Teresa. She was so miserable and in such a low state after the accident. I had to make the suggestion, and the more I thought of it the better it seemed. Teresa would not go to sleep now. She wanted to talk about Aunt Patty and her home in the country.

'I don't know much about it myself yet. I haven't been there when it was a home. It has always been an empty

149

house to me. They only moved in when I came to Colby, so I only know about it from Aunt Patty's letters.'

'Tell me about Aunt Patty. Tell me about how she came to meet you from Africa in that hat with the feather.'

So I told her, as I had told her before, and I heard her laugh contentedly beside me, and I knew that the prospect of the summer holiday was doing more to restore her than anything else could have done.

*   *   *

The next day Emmet arrived to take us back to the school. Mrs Keel saw us off with two of the servants and as we were about to get into the carriage Sir Jason appeared.

I said: 'Thank you for your hospitality. Teresa, please thank Sir Jason.'

'Thank you,' said Teresa obediently, her eyes still shining with anticipation of the summer holidays.

'It was a great pleasure,' he said. 'I so much enjoyed our dinner.'

'A culinary masterpiece,' I replied. 'Again thank you and everyone concerned. Come along, Teresa.'

'I trust we shall meet again soon,' he said looking at me.

I smiled vaguely and settled Teresa, taking my seat beside her. Emmet whipped up the horse and we moved away. Sir Jason was looking straight at me rather pleadingly, I thought, and again I felt a twinge of that pity for him which would, I am sure, have amused him, had he known of it.

Daisy Hetherington was waiting to receive us. She greeted me and her eyes went immediately to Teresa.

'You look none the worse for your adventure,' she said. 'Come along in. What does the doctor say, Miss Grant? Is Teresa to rest for a while?'

'Yes, for today. I will take her to her room. She should rest in bed for today, and tomorrow we will see.'

'When you have dealt with her, come to my sitting room, Miss Grant. I want to talk to you.'

'Certainly,' I replied.

I took Teresa to her room and helped her to bed.

'Will you ask Miss Hetherington now?' she whispered conspiratorially.

'Yes,' I said. 'At the first opportunity.'

'And will you let me know . . . at once?'

'I promise.'

I saw Charlotte and the Verringer girls on my way to Miss Hetherington.

I said to them: 'Teresa is back. She may be a little shocked. I want you all to be very careful. Don't refer to the mishap unless she does. Is that clear?'

'Yes, Miss Grant. Yes, Miss Grant. Yes, Miss Grant.'

There was even an understanding affirmative from Charlotte. That little bit of authority had worked wonders.

'You three ride very well,' I went on. 'You happen to be especially good horse-women.' I was looking at Charlotte, who turned pink with pleasure. 'You must understand that everyone cannot be as good. Their talents might lie in other directions.'

I passed on. I did not think Charlotte would taunt Teresa with cowardice if she refused to ride for a while. I really did believe that I had got through to her because of her love of horses – in a small way perhaps but it was a beginning. I fell to thinking then that many people behaved badly through a desire to assert themselves, and when their success was acknowledged there ceased to be that necessity. It was a point I should like to discuss. Certainly not with Daisy Hetherington but with Eileen Eccles, Aunt Patty . . . and it might be interesting to hear Sir Jason's views.

Daisy was waiting for me.

'Oh, Miss Grant, do sit down. What an unfortunate thing to happen! And there of all places . . .'

'It was better than happening in the isolated country,' I reminded her. 'At least we got Teresa attended to very quickly.'

'I gather it is only bruises.'

'No bones were broken. She was lucky. Of course she is shocked.'

'Sometimes I wish I had never taken Teresa Hurst.'

'She is a very pleasant girl.'

151

'She seems to have some fixation for you, Cordelia. Be careful. These obsessions can become tiresome.'

'The fact with Teresa is that she is lonely. She feels unwanted because of her home situation. By the way she is very depressed about the summer holidays and I, rather rashly I'm afraid, promised to take her home with me if all were agreeable.'

'Take her home!' cried Daisy. 'My dear Cordelia!'

'It seemed a good idea in the middle of the night when the poor child was so depressed, and after what had happened I promised . . .'

Daisy smiled slowly. 'It was extremely good of you and I am sure Patience would raise no objections.'

'Then I have your permission?'

'My dear Cordelia, nothing would please me better than to have the child somewhere else for the summer holidays. It is an added burden when they stay at school . . . and not worth the price they pay for it. Imagine . . . the child here all that time and no others of her age. And a responsibility. As far as I am concerned I would give a whole-hearted Yes. There are the parents.'

'They are in Rhodesia.'

'I am thinking of the guardians here. The cousins . . . I will write to them and ask for their permission for Teresa to stay with you. I will tell them that your aunt with whom you will be staying is an old friend of mine and I can vouch for Teresa's being in the best possible place, since she cannot be with her own parents.'

'Oh thank you, Miss Hetherington. Would you mind if I went to tell Teresa right away. She is so anxious.'

'Yes. And there is one other thing, Cordelia. I was uneasy about your spending a night at the Hall.'

'I know you were and it was good of you to be concerned.'

'I feel as responsible for my staff as I do for my girls . . . Did you dine with Sir Jason?'

'Yes.'

'He has a reputation for being rather . . . free with women.'

152

'I can well imagine that.'

'I hope he was in no way offensive.'

'No. As a matter of fact after dinner Mrs Martindale called. I left them and went to Teresa to relieve Mrs Keel who had kindly offered to keep vigil while I ate.'

Daisy was obviously relieved.

I went straight to Teresa.

'The first hurdle is over,' I said. 'Miss Hetherington gives her whole-hearted consent. There now remain the cousins. She will write to them today.'

'They will say "Yes please." We have nothing to fear from them. Oh, Miss Grant, I am going to spend my summer holidays with you and Aunt Patty!'

A Summer Interlude

***

We had heard from the cousins and they were delighted with the arrangements and expressed assurance that as Miss Grant was so highly recommended by Miss Hetherington, she would take good care of Teresa.

'As if they cared,' said Daisy. 'You can read the relief oozing out of their words.'

Aunt Patty wrote that she thought it was an admirable suggestion and Teresa could have the room next to mine. She had made curtains of sprigged muslin – delphinium blue in colour – and a bedspread to match. Very pretty but Violet said they wouldn't stand up to the wash. Trust Violet! She could not wait to meet us at the station.

I showed the letter to Teresa who from then on dreamed of a room with delphinium blue sprigged muslin curtains.

She had not mounted a horse since her accident. The general opinion was that she should, but I told Miss Hetherington that she had had a great shock and that she was seized with trembling every time the subject was broached, and we did not yet know the full effects of her fall. So we decided that we would let Teresa have her way.

Charlotte and her cronies did not taunt her as I feared they would. It might have been that my words had had some effect on them or perhaps they were too excited about the coming break.

I saw nothing of Sir Jason. I heard that he had gone to London and I began to realize that there had been nothing of any great significance in our encounter. He had been ready to turn it into what he would call an adventure – just a light-hearted passing *affaire*; and as I had not responded with enthusiasm, he, preferring easier conquests, had not thought it worth while to pursue the project. I was ashamed of myself for thinking so much about him. I must stop thinking of it. I must dismiss the incident in the courtyard as I had tried to in the case of my encounter with the stranger in the forest. One had to accept people's idiosyncrasies and try not to find a reason for them when it was quite impossible to know what was going on in other people's minds. As for allowing oneself to be disturbed – even faintly – by a man of Jason Verringer's reputation, that was the utmost folly. I would proceed to forget all about him.

The rest of the term slipped by and as soon as we were in July the girls talked of little else but the coming summer holidays – the longest of the year and the most looked forward to.

The day came when we steamed into the station and there was Aunt Patty in a biscuit-coloured creation covered with blue-and-yellow flowers perched on her head. I watched Teresa's eyes shine with excitement, and I knew that Aunt Patty was going to live up to my picture of her.

'Oh there you are.' I was held in that lavender-scented embrace which brought back memories. 'And this is Teresa.'

Teresa was caught up in Aunt Patty's arms.

'Well, here we are in Moldenbury. Violet's in the dog cart. She wouldn't leave the horse. Tom will take your bags. Here you are, Tom,' she said to the railway porter. I couldn't help smiling. It was typical of Aunt Patty to be on friendly terms with everyone in record time and she seemed as at home here as she had at Grantley. 'Here we are. Vi! Vi! You can leave the horse and come and greet our girls.'

Violet looked just the same as ever, with her brown hair escaping from a brown hat which looked more sombre than it actually was in comparison with Aunt Patty's glory.

'The girls are here, Violet. This is Teresa.'

'Hello, Teresa,' said Violet as though she had known her all her life. 'And Cordelia.' We embraced rather emotionally. I was very fond of Violet and I knew she was of me.

155

Violet drove the dog cart and Teresa and I sat opposite Aunt Patty as we jolted along the lanes.

Aunt Patty talked all the time. 'You'll love the house. Not Grantley, of course. We had a big house before we came here, Teresa. It seems such a change, but for the better. There's something about small houses . . . they're warm and cosy. Do you remember how the wind used to whistle through those windows at Grantley, Cordelia? My goodness, you felt as if you were going to be blown sky-high. Nothing of that here at Moldenbury, even though the wind howls and it can do that sometimes . . . we're as warm as toast. Do you like toast, Teresa? I'm rather a one for it. There's nothing like a round of toast with the butter well soaked in. We always stand it over a basin of water, don't we Cordelia? Just as my grandmother used to do. I'm a bit of a one for old customs, Teresa. Old ways are best, my grandmother used to say, and somehow I think she's right.'

She chattered all the way and then we tumbled out of the trap and went into the house.

It was the beginning of the ideal holiday for Teresa and for me, because her obvious happiness made everything doubly enjoyable. I was so proud of Aunt Patty who had the secret of spreading happiness about her; and how we used to laugh to see Violet looking over her spectacles and raising her eyes to Heaven and continually asking us to look what your Aunt Patty is up to now.

Violet was the perfect foil for Aunt Patty, always looking on the black side, constantly questioning Aunt Patty's wisdom, always appalled by her impetuosity but loving her as fiercely and devotedly as any of us.

Teresa had never been in such a household before. She was changing. Her timidity dropped from her. For what was there to be afraid of here? There was always so much to do and strangely enough she was with Violet more than any of us.

Her love of flowers and plants had quickly been noticed and, as Violet did the gardening, Teresa was soon helping her. They talked constantly of the kitchen garden and the

156

flower beds, while Aunt Patty and I silently looked on and, when Violet said the wasps would get most of the plums and a plague of greenfly was making short work of the finest roses, even Teresa laughed at Violet's pessimism with the rest of us.

Teresa would go with Violet to cut the vegetables we would have that day and she and Violet would talk of planting and pruning as though Teresa were going to be with us for ever.

Aunt Patty had very quickly become well-known throughout the village and was deeply involved in all its activities. It was what she had always wanted and had never had time for at Grantley. Her new role became her. She was a born organizer and was to have a big part in the summer fête which would take place during these holidays. Everyone was drawn in. Violet and Teresa were to have the flower stall. I had the white elephant with Aunt Patty and the preparations for that event went on for days.

I was amazed to see Teresa's enthusiasm.

There was in the village a retired Major who ran a riding-stable and I think that because she wanted to show her gratitude to me, I was able to prevail on Teresa to mount a horse again. I had explained to the Major what had happened and he produced a mare whom he called Snowdrop, explaining that she was rather long in the tooth and had a mouth like leather on account of being pulled on so hard. 'I get all my beginners started on Snowdrop,' he said. 'She can be as stubborn as a mule but she is safe as houses.'

So I took Teresa out on Snowdrop and, after the first morning, she was ready to ride again. I looked on that as a great achievement.

The weeks flew past – long days of sunshine for it was a good summer, and when it rained there was always something to do in the house. I had wondered how we were going to entertain Teresa at such times but I need have had no qualms about that. She was off with Violet to the potting shed and in the evenings they would pore over seed catalogues together.

157

'I always wanted a piece of garden of my own,' said Teresa.

'That's easily arranged,' said Aunt Patty. 'Surely there's somewhere in this big garden.'

Violet considered seriously and said: 'What about that bit by the rockery. We've never got round to doing much with that. Yes, that's it. What could you plant there?'

She and Teresa went into a deep discussion before Teresa cried out in dismay: 'But I'm only here for the holiday.'

Violet looked disconsolate but Aunt Patty was ready for the occasion. 'Why bless you, my dear, that'll be your bit of land for as long as you want it. I hope you're not going to tell us you don't want to come again.'

Teresa was so moved she almost sobbed: 'Oh, but I do. I do. I can't bear it if I don't.'

'Well, that's settled,' said Aunt Patty. 'What do we call this garden? Teresa's Treat. Teresa's Treasure.'

'Teresa's Tribulation by the look of that soil,' said Violet. 'There's a lot of alkali in it.'

And we all laughed and started to plan Teresa's garden. I knew Teresa well and I guessed she was not so much thinking of her garden but that she was coming again.

Aunt Patty had naturally been interested in the school and during the first days of the holiday she talked a good deal about it. This was while Teresa was with Violet in the garden because there must be some things which I could not talk of before one of the pupils.

Aunt Patty listened avidly. She wanted to know just how Daisy Hetherington ran her school. She had a great admiration for her and was in no way envious because Daisy had succeeded where she herself had failed. In fact Aunt Patty did not think she had failed.

'I like it here, Cordelia,' she said. 'This is what I always wanted. I sold out at the right time. I've enough to be comfortable on . . . without great luxury of course . . . but what is luxury compared with comfort? We're very happy here, happier even than we were at Grantley. There were silly niggling worries there. Parents can be difficult, some of them, and my goodness, pupils can be too.'

I told her about the rebellious Hon. Charlotte and her henchmaid Eugenie Verringer: 'The niece of the man who owns the Hall, and the school too, and much of the neighbourhood. He has two nieces, Fiona and Eugenie, and they are both at the school. Eugenie is the difficult one.'

She wanted to hear about Teresa's accident and I told her without mentioning the tête-à-tête dinner with Sir Jason. I did not want to talk about that any more than I did about that other adventure.

Aunt Patty said: 'Did you ever hear from those girls who were with you at Schaffenbrucken. You used to talk about them so much at one time. The ones who were your particular cronies, I mean.'

'No. We said we'd write but we didn't. You mean to . . . and then something happens and you forget. The days pass and all that seems so remote now.'

She had aroused memories. I was thinking of us all lying there on the grass of the forest, lying back supporting our heads on our arms . . . when he had appeared.

'Someone has to be the one to write,' said Aunt Patty. 'Do you have their addresses?'

'Yes, we all exchanged addresses.'

'What were their names. I am trying to remember. There was a German girl, a French girl and an English one.'

'That's right. Lydia Markham was the English one. Then there was Monique Delorme and Frieda Schmidt. I wonder what they are doing now.'

'Write to them. Perhaps you'll find out.'

'I will. I'll write today.'

And I did.

The days passed with incredible speed. They were so full. We went for a picnic, taking the trap with us and rattling along the lanes. Violet packed a hamper and grumbled about the rattling of the trap which would turn the milk, she said, and when she was proved right, that was a great joke.

159

We sat in the middle of a field, boiled a kettle and drank milkless tea and were tormented by flies, alarmed by wasps and played guessing games.

'That's picnics for you,' said Violet when we found ants swarming over the sponge cake.

And it was such a happy day.

Drowsy with sun we rattled home again and stretched ourselves in the garden and talked of picnics we had known. Aunt Patty had some hilarious stories to tell while Violet was characteristically lugubrious and I marvelled to watch Teresa, intent one moment, listening avidly and rolling about in uncontrollable mirth the next.

There were summer evenings when, if it was warm enough, we had supper in the gardens. They were lovely days. When I think of them I see Aunt Patty in a hat trimmed with poppies sitting in the garden supporting a basin on her knees while she shelled peas very deftly and dropped them into it. I see Teresa, lying on the grass, her eyes half closed; I can hear the buzzing of Violet's bees. I recall evenings redolent with the scent of night stock and perfect peace.

I was delighted to receive a letter from Frieda. It was to be expected that she would be the first to reply. Frieda had always been meticulous. She wrote that she was very pleased to hear from me. She herself had one more term before she would be leaving Schaffenbrucken. They missed me, particularly as Lydia had left rather sooner than she had expected to. To read Frieda's letter took me back, and the school had not changed apparently since I was there.

I had not known that Lydia was leaving so soon. I thought she was to have another year. There must have been some reason. I daresay I should hear from her.

'There you are,' said Aunt Patty. 'Each of you waiting for the other to write. Somebody has to make a move. That's life for you. I reckon you'll be hearing from the others. Lydia is not so far away, is she?'

'No, she is in Essex . . . and London of course.'

'Quite near us. She might be popping over to see you.

160

That would be nice. I think you were rather specially fond of her.'

'Well, we had more in common. I expect it was because she is English.'

'That would be it. You'll hear, you see.'

A week later there was a letter from Monique.

She was leaving at the end of next term also, at the same time as Frieda. 'I'm glad at least she is staying on with me. It saves my being all alone. Fancy your teaching now. I was sorry about Grantley. It sounded so grand. I think I shall be marrying Henri soon after I leave Schaffenbrucken. After all, I'll be quite old by then. It was lovely to hear from you. Please do write again, Cordelia.'

'There,' said Aunt Patty. 'What did I say?'

Strangely enough there was no reply from Lydia, but I didn't think about this until I was back at school, when I wrote to Aunt Patty asking her to send the letter on if Lydia should write. It seemed strange that she, who was nearer and with whom I had been on more friendly terms, should have been the one not to answer.

It was not surprising that I forgot about Lydia during the rest of that holiday, for something happened which drove all thought of my old friends from my mind.

I was reading in my room one afternoon when Violet came in in a flutter of excitement.

'There's a gentleman. He's called to see you. He's with Patty in the garden.'

'A gentleman . . . ? Who . . . ?'

'Sir Something Something,' said Violet. 'I didn't quite catch his name.'

'Sir Jason Verringer?'

'Yes, that sounds like it. Your Aunt Patty said to me, Violet, this is Sir Something Something. He's come to see Cordelia. Do go to her room and tell her he's here.'

'He's in the garden, you say?'

I looked at my reflection in the barbola mirror which I had admired when it was in Aunt Patty's room and which had been transferred to mine.

Colour had deepened in my cheeks.

161

'What on earth is he doing here?'

I looked askance at Violet. How foolish of me. As if she would know.

I said: 'I'll come down at once.'

When I appeared, Aunt Patty in the enormous sun hat she wore in the garden and which made her look like a large mushroom, sprang up from the chair in which she had been sitting.

'Ah,' she cried. 'Here is my niece.'

'Miss Grant . . . Cordelia,' he said and came towards me, his hands outstretched.

'You . . . you came to see us,' I stammered in a bemused state.

'Yes, I have come from London and as I was passing . . .'

Passing? What did he mean? He did not pass Moldenbury on his way from London to Devon.

Aunt Patty was watching us with her head on one side which indicated particular absorption.

'Would you like tea?' she asked. 'I'll go and see to it. You can sit in my chair, Cordelia, you and er . . .'

'Jason Verringer,' he said.

'Can have a little chat,' finished Aunt Patty and disappeared.

'I am surprised that you called here,' I began.

'Shall we sit down as your Aunt suggested. I called to say goodbye. I am going abroad and shall not be in Colby for some months. I felt I should explain this to you.'

'Oh?'

'You look surprised. I didn't want to go off without telling you.'

I stared straight ahead at the lavender, considerably depleted as Violet had gathered most of it to make little sachets which scented Aunt Patty's clothes and cupboards.

'I am surprised that you should have thought it necessary to come here.'

'Well, we are rather special friends I thought and, in view of everything that has happened, I wanted to let you know. I have so recently become a widower and the death of

162

someone with whom one has lived closely for many years is shattering . . . even when death is expected. I feel the need to get right away. I have several good friends on the Continent whom I shall visit. I shall do a sort of Grand Tour . . . France, Italy, Spain . . . so I thought I should like to say *au revoir* to you.'

'I can only say that I am surprised you should have come so far to do that. I should have heard the news in due course when I return to the school, I daresay.'

'But of course I wanted you to know I was going, and particularly how much I shall look forward to seeing you when I come back.'

'I am unexpectedly flattered. They will be bringing out the tea soon. You will stay for that?'

'I shall be delighted to. It is such a great pleasure to talk to you.'

'When do you leave?' I asked.

'Next week.'

'I hope you will have an interesting journey. The Grand Tour used to be the high spot of a young man's life.'

'I am not so young, nor am I looking for high spots.'

'You just feel the need to travel after your bereavement. I understand.'

'One has certain misgivings when people die.'

'You mean . . . conscience?'

'H'm. One has to come to terms with that, I suppose.'

'I hope it is not proving too formidable an opponent.'

He laughed and I couldn't help laughing with him. 'It is so good to be with you,' he said. 'You do mock me, don't you?'

'I am sorry. I should not . . . on such a subject.'

'I know of the rumours which are circulated about me. But I want you to remember that rumour is a lying jade . . . very often.'

'Oh, I don't take notice of rumours.'

'Nonsense. Everybody takes notice of rumours.'

'But you are the last person surely to be concerned about them.'

'Only on the effect they may have on someone whom one

163

is trying to impress.'

'You mean you are trying to impress me?'

'I am . . . most fervently. I want you to consider that I might not be as black as I am painted, though the last thing I should want you to do is consider me a saint.'

'Rest assured I should find that very difficult to do.'

We were laughing again.

'It was a wonderful evening we had together,' he said wistfully.

'It was kind of you to allow Teresa and me to stay at the Hall. Teresa is with us now.'

'Yes. I heard that you brought her with you.'

'They will all be coming out to tea very soon.'

'I should like to go on talking to you. There is so much I want to say.'

'Here is Teresa now.' I went on: 'Teresa, we have a visitor. You know Sir Jason Verringer.'

'Of course,' said Teresa. 'He's Fiona's and Eugenie's uncle.'

Jason laughed. 'I have achieved fame in Teresa's eyes,' he said. 'The uncle of Fiona and Eugenie! It is only reflected glory of course.'

'It is gratifying to be recognized no matter what the reason,' I said.

Aunt Patty and Violet appeared and tea was served.

There was talk about the village life and Aunt Patty's descriptions were apt and amusing. Teresa handed round the food like a daughter of the house and I was amazed afresh at the change in her. It was a conventionally pleasant scene. Tea on the lawn and a visitor who happened to be passing and who had called in.

But I could not get over the strangeness of his being here and wondering what was the real motive for his call. To see me, of course. But why? I was a little annoyed with myself that I should find the question so stimulating. Aunt Violet asked if he had come in on the three forty-five and he said that he had.

'Then you'll be catching the six o'clock.'

'Unless,' put in Aunt Patty, 'you are spending some time

164

here. When we were at Grantley we could have put you up. Here alas, we are short of rooms. There is, of course, the King's Arms in Moldenbury itself.'

'The food's poor so I've heard,' said Violet.

'But they do excellent roast beef,' added Aunt Patty. 'They're noted for it.'

'I did ask the fly to call for me at a quarter to six,' he said.

'Well then you haven't much time left, have you,' said Aunt Patty. 'Cordelia, why don't you show Sir Jason the garden.'

'What an excellent idea,' he said.

'It's not at its best now,' put in Violet. 'Early spring's the best time. The flowers are beginning to get that tired look. The sun's been particularly fierce this year.'

'I am sure Cordelia will find something pleasant to show our guest,' said Aunt Patty. 'Come, Teresa, help me with the tray. Violet will see to the rest.'

'You must allow me to carry the tray,' said Jason.

'Get away with you,' said Aunt Patty. 'If you knew the number of trays I've carried in my life . . .'

'Astronomical, I expect,' said Jason, picking up the tray. 'Now show me the way without more argument.'

Aunt Patty waddled in front of him. I watched them disappear into the house, smiling to myself.

In a few moments he was at my side.

'What a charming lady your aunt is! So merry . . . and so tactful.'

'Come then. I'll show you the garden.'

He walked in silence for a few seconds. I said: 'Teresa is developing this patch. There is a great change in her. Poor child, she felt unwanted.'

'I shall miss you,' he said.

'Miss me? You talk as though you see me every day. We have only met a few times . . . and how long is it since the last time I saw you?'

'I felt that you were displeased with me in some way.'

'Displeased? I have thanked you several times for your hospitality to Teresa and me.'

'Our happy evening was rather suddenly interrupted.'

'Oh yes . . . when your friend arrived. I quite understood that.'

'I don't think you did.'

'Well, it wasn't important. The meal was over and I was thinking that it was time I returned to Teresa.'

He sighed. 'There are many things I would like to explain to you.'

'There is no reason why you should.'

'There are reasons. When I return we must meet. I am desperately anxious for us to be good friends. There is much I want to tell you.'

'Well, I hope you will have a pleasant trip. The fly will be here very soon. You mustn't miss your train.'

He laid a hand on my arm. 'When I return, I want to talk to you . . . seriously. You see it is so soon . . . after . . . and there are certain difficulties which have to be settled. Cordelia, I shall return and then . . .'

I avoided his eyes. 'Oh, there's Violet,' I said. 'She must be looking for you. That means the station fly is here.' I called: 'We're coming, Violet. The fly's here, is it?'

I walked with him across the lawn. He held my hand firmly in his and was trying to tell me something. He was asking me to wait until his return when he would be in a position to continue our relationship. It was the way in which he would behave to any young woman. But it seemed strange that he had come out of his way to tell me he was going away.

We stood waving until the fly disappeared.

Aunt Patty was thoughtful.

When we were alone together she said: 'What an interesting man! It was nice of him to call and tell you he was going away.' She looked at me intently. 'He must have felt that you were a very special friend . . . to come all that way.'

'Oh, he was in the neighbourhood, I expect. I have only met him a few times. He is a sort of lord of the manor and probably feels he ought to take an interest in all the vassals.'

'Do you know, I quite liked him.'

166

I laughed. 'I gather from that remark that you are rather surprised that you do.'

She was looking into the distance.

'It was courteous of him to call,' she said. 'I have no doubt he had his reasons.'

Rooks' Rest

❋

When I went back to school, I quickly slipped into the old routine and it felt like coming home. In a few days even the girls settled down. Teresa had changed considerably; she had almost lost that scared look she had had before and was able to mingle more easily with the other girls.

Daisy Hetherington wanted to know how she had behaved during the holiday and I was delighted to be able to tell her that everything had worked out very well indeed.

'Teresa's trouble was that she was lonely and felt unwanted,' I explained. 'As soon as she saw that we were glad to have her, she changed and became just a normal happy girl.'

'How fortunate if all our troubles could be so easily solved,' said Daisy, but she smiled, well pleased, and I said that if there was no objection she was invited for Christmas.

'I daresay those cousins will be as ready to forsake their duties at Christmas as in the summer,' was Daisy's comment.

Then she went on to discuss the term's work.

'We put on a little entertainment at Christmas,' she said. 'I know it seems far away but you'd be surprised how much preparation is needed and it gives the girls something to think about instead of mooning nostalgically over the summer holidays. I thought you with Miss Eccles and Miss Parker could put your heads together, and of course Miss Barston for the costumes. We do it in the refectory one night and then we have been invited to repeat it at the Hall when some of the people from the village come to see it. This year I understand Sir Jason will be away and, as he has said nothing about lending us the Hall, I suppose we shan't have it there this time. He did tell me that he planned to stay away some time.'

I said I would consult with Miss Eccles and Miss Parker and we would submit the results of our conference for her approval.

She bowed her head graciously and said that it would not be quite the same with no performance at the Hall. 'It makes a difference to the neighbourhood when the squire is not in residence.'

I was to agree with her as the weeks passed. I would ride now and then past the Hall and remember the day of Teresa's accident and that twilit tête-à-tête in the courtyard. I found it hard to stop thinking about him and wondering why he had taken the trouble to come to Moldenbury to say goodbye to me.

I guessed that when he came back Marcia Martindale would expect him to marry her and it occurred to me that he might have wanted to get away to make up his mind what he must do. He had said something about coming to terms with his conscience. Was he referring to the death of his wife or his obligations to Marcia Martindale? It could be either . . . or both. My presence bothered him – just as his bothered me.

But I could forget him now that he was no longer there. I felt free. I very much enjoyed my work; I got on well with Daisy and my fellow teachers and I believed I was getting somewhere with the girls.

Daisy told me that she had a waiting list this term.

'More applicants than I have room for,' she said complacently. 'I think they are beginning to realize that they get the Schaffenbrucken treatment here. And of course there are so many parents who are against sending their daughters abroad . . . especially when they can get the desired result in England.'

Daisy was implying that my presence was an asset to the school and I couldn't suppress a rather smug feeling of satisfaction.

The term went on. English lessons, deportment, social graces, dancing waltzes and cotillions, taking the girls for

169

their rides. Each day had its little drama such as who should be chosen for Prince Charming and Cinderella; whose drawing would be selected as the best of the month; who should be chosen by Mr Bathurst to partner him in the waltz he was teaching. Mr Bathurst was a young man of dark Italianate good looks and was a great favourite with the girls, and there was always excitement on the days when he came to the school to take the dancing class, which resulted in much romantic speculation. His visits were awaited with great anticipation and he was jealously watched, and the elder girls vied for the favour of being chosen by him to demonstrate the steps.

Autumn came. It was the time of Hunter's Moon. A whole year since I had gone into the forest and met the stranger! It seemed longer. I suppose that was because so much had happened. I was beginning to convince myself that I had imagined the whole thing; and I should have loved to see Monique, Frieda or Lydia again so that I could assure myself that we really had all been in the forest together on that day.

Fiona Verringer was at length chosen to play Cinderella and Charlotte was Prince Charming. They were the inevitable choices because Fiona was so pretty and Charlotte so tall. Charlotte was delighted and far more manageable than before, being absorbed in her role.

During November we were rehearsing and Mr Crowe, the music master, wrote some songs for the girls to sing and there was great activity in Miss Barston's class putting the costumes together.

One morning I went into the town and in the little draper's shop I came face to face with Marcia Martindale. She seemed quite a different person from the heart-broken woman I had met in the courtyard. She was serene and friendly and asked me to call.

'I should be so pleased if you would,' she said. 'One doesn't see many people and it would be a great treat. Do you ever get a few hours free?'

I said I had a free afternoon on Wednesday unless something happened, such as one of the other mistresses

170

being indisposed. Then I should be expected to take her class.

'Shall we say Wednesday then? I'll be so delighted if you can come.'

I accepted, I have to admit, with alacrity for I was very eager to discover more about her. I tried to pretend to myself that her relationship with Jason Verringer was of no interest to me, but that I wanted to make her understand that circumstances had thrust me into the position of dining with him – as she had found us on that night when she had been so clearly distressed.

So I went to tea with Marcia Martindale.

It was a very unusual afternoon. The door was opened by a little woman with a sharp dark face rather like an intelligent monkey's. She had hair which was almost black, stiff and coarse, and stood out *en brosse* round her small face; her eyes were small and very dark; they seemed to dart everywhere, missing nothing.

She said: 'Come in. We're expecting you.' And she smiled, showing large white teeth, as though my coming was some tremendous joke.

She took me into a drawing room most graciously furnished with Queen Anne furniture which suited the house.

From a sofa Marcia Martindale rose and held out both her hands to me. She was dressed in a peignoir of peacock blue silk. Her hair was loose and about her forehead was a velvet band with a few brilliants in it which might have been diamonds. There was a similar band about her throat. She looked dramatic as though she were about to play some tragic role like Lady Macbeth or the Duchess of Malfi. Yet again she was quite unlike the woman I had so recently met in the draper's.

'So you have come,' she said in a low voice; then raising it a little. 'Do sit down. We'll have tea now, Maisie. Will you tell Mrs Gittings?'

'All right,' said the woman who was clearly Maisie, with more alacrity than respect. In her cockney voice was a jaunty suggestion of equality. She was a striking contrast to

171

Marcia Martindale. She went out as though she were finding it difficult to suppress her mirth.

'My friends get used to Maisie,' said Marcia. 'She was my dresser. They get very familiar.'

'Your dresser?'

'Yes. I was in the theatre, you know, before I came here.'

'I see.'

'Maisie remembers the old days. It was good of you to come. Particularly as you have so little free time.'

'We're busy at the moment. We are putting on a pantomime for Christmas.'

'Pantomime?' Her eyes lighted up and then became contemptuous. 'I started in it,' she went on. 'It gets you nowhere.'

'I think it is most interesting that you were an actress.'

'Very different from being a schoolmistress, I daresay.'

'They are poles apart,' I agreed.

She smiled at me.

'You must miss the theatre,' I went on.

She nodded. 'One never really gets used to not working. Particularly if . . .'

She shrugged her shoulders and at that moment there was a tap on the door and a squat, middle-aged woman trundled in a tea trolley on which were sandwiches and cakes and everything we should need for tea.

'Over here, Mrs Gittings,' said Marcia in rather loud ringing tones. And then more quietly: 'That's right. Thank you.'

Mrs Gittings gave me a look and a nod and went out. Marcia surveyed the tea trolley as though it were John the Baptist's head on a charger. I did not know why these allusions kept occurring to me. It was simply because everything here did not seem quite natural. I wished Eileen Eccles were with me. We should have a hilarious time laughing over it all I was sure.

'You must tell me how you like your tea. I do think it is *so* good of you to come. You can't believe what a pleasure it is to have someone to talk to.'

172

I said I liked it weak with a little milk and no sugar. I stood up and took the cup from her. Then I sat down. There was a little table beside me on which I set my cup.

'Do have one of these sandwiches.' She seemed to glide towards me, holding out the plate, even infusing a certain amount of drama into that ordinary action. 'Mrs Gittings is *very* good. I'm lucky. But I do miss the theatre.'

'I can understand that.'

'I knew you would. I expect you wonder why I bury myself in the country. Well, there is the little one. You must see Miranda before you leave.'

'Your little girl? Yes, I should like that.'

'It's for her sake, really.' She threw back her head with a gesture of resignation. 'I shouldn't be here otherwise. Children break into one's career. One has to make a choice.'

There were many questions I should have liked to ask, but I supposed they were all too personal. I became intent on stirring my tea.

'You must tell me *all* about yourself,' she said.

I told her briefly that I lived with my aunt and that this was my first post; but I sensed that she was not really listening.

'You are very young,' she said at length. 'Not that I am much older than you . . . in years.'

She sighed and I presumed she was referring to her superior experience of life. I felt she was probably right about that.

'And,' she said, coming to the point which I was sure was the reason why she had been eager for me to visit her, 'you have already become friendly with Jason Verringer.'

'Well, hardly friendly. There was that accident and I had to stay at the Hall with the girl who had been thrown from her horse. You remember you came when I was there.'

She regarded me steadily. 'Oh yes. Jason went to great lengths to explain. He was most apologetic. But I told him that in the circumstances he *had* to entertain you.'

'It wasn't a matter of entertaining. I would have been perfectly happy with a tray in the sick room.'

173

'He did say that was out of the question . . . A guest in his house and all that.'

'He seems to have gone into the matter pretty thoroughly.'

'Of course he would enjoy your company. He likes intelligent women . . . if they are pretty as well, which you undoubtedly are, Miss Grant.'

'Thank you.'

'I understand Jason very well. In fact when he comes back . . . Well, there is an understanding you see. There is the child, of course, and his poor wife . . . That's over now . . .'

I understood that she was telling me I was not to take seriously the attention Jason Verringer had bestowed on me. I wanted to tell her not to worry. I should certainly not attempt to be a menace to her and I was really quite indifferent to the plans she had made with the odious man.

I said coolly: 'I am absorbed in my career. I was going in with my aunt at one time but that came to nothing. The Abbey is a most interesting school and Miss Hetherington a wonderful woman to work with.'

'I am so glad you are happy. You are different from the others.'

'Which others?'

'The mistresses.'

'Oh, you know them?'

'I have seen them. They look like schoolmistresses. You don't exactly.'

'I am one, nevertheless. Tell me about the parts you played.'

She was nothing loth. Her greatest success had been Lady Isabel in *East Lynne*. She stood up and burying her face in her hands declaimed: 'Dead. Dead. And never called me Mother.'

'That was the deathbed scene,' she told me. 'It used to entrance the house. There wasn't a dry eye in the place. I played Pinero's *Two Hundred a Year*. Lovely. I liked drama best. But there was nothing to touch *East Lynne*. That was a certain success.'

174

She then gave me little extracts from other parts she had played. She seemed quite a different woman from the one I had first seen on the lawn with the child or in the draper's shop. In fact she seemed to change her personality every few minutes. The quiet fond mother; the lonely woman pleading for a visit; the heart-broken mistress of the courtyard scene; the charming hostess; and now the versatile actress. She slipped from role to role with perfect ease.

We talked about Cinderella which we were doing at school. She had played in it once. 'My first part,' she cried ecstatically, clasping her hands about her knees and becoming a little girl. 'I was Buttons. You must have a good Buttons. It's a small but effective role.' She looked upwards with adoration at an imaginary Cinderella. 'I was a very good Buttons. It was then people began to realize I had a future.'

The door opened and Mrs Gittings came in leading a little girl by the hand.

'Come and say Hello to Miss Grant, Miranda,' said Marcia slipping easily into the part of fond parent.

I said Hello to the child who surveyed me solemnly. She was very pretty and had a look of her mother.

We talked about the child and Marcia tried to make her say something but she refused, and after a while I looked at my watch and said I should have to be back at school in half an hour. I was sorry to hurry away but she would understand.

She was the gracious hostess. 'You must come again,' she said, and I promised I would.

Riding back to the Abbey I thought how unreal everything had seemed. Marcia Martindale appeared to be acting a part all the time.

Perhaps that was to be expected since she was an actress. I wondered why Jason Verringer had become enamoured of her and what part he could play in such a household. I felt there was something very unpleasant about the whole matter and I wanted to put them both out of my mind.

*   *   *

175

The term passed with greater speed than the previous one, which might have been because I was becoming so familiar with the school. Lessons, rehearsals, gossip in the calefactory, little chats with Daisy . . . I found it all absorbing.

There was no doubt that I was a favourite with Daisy who, I knew, congratulated herself on having imported a Schaffenbrucken product into the establishment; and I really believed she attributed the growing prosperity to my presence.

She would ask me to her sitting room and over cups of tea talk about the school and the pupils. She was delighted in the change in Teresa Hurst and was relieved that I could be relied upon to take her off her hands when the cousins defaulted.

As the term progressed the main item of conversation was the coming pantomime.

'The parents come to see it, so it is very important that we have the right kind of entertainment,' Daisy said. 'Parents are not very perceptive where their own daughters are concerned and are apt to think that they are budding Bernhardts – but they can be highly critical of others. I want them to notice how well *all* the girls enunciate, how they move with a particular grace, how they enter a room and are free from any gaucherie. You know what I mean. I should think a good many parents will come to see the pantomime. They will have to make their own arrangements, of course. The hotel in Colby will be full, but some of them can stay a few miles off at Bantable. There are some big hotels there. They can then travel back with their daughters. We have never had as many as we did for the Abbey Festival. That was last year. We'll do it again next. It should be in June. Midsummer Night is the best. It's light then and of course it is so effective among the ruins. Such a wonderful setting. It was most impressive . . . quite uncanny in fact. The seniors were in their white robes. You really would have thought the monks had come to life again. We had some lovely singing and chanting. It was a great occasion. I daresay we have some of the costumes put away somewhere. I must ask Miss Barston.'

176

'An Abbey Festival with the girls dressed as monks. That must have been really exciting.'

'Oh it was. The Cistercian robes . . . and I remember we had torches. I was terrified of those torches – though I must say they did add something to the scene. Girls can be so careless. We came near to having an accident. It would be better if we could do it in the light of a full moon. But that's for the future. Now let us concentrate on Cinderella. I hope Charlotte will not show off. Other parents won't like it.'

'I am sure she will do very well. And Fiona Verringer is going to make a charming Cinderella.'

And so we went on.

The term progressed and I did not see Marcia Martindale during it, but I did on two occasions meet Mrs Gittings wheeling the child through the lanes. I stopped and talked to her. She seemed devoted to the child and I liked her. She was a rosy-cheeked homely woman with an air of honesty, quite a contrast to the flamboyant actress and her truculent cockney dresser.

I talked to her and I confess to a curiosity to know how she fitted into such a household. She was not the sort of woman to talk much of her employers but one or two revealing observations slipped out.

'Mrs Martindale be an actress twenty-four hours of the day. So you can never be sure whether 'tis what she means or whether she be playing a part, if you get my meaning. She'm fond of the child but forgets her sometimes . . . and that's not the way for children.' And of Maisie. 'She be such another. Got her two feet on the ground though, that one. I don't know. It be like working in some sort of theatre . . . not, mind you, Miss Grant, as I've ever worked in one. But I say to myself, Jane Gittings, this b'aint no theatre. This be a real live home and this be a real live child. And if they forget it, see you don't.'

On the other occasions when I saw her – that was nearer the break-up for the Christmas holiday, she told me she was going to stay with her sister on the Moor just over the holiday. 'Mistress, her be going to London and her'll take Maisie with her. That gives me a chance to take the little

177

'un with me. My sister's a one for babies. I reckon it was a real pity she never had one of her own.'

Somehow I could not imagine Marcia Martindale as mistress of the Hall. But it was no concern of mine and there was plenty at this time with which to occupy myself.

Cinderella was a continual source of panic and joy. Fiona had a pretty singing voice and we had found an exuberant wicked stepmother and two ugly sisters whose spirits were difficult to restrain, and who were determined to add touches of their own, to the despair of Eileen Eccles. Then Charlotte's costume didn't fit in a manner to please Miss Barston and there was pandemonium about that.

'For Heaven's sake!' cried Eileen. 'It can't be worse at Drury Lane!'

There was the task of decorating the school and setting up a post box so that the girls could send Christmas cards to each other. On the morning before Cinderella was performed we had our postal delivery and two of the younger girls had postman's caps and very solemnly opened the box which had been set up in the refectory, and the cards were delivered to the various classes. There were gasps of oohs and ahs and much embracing and many expressions of heartfelt thanks.

A record number of parents came to watch Cinderella; they applauded wildly, declared it was charming and much better than last year's Dick Whittington, and it didn't matter in the least that one of the ugly sisters fell sprawling on the stage and her shoe went hurtling into the audience and that the second ugly sister forgot her lines and the prompter's voice was so loud that it could be heard all over the hall.

Everyone said it was delightful. Daisy was congratulated.

'Your girls have such beautiful manners,' said one parent.

'I'm so glad you notice,' replied Daisy smiling. 'We are so insistent on deportment. More so I believe than in so many of these fashionable finishing schools.'

It was triumph indeed.

178

The girls had gone and Teresa and I would be departing on the next day for Moldenbury. Another term was over. It had been a very interesting and pleasant one and it was partly due to the fact that Jason Verringer was absent. That fact gave a certain peace to the surroundings.

*   *   *

Christmas was a real success. Teresa had so looked forward to it that I feared she might have set her hopes too high and suffer disappointment.

But no, everything went perfectly.

We arrived a week before the Day and I was glad of that because it gave Teresa time to enjoy the anticipation of Christmas and all the preparations which I had often felt were more enjoyable than the feast itself.

She was able to help Violet with the pudding and the Christmas cake. All of which Violet said should have been done by this time. But there was Teresa sitting on a chair stoning raisins and shelling nuts, watching Violet like a dedicated priestess stirring the pudding and calling everyone in to have a stir, even the man who helped in the garden three times a week.

'Everyone must have a stir,' said Violet mysteriously. 'Otherwise . . .'

She did not finish the sentence but the silence was more ominous than words could have been.

Then there was the smell which seemed to pervade the house while the puddings bubbled away in the copper in the little laundry room and Teresa was there when Violet, with the long stick which was used for pulling out clothes, expertly stuck the end through the loops in the pudding cloths and triumphantly lifted them out while we all looked on in wonder. There was the all-important little taster – a small basin with just enough for four in it. We would taste that after dinner and give our unbiased verdict.

It was wonderful to see Teresa's delight in these small happenings, and her face was very serious when her portion of the taster was placed before her. We tasted – all eyes on Violet, the connoisseur of Christmas puddings.

179

'A little too much cinnamon,' she said. 'I guessed it.'

'Nonsense,' said Aunt Patty. 'It's perfect.'

'Could have been better.'

'It's the best pudding I ever tasted,' declared Teresa.

'You didn't taste last year's,' said Violet.

'Well, I can't see anything wrong with it,' insisted Aunt Patty. 'I only hope next year's is half as good.'

'So do I,' said Teresa.

And there was a little silence which Aunt Patty quickly filled. Teresa had found a way into this home and she was welcome. I think both my aunt and Violet were gratified and delighted that she enjoyed being with us so much. But we had to admit that at any time she could be sent for by relations or even her parents.

I hoped Teresa did not notice the pause and we went on with the inquest on the taster.

Then there was the decorating. Aunt Patty had left this for us to do so that Teresa could share in it. We picked holly and ivy which was hung in the rooms and we made a wreath to hang on the door. We went carol singing with the church party and to Midnight Service on Christmas Eve after which we came back to hot soup at the kitchen table and, when we had finished it, Aunt Patty bustled us off to bed.

'You'll want to sleep late if you don't get off to bed,' she said, 'and that will shorten the great day.'

In spite of our late night we were all up early on Christmas morning. The presents were lying under the tree and would be distributed after dinner which would be eaten at one o'clock. Aunt Patty, Teresa and I went to church; Violet stayed behind to cook the goose. After service many of us congregated in the porch to wish each other a happy Christmas and then Aunt Patty, Teresa and I walked home across the fields humming *Come All Ye Faithful.*

We all declared the goose was done to a turn, except Violet who insisted that it had been in the oven five minutes too long; the pudding lived up to the expectations established by the taster and the opening of presents began. Aunt Patty had woollen gloves for Teresa and Violet's offering was a scarf to match. I had bought her brushes and

180

paints because rather to our surprise she had begun to improve with her art. She was not as good as Eugenie Verringer, Eileen had said, but her progress was remarkable. We were touched because she had painted pictures for us all and had had them framed in Colby. There was a bowl of violets for Violet – very appropriate, we all declared; for Aunt Patty there was a garden scene with a girl seated on a chair wearing an enormous hat which covered her face, which was a mercy for I was sure that Teresa would never have managed anything so demanding; and for me a landscape with a house in the distance which looked a little like Colby Hall.

In the afternoon Aunt Patty and Violet dozed while Teresa and I went for a walk, skirting the woods where the pale wintry sunshine glinted through the bare branches of the trees and taking the path across the stubbly fields, revelling in the smell of the damp earth and watching the jackdaws and rooks looking for food on the broken soil.

We did not speak much but there was a contentment about us both.

In the evening there were visitors. Aunt Patty had made many friends in the village and we played childish games like In the Manner of the Word and Animal, Vegetable and Mineral, refreshing ourselves with sandwiches and Violet's parsnip and ginger wines.

Then there was Boxing Day when the postman and dustman came for their Christmas boxes, solemnly presented in sealed envelopes with Merry Christmas written on them; and visiting the vicarage in the afternoon for muffins and tea and Christmas cake with icing on top.

Violet, being a little gratified because the icing was a trifle hard, wondered whether she ought to tell the vicarage cook to put a drop – not much mind you – of glycerine in it next year to soften it.

This problem occupied her all the way home. Should she or shouldn't she? And we all took sides over this matter although I suppose none of us – except Violet – cared either way.

But that was how it was. There was so much delight and

181

pleasure in the simple things. I watched Teresa's animated face and felt ashamed of myself. I had known so many Christmases like this but I had never really appreciated them before.

The holidays were over and there was Aunt Patty waving goodbye on the platform, cherries bobbing on her hat and Violet telling us that she was sure the sandwiches she had packed for the journey would be dry before we ate them.

'See you at Easter time,' called Aunt Patty.

'Hot cross bun time,' added Violet.

I looked at Teresa. She was smiling, clearly looking forward to Easter and hot cross buns.

*　　　*　　　*

That term seemed dull compared with the others. The first had been exciting because I was settling in and I had had my encounters with Jason Verringer. During the term leading up to Christmas I had been busy with rehearsals and so on. Now that was over and this term seemed like an anticlimax. For one thing Jason Verringer was still away. Fiona and Eugenie had naturally been at the Hall for Christmas and an elderly cousin and her husband had come to take charge of them. I gathered from Teresa that they had done very much as they liked and that the elderly cousins had quickly given up trying to exercise control.

When I asked them how they had enjoyed Christmas, Eugenie had laughed and said with a rather malicious twinkle in her eyes: 'It was quite interesting, Miss Grant!' and Fiona replied demurely: 'We enjoyed it very much thank you.'

Eugenie and I were in a state of what I called armed neutrality – and of course Charlotte Mackay was with her in this. They had never forgiven me for preventing their sharing a room and they would, I knew, discountenance me if they had the chance, but now they did seem to respect my authority and of course I held over them the threat of curtailing their riding if they did not behave well.

It was different with Fiona. She was a docile girl, very pretty and easily led and I was sure if left alone would not

182

have looked for trouble. Teresa was my stalwart ally and the rest of the girls in my section were ordinary kind-hearted creatures who might be led astray by others but were quite ready, and really preferred, to be amenable. I think they were all a little impressed by the change in Teresa and I tried to imagine what descriptions she gave of Aunt Patty's house. I suspected that she made a visit there sound like a trip to the Promised Land.

However, I was becoming more and more aware that I had the special gift of winning the respect of my pupils without a great deal of effort, which is one of the primary needs of any who wish to teach.

So the term went smoothly, too smoothly perhaps, and I, like Teresa, was looking forward to returning to Moldenbury.

Halfway through January the snow came and it was difficult to keep the rooms warm in spite of big fires. The bitter North wind seemed to penetrate even the thick walls of the Abbey, and the ruins, white with snow, were fantastically beautiful – and even more uncanny in moonlight. The girls enjoyed it; they built rival snowmen, had snowballing battles and tobogganed down the slight incline above which the Abbey stood. The roads were treacherous and for over a week no vehicle could reach us. Daisy was, of course, prepared for such an emergency and there was plenty of food, but the girls enjoyed feeling cut off and many of them were hoping that the icy conditions would continue. Some of the servants were saying that Devon had never known such weather and what was the world coming to?

'Disaster,' commented Eileen Eccles. 'When the temperature in Devonshire falls below freezing, the world is coming to an end. Some of them ought to be transported to the north of Scotland; then they would learn what winter is.'

Before the end of the month the thaw set in, and I went into the town. Mrs Baddicombe the postmistress detained me for a gossip as no one else was in the shop, which served groceries and many other things besides being a post office.

183

Eileen had warned me that Mrs Baddicombe was what she called 'the town recorder' in as much as she knew all that was going on and her mission in life was to make sure that she spread the news throughout the community with as much speed as possible.

She was a tall spare woman with dull opaque eyes and a great deal of pepper and salt hair, which she wore piled high on her head with a frizzed fringe. She talked incessantly while she weighed parcels and handed out stamps or dealt with the commodities of the store.

'Oh, Miss Grant, it be nice to see 'ee. How have 'ee been getting on at the school during this terrible weather? I said to Jim (Jim was her husband who sometimes helped in the shop and was noted for his somewhat taciturn silences. 'His refuge against that flow of talk,' said Eileen.) weather be terrible. I didn't see a soul in the shop for days.'

I said we had managed but Miss Hetherington would like the goods sent up as soon as possible and I had an order for her.

'Jim will bring 'em up as soon as he can. There's everybody wanting things now. Fair run out they had. Who'd have thought we'd have such weather here in Devon. It's the worst for fifty year they'm telling me. Her from Rooks' Rest have sent up this morning. She don't come herself . . . oh no . . . too grand. Sends that London woman. Never could abide her. Looks like she's laughing at you all the time. That's London, I suppose. Thinks she's smarter than we be. Oh no, Madam hardly ever comes in herself. Why, you'd think she was my lady already.'

'Oh . . . you mean Mrs Martindale.'

'That's her,' Mrs Baddicombe leaned forward and lowered her voice. 'I reckon we'll have her up at the Hall soon. Hm . . . well, least said soonest mended. Her ladyship now, she was a lovely lady. Never saw much of her lately . . . but to go like that . . . and her in Rooks' Rest, his house . . . all at the disposal of Madam if you please. And there is she having the baby and all that. I reckon it's real disgraceful. Of course, you know they've got the devil in them.'

184

I ought not to be listening. It would be more dignified to make my excuses and yet, to tell the truth, I found the opportunity to discover something irresistible.

'Well, you've not been here long, Miss Grant, and you're up at that school and that Miss Hetherington, she be a fine lady, places her order regular and there's no question about paying . . . That's what I like. Not that Hall bills ain't paid. I wouldn't say that – but the goings on! They've always been a wild lot . . . got the devil in them. Well, he's gone away to make a respectable delay. Couldn't marry her right away could he? Even he has to wait a year for decency's sake. I reckon come Easter we'll have the church bells ringing for them. A wedding when the last time they was tolling for a funeral.'

'Well, Mrs Baddicombe. I'd better be going . . .'

It was a feeble attempt and Mrs Baddicombe was not easily dismissed.

She leaned further over the counter.

'And how did her ladyship die? Well, it happened nice and convenient, didn't it? Madam has the little bastard and her ladyship takes her dose of laudanum. But this be Verringer land and there's no gainsaying that. The things that goes on . . . and them two young ladies up at the school. Miss Eugenie's got a lot of Verringer in her. But I reckon there'll be trouble when he marries her. There's so much people will stand and no more. I reckon they ought to take another look at her ladyship.'

Someone had come into the shop and Mrs Baddicombe started back.

It was Miss Barston who wanted stamps and sewing cottons.

I waited while she was served, said goodbye to Mrs Baddicombe, and Miss Barston and I came out of the shop together.

'That woman is a pernicious gossip,' said Miss Barston. 'I always discourage her when she starts on me.'

I was a little ashamed. I should have done the same, but I was very eager to learn all I could about Jason Verringer and Marcia Martindale.

185

After the snow the weather turned mild and almost springlike. I met Marcia Martindale in the town. She stood talking for a little while and told me how wretched she had been when snowed up, and reproached me for not coming to see her. I made an appointment to call the following Wednesday if no sudden duties were imposed on me.

I rode over. It was a dampish day with a reluctant sun glinting out now and then through the clouds. I glanced up at nests in the elms and passed under the porch with the golden jasmine trailing over it and rang the bell.

It was opened by Maisie who said: 'Come in, Miss Grant. We're expecting you.'

Marcia Martindale rose to greet me; she was dressed in black, soft and clinging; she had a magnificent figure; and about her neck was a heavy golden chain; and she wore gold bracelets, three on each wrist.

She looked like a character from a play but I could not think which. She took both my hands in hers. 'Miss Grant, how good of you to call.'

'I reckon my lady needs a bit of cheering up,' said Maisie grinning at me. 'She's in mourning today.'

'Mourning?' I said and my heart beat with fear. I thought something had happened to Jason Verringer. 'For er . . .'

Maisie winked. 'For the past,' she said.

'Oh, Maisie, you are a fool,' said Marcia. 'Get off with you and tell Mrs Gittings to bring us tea.'

'She's doing that,' said Maisie. 'She heard Miss Grant come.'

'Do sit down, Miss Grant. I am sorry you find me in this sad state. It is an anniversary.'

'Oh dear, would you rather I went and came another time?'

'Oh no, no. It is so *cheering* to have you. I hate being shut in, which is what happened with all that snow. I was nostalgic for London. It is rather quiet here; all this waiting.'

I replied that the snow had been restricting but that the girls had enjoyed it.

She sighed. 'It is five years ago that it happened.'

'Oh?'

'A great tragedy. I'll tell you about it . . . after they've brought the tea.'

'How is the little girl?'

She looked rather vague. 'Oh . . . Miranda. She is well, Mrs Gittings is so good with her.'

'I thought she was. I've seen them once or twice in the lanes. She took her away for Christmas, didn't she?'

'Yes. I was in London. I had to have Maisie with me. One needs a maid. And for all her faults Maisie is very good with hair and clothes. She's devoted to me, though sometimes you wouldn't think it. And Mrs Gittings just loves having Miranda. She takes her to some relations on Dartmoor. She says the moorland air is good for the child.'

'I am sure it is.'

'Ah, here is the tea,'

Mrs Gittings wheeled in the trolley as she had on an earlier occasion, nodded to me and I asked if she were well and had enjoyed Christmas.

'It was wonderful,' she said. 'Miranda loved it and you should have seen my sister. She loves little ones. Always asking when we're coming again.'

'I have promised Mrs Gittings that she shall take Miranda soon,' said Marcia.

Mrs Gittings smiled and went out.

'Such a good soul,' said Marcia. 'I can trust her absolutely with Miranda.'

She poured the tea and said: 'Well, you have discovered me in the midst of my mourning. I am sorry if I am a little depressing. It was so tragic.'

'Yes?'

'Five years today when I said goodbye to Jack.'

'Jack?'

'Jack Martindale.'

'Was he your . . . ?'

'My husband. We were so young . . . very very young . . . striving then, both of us. I had had my successes. It was in *East Lynne* that we met. He was Archibald to my Isabel.

187

Young love is rather beautiful, don't you think, Miss Grant?'

'I cannot speak from experience, but I expect it is.'

'Oh, you must be a late starter.'

'I probably am.'

'Well, my dear, be thankful for that. When one is young, one can be so impulsive. But between Jack and me it was right from the very beginning. We were married. I was just seventeen. It was idyllic. We played many roles together. We brought something to our parts. Everyone said so. But then I began to surpass him. Jack loved me passionately but he was a little hurt. You see I was the one the audiences came for. Without me he could not draw audiences at all.'

She rose and stood with her back to the window, her arms across her breast. She looked very dramatic.

'So he went away. I didn't try to stop him. I knew he had to make his own way. There was this chance to go to America. It was for him alone. Some manager had seen him . . .'

'And he didn't want you too?'

She looked at me coldly. 'It was a male lead he was searching for.'

'Oh, I see.'

'You wouldn't understand about the theatre, Miss Grant.' She was still rather cold. 'However Jack went.' She stood for a moment tense. It was like the end of the act when the curtain is about to fall and the time has come to deliver the last telling line.

'The ship was struck by an iceberg . . . three days out from Liverpool.'

She dropped her hands and walked to the tea trolley.

'It's a very sad story,' I said, stirring my tea.

'Miss Grant, you can have no idea. How could you . . . living as you do so quietly . . . teaching . . . You can't imagine how an artist *feels* . . . shut up here . . . after such a tragedy.'

'I can very well imagine how anyone would feel after such a tragedy. One does not necessarily have to be an artist to feel grief.'

'Jack was lost. I went on working. Nothing could stop that. And then . . . it must have been two years later I became friendly with Jason. He has a pleasant house in London. In St James's . . . and he was always interested in the theatre. He used to come often to watch me. He's a very exciting man . . . when you get to know him. He was crazy about me. Well, you can guess how it happened. Of course I shall never forget Jack, but Jason is here and that place of his is very attractive. He seemed a little tragic too. That family of his, always living in that mansion for hundreds of years and then there were no heirs and that disastrous marriage of his. Then there are only two girls. You know what I mean. Of course it was a sacrifice for me. A child is so restricting. There is all the time while you're waiting for it to be born, to say nothing of the discomforts. And then when it comes . . . But I did it . . . for Jason . . . and I think I can be happy when everything is settled.'

'You mean when you marry Sir Jason?'

She smiled at me. 'It can't be just yet, of course. There had to be this interval. People in a place like this . . . you know, so narrow. They say all sorts of cruel things. I said to Jason, "What do we care?" But he said we had to step warily. There was a lot of talk, you know, and most unpleasant talk.'

'Gossip can be dangerous,' I said, with a touch of conscience, having so recently indulged in it with Mrs Baddicombe.

'Devastating,' she said. 'I was in a play once about a man whose wife died . . . rather as Lady Verringer did. There was Another Woman.'

'I suppose it is a not unusual situation.'

'Men being men.'

'And women women,' I said, perhaps a trifle coolly.

'I agree. I agree.' She rose from the trolley and paced to the window. She stood there for a few moments, and when she turned she was in a different role. She was no longer mourning a husband. She had become the bride of a new one.

'Well,' she said, turning to me and smiling. 'The wheel

189

turns. Now I have to make Jason happy. He dotes on little Miranda.'

'Oh does he?'

'When he is here. Of course, he has been away such a long time. But when he returns we shall have wedding bells. The waiting is irksome. But he had to go. It is not easy with me being here . . . so close . . . and all the talk.'

'No, I suppose not.'

'I might even join him before he comes back. He can be very persistent and he is trying to persuade me to go to him.'

'All I can do is wish you well.'

'There will be horrid gossip, but one lives that sort of thing down, doesn't one?'

'I suppose one does.'

There was a tap on the door and Mrs Gittings appeared with Miranda.'

'Come here, my darling,' said Marcia, now the doting mother.

The child approached but, I noticed, clinging very tightly to Mrs Gittings' hand.

'My little one, come and say how do you do to Miss Grant.'

'Hello Miranda,' I said.

The dark eyes were turned to me. She said: 'I've got a corn dolly.'

'A what, darling?'

Mrs Gittings said: 'It's hanging on the wall in my sister's cottage. Miranda always says it is hers.'

'How old is she?' I asked.

'Nearly two,' said Mrs Gittings. 'Quite a big girl, aren't you, pet?'

Miranda laughed and snuggled up to Mrs Gittings' skirts.

It was quite clear who had Miranda's affection in that house.

I felt a great desire to get away. I was tired of hearing of Jason Verringer and his affairs. It was all rather distasteful and there was an air of such unreality in that house that I

190

never wanted to see any of them again – except perhaps Mrs Gittings and the child.

After a while Miranda was taken away and I left. I had the excuse that I must get back to the school. As I rode home I thought what a pity it was that the school was so close to the Hall and a part of it really. It made escape difficult. But I certainly would not again visit Rooks' Rest in a hurry.

It must have been only two weeks later when I ran into Mrs Gittings with Miranda in the town. Her rosy face lit up with pleasure when she saw me.

'Why, it's Miss Grant,' she said. 'Lovely day, isn't it? Spring's on the way. I came in with Miranda in the dog cart. She loves that, don't you, Miranda? We've got one or two bits of shopping to do before we go away.'

'Oh, are you going away?'

'I'm taking Miranda with me down to my sister.'

'You'll love that. Miranda too.'

'Yes. She'll see her corn dolly, won't you, pet? And Aunt Grace, that's my sister. Very fond of Miranda, she is, and Miranda's fond of her. It'll be lovely on the moors. I was brought up there. They say you always want to go back to your native spot.'

'How will they get on without you at Rooks' Rest?'

'They won't be there. The house is to be shut up till I'm told when to go back.'

'So Mrs Martindale is going to London, is she?'

'Farther than that, she says. She keeps rather quiet about it, but sometimes it comes out. She is going to him.'

'To him?'

'To Sir Jason. Somewhere on the Continent. Maisie will go with her.'

'Do you think they will get married out there . . . wherever it is?'

'Well, that's what she seems to have in mind.'

'I see.'

'I can't wait to get to the moors. It was nice seeing you, Miss Grant. I think Miranda quite took to you.'

I said goodbye and felt faintly depressed.

191

What a sordid affair, I thought, as I rode back to the Abbey.

* * *

Teresa came to me in a state of great distress.

'It's the cousins,' she said. 'They want me to go to them for Easter. Miss Hetherington sent for me in her study. She said she's just heard. I said I don't want to go but Miss Hetherington says I'll have to.'

'Oh Teresa,' I said. 'Aunt Patty and Violet will be so disappointed.'

'I know.' There were tears in her eyes. 'Violet was going to show me how to make hot cross buns.'

I said: 'Perhaps we can arrange something. I'll go and see Miss Hetherington.'

Daisy shook her head grimly.

'I have often wondered about the wisdom of your taking Teresa home with you. I know Patience and Violet and the effect they'd have on a girl like Teresa. Poor child, she was almost demented when I told her.'

I said: 'Surely it can be explained to them.'

'I don't think they'll change their minds. It's not that they want her. I can read between the lines. They feel they look remiss in the eyes of the parents as they are supposed to be looking after her, and two vacations away from them is a bit too much. She'll have to go for Easter and then perhaps it can be arranged that you take her in the summer holidays which are the longer ones.'

'We shall be so sad. You see, she quickly became part of the household.'

'That's the trouble. One has to be careful with girls like Teresa. They become so intense. She became too involved too quickly.'

'It was just holidays she had with us in an ordinary little home.'

'My dear Cordelia, no house is ordinary with Patience in it.'

'I know. She is quite the most wonderful person. I was so happy for Teresa to have a share in all that.'

192

'You're too sentimental. Let Teresa go for Easter and I am sure it will be all right for the summer.'

'Couldn't we explain to them?'

'Explanations would make it worse. They'd feel more guilty. They are just making this gesture to preserve their kindly image with the parents. We'll have to let them this time. And perhaps Teresa will make it so that they don't want her again for a very long time.' Daisy smiled grimly. 'Oh come, Cordelia, it's not so tragic as all that. Just this once. Teresa has to learn that life is not a bed of roses. It'll be good for her and make her all the more appreciative of Moldenbury next time.'

'She's appreciative enough already.'

Daisy shrugged her shoulders. 'She'll have to go,' she said firmly.

Poor Teresa was heart-broken and her grief cast an air of tragedy over the rest of term.

When I waved her off with the rest of the girls the day before my departure we were both of us on the verge of tears.

*   *   *

It was a sad household at Moldenbury. Teresa would have been very gratified to see how we missed her.

Aunt Patty said: 'Never mind. She'll be here for summer and those are the long holidays.'

'We shan't see her again,' said Violet prophetically.

Everyone in the village asked where she was. I had not realized what a part of the household she had become. We decorated the church with daffodils and I was regretful thinking of how she would have enjoyed that. The hot cross buns did not seem nearly such a treat as they would have done had she been there.

'She loved it so much here,' I said, 'and she made us all realize how fortunate we are to have each other.'

'I always knew that, dear,' said Aunt Patty, solemn for once.

I went for long walks and thought about Marcia Martindale on the Continent with Jason Verringer. I imagined

193

them on the canals of Venice, strolling beside the Arno in Florence, riding down the Champs Elysées, visiting the Colosseum in Rome . . . all places I longed to visit.

I thought rather maliciously: They are worthy of each other, and I am sure they will get all the happiness they deserve.

It was the day after Easter Monday, in the mid afternoon, and I was in the sitting room reading when I heard the gate click. I got up and looked out of the window. Teresa was coming up the drive carrying a suitcase.

I dashed out. 'Teresa!' I cried.

She flew at me and we hugged each other.

'Whatever are you doing here?' I asked.

'I just came,' she replied. 'I got on a train and came. I couldn't stand it any longer.'

'But what of the cousins?'

'I left a note for them. They'll be glad. I was such a nuisance to them.'

'Oh Teresa,' I cried, trying to sound stern but only conveying my pleasure.

I called up the stairs. 'Aunt Patty. Violet. Come down at once.'

They came running. For a few seconds they stared at Teresa. Then she flung herself at them and the three of them were in a sort of huddle while I stood looking on and laughing.

I said: 'It's really rather awful. She's just walked out on the cousins, leaving a note.'

Aunt Patty was trying not to laugh and even Violet was smiling.

'Well, I never!' said Aunt Patty.

'She just packed a suitcase and came.'

'All that way by herself,' said Violet looking shocked.

'She's nearly seventeen,' I reminded them.

'I knew the way,' said Teresa. 'I had to go to London first. That was the tricky part. But the guard was helpful. He showed me.'

'What about those cousins?' asked Violet. 'They'll be out of their minds with worry.'

194

'With relief,' said Teresa.

'And you just left a note,' I said.

Teresa nodded.

'I'll write to them immediately explaining that you arrived safely and I'll ask their permission to let you stay for the rest of the holiday,' I said.

'I shan't go back if they say No,' said Teresa firmly. 'I couldn't bear to think of you all eating hot cross buns without me.' She turned to Violet. 'How did they come out this year?'

'Not as good as last,' said Violet predictably. 'Some of them lost their crosses in the baking.'

Teresa looked mournful and Violet went on. 'We could make another batch. There's no law I know of that says you can only eat them on Good Friday.'

'Oh, let's do it,' said Teresa.

She was back. It was wonderful and we were all delighted.

In due course I received a letter from the cousins thanking me for my interest in Teresa. They knew how she had enjoyed the holidays spent at my home, but their great concern was not to impose, and if I found I had had enough of Teresa I was to send her back to them at once. I had asked their permission for her to spend the summer holiday with us and it was graciously – and I felt eagerly – given.

When I showed the letter to Teresa she was overcome with joy.

We went into the village where she was warmly greeted by almost everyone and reproached by some for missing the Easter services.

She was pink with pleasure.

So it was a happy holiday after all. But soon it was time for us to return to school – and that was the end of the peaceful days.

The Ruby Earring

*

The moment I stepped off the train I was aware of him. Emmet was there to take us back to the school but as we came into the station yard, I saw the Verringer carriage with him beside it.

He came forward, hat in hand.

'Miss Grant, what a pleasure to see you. It has been so long.'

I was taken aback, not expecting to see him so soon, but I confess I had been wondering whether he would have returned by the time we got back to school.

'So . . . you have come back,' I said, and thought how foolish such a statement of the obvious must seem to him, and it would of course expose my embarrassment.

'I have my carriage here,' he said. 'Give me the pleasure of taking you back to the Academy.'

'That is kind of you,' I replied. 'But Emmet has the school carriage here to take us.'

'It is something of an old rattler, isn't it? You'll be more comfortable in mine.'

'We'll be quite all right with Emmet, thank you.'

'I shall not allow it. Emmet, you can take the baggage and perhaps Miss er . . .'

He was looking at Teresa who returned his gaze defiantly.

'I was going to say perhaps you would do me the honour of riding in my carriage,' he went on with a faint hint of mockery.

'I shall ride with Miss Grant,' said Teresa.

'That's an excellent idea. Emmet, I'm taking both the ladies.'

'Very good, Sir Jason,' said Emmet.

196

I felt angry but it would have looked ridiculous to make a fuss, like making an issue about something which was not really very important. But I had a feeling that everything which brought me into touch with him was important. I felt furious with myself for not refusing in a way which would have been polite and coolly conventional and at the same time conveying to him that I had no wish to be under an obligation to him.

'This is pleasant,' he said. 'You can both sit beside me. There's plenty of room, and it's the best way to enjoy the scenery. *I* shall enjoy showing you how my bays perform. I am really rather proud of them.'

And there we were seated beside him, turning out of the station yard into the lanes.

I said: 'I trust you had a pleasant tour.'

'Well, one gets a little tired of being away from home. Homesick, I suppose. One broods on what one has left behind. Did you and Miss er –'

'Hurst,' I said.

'Miss Teresa, yes, I remember. Did you enjoy your holiday?'

'Very much, didn't we, Teresa?'

'The last bit,' answered Teresa.

'Oh . . . not until the end?'

Teresa said: 'The last bit was with Miss Grant, the first with my cousins. That was the bit I didn't like at all.'

'I can understand how enjoyable it must have been to be with Miss Grant. I envy you.'

I looked straight ahead. 'It is to be hoped we don't meet another carriage in this lane,' I said.

'Ah, memories return. If we do . . .'

'You will insist on their going back.'

'But of course. I hope I shall see something of you this erm. I heard from Miss Hetherington that there is going to be a midsummer pageant. They might involve us at the Hall as well as the school, as it is concerned with the Abbey.'

Us? I thought. Who is Us? Does he mean himself and Marcia Martindale. Is she Lady Verringer by now?

'I remember the last one but one. That was some years

197

ago. It was commemorating something. We have some costumes tucked away somewhere. We had actors down last time and they left the things behind. Monks' robes. I must tell Miss Hetherington about them.'

'That will be interesting,' I said coolly.

We had come through the narrow lane.

'Safe,' he said, looking at me sideways. 'You are relieved that I shall not embarrass you with a show of arrogance and selfishness.'

He pulled up suddenly.

'Just so that you can admire it for a few moments,' he said. 'Looks grand, doesn't it? It must have looked very much like that six hundred years ago. You'd never guess from here, would you, that it is a ruin?'

'I can see the school,' said Teresa.

'No ruin, thank heaven. I don't know what we should do without our good Miss Hetherington, her pupils and her wonderful mistresses.'

'I should not have thought they made a great deal of difference to you at the Hall.'

'Oh they do. They add a spice to life. And think how useful to my wards. Where else would they get such an excellent education? Where else would they get that whiff of culture. It would mean sending them to an establishment abroad. How much more convenient for them to be a short ride away from home.'

'Miss Hetherington would be gratified by your comments.'

'I have made them to her time and time again.' He glanced at me. 'But I have never felt this so strongly until lately.'

'I daresay those sentimental thoughts came while you were away. It is said that absence makes the heart grow fonder.'

'Absence did make mine, I'll admit.'

'Shall we go? Miss Hetherington will wonder what has happened when she sees Emmet returning without us.'

'Do you think he is already there?'

198

'He has taken the short cut,' said Teresa. 'You took the long way round, Sir Jason.'

We went on and in a short time arrived at the school.

Miss Hetherington came out to meet us. She did look a little disturbed.

'Oh, there you are, Miss Grant. I wondered. And Teresa . . .'

'I was at the station,' said Jason Verringer. 'I saw the ladies and thought it would be discourteous of me not to offer them a lift. Now that I have safely delivered them I'll say *au revoir*. By the way, Miss Hetherington, we have some monks' costumes up at the Hall. Residue of the last affair. I'll get someone to look through them or perhaps one of your people could do that. You might find them useful.'

'Thank you. I shall most certainly take advantage of your kind offer, Sir Jason. Are you sure you won't come in?'

'Not now, but I will call later. Good day to you, ladies.'

With a gallant gesture he swept off his hat and then his horses were trotting away.

'Teresa,' said Miss Hetherington, 'you'd better get to your room. I suppose you met Miss Grant at the station?'

Teresa was silent and I said quickly: 'I'll explain. You go along Teresa.'

'Emmet has taken your bags up,' said Daisy. 'Come into the study.'

I followed her and when the door was shut I told her about Teresa.

'She left them and travelled on her own! I shouldn't have thought Teresa would have had the courage to do that.'

'She's grown up quite a lot lately.'

'She evidently hated it with the cousins. I wrote to them and it was all amicably settled. They were really rather relieved. I think that much was obvious and I got their permission for her to spend the summer holiday with us.'

Daisy nodded.

'Her travelling on her own like that was not our responsibility,' she said. 'I hope Teresa is not getting too fond of

199

you, Cordelia. You have to be careful with these impressionable girls.'

'Actually I think she is more with Violet than with me. It is amazing how they get on.'

She nodded. Then she said: 'And Sir Jason . . . I was surprised to see you in his carriage . . . and seated next to him.'

I explained: 'It was as he said. He was there. He was so persistent. I couldn't refuse his offer without seeming impolite and . . . uncivilized.'

'I understand. Be careful of him. He's a dangerous man.'

'Dangerous . . . in what way?'

'I mean it would be unwise for a young woman in your position to become too friendly with him.'

'I am not likely to do that.'

'I hope not.'

'Did he marry Mrs Martindale, or is that to come?'

'There has been no marriage . . . yet. There is a good deal of speculation as there has been since Mrs Martindale came to Rooks' Rest.'

'She is there now, is she?'

'Oh yes. She has been back for about three weeks. So has he, and people are waiting for the next development. The general opinion seems to be that they will be married. The unpleasant rumour that he helped his wife to her death so that he could marry Mrs Martindale still persists. I don't like that sort of gossip about someone so close to the school. It is a pity the place belongs to him and he shows an interest in it. I am sure all those rumours are nonsense. He might be all sorts of rogue but he isn't the sort to murder his wife. But until he marries and settles down, I am afraid these rumours will persist. In the meantime it is well for our people to remain as aloof as possible.'

'I agree,' I said. 'And it is certainly what I intend to do.'

Daisy nodded, satisfied. 'It is not easy,' she went on, 'he being our landlord and this connection between the Hall and the Abbey.'

Later I saw Eileen Eccles in the calefactory and I looked in to have a word with her.

200

'Welcome back to the grindstone,' she said. 'Had a good holiday?'

'Very good, thanks. And you?'

'Lovely. It's a long time to wait for the summer break. I always think this term is the most difficult. I suppose it is because the longing to get away is more acute than usual.'

'Oh please,' I laughed. 'It hasn't begun yet.'

'I think it will be a grim one. Just think we are going to have that appalling Midsummer thing. I was here for the last one and you have no idea until you have suffered it what a ghastly business it is. Musical interludes, singing under the shadow of the great nave, prowling about in white, the robes of our founders . . . staging a little pageant . . . a play probably – act one the building of the Abbey; act two the Dissolution; and act three the rising of Phoenix – our own dear Academy for Young Ladies.'

'In any case you can laugh at it.'

'Laugh, my dear Cordelia. One must either laugh or weep.'

'I daresay we shall do more of the former during the proceedings.'

'And after that – glorious freedom. Keep your eyes on that all through the weeks of toil and conflict: the light at the end of the tunnel. By the way, you came back in style.'

'Oh, you knew about that then?'

'My dear Cordelia, everyone knows. There you were seated beside him for everyone to see. This is not only the home of clotted cream and cider, but of scandal and gossip. And they are two of its major industries.'

'There is no need for scandal concerning me, I do assure you.'

'I'm glad. I shouldn't like you to be stabbed with a poniard and your grisly remains buried beneath the ruined chancel . . . or perhaps your body thrown into the fish ponds one dark night. Madam Martindale looks to me as if she might employ the methods of the Borgias or Medici if the mood took her.'

'She certainly does seem a little theatrical.'

'And determined to reach her goal, which, my dear

201

Cordelia, is the Hall and the title that goes with it. For these benefits she is prepared to take Sir Jason too, and it might well be woe betide any rivals for that desirable *parti*.'

'You talk such nonsense,' I said laughing. 'I can assure you that a ride in a carriage does not constitute a proposal of marriage – or intentions to such a thing.'

'I thought he might have his eyes on you, nevertheless. You are not without personal charms.'

'Oh, thank you! You said that gossip and scandal were the products of this place. *I* think some people suffer from an excess of imagination. I have seen very little of this Jason Verringer and what I have I don't like very much.'

'Keep it that way, Cordelia. Be a wise virgin.'

I laughed with her. It was rather good to be back.

*　　*　　*

In spite of my assurances to myself that Jason Verringer did not concern me in the least, during the days which followed I was finding more and more that this was not so. Whenever I went out I looked for him; once I saw him coming from the Hall and turned and galloped as far from the place as possible. I believe he saw me but as he was on foot he had no chance of catching up with me . . . if he had been of a mind to do so.

Then when I rode out from school on my free periods very often I would meet him and I realized that he contrived these meetings. In my position it was natural that my outings must occur at regular times and he quickly discovered when.

This alarmed and yet intrigued me; and if I were perfectly honest with myself I would admit that I was far from indifferent to him, which was the state of mind I was striving for.

He was intruding, not only on my free afternoons but into my thoughts. Whenever his name was mentioned – which was frequently for one could not go into one of the shops without hearing something about him or his affairs – I would pretend not to be interested, when all the time I was trying to glean as much information as I could.

202

I was very inexperienced of the world and of men. The only encounter had been with Edward Compton, and as I grew farther away from that the more like a dream it seemed. Perhaps if I had been more worldly I would have been more alarmed than I actually was. The fact was that I was allowing myself to be drawn into his orbit and he – a man who had a wide knowledge of my sex – understood my feelings and determined to exploit them.

He was attracted by me from the moment he had seen me riding with Emmet, and when he was attracted by a woman he was not the man to deny himself the pleasure of pursuit.

Therefore he now pursued me.

My acid manner did not deter him in the least. On the other hand, if I had been wiser, I should have known it made him all the more determined.

From a man who was on the point of marriage with another woman this was deplorable. I refused to accept it and told myself that his manner towards me was the same as it would be towards any woman who was young and moderately good-looking. There was nothing special about it.

But of course it was not so.

Once I was riding out for my afternoon's exercise when he came cantering up beside me.

'What a pleasant surprise,' he said ironically, for he had clearly been waiting for me. 'I am sure you won't have any objection to my riding with you.'

'Actually I prefer to ride alone,' I said. 'One can go at one's own pace.'

'I will adjust mine to yours. What a glorious afternoon! The more so for me, I might say, since I have met you.'

I shrugged that aside and said I should really return to the school very shortly. 'There is a great deal to do,' I added.

'What a pity. Is it the Midsummer orgy?'

I laughed in spite of myself. 'I don't think Miss Hetherington would like to hear it called that.'

'I want someone to go through the costumes I have, to

203

see if they will be of any use. Will you come to the Hall? I'd like to show them to you.'

'That would be Miss Barston's department. She is the needlework mistress.'

'They don't need to be made. They are already done.'

'Perhaps they need a little renovation and refitting for whoever is going to wear them. I will tell Miss Hetherington that you want Miss Barston to call.'

'I was hoping you would come. After all it is a matter of how the costumes should be worn . . . and all that.'

'How many ways are there of wearing Cistercian robes, I wonder?'

'You would know. That is why I want you to come.'

'It really is Miss Barston you need.'

'I do not need Miss Barston. I need Miss Grant.'

I glanced at him in cold surprise.

'Yes,' he went on. 'Why are you so aloof? Are you afraid of me?'

'Afraid of you! Why should I be?'

'Well, I am represented as a big of an ogre, am I not?'

'Are you? I thought you were a widower who is about to remarry.'

He burst out laughing. 'Oh, that's it!' he said. 'The tales they tell about my family are really quite amusing. Now there is only myself, I have to bear the whole brunt. Once my brother shared it with me.'

'Your life is so colourful, I suppose. You certainly provide the neighbourhood with something to talk about.'

'So I have my uses. Cordelia, why can't we be . . . friends?'

'One doesn't just make up one's mind to be friends. Friendship is something that grows.'

'Well, give ours a chance to grow, will you?'

My heart was beating faster than it should. He certainly had a potent effect on me.

'Everything has its chance,' I said.

'So even I have . . . with you?'

I spurred up my horse and broke into a canter. I turned off and galloped across a field.

204

He was beside me all the way. I had to pull up as we came to the road.

'Exhilarating,' he said.

I agreed.

'I have to return now. I mustn't be late. I have a class starting in an hour and I have to get back and change.'

He nodded and rode beside me. He did not come right up to the school. I wondered whether he was aware of the gossip and did not want it to get to Marcia Martindale's ears, or whether he thought it would displease me and make me refuse to ride with him again.

I went into the school, changed into a blouse and skirt and hurried to my class.

But I could not stop thinking of him.

*   *   *

Two days later during my afternoon break I did not go riding. I was sure that if I did I should meet him again. So I took a stroll through the ruins of the Abbey.

There it was quiet and peaceful and yet at the same time I was aware of a sense of warning as I always was when I was alone among the ruins. I suppose it was the brooding atmosphere of antiquity, the realization that once this had been a flourishing community of saintly men going about their work . . . and then suddenly the blow had fallen and in place of all that calm beauty and sanctity there was ruin. It was still beautiful, of course. That could not be completely destroyed. A thing of beauty was a joy forever – even when vandals had done their best to destroy it. But so much of the Abbey remained, and how impressive it was with those stone walls – roofless as they were – reaching to the sky.

I walked through the transept and the nave looking up at the blue sky above me. I passed through the narthex on the west side of the basilica and, skirting the chapel and the Abbot's House, I left the ruins a little behind me and came to the fishponds.

I stood for a little while watching the water which flowed from one pond to another. There were three of them, the

205

second lower than the first, the third lower than the second, so that where they flowed into each other there were waterfalls. It was very effective and beautiful to watch.

I was standing by the water, deep in thought, when I heard a footstep and turning sharply saw Jason Verringer.

He approached smiling, hat in hand.

'What made you come here?' I demanded and then realized the folly and impertinence of such a question. After all, the abbey lands belonged to him. He could go where he wished.

He was still smiling.

'Guess,' he said. 'Only one . . . not the usual three . . . because the answer is obvious. I'll tell you. To see you.'

'But how did you know . . . ?'

'Very simple really. You weren't riding so the chances were that you were walking. Where would you walk? Well, the ruins are irresistible, aren't they? So I tethered my horse not far from here and was walking through the ruins when I saw you admiring the ponds. They are worthy of attention, aren't they?'

'They are. I was imagining the monks sitting here fishing.'

'As the worthy Emmet does, I believe, and provides you with the fish you eat at the table.'

'That's true.'

'It is one of the privileges Miss Hetherington has extracted from me.'

'I am sure she is most appreciative.'

'She always seems so. I am devoted to her really. When the school is not in residence it is extremely dull.'

'Surely not, with the estate and . . . all your activities.'

'There is still something missing . . . something very attractive.'

I laughed. 'You exaggerate, of course. And in any case you were abroad most of the winter.'

'Just this year, yes. The circumstances were rather different from usual.'

'Yes, of course. Do you ever fish in these ponds?'

He shook his head. 'I know some of my people do. The

206

fish, I am assured, is excellent and occasionally some of it finds its way to our table.'

I nodded and looked at the watch pinned to my blouse.

'It isn't time yet,' he said. 'Why is it that when we meet you always become very interested in when we shall part?'

'A schoolmistress's life is run by time. You must know that.'

'The monks lived by bells. You are like them.'

'Yes, I suppose so. And the time I take off in the afternoon is between classes.'

'Which makes it easy to know when you will be available. You should come and dine with me one night at the Hall.'

'I think Miss Hetherington would consider that somewhat indecorous.'

'I was not asking Miss Hetherington. Does she rule your life?'

'A headmistress in a school of this nature would have a great influence on the behaviour of her staff.'

'In choosing their friends? In deciding what invitations they should accept? Oh come, you are in an Abbey, I know, but it is only the ruins of one. You are not a nun taking your vows.'

'It is kind of you to invite me but it is impossible for me to accept.'

'There might be a way.'

'I can see none.'

We had been walking along by the side of the ponds and he stopped suddenly and turning to me laid his hands on my shoulders.

'Cordelia,' he said, 'suppose Miss Hetherington was agreeable, would you then come and dine with me?'

I hesitated and he said: 'You would.'

'No . . . no . . . I don't think it would be very . . . suitable. Besides, as it is out of the question, I see no point in discussing it.'

'I am really getting rather fond of you, Cordelia.'

I was silent for a moment and started to walk. He slipped his arm through mine. I wished he would not touch me. He

207

made me feel very embarrassed and uneasy.

'You are fond of a number of people I daresay,' I replied.

'That is an indication of my affectionate nature. What I mean is that I am getting particularly fond of you.'

I released myself and said: 'It really is time I went back. I was only taking a short walk through the ruins.'

'Oh, I know you hear tales of me, but you mustn't let them affect you. They have been going on for hundreds of years. I am here at the moment so I am the central figure in all the scandals. All my ancestors have shared the same fate, Monsters of Iniquity. That's what they have all been made out to be. We always laughed at the stories circulated about us. Let the people amuse themselves at our expense, we used to say. Their lives are dull. Let them live vicariously through us. Why there is even a story about these fish ponds. Have you heard yet that my great-great-great-grandfather was said to have murdered a man and thrown his body into these very ponds?'

I looked at them and shuddered.

'The ponds flow into the river,' he went on, 'and it is fast moving at this point because of the flow from the ponds. I'll show you. Come to the end there and you'll see. The river is only a few miles from the sea . . . so the poor victim was carried away and his bones now lie somewhere at the bottom of the ocean.'

We had come to the last pond and he proved what he had said. The river was certainly fast at that point rushing along its way to the sea.

'This wicked Verringer wanted another man's wife, so he brought him to the ponds, hit him on the head, threw him in and let his body float, by way of the ponds, to the sea. Unfortunately for him there was a witness to the evil deed. That is how we know it took place. Much he cared. He married the lady of his choice and she became one of us. You see, we are a wicked clan.'

'You happen to have some records of your family's action if they have only been handed down by word of mouth. It may well be that if we could all trace our family history back so far, we should find skeletons in cupboards.'

208

'That's a kindly thought. It is pleasant to contemplate that we are not the only villains.'

There was a sound from above. I turned and saw Teresa standing on the slope which led down to the ponds.

'Are you looking for me, Teresa?' I asked.

'Yes, Miss Grant,' she answered. 'Miss Barston has a headache and she wants you to sit with her class this afternoon if you are free. She says all you will have to do is watch them. She has set them work.'

'Yes, certainly. I'll come back at once. Goodbye, Sir Jason.'

He took my hand and kissed it after bowing to Teresa. 'It has been a very pleasant afternoon for me,' he said.

I joined Teresa. She said: 'I saw you hadn't gone riding so I guessed you were walking in the ruins.'

'I went down to the ponds and happened to meet Sir Jason there.'

Teresa said: 'I had to interrupt you. Miss Barston said . . .'

'Of course you did, Teresa.'

'I hope you didn't *mind*.'

'Of course not. As a matter of fact I was trying to get away.'

She nodded and looked rather pleased.

*   *   *

His pursuit of me was becoming obvious and people were noticing. He had the temerity to call at the school and suggest to Miss Hetherington that I call at the Hall to inspect the costumes. She told me that when she reminded him that that was a task for Miss Barston he replied that he thought the girls who would wear the costumes should be taught to carry them off with dignity, and that with the special training I had had I should be the one to inspect them.

'It was so blatant,' said Daisy. 'He knew it and he knew I knew it too. I couldn't help laughing . . . at which he joined in. I said firmly: "No. It must be Miss Barston", and he said he would let me know when it would be convenient. I fancy

209

we are not going to hear any more about that. I don't know what to say to you, Cordelia. He has obviously got some interest in you. You are young and good-looking and to put it frankly he is a rake. But he really should provide his own women and not look for them in respectable quarters. He has set that women up at Rooks' Rest and, surely he knows, that in itself – if he were not who he is – should be enough to exclude him from our premises. Unfortunately he is our landlord. He could turn us out at a moment's notice if the whim took him. Moreover we have two pupils from the Hall. They take all the extras and are most profitable. It's a teasing situation. Do you think you can handle it? You are a sensible young woman.'

'I think I can. He sometimes waylays me when I ride and the other day I came upon him at the fish ponds.'

'Oh dear . . . Of course he has every right to be here. We can't ban him from his own property.'

I felt myself glowing with excitement. It was rather like a battle and I was deeply involved. I could not, with honesty, say that I deplored his pursuit of me. It was flattering in the extreme and I should be a very unusual woman if I were averse to flattery.

When I next went into the town Mrs Baddicombe cornered me.

'Oh. I do reckon it'll be wedding bells pretty soon,' she told me confidentially. 'I do hear there be preparations up at Rooks' Rest. Mrs Gittings were in here yesterday . . . going today she is, taking the little 'un to her sister's place down on the moors. Real pleased she was. There's nothing she likes better and you can see why. It must be a very odd sort of household up there at the Rest.'

'I know Mrs Gittings always enjoys visiting her sister.'

'I reckon if it wasn't for the little 'un she wouldn't be working at the Rest. She do live for that child. Poor little mite. 'Tis a mercy someone has a little thought for her. Reckon they want her out of the way for the wedding. Stands to reason the likes of she . . . well she should be putting in an appearance *after* the ceremony . . . no before.'

210

'So you think the fact that Mrs Gittings is going away with the child means . . .'

'Of course it does, me dear. There'll be a wedding, no mistake. Parson won't like performing the ceremony likely as not, but what can he do? Don't want to lose his living, do he?'

'You can't be sure this is because of the wedding,' I began.

'What else? And if it ain't time now, when is it? 'Tis a year since that poor saint went. He's waited his year, and remember there be no male heir for the Verringers as yet. That's got to be thought on. You mark my words, that's what it all means.'

I came out of the shop feeling depressed. Could Mrs Baddicombe be right? Surely if he were on the brink of marriage he would not show such obvious interest in me?

A few days later Miss Hetherington sent for me.

'Here is a note from Sir Jason,' she said. 'He said he wants you to go to the Hall to discuss the progress of Fiona and Eugenie.'

'Go to the Hall . . . me! Surely he would want to speak to you about that.'

'So I thought, but he goes on to say that he is concerned about Fiona's being launched into society, which will be next year when she is due to leave us, and he thinks that with your Schaffenbrucken training he can talk to you about these matters and the special coaching she needs.'

'But I know nothing of the launching of girls into English society.'

'He was defeated over the monks' costumes, but he never gives up. I am wondering what to tell him.'

'I suppose I could go to the Hall.'

'My dear Cordelia, I do wonder if it would be wise.'

'I think it will be all right. I gather that his wedding is imminent.'

'Is it?'

'According to Mrs Baddicombe.'

'She is an excellent news agency,' said Daisy, 'but I believe she does not always send out true messages.'

'According to her, Mrs Gittings has departed with the child who might prove an embarrassment in the circumstances.'

Daisy shrugged her shoulders. 'I do wish he would behave more reputably. But as long as it has no adverse effect on the school I suppose it is no concern of ours.

'I can't see how the school can be affected by his conduct. Suppose I went and took the girls with me. They would be there as chaperones.'

'H'm,' snorted Daisy. 'Really this is ridiculous. The annoying part about it is that he knows it and I believe he is laughing at us.'

'He is teasing us, I think,' I said. 'After all, I suppose he will soon be married and perhaps he will change then.'

'That is a statement I would challenge very strongly. They say leopards never change their spots.'

'They say also that reformed rakes make the best husbands.'

'Oh dear, it really is rather absurd. Do you think you can handle it, Cordelia?'

'Yes, I do. I'll take the girls with me and insist on their being present.'

'I am sure he will try to outwit you in some way.'

'He has done that on one or two occasions, but I think he will get tired of it when I show him clearly that I do not want his company.'

She looked at me very steadily. 'You do show him that, Cordelia?'

'But of course.'

'They say he is a very attractive man. I don't know much about these things myself, but I do know that in some quarters rakes are said to be attractive.'

'That's a romantic fiction, Miss Hetherington. It doesn't apply to real life.'

'You seem very certain.'

'I am about him.'

'Well, then go with the girls and see what comes of it. I can't see why he can't discuss their future with me.'

That was how I came to be at the Hall on that afternoon

212

in May which was to prove so important in the future.

I set out with Fiona and Eugenie in the early afternoon and we soon covered the few miles between the school and the Hall.

Fiona was reserved but charming; Eugenie was her usual brash self – a little peevish because she was missing the afternoon ride when she would have gone off with the party of girls among whom would be Charlotte Mackay.

When we reached the Hall we went straight to the stables. Jason Verringer was there as though impatiently awaiting us.

He helped me to dismount. 'Just on time,' he said. 'I do like punctuality and I guess Miss Grant is the same.'

One of the grooms had come forward to take the horses. Eugenie patted hers and told the groom what she wanted him to do.

'I have two new horses,' said Jason to Eugenie. 'I'm rather proud of them. I'll show you, Eugenie, before you go.'

'I'd love to see them,' cried Eugenie, looking animated and pretty suddenly.

'You shall.'

As I turned I saw something lying on the cobbles and stopped to pick it up. It was an earring – very large, rather bizarre with what might have been a ruby the size of a pea surrounded by diamonds.

'Look at this!' I cried.

I held it out in the palm of my hand and the girls came to peer at it.

'I know whose it is,' said Eugenie. 'I've seen her wearing them. It's Mrs Martindale's.' There was something malicious in her eyes which ill became one so young. 'It is hers, isn't it, Uncle Jason?'

'I suppose it could be,' he said.

'She wouldn't like to lose it,' said Fiona. 'What use is one without the other?'

'Shall I give it to you to give to her, Uncle Jason?' said Eugenie with a smirk. 'Or I could take it to her. I could easily drop it in when I ride by tomorrow.'

213

'Do that,' said Jason Verringer. 'If it is really hers she'll be glad to have it.'

'I don't see who else it could belong to,' said Eugenie. 'Do you, Miss Grant?'

'I'm sure I don't know,' I said. 'I certainly have never seen it before.'

Eugenie put it into her pocket. 'Show us the horses, Uncle Jason,' she said.

He looked at me and lifted his shoulders.

'Oh, here's Mrs Keel. Mrs Keel, do take Miss Grant to the sitting room. Are those books from the library there?'

'Yes, Sir Jason.'

'Good. We'll be there in a minute. The girls are impatient for a glimpse of the new greys.'

He started to run across the yard with the two girls at his heels. I wanted to go after them but Mrs Keel was talking to me.

'Miss Eugenie is crazy about horses. She always was. Would you come with me, Miss Grant.'

I felt foolish. I guessed that he had planned just this. However, the girls had only gone to look at the horses and there was only one thing I could do and that was follow Mrs Keel into the house.

We went into the great hall through which I had passed on that memorable occasion when I had dined with him and sat afterwards in the twilit courtyard.

We went up the great staircase with its beautifully carved newel posts displaying prominently the Tudor roses and slightly less so the fleurs-de-lys, and I was shown into a panelled room with rich red carpets and heavy red velvet curtains. There was a big carved table under a latticed window and on this had been piled several volumes. On a smaller table was a silver tea tray on which were cups and saucers.

'If you'll take a seat, Miss Grant. They won't be long and I'll bring the tea when it is rung for.'

'Thank you,' I said, and she went out and left me. I felt uneasy. Here was I, alone in this house and only just arrived.

214

I looked round the room. This was his special sanctum. There were two beautiful paintings on the walls. One of a woman – a Verringer obviously. It looked like a Gainsborough. There was a certain unmistakable look about it. The other was a landscape. There was a bookcase with glass doors. I looked at the books. Some poetry. How extraordinary! I could not imagine his reading poetry. The others were mainly history.

'Assessing my reading habits?'

I had not heard him come into the room. I swung round and saw to my dismay that he was alone.

'Where are the girls?' I demanded.

'You're going to be a little bit put out, I believe. Don't blame them. You know how girls are about horses.'

'I thought they were coming here to discuss . . .'

'It was you who were going to do that. I didn't suggest they come in the first place. In fact I think it is better that they are not here. We can talk more frankly about them. Eugenie was mad to try out the horses and she carried Fiona along with her, so I said they might take them out and ride them in the paddock for half an hour. They'll come in for tea.'

He was smiling at me with just a hint of mischievous triumph in his eyes.

So he had won again.

I was determined now to show my displeasure. In fact, if I were honest I would admit that I was glad to be rid of the girls. Eugenie could be really unpleasant and Fiona was inclined to behave as those with her and, although she was quite a docile girl when she was alone, she was slightly less so in the company of Eugenie and Charlotte Mackay.

'What is it you wish to discuss?'

'Sit down. Would you like to look at my books? I have something interesting to show you. I had them brought up from the library. I thought it would be more comfortable up here, but there are others in the collection and, as you are so interested in the Abbey, I thought I'd have them brought up to show you.'

'I should like to see them of course, but first shouldn't we get on with the reason for my coming. What are you worried about concerning Fiona?'

'Worried? Certainly not worried. Just asking for help, that's all.'

'But you have something in mind?'

He looked at me intently. 'My mind teems with possibilities.'

'Then please let me hear them and I will see if there is anything we can do at the school to help.'

'It is a problem for me, having the care of two girls. Particularly now they are coming of age.'

'I can understand that.'

'A man . . . on his own . . . it is not easy.'

'I can see it would have been less difficult if your wife had lived.'

'There wasn't much she could do. She was an invalid for years, you know.'

'Yes, I did know.'

'I've no doubt you have had my complete dossier presented to you . . . from that wicked old postmistress. I wonder I keep her there.'

I was rather shocked to think that Mrs Baddicombe should be so malicious about him, when she owed her livelihood to him, as I supposed most people in the area did.

'Wouldn't it be possible for you to . . .' I began.

'Appoint a new postmistress. Certainly. This is like a little kingdom here, Cordelia. It is almost as feudal as it was in the days when my ancestors bought the abbey lands. The lands extend to the town which has only sprung into existence during the last hundred years or so. My great grandfather was deeply concerned with building projects. He rented them and increased his properties. I know that wicked old woman serves out gossip with her stamps.'

'You know this and you allow it?'

He laughed. 'Let her enjoy her life, poor old lady. The Verringers provide the spice in her dull diet. Mind you she has a certain amount to call on and for the rest . . . a fertile imagination.'

216

'How do you know about all this gossip?'

'You think that I am a careless good-for-nothing concerned only with pleasure, which you imagine as attending balls, gambling clubs and indulging in the company of obliging ladies. There are all sorts of pleasures, Cordelia. Running an estate is one of them, delving into the past another. You see, my character has many facets. I can change it in a flash. There is quite a lot to know about me, I assure you.'

'I never doubted that. Shall we get down to the business for which I came? Tell me what extra tuition you would like for Fiona?'

'I want her to leave the Academy as a young lady ready for society.'

'Do you think we can make her so?'

'I think you can.'

'How?'

'I should like her to emerge . . . exactly like you.'

I felt myself flushing. 'Really, I don't understand . . .'

'Poised, articulate, cool, inviting interest. Humorous . . . in fact devastatingly attractive.'

I began to laugh but I knew my eyes were shining. I had said that I liked flattery and it was certainly true.

'Why do you laugh?'

'Because *you* are laughing at me.'

'I am deadly serious. If I had to launch you into society I would know that I had an easy task.'

'I disagree. A penniless schoolmistress would not get very far in your sort of society.'

He had come to my side. He took my hand and kissed it.

I said: 'This is absurd. If you behave like this I must leave at once.'

He looked at me slyly. 'You will have to wait for the girls.'

I put my hands behind my back for they were shaking a little.

'I thought you asked me here for a serious purpose.'

'I am very serious.'

'Then your behaviour is very extraordinary.'

217

'I thought it was very restrained.'

'I mean your absurd compliments and insinuations. Please, no more of them, I find them offensive.'

'I was only speaking the truth. Isn't that what you teach your pupils to do?'

I sat down with a show of dignity.

'I suspect that this talk about guiding Fiona's future is nonsense.'

'I'll confess I don't find it a very interesting subject.'

'Then why did you ask me to come here?'

'Because I wanted to talk to you.'

'Then why didn't you state your real purpose?'

'If I had, my wish would not have been granted.'

'So you lied.'

'Only white lies, really. Who in a lifetime has not had to resort to those at some time? Even you perhaps.'

'Tell me what your purpose is.'

To be with you.'

'But why?'

'You must know that I find you irresistibly attractive.'

'Is that the way a prospective bridegroom should talk to another woman. I feel sorry for Mrs Martindale.'

'You need not. There is a woman who is infinitely capable of taking care of herself. You are thinking that she and I are going to marry. Is that it? The hot news from the indefatigable Mrs B. of the post office. Cordelia, I am not, and never was, going to marry Mrs Martindale . . .'

'But what of the child . . .'

'You mean her daughter. Oh, is that child said to be mine? Mrs B. again. She should be writing fiction.'

'So . . . Well, it is no concern of mine. In fact, you must think me rather impertinent to talk as I have. Please forgive me.'

'Most willingly.'

'Do you have nothing to say about Fiona, and are you satisfied with the tuition she is receiving at this moment?'

'She does seem a little colourless, but that is not the fault of the school. She is naturally so. And Eugenie is inclined to be aggressive. There is a lack of charm in both of them –

but perhaps I am comparing them with . . . others. I really wanted to talk about the Abbey and the coming celebrations. It is not so much the costumes, but I thought you would be interested in some old accounts of the Abbey and that you might care to teach the girls something about it. I was appalled by the ignorance of both Fiona and Eugenie on the subject. And there is to be this pageant. I have delved into the archives and found these. We have many accounts of the early days here and apparently when my ancestors acquired it there was much of it intact, including lots of records which were not destroyed, and they were placed in our library. I thought you might be interested to see them.'

'I should be most interested.'

'Come to the table then and I will show you some of the old plans of the place. There are some very good drawings done by the monks about a hundred years before the Dissolution.'

He drew two chairs up to the table. I sat down and he pulled a great tome towards us.

'What do you know about the monks of Colby?' he asked.

'That they were Cistercians . . . little else.'

'Then I'll tell you a little. They came into existence round about the twelfth century and our abbey was built in the 1190s. Do you know where their name came from?'

'No.'

'From Cîteaux which was a desolate and almost inaccessible forest bordering on Champagne and Burgundy. Here is an old map. I'll show you. St Bernard, the founder, was the Abbot of Clairvaux, the first of the monasteries.'

I turned to look at him. He had indeed changed. That he was immensely interested in the Abbey was obvious, for he had thrown off that blasé worldly manner. He looked younger, almost boyish in his enthusiasm.

'They were a noble band of men,' he said. 'Their aim was to devote themselves entirely to their religion. Perhaps it is nobler to go into the world and try to improve it than to

219

shut oneself away in meditation and prayer. What do you think?'

'Yes, I think the braver course is to go out into the world. But so few people improve it when they do and a love of power gets between them and their ambitions.'

'Ambition,' he said. 'By that sin fell the angels. Lucifer was proud and ambitious, and as I have told you he is believed to have been a member of our family. Ask Mrs Baddicombe.'

I laughed. 'Please go on. It's fascinating.'

'The aim of the Cistercians was to live as simply as possible. Everything was to be plain. They always built in remote places, far from the towns. This must have been isolated once. Can you imagine it? The precincts were surrounded by a strong wall and always near water. Some were built on either side of a stream. We have the river nearby and that gives us our important fish ponds. The monks had to have a supply of fresh food. In the walls were watch-towers. I suppose they had to keep a lookout for despoilers. Look. Here is a map. You'll recognize much of it. Here are the barns, the granaries, shambles, work shops. This is the inner ward and this the outer.'

'Oh yes,' I said. 'It is indeed recognizable.'

'Here's the Abbot's House; the guest house is next to it. People were always calling at the Abbey and no one who needed food and shelter was ever turned away. Look at the nave. There were eleven bays. You can see it clearly in this map. You see, you enter by the narthex. And here is the transept. Look at the stall divided by a wall once . . . the monks one side and the *fratres conversi* on the other. They were the novices . . . Some of their quarters help to make up the Academy. They were not so badly damaged as the rest of the Abbey.'

'What a wonderful map!'

'As it was in those days. And I have another as it appeared after the Dissolution. My family had that one done. Look, here is the calefactory, the day room.'

'Our common room today.'

He turned to me and said: 'I am glad you are so interested.'

'I find it fascinating.'

'So many people are enamoured of the present and never want to look back to the past. Yet it is by studying what happened then that we are often better able to deal with the events of today.'

'Yes, I suppose that's true. Thank Heaven they won't come along now and demolish our school.'

'I should like to see anyone try with Miss Daisy Hetherington in command.'

I laughed. 'She is a very fine woman.'

'We'll put our heads together over this pageant and get some really authentic touches.'

'I think you should consult Miss Hetherington.'

He looked at me in dismay and we both started to laugh again.

'It has been very illuminating,' I said.

'And you are surprised that I should be interested in such a serious subject.'

'I am sure you can be very serious. There must be a great deal of work on the estate.'

'It needs constant attention.'

'Yet you were able to leave for long stretches at a time.'

'I did, didn't I. I don't often do that. I have good people . . . one very good man, Gerald Coverdale. You should meet him.'

'I doubt he would have much to talk about with me.'

'You would be interested to hear about the estate. It is a little community of its own, like a town . . . more than that, like a kingdom.'

'And you are the king.'

' "Uneasy lies the head that wears a crown." '

'I am sure you would never be uneasy.'

'You mistake me. There is so much about me that you have to learn. You have dismissed me as frivolous, immoral, bent on pleasure. That is only a part of me. When I come to think of it, I have some very good points.'

221

'It is said that good points should be discovered by others, not by ourselves.'

'Who said so? Miss Cordelia Grant, I'll wager. It sounds like one of the homilies you declaim to your classes.'

'They do say that schoolteachers are recognizable wherever they go.'

'Perhaps there is something in that.'

'We are inclined to be tutorial and give the impression of knowing all.'

'Sometimes that can be charming.'

'I can see you are determined to flatter me this afternoon. Tell me about the estate, this little kingdom with the uneasy-headed king.'

'We have to keep it in working order. There are the farms and the factory.'

'The factory? What factory is that?'

'The cider factory. We employ most of the people round here in some capacity or other.'

'So they are dependent on you for their livelihood?'

'On the estate rather than on me. I just happen to have inherited it. The Verringers have always taken their duties to the estate seriously, and although I say it of my own family, we have been good landlords. We have made it a duty to care for our people. That is why the cider factory was started about a hundred years ago. We'd had several bad harvests and lots of the farms were not paying their way. It looked as though there would not be enough work for a number of people. The cider factory seemed a good idea. Most of them were making it in their own homes, so we started it and we employ about a hundred people in the neighbourhood.'

'You are in a way the benefactors.'

'We always liked to think of ourselves as such.'

'The people should be grateful.'

'Grateful. Only fools expect gratitude.'

'I see the cynic has reappeared.'

'If truth is cynicism then he is never far away. I always like to face the facts. It is a peculiar trait of human nature that people dislike those who help them.'

222

'Oh no.'

'Oh yes, my dear Cordelia. Just consider it. Who have always been the Verringers' bitterest enemies? Our own people on the estate. Who have endowed us with satanic qualities? The very same. Mind you, I am not saying that we do not possess those devilish habits, but it is our own people who are our own most vicious critics and, when our exploits are not startling enough, magnify them. The fact is, people hate feeling they owe anything to anyone, and although they take help, they hate themselves for being in a position to have to take it. As it is the hardest thing on Earth to hate oneself, that hatred is transferred to the helper.'

I was silent. I thought of Mrs Baddicombe who owed her living to the fact that she had been appointed postmistress by the Verringer estate and could not hide the venom in her voice when she discussed them.

'Perhaps you are right . . . in some cases,' I said. 'But not all.'

'No one is ever right in all cases. There must be exceptions.'

We smiled at each other and I felt a glow of happiness. I was glad that the girls had gone off to try the horses and I was hoping that they would not return just yet.

'It is a pleasure to be able to talk to you reasonably . . . seriously. In the past our encounters have been verbal battles. Amusing, stimulating, but this is a great pleasure to me. I want to talk to you about the estate. How I want to improve it. What plans I have for it.'

'I doubt I should understand them.'

'That's why I want to talk to you . . . to make you understand . . . and to tell you about my life and myself. Do you know, this has been one of the happiest afternoons I have ever known.'

I laughed. He had broken the spell. 'That is going too far,' I said.

'You laugh. But it is not so. I have had moments in the past when I am happy. But happiness is just moments, isn't it? From the time I came into this room and found you

223

here, I have been happy. That must have been for twenty minutes. That's quite a stretch.'

'It seems a very short time to me.'

'I knew it would be good to talk to you. I knew you would understand. You make me see life differently. I wish we could meet often.'

'That would not be easy. Miss Hetherington would be most disapproving.'

'For Heaven's sake why?'

'I am employed by her and it would not be seemly for one of her mistresses to be too friendly with someone of the opposite sex living in the neighbourhood, particularly . . .'

'A man of my reputation. I doubt Mrs Baddicombe would approve either. But then what a scoop for her!'

We were laughing again.

'Cordelia,' he said seriously, 'you know I am falling in love with you.'

I stood up, but he was beside me. He put his arms round me and kissed me. I was trying to force myself to struggle free and not to accept the fact that I wanted to stay close to him.

'This must not be,' I began.

'Why not?'

'Because I am not . . .'

'I love you Cordelia. It started the moment I saw you in the driving seat with Emmet.'

'I must go. Oh, where are those girls?'

As though in answer to my question I heard their voices. I withdrew myself and went to the window. I said: 'They are coming.'

'We'll talk more of this,' he said.

I shook my head.

'Think about me,' he said.

'I can scarcely avoid doing that.'

'Try to understand. I want a happy family life. I have never had one. My frustrations, my disappointments have made me what I am. I want to be different.' He was speaking earnestly now. 'I want to live my life here, with my wife and the children we shall have. I want to make the

224

estate the best in the country and above all I want to live at peace.'

'I think your desires for these things are very natural but . . .'

'Then help me to achieve them. Marry me!'

'Marry you! But a short while ago you were about to marry Marcia Martindale.'

'No. That was the Baddicombe version.'

'You can't be serious. You are amusing yourself at my expense.'

'I am serious.'

'No . . . not with Mrs Martindale living so close . . . I know very well that you and she . . .'

The girls burst into the room.

Eugenie looked radiant. 'They are superb, Uncle Jason,' she cried. 'I tried them both.'

'Have we been too long,' asked Fiona.

'No. You could have stayed longer,' he said ironically.

'I'm gasping for tea,' said Eugenie.

'Then ring for it,' he said.

She did and it came; and Fiona poured out. Eugenie talked all the time about the horses, but I was not listening and I was sure he was not either.

I was wildly exhilarated and horribly sceptical as we rode back to school. Eugenie was still talking about the horses and said she was going to take Charlotte Mackay over to see them.

In the Devil's Den

*

I spent a sleepless night trying to remember everything he had said. Had he really been serious? I kept seeing his face alight with enthusiasm. I thought of the way in which his eyebrows turned up slightly at the ends; the way his dark hair sprang from his rather high forehead; the brilliance of his eyes when he talked of love.

How did I feel? I could not exactly say. I was too bewildered. All I knew was that I wanted to be with him, that I had never felt so excited in my life as I had been sitting close to him, listening to his enthusiasm for the Abbey; and then when he had kissed me I had been quite unprepared.

He was very experienced; he would know what effect he had on me. Whereas I had never known anything like this before.

I was able to stand up to him in our verbal battles and that was because I had always found it easy to express myself lucidly. After all, wasn't I teaching English? It was when it came to understanding my emotions that I was a novice.

I must curb my elation. I must remind myself that he probably talked to every woman he was trying to seduce as he had to me. I was very well aware of his intentions and I must be careful.

The next day Daisy called me to her room to ask how the meeting went.

'I didn't get a chance to talk to you last night,' she said, 'but I gathered all went well.'

'Oh yes, very well. He really wants to help with the Abbey pageant. He showed me some interesting maps and he is certainly knowledgeable about the history of the

226

Abbey. I really think he wants to make sure we don't commit any anachronisms.'

'Did he say anything about the costumes?'

'He may have mentioned them. I think he will be very happy to lend them.'

'So we misjudged him really.'

'Well, the girls did go off to look at horses.'

'So you were alone with him?'

'Not for long. That was when he showed me the maps and books.'

She nodded. 'By the way,' she said, 'something rather interesting has turned up. You know I was looking for a maid since Lizzie Garnett left last term.'

'Oh yes. Have you got someone?'

'Yes, and the strange thing is that she was at Schaffenbrucken.'

'Oh!'

'That was why I selected her. I had one or two to choose from. You know I put an advertisement in the Lady's Companion. I didn't have many letters. Most of them couldn't put pen to paper if they tried. It may be that those who can write wouldn't make the best maids. However, I liked the sound of this letter and the fact that she had worked at Schaffenbrucken I must admit interested me and decided me in her favour. I wonder if you knew her.'

'What is her name?'

'Elsa something. Yes . . . Elsa Kracken.'

'Elsa,' I said. 'There was a maid called Elsa. But then it is a fairly common name. I don't think I ever heard her surname.'

'It will be amusing if you knew her from Schaffenbrucken.'

'Is she English?'

'She wrote in English. The name doesn't sound quite . . .'

'Elsa,' I said. 'Yes . . . she was rather a talkative girl . . . not much of a servant but everybody liked her.'

'I thought she wrote a good letter.'

'When does she arrive?'

'At the end of the week.'

I was thoughtful. The conversation had brought back memories of Schaffenbrucken. It was Elsa who had told us about the legend of Pilcher's Peak and that if we went out at the time of Hunter's Moon we should meet our future husbands.

It would be quite a coincidence if she should be the one. But it might well be another Elsa.

*   *   *

It was not long before I met her. I was coming upstairs and there she was coming down.

'Elsa!' I cried. 'It is you, then.'

She turned so white I thought she was going to faint. She clutched at the banister and stared at me. I might have been a ghost.

'Cordelia Grant. We met at Schaffenbrucken.'

'Cordelia Grant.' She whispered my name. 'Why . . . of course.'

'I confess I am not so surprised as you are,' I said. 'Miss Hetherington did tell me that someone named Elsa was coming and that she had worked at Schaffenbrucken. I thought of you, but didn't really believe it possibly could be.'

The colour was returning to her face. She was smiling and looked more like the jolly girl I had known.

'Well, fancy that. The age of miracles is not past. What are you doing here?'

'Working,' I told her. 'I'm teaching.'

'Oh, but I thought . . .'

'It all changed. When I left school I had to find a post. My aunt knew Miss Hetherington and I came here.'

'Well, I never did!'

She started to laugh. 'They were good days at Schaffenbrucken,' she said.

'Oh yes. You remember the girls . . .'

'Your special friends. There was that French girl and the German girl and that Lydia . . . wasn't that her name?'

'Yes, I think Frieda and Monique will be leaving this

228

year. Probably have left by now. I wrote to Lydia but I didn't hear from her.'

'Too busy with her affairs, I daresay.'

'Well, she left Schaffenbrucken soon after I did, I gathered.'

'Oh, did she now?'

'But Elsa, where have you sprung from?'

'I came to England. I left the term after you did. I got a job over here . . . that didn't last so long and then I applied for this. What a life!'

'Miss Hetherington is rather particular. You'll have to do your work properly.'

'Do you mean I didn't at Schaffenbrucken?'

'I only remember your doing a lot more talking than anyone else.'

'Oh, this is like the old days. I can't tell you how pleased I am to see you.'

'You looked as if you'd seen a ghost a moment ago.'

'I was shaken all of a heap, as they say. It was such a surprise. Now I'm realizing what a nice one it is.'

'Well, I shall be seeing you about, Elsa.'

'I'm looking forward to getting to know the girls. It was you girls that I liked at Schaffenbrucken.'

'Miss Hetherington won't want you to be too friendly with them.'

Elsa winked at me and went on downstairs.

*　　　*　　　*

Sir Jason sent a message over to the school to say that he had discovered some very interesting information which he thought would be very useful when compiling the commentaries for the pageant. If Miss Grant would care to come over he would be delighted to show them to her.

Daisy called me to her study to tell me. She immediately noticed my embarrassment.

She said: 'I think you ought to go, but take Miss Barston with you. I do think he is trying to become too friendly and one has to be careful. I haven't told you about Miss Lyons,

229

have I? That was some years ago. She was a pretty dainty little thing. She taught dancing – that was before Mr Bathurst's time. Sir Jason noticed her. I don't know what happened. He pursued her a bit and the poor child was most unworldly. She must have believed all he told her. She was very unhappy when she discovered the sort of relationship he was after. Of course his fancy for her was only passing. You and I know what such men are, but poor Hilda Lyons believed in beautiful romance. She became quite depressed and almost suicidal. I had to send her away – and in the middle of term! You are a different kettle of fish.' She smiled with rare humour. 'Not that I am really comparing you with that useful object. It is just in the nature of the metaphor. I know you will take great care. He has a fancy for you but you are not in the least like poor Hilda . . . or that Martindale woman for that matter. He evidently likes variety and has all his lines in the river at once . . . if you know what I mean.'

'I think I understand very well,' I said. 'I think, too, that I know how to deal with Sir Jason.'

'The rather annoying part of all this is that we have to, as they say, keep on the right side of him. If he became spiteful . . . imagine what he could do.'

'In spite of his many failings I don't think he would be that.'

Oh?'

'Well, I was thinking of all the gossip in the town about him over his wife's death and his association with Mrs Martindale. He knows it and yet he is very lenient with those people. I suppose he could put the fear of God into them if he wanted to.'

'H'm,' said Daisy. 'Well, my dear, you can't very well refuse to go, and Miss Barston will be a good chaperone.'

'I'll go over this afternoon.'

'That's right. If you go about two you can be back at four. I believe you have a class at four thirty.'

'Yes. The last of the day.'

The matter was closed as far as Daisy was concerned. I must admit that I was not altogether displeased to be riding

230

over to the Hall, although every day it seemed I learned something more about him and it was mostly derogatory. Now the dainty pretty Hilda Lyons had put in an appearance.

Mrs Keel greeted us. No doubt she had her instructions.

'I was to take you to the rooms which Sir Jason particularly wanted you to see. He will be with you in five or ten minutes.'

'Thank you, Mrs Keel.'

'He will be glad Miss Barston has come. He has something special to show her. It is in the library. I'll take you there, Miss Barston, and then you can join Miss Grant when you have seen them.'

'I shall be most interested to see whatever it is,' said Miss Barston.

Mrs Keel took us to the library where several old manuscripts were laid out on the table. Miss Barston was immediately absorbed.

'I'll just take Miss Grant up and come for you later, Miss Barston, when you've had time to look through those papers. There are some drawings there of costumes . . . last century, I think Sir Jason said. Miss Grant, will you come with me?'

I followed her out of the library. We went along a corridor and came to a stone staircase.

'I don't know whether you have been to this part of the house before, Miss Grant.'

I said I hadn't.

'This staircase leads to a set of apartments which we don't use. They have a historical significance, Sir Jason says.'

'How interesting.'

Mrs Keel opened a door. I was in a long low room with heavy beams across the ceiling. The windows were small but we were at the top of the house and it was fairly light.

'It's quite an apartment,' said Mrs Keel. 'A little separate from the rest of the house. I'll bring Miss Barston up when she's finished with the drawings.'

She went out leaving me a little uneasy. Miss Barston

231

had come as chaperone and I was already separated from her.

What could he possibly want to show me up here?

I walked round the place. It was like a sitting room with heavily carved chairs and a settle. I saw a communicating door. It led to a bedroom. In this was a four-poster bed, a court cupboard and some chairs. I was startled to see that the windows were barred. They made it look like a prison.

I thought I should find my way down to Miss Barston and we would see what we had to see here together.

I came out of the bedroom and there he was smiling at me.

I said as calmly as I could: 'Good afternoon. Mrs Keel brought me up here.'

'I know. I saw you coming with your companion, so I arranged for her to go to the library.'

'What is it you want to show me in this place?'

'Did you notice anything unusual about it?'

'Only that the windows in there are barred.'

'It was a sort of prison at one time. Come and sit down.' He led me to the settle and we sat side by side. I was aware of him very close and it made a tension in the atmosphere. What a fool I had been to allow myself to be separated from Miss Barston. I had walked straight into the trap, aware all the time that it was being set for me. There was something about Mrs Keel that was so conventional that she made everything appear so normal. She had done this once before.

'Well, why have you brought me here?'

'I knew you'd want to see it. You were so interested when I told you the story.'

'What story was that?'

'About our devilish ancestors. This is said to be the apartment where our satanic prisoner was kept when the wicked Verringer was trying to force him to marry his daughter. It's called the Devil's Den.'

'Very interesting,' I said. 'Is that all you wanted to show me?'

'I have a great deal to show you.'

232

'Then I am sure Miss Barston will be interested too. Shouldn't she be brought up?'

'You wouldn't spoil her pleasure in those magnificent drawings. These rooms are used on certain occasions only. Would you like me to tell you about it?'

'Yes.'

'There is said to be a certain quality . . . an aura . . . about them. Perhaps you can sense it.'

I looked round the room. What I was aware of was the isolation, and those bars across the window of the bedroom gave it a somewhat sinister atmosphere.

'There is said to be an aphrodisiacal ambience in these rooms . . . something which was left by the Devil when he honoured us.'

I laughed to hide my uneasiness. I was embarrassed that he should talk to me in this manner and I guessed he was leading up to something which put me on my guard and yet at the same time excited me. There was something about him which was different from anyone else I had ever known and, while it alarmed me, it fascinated me.

'The story goes back into the past,' he went on. 'If childless couples slept here, it was said, they were sure of . . . fertility. Such an important person as the Devil couldn't live somewhere for even a short space of time without leaving something behind, could he?'

'Well, I suppose if you believe that sort of thing it is very interesting.'

'You would believe, wouldn't you?'

'No.'

'What about your stranger in the forest? You see, at some time we all have odd inexplicable experiences. Mrs Keel always comes up here with the servants when they clean. She says the silly girls imagine things. One of them said she saw the Devil and he forced her to get into the bed with him. It turned out to be that she had been sporting with one of the stable boys and as he would have none of it, he Devil seemed a good substitute.'

'You see, people fit these legends to suit themselves.'

'My brother and I used to come up here sometimes. We

stayed here one night . . . just to show we were not afraid. Then he wagered me that I wouldn't sleep here alone.'

'And of course you did and saw the Devil.'

'Yes and no. I came, but his Satanic Majesty did not deign to put in an appearance on that night.'

'I am sure Miss Barston would love to see it. Shall we go down to her?'

'I have instructed Mrs Keel regarding Miss Barston.'

'There doesn't seem to be anything much to see up here,' I said. 'Apart from the legend it might be an ordinary apartment.'

'There is so much I want you to see.'

'Well, show me.'

'It is a matter of understanding. You know how very much I am attracted by you.'

'I have noticed that you are inclined to appear rather frequently.'

'How else could I get you to realize what a fine fellow I am?'

'You don't have to appear so frequently to keep me informed of that. I am constantly hearing of you. As we have said before, you are the main topic of conversation in the neighbourhood. But what I can only call your waylaying me and contriving meetings like this is rather embarrassing. You must really understand that I am not one of your Mrs Martindales or Miss Lyons . . .'

'Good Heavens!' he said. 'That goes back a long way.'

'You can be sure it was duly noted when it occurred.'

'Obviously. Hilda Lyons, a pretty little thing but no conversationalist.'

'She was a schoolmistress, I believe. Understandably she lacked the glamour of someone like Mrs Martindale.'

'Not necessarily. Take Miss Grant for instance.'

'It is her future which interests me most.'

'And me,' he said, looking earnest suddenly.

I stood up but he was beside me. He put an arm about me.

'Please . . . don't touch me.'

He took me by the shoulders and turned me to face him.

234

'You have a tremulous mouth,' he said. 'It betrays you.' Then he kissed me. He frightened me. I felt he was going to crush my body. It was such a violent embrace.

I fought him off.

'You are insufferable . . .' I panted.

'Which is rather nice, eh?'

'Please do not use those tactics with me.'

'I know you are not Mrs Martindale or yet Miss Lyons. You are far more attractive . . . far more passionate . . . far more desirable than either.'

'Your past mistresses are of no interest to me.'

'You do not always speak the truth do you? I thought schoolmistresses were supposed to. I'll tell you something. They are of the utmost interest to you.'

'Do you always tell people what they must think, what they must do?'

'Always.'

'Not in this case.'

'I realize I shall have to work hard on it.'

'And bring no results. I am going down now. And please do not bring me here again on false pretences. I shall not come. You make take what revenge you like. I am not coming when you beckon.'

'Then I shall have to resort to pleading.'

'Nothing will make me come here again.'

'Don't make rash vows, Cordelia, because you are the sort of woman who would hate to break them. Come and sit down. I promise I won't kiss you, touch you, or do anything which could cause offence while we talk.'

'Please say what you have to say and say it quickly.'

'You are a very attractive girl. You have all the social graces. After all, didn't you spend – how many years was it? – at that place in Switzerland? Perhaps it has done something. I don't know. I suppose that firmness of character, that unswerving desire to do what is right, were there all the time. What they have done is turn you into a young lady who would grace any circles.'

'Well?'

'Even a place like this.'

235

'Really!' I said with sarcasm.

'I mean it.'

'Then I am indeed flattered, and on that note I will take my departure.'

'I have not finished yet and, as you have learned at that magnificent place whose name for the moment escapes me, young ladies do not move away when their hosts are speaking to them. They stay and listen and appear to be animated; in fact they give the impression of paying attention even though their thoughts are far away. Is that correct?'

'It is.'

'Then follow the rules of the school. I might even marry you.'

'Really, sir. Your condescension overwhelms me. But I should have to decline.'

'Why?'

'I should have thought that was obvious, and polite young ladies never talk of unpleasant matters.'

'Look at this place. You would be in your element. After all what was the business of Schaffenbrucken if not to prepare you to take your place at the head of some rich man's table?'

'So you *have* remembered the name. I am so glad. That was indeed the purpose of Schaffenbrucken, but there are always the rogue pupils who are meant for another destiny.'

'You mean schoolteaching?'

'In some cases, obviously, yes.'

'Don't be foolish, Cordelia. You are not going to teach silly girls all your life, are you? Are you going to be another Miss Hetherington?'

'Miss Hetherington is a very great lady. If I were like her, I should think I had done rather well.'

'Nonsense. You're not a schoolmarm underneath. Don't think I don't know women.'

'I think you know a great deal about them . . . physically. Mentally I imagine you know very little. Certainly you do not seem to know much about me.'

236

'You'd be surprised. You are at the moment the virgin schoolmistress . . . prim, clinging to conventions, completely ignorant of the world. My dear Cordelia, beneath that schoolmistress is a passionate woman eager to escape . . . to life.'

I laughed and he laughed with me, but he said with feigned reproach: 'You find me amusing?'

'Very. And I know your interest in me is directed to one goal.'

'You are right.'

'And that goal is seduction. Do you have formulae? This one for Marcia Martindale. This for Miss Lyons. Now here is Cordelia Grant. Which number for her?'

'You are very cynical. Don't you give me credit for any deep feelings?'

'No.'

'My dear girl, you do delight me, you know. Really, I would marry you.'

'Aren't you being rather rash. A penniless schoolmistress . . .'

'I have no need of money.'

'Nor have I. I am content with what I have. So you see it is no use your bringing me here and in your satanic manner showing me the riches which would be mine.'

'Everyone likes riches.'

'One can do much with money, yes. But in this case think of the price one would have to pay to be Lady Verringer, and grace your halls. You!'

'You are unconvincing. You are trembling with excitement at the prospect.'

'That's not excitement,' I retorted. 'It's rage.'

I rose but he gripped my arm firmly and forced me to sit down.

'You know my problem. I need an heir. A son . . .'

'I have heard that mentioned too.'

'I want a son. I would marry you if you would give me a son.'

I stared at him incredulously and then I said: 'Oh . . . I understand now. You want proof before you commit yourself. How wise! Other people marry and hope for children, but that is not the way of the Verringers. Am I right?' I burst out laughing. 'I can't help it,' I went on. 'I just pictured your chosen women . . . kept at Rooks' Rest until they showed what they could do. Like a harem or a Restoration play perhaps. Imagine it.'

He was trying not to laugh but he couldn't help it and for a moment we gave ourselves up to our mirth.

I said: 'It will be most amusing. At present you only have one there. That's very tame. I can see them all in various stages. Who shall produce the boy and win the prize? Poor Marcia. Hers was only a girl. What a shame!'

I had seized the opportunity and made for the door. He was there before me and stood with his back to it facing me.

He said: 'Cordelia, I want you. I fall more and more in love with you every time we meet. It's important to me.'

'I should like to join Miss Barston.'

He stood aside and I tried to open the door. It was locked.

I turned to him; he was smiling at me and I thought: Yes, indeed, they are sons of the devil. I was really frightened now because I saw the purpose in his face, and I knew he was even capable . . . of this.

'Well,' he said, mockingly. 'What now?'

'You will open this door,' I said, trying to sound firm but being somewhat unconvincing I was afraid.

'No, Miss Grant, I will not.'

'Let me out of here at once.'

'No, Miss Grant.'

'You lured me up here.'

'You came willingly with my housekeeper.'

'What is she . . . a sort of procuress?'

'She is obedient to my wishes as I expect all my servants to be. You are not so calm now, are you, Cordelia? Do I sense little tremors of expectation? I will show you what you were meant to be. We'll call forth that wonderful passionate woman. We'll let her sweep aside the prim schoolmistress.'

'You will let me out of here at once.'

238

He shook his head. 'I have wanted you for a long time. I wanted you . . . willing.'

'Willing? Do you think . . . ?'

'Once you really know how happy I can make you, yes. But you are rather stubborn, aren't you. That schoolmistress façade is quite formidable. I began to see that I should have to help you break out.'

With trembling hands I looked at the watch which was pinned to my blouse.

'Always the time!' he said. 'What do we care for time on occasions like this?'

'I should be leaving now.'

'Not yet.'

'Don't you realize . . . ?'

'I realize one thing. It obsesses me. I want you and if you are so stubborn as to turn away from what is the best thing for you, I shall have to insist on bringing you to reason.'

'I hate you,' I said. 'Can't you see that. You expect every woman to fall into your arms. Not this one. And if you dare touch me, you are acting like a criminal and I shall see that you are punished for it.'

'What fire!' he taunted. 'What rage! Cordelia, you and I are lovers . . .'

'Haters for my part,' I spat out.

'If you are going to fight . . . fight. But you will soon see how much stronger I am than you. Come, let me take your coat. You look flushed and overheated. My dear love, Cordelia, you are going to be so happy . . . We *both* are.'

He was forcing me out of my coat. I kicked out at him and he laughed.

'Are you really capable of this?' I stammered. 'I am not one of your servants, you know, or one of your tenants who are afraid to stand up to you. My family will avenge this and so will I. Rape is not within the law, Jason Verringer, even for men like you.'

He took me by the shoulders and laughed at me.

'I would insist that you came here willingly, that you provoked me, enticed me, which is true.'

'You are a fiend.'

239

'I warned you of my great ancestor.'

Catching him suddenly off his guard, I broke away from him. I ran to the window. There were no bars across this one. He was close behind me and in desperation I beat on the glass with my bare hands.

The glass shattered. The blood ran down my arms onto the sleeves of my dress, spattering my bodice.

'Oh my God,' he cried. He was sobered. 'Oh Cordelia,' he went on almost sadly. 'Do you hate me so much?'

I felt bewildered. My emotions were so mixed that I did not know what I felt. I was afraid of him, yes, but at the same time I wanted to be with him. It was a thought I would not admit into my mind but I did believe half of me wanted him to carry me into the room with the barred windows. Yet I had made this futile attempt to break the windows to escape. I was brought face to face with the fact that I did not know myself.

He was looking at my bleeding hands and his mood had changed. It was all tenderness now. He said: 'Oh Cordelia, my dear Cordelia!' and held me against him for a few seconds. I drew away from him. I could feel the tears on my cheeks. I wanted him to hold me tightly and to tell me that in some ways he knew me better than I knew myself. I was not the practical schoolmistress I made myself out to be. There was some part of me striving to get out.

He had taken my hands in his. 'These must be attended to immediately,' he said.

He put an arm about me and led me to the door; and taking a key from his pocket unlocked it.

We went downstairs. Mrs Keel came out of the library with Miss Barston behind her.

Miss Barston said: 'We shall be late, Miss Grant. Oh . . .' She had seen my wounds.

'There's been an accident,' said Jason Verringer. 'Miss Grant cut her hands on a window. Mrs Keel, get something to put on this . . . some bandages . . . You have some lotions . . .'

'Yes, Sir Jason.'

I sat down in a chair. I was aware of Miss Barston's

240

scrutiny. Jason was quite calm. I was amazed and my anger against him returned.

'You do look queer, Miss Grant,' said Miss Barston. 'You have cut yourself badly . . .'

'I don't think it is as bad as it looks,' said Jason. 'When the blood is washed away we'll see what harm has been done. The cuts don't appear to be so very deep. The great thing is to clean the wounds. Mrs Keel is quite knowledgeable about these things. There are often such accidents in the kitchen and she always manages to deal with them. How do you feel, Miss Grant? Ah, you look better now. Mrs Keel won't be long.' He turned to Miss Barston. 'I was showing Miss Grant one of the apartments tied up in our family legends . . . We were saying you would be interested to see it. Then this happened. I'll send someone over to Miss Hetherington to tell her you'll be a little late returning. Then you can wait and go back with Miss Grant in the carriage. Miss Grant is certain to feel a little shaken after this. One of the grooms can take your horses over when he goes with the message to Miss Hetherington.'

How neatly he explained everything and how lightly he managed to introduce normality into the accident. I admired him while I deplored his expert manner in extricating us from an embarrassing situation. No doubt he had had a great deal of practice. I hated him for his suggestion and for his attempt to force me, and I was really rather amazed that he had so quickly given up his intentions at the sight of my blood.

I hated him, I assured myself vehemently . . . far too vehemently.

* * *

I was completely shattered by the experience and could not bring myself to talk of it. I answered questions as briefly as I could. Sir Jason had been showing me some of the apartments, I had unthinkingly put out my hands and broken the glass, cutting myself. Yes, certainly I had felt most embarrassed. I did not know whether it was particularly valuable glass. Yes, I must have put my hands out with some force.

241

No, Sir Jason did not seem put out. He was most concerned about the damage I had done to myself. His housekeeper had bound up my wounds after carefully washing them and applying something; and Sir Jason had sent us back in his carriage.

Daisy looked at me quizzically, but she did not probe. I think she had some idea that if she did, something unpleasant might emerge and wisely she left it alone.

I was excused lessons for a day.

'That sort of thing is a bit of a shock,' said Daisy.

So I lay on my bed alone in my room and went over everything that had happened. The man was a monster, that much was clear. I must never be alone with him again. I had saved myself from what was called 'a fate worse than death'. The phrase had always made me laugh but I was a little more sober about it now. My imagination would not give me any rest. I kept thinking of what would have happened if I had not put my hands through the glass. I dreaded that happening . . . or did I?

What had he said about a prim schoolmistress? Was I one? I supposed I was to some extent. My post made me so and I should get more so every day. I saw myself years ahead – white-haired, dignified like Daisy Hetherington . . . and as efficient. I could be sure of that, even though I did have my foolish moments. Had Daisy ever . . . ?

Alone with my thoughts I could at moments be honest. He was right. There was another woman beneath the schoolmistress. He knew she was there and he had done his best to release her. Yet he had been halted in his determination by the sight of a little blood. There had been a concern, a tenderness . . . Oh, how foolish. I was trying to make excuses for him.

Stop thinking of him, I admonished myself. And never give him such an opportunity again.

It was three days after the incident. My wounds were healing thanks to the prompt treatment I had received and the lotion Mrs Keel had given me. I felt calmer, getting more in command of myself, telling myself that I had given up to foolish emotions because I had been overwrought.

I saw him now as he was – an arrogant sensual rake who thought any woman who appealed to him was fair game.

Not this one, I said to myself firmly.

I went into the town and called at the post office to buy stamps. Mrs Baddicombe was serving someone but she looked up with pleasure at the sight of me.

She finished serving and waited until the bell over the shop door rang as the customer left.

'Well, Miss Grant, it is nice to see 'ee. How's the hands? I heard about your accident. Nasty, wasn't it?'

I flushed slightly. Did the woman know everything?

'They're getting better,' I said. 'It wasn't very much.'

'And is all well with the young ladies? Have you heard the news?'

'News? What news?'

'She be gone . . . disappeared . . . gone clean away.'

'Who would that be?'

'That Mrs Martindale, of course.'

'Where has she gone?'

'That's what we'd like to know.'

'I believe she pays frequent visits to London.'

'Well, this time she be gone for good and all.'

'How do you know?'

'The house be all shut up and Mrs Keel at the Hall has sent servants down to clean it up. They do say Gerald Coverdale be going to move in. That house of his ain't big enough now he be married with two children. They say he have had his eyes on it for some time. It can only mean she's gone for good.'

'But how can you be *sure*?'

'I had her what does for the Coverdales in here only this morning. She says Sir Jason has told 'em they can move in when they like. I do wonder what's happened to *her* . . . hat Mrs Martindale.'

'I don't think she can have gone off just like that.'

Mrs Baddicombe lifted her shoulders. 'There's no knowing. She was got rid of fast.'

There was speculation in Mrs Baddicombe's inquisitive little eyes and I felt I could not remain in her shop. I wanted

243

to get away to think about what she had said. What was she hinting?

I said quietly and quickly: 'I expect we shall know in due course. I just wanted some stamps, please Mrs Baddicombe. I have to get back quickly.'

I came out into the sunshine. A sudden fear had seized me. Why? Surely if Marcia Martindale wanted to leave in a hurry, there was nothing in that to arouse my concern.

*   *   *

Miss Hetherington called a conference to discuss what she grandiloquently called 'The Pageant'. She reminded us all that time was short and it would be most effective if it took place on Midsummer's Eve. That left us about a month for preparation, which was not long, but she did not care for these things to go on too long because they had a way of interfering with school work, as we had seen recently in the case of Cinderella.

'We have some costumes,' she said. 'Those which have been used in previous pageants, and Sir Jason Verringer has promised to lend us others. Naturally we must have monks . . . and some of the seniors can take those parts. The smaller girls will look incongruous in the habits. We shall do the usual three-act piece. The beginning leading to the Dissolution; the Elizabethan age and revival; and today with the school. All the girls can take part in singing the school song, etc. If it is warm and fine it will take place out of doors. There will be a full moon, which is ideal. The ruins will make a wonderful setting. I hope and pray it will not be wet. Then it will have to be in the refectory hall or perhaps Sir Jason would offer us the ball-room at the Hall. That is really very suitable but I should have to wait for him to offer. Mr Crowe, you could get down to work on the singing. There should be quite a lot of that so that everyone can join in. Miss Eccles, you could do the settings, and Miss Grant of course will choose the pieces for recitation and direct the players. Miss Parker, I think for the final part they might do a few attractive physical exercises. We could have a few folk dances, Mr Bathurst. We must make an

244

interesting evening and, if it is a success, we could repeat the highlights just before break-up when the parents could come. Not many of them would want to make the journey in mid-term even to see their offspring perform. The thing is to get into action without delay. Any questions?'

There were a few and there was no talk of anything else in the school but the pageant. I threw myself into it with fervour, trying to forget those alarming yet stimulating moments in the Devil's Den. I knew that he had been on the verge of treating me barbarously and I continued to be amazed that the sight of my injuries had had such an immediate effect on him and brought out that little decency which must be in him. Perhaps he had really believed until then that I had *wanted* him to seize me, to possess me as he had clearly threatened to do. Perhaps I did. Yet, I had made that desperate gesture, almost without thinking, for it would have been quite impossible for me to have escaped by the window.

I could not forget it. It was there in my dreams.

And now Marcia Martindale had gone. What could that mean?

He called at the school and was closeted with Miss Hetherington in her study. I was summoned with Eileen Eccles. I avoided looking at him as much as possible. He asked about my hands and I told him they were recovering fast. We talked about the pageant, and I believe I was quite cool and certainly aloof. He tried to make me look at him and it was always as though he were pleading for forgiveness.

Daisy went to the gates to see him off and during the next days I did not go out riding alone. I was afraid of meeting him and I kept reminding myself that I must never again be alone with him.

I learned from Teresa that the new maid, Elsa, was voted 'very jolly' by most of the girls. She was not like the others. She never complained about untidy bedrooms and, when she knew that Miss Hetherington was going to make an inspection, she had hastened into Charlotte's room and tidied up. They thought that was 'very sporting'.

245

She seemed to like that threesome particularly and was always gossiping with Fiona, Eugenie and Charlotte. I was surprised, for Charlotte was not the sort to talk to servants but evidently even she had been won over by Elsa.

'I remember her well,' I told Teresa. 'She was like that at Schaffenbrucken, a great favourite with the girls.'

It must have been about a week after the departure of Marcia Martindale that the rumours started. Mrs Baddicombe, I was sure, had kept up her comments on the strangeness of the situation, and when one of the baker's boys delivering to the post office told her that he had driven his cart past Rooks' Rest and seen a lady standing at the door with a child in her arms, Mrs Baddicombe was determined to wring as much drama as she could from the situation.

The lady seen by the boy was probably Mrs Coverdale who had a young child, and it was quite natural that she should be at the door holding her youngest child in her arms.

However, Mrs Baddicombe would not accept such a simple explanation.

'Poor Tom Yeo! He was struck all of a heap. Said his hair stood on end. She was surrounded by a misty light, and she held up her hands as though calling for help.'

'I hope she didn't drop the child,' I said. 'And why didn't Tom Yeo go to help her or at least see what she wanted?'

'Why, bless you, Miss Grant, have you ever come face to face with that what's not natural?'

'No,' I admitted.

'If you had, you'd understand. Poor Tom, he just whipped up his horse and got off fast as he could.'

'But the Coverdales have moved in, haven't they?'

'Not yet they ain't. Like as not won't want to now.'

'Mrs Baddicombe, what are you thinking?'

'Well, she did go rather sudden, didn't she?'

'Mrs Baddicombe,' I said seriously. 'You ought to be careful.'

She drew herself up and looked at me suspiciously. 'Careful? Me? Ain't I always careful?'

246

'I'd like to know what you're hinting.'

'Plain as the nose on your face, Miss. She comes here . . . and then when she's not wanted no more . . . she goes.'

'Not wanted?'

Mrs Baddicombe smirked. 'I read between the lines . . .' she said.

'And compose the script,' I added angrily.

She looked at me blankly.

'Good day, Mrs Baddicombe,' I said.

I was trembling as I stood outside the shop. I thought how foolish I had been. I should now be cut off from the information she had to offer; and although half of it might be false, I wanted to hear what was said.

The extent of my foolishness was obvious when Eileen Eccles met me in the calefactory and said: 'You're becoming involved in the dramas of Colby, Cordelia. The Sibyl of the post office whispered to me that she thinks you are "sweet on" Sir Jason Verringer, and she has known for some time that he had his eyes on you, and ain't it a funny thing that poor Mrs Martindale, who has had her hopes raised for so long, should, as if by magic, disappear when she is not wanted.'

'What nonsense!' I said flushing scarlet.

'The trouble with that sort of talk is that it often has an element of truth in it. I certainly think the libidinous Sir J. has had his eyes on you, and there is no doubt that at one time Mrs Martindale was his very good friend. So far so good. On this flimsy foundation Mrs B. weaves her fantasies. Nonsense, yes, but founded on a certain fact, and that is where the danger lies.'

'You're warning me,' I said.

She put her head on one side and regarded me with mock seriousness. 'You know best what you want to do,' she said. 'All I can say is that he has a reputation of sorts. There were rumours about his wife's death. Now there are rumours about the disappearance, as they call it, of his lady friend. He is rumour-prone, and in our profession rumour can kill careers. I would advise . . . but I expect that you know as well as I do that advice is something to be given

247

freely and taken only if it suits the recipient's inclinations. I'd keep away from him, and after the summer holidays it may have died down.'

I looked fondly at Eileen. She was a good friend and a sensible woman. I wanted to tell her that I needed no warning. I had decided never to be alone with Jason Verringer again.

*   *   *

Miss Hetherington summoned me to her study. She was so disturbed that she was unable to hide it completely and was slightly less than her usual unruffled self.

'A disgraceful display!' she said. 'I've sent for you, Cordelia, because Teresa is your special protégée.'

'Teresa! What has she done?'

'She has attacked another girl.'

'Attacked!'

'Indeed yes. Physically . . . attacked!'

'What girl? Why?'

'The girl in question is Charlotte Mackay. The reason neither of them will say. I expect it is some trivial disagreement, but that a pupil of mine should actually resort to violence . . .'

'I can't believe that of Teresa. She is really rather gentle.'

'She has been more assertive of late. She threw a shoe at Charlotte Mackay which hit her above the temple. There is quite a deep cut. The girls were frightened when they saw blood and called Miss Parker who happened to be passing.'

'Where are they now?'

'Charlotte is lying down. Fortunately it missed her eye. Heaven knows what damage might have been done. As it is, thank God, it is only a cut. Teresa is locked in the punishment room. I shall decide her punishment later. But what shocks me is that there could be such behaviour here. I only hope the parents don't hear of it.'

'Shall I go and see Teresa?'

'She is very sullen and refuses to say anything. She sits there with her lips tightly shut having said that Charlotte deserved it.'

248

'Charlotte is, of course, a very aggravating girl. Her character is not the most pleasant and I know that in the past she has teased Teresa a good deal.'

'The girl never attacked her before.'

'No . . .'

'She's got a lot more spirit than she had, and I thought that was a good thing. Now . . . I'm not so sure. Yes, go and see her, and try to find out the reason for this extraordinary and unacceptable conduct.'

I unlocked the door of the punishment room. It was a small cell-like place which had been used for storage by the lay brothers. The rather repelling name suited it. There were three desks there and a table and chair. Girls were sent there to learn or write lines, and it was used when an offence was considered more than a venial one.

Teresa was sitting at one of the desks.

'Teresa!' I cried.

She stood up uncertainly and looked at me almost defiantly.

'Tell me about it,' I said. 'I'm sure there is an explanation.'

'I hate Charlotte Mackay,' she said.

'You don't really. She's just a silly arrogant girl most of the time.'

'I hate her,' she said. 'She's wicked.'

'Tell me exactly what happened.'

She was silent.

'Miss Hetherington wants an explanation, you know.'

Still she was silent.

'There must be a reason. Was it perhaps some little thing, and you remembered all your anger with her in the past . . . ? Was it the last straw?'

She said: 'It wasn't little.'

'What was it then?'

Again that silence.

'Perhaps if you could explain, Miss Hetherington would understand. She is just, you know. If you have a good reason she will realize that for the moment you lost control. We all know how trying Charlotte can be.'

249

But she would not tell me. I tried again and again but although I was sure of her affection for me I could get nothing out of her.

'She's wicked,' was all she would say. 'She's wicked and a liar and I hate her. I'm glad I did it.'

'Don't tell Miss Hetherington that. You must be penitent and say you're sorry and you must never do such a thing again. I daresay you'll have some lines to write after this. You'll probably have to spend all day tomorrow here doing your penance.'

'I don't care. I'm glad I hurt her.'

I sighed. That was not the right attitude, and I was very disconcerted that Teresa refused to tell even me what had happened.

I had to go back to Daisy and admit defeat.

*   *   *

Uneasy days passed. Charlotte made the most of her injury. Once I went to her bedroom and found Fiona and Eugenie there with Elsa. They were sitting on the beds laughing.

It was hard to reprove them when I remembered that only a short time ago I might have figured in such a scene at Schaffenbrucken.

I continued to avoid Jason Verringer but I did go out alone sometimes. When I rode into the town I took a long route round so that I did not go too near the Hall. This led me past Rooks' Rest. I saw signs of activity there and guessed the Coverdales were moving in.

I hesitated about going into the post office but should have to do so one day, and the time came when I boldly went in. Mrs Baddicombe was overjoyed to see me. She showed no rancour over my coldness during our previous encounter. She kept me waiting until she had served two customers and then gave me that lively curious look and leaned over the counter with an air of intimacy.

'Nice to see you, Miss Grant. I hear there's to be grand doings up at the school with that pageant.'

250

'Oh yes,' I replied. 'It's the anniversary of the building of the Abbey so a rather special occasion.'

'Fancy that! All them years ago. I was saying to Mrs Taylor when she was in this morning that I wondered how the little mite Miranda was getting on. Happy enough, I'll bet. That Jane Gittings dotes on her and so does Ada Whalley.'

'Who is Ada Whalley?'

'Jane's sister. The Whalleys lived here in Colby for years. Old Billy Whalley was manager of the cider place. Did well for himself. Brought up on the moors he were and the girls was with their grandmother there when they was little. When he retired he went to the cottage on the moors. His mother was dead then. Jane had married Gittings and Ada went with him to keep house for him. Down at Bristonleigh, it was, right on the edge of the Moor. They was always talking about the Moor, those Whalleys were. Percy Billings was sweet on Ada at one time, but nothing came of it because she had to look after the old man and then Percy all of a sudden marries Jenny Markey.'

'Quite a little saga.'

'Well so it be, me dear. Ada would have made a good mother. I'll reckon she'll look after that little Miranda, her and Jane Gittings between them. Jane didn't have no children neither. Funny how some 'as 'em and some don't . . . and it's more likely them that don't want them as gets them. Look at Sophie Prestwick. Easy to see what she's been up to. There'll have to be a quick wedding there, mark my words. So Sophie larks about and gets caught . . . and them that wants 'em can't get 'em. Take Sir Jason for instance . . .'

She was looking at me slyly.

I told her what stamps I wanted, and almost reluctantly she took out her folder and gave them to me.

'Well, be seeing things won't we, now the lady in the case has passed on, you might say.'

'Passed on?'

'We don't know where to, do we? All we know is that she ain't with us now. I'll tell you one thing, Miss Grant,

251

nothing stands still does it? Life moves on. I often say to myself: well, I wonder what next?'

'You seem to be well informed on everything that goes on,' I said ironically.

'It's in the nature of the post office, you might say. As I always say to Baddicombe: There's not much to this job . . . you work hard and you don't get much . . . but I says to him, I says: There's people . . . and that's what makes it worthwhile.'

She raised her eyes and with the air of a benefactress to mankind, put her folder in a drawer.

I went out feeling relieved that she had shown no displeasure and wondered whether at our last meeting she had even grasped my disapproval.

In the afternoon I went for a walk through the ruins, keeping a wary eye out for Jason Verringer in case he had decided to take a walk there. He might easily do so for I guessed he was trying to catch me, and would do so sooner or later.

I came to the ponds and looked at their waters rushing to the falls as they reached their lower depths. They made a soothing sound and I walked along beside them to the river and then started to wander along its bank.

I realized that I must turn back or be late so I retraced my steps and, as I came in sight of the fishponds, I saw Teresa.

I called to her and she came running towards me.

'Are you taking a walk too?' I asked.

'Yes. I saw you coming this way.'

'We have to start back now. I mustn't be late for class, nor must you. Did you manage your lines?'

'Oh yes. I had to learn "Once more unto the breach" right down to "God for Harry, England and St George".'

'Quite a long piece.'

'I knew most of it already.'

'Oh, Teresa, I'm sorry that happened. Are you sure you don't want to talk about it?'

She nodded firmly.

I sighed. 'I thought you might have felt you could confide in me.'

252

She remained silent and a look of mulish obstinacy crossed her face.

We walked in silence.

'Have you a part in the pageant?' I asked.

'No. Well, only at the end . . . doing exercises and singing the school song. Miss Grant . . . there is something I want to ask you.'

I breathed a sigh of relief. I thought: Now she is going to tell me what Charlotte had done to offend her so deeply.

'Well, Teresa?'

'It's hard to say because I think you like him . . . I think you like him quite a lot.'

'Who? What do you mean?'

'It's about Mrs Martindale.'

I felt my voice shake a little as I said: 'What about her?'

'I – I think she's dead. I – I think she was murdered.'

'Teresa! How can you say such a thing. You really mustn't'

'I haven't told anyone else.'

'I should hope not.'

She stopped and putting her hand in her pocket held it out to me. As the fingers unclosed I saw an earring. It was so bizarre and colourful that I immediately recognized it.

'It was hers,' she said. 'I saw her wearing it.'

'Well?'

'I found it here . . . by the ponds . . . It must have come off . . . in a struggle.'

'My dear Teresa, you are imagining too much. You're like Mrs Baddicombe.'

'It's her earring. I know because Eugenie had it to return to her not long ago. She showed it to us then. I found this . . down there by the water . . . She must have dropped it.'

'Well, she dropped it. She lost it. People do lose earrings and the fact that she lost this one before shows that there was something faulty about it.'

'I think this dropped off when she was thrown into the river.'

'Teresa! What has come over you? First you attack

253

Charlotte Mackay and now you are making these wild accusations about . . . about whom, Teresa?'

'About him. I'm afraid you like him, Miss Grant. I know that women are supposed to. But don't . . . I – I . . . can't bear it that he should . . . talk to you . . . and bring you into all this. It spoils everything . . . all the fun we have with Aunt Patty and Violet. Miss Grant, please don't take any notice of him. He's a wicked man. Eugenie says . . .'

'Have you said anything to anyone about this, Teresa?'

She shook her head violently.

'Promise me you won't'

She nodded firmly.

'It's nonsense,' I went on. 'There is a lot of evil gossip. Mrs Martindale left because she was tired of the country.'

'Why didn't she *say* she was going?'

'Why should she? It was no concern of anyone but herself. No doubt she told anyone who would be concerned.'

'Oh, Miss Grant, don't be in it. Let them do what they like, but let *us* stay away from it. Let's think about the summer and the bees and the flowers and Aunt Patty's hats and Violet's apple pies.'

'Teresa, calm down,' I said. 'You are imagining all this. I shouldn't be surprised if Mrs Martindale came back.'

'She can't. He wouldn't have her. He's finished with her now. That's what he's like. He casts off people when he's finished with them . . . and kills them. There was his first wife.'

'This is all so much gossip.'

'It's true.'

'No.'

'It *is* true,' said Teresa, 'and I'm afraid. I don't want you –'

I put my arm round her. 'I am not concerned in this,' I said soothingly. 'This man is nothing to do with us. He just happens to own the Abbey lands, that's all. Everything is as it was before. You're coming home with me for the summer holidays and we'll have a wonderful time.'

'Oh yes . . . yes.'

'Make sure you don't do anything that might make Miss Hetherington angry. She might decide to punish you by keeping you at school.'

Teresa had turned white.

I said quickly: 'Oh, she wouldn't do that. But don't run the risk. And, Teresa, not a word of this to anyone. It's not true . . . but it would be wrong to talk of it. You haven't, have you?'

'Oh no, no.'

'And that earring . . .'

She held out her palm. It lay there, the ruby a vivid red glistening in the sunshine.

I wondered what should be done with it and what effect it would have if people knew it had been found by the fish ponds.

I did not have to wonder long for with a quick movement Teresa lifted her arm and flung the earring into the water.

Shocked, I turned to her. 'Teresa,' I cried. 'Why did you do that?'

'It's all over,' she said. 'Don't let's say any more about it. I won't . . . if you don't.'

I felt very disturbed and at the same time relieved that I did not have to take some action about the earring.

Quietly we walked back to school. I thought Teresa seemed calmer and happier than she had since the affair with Charlotte.

Midsummer Moon

*

I was haunted by doubts. I found sleep impossible. How had the earring come to be down there by the fish ponds? Only if the owner had been there.

She might have walked to the fish ponds. It was some way from Rooks' Rest and I had never seen her out walking; she was not the sort of person to take long tramps in the countryside.

Just suppose she was dead. Suppose she *was* murdered. What of Maisie? Where was she? Were the scandal-mongers suggesting that she too had been murdered? Perhaps the idea of one body being thrown into the ponds was plausible. But two? I remembered then that Jason Verringer had told me how an ancestor of his had once disposed of a rival by throwing his body into the fish ponds after killing him. 'The river is swift running and only a few miles from the sea.' He had said something like that.

And then the child? What of the child? She was in the care of Mrs Gittings on Dartmoor, but she could not stay there indefinitely without arrangements being made.

It was a lot of nonsense. It had its roots in the post office and had grown to this through other mischief-makers. But Jason Verringer was ruthless. He had shown me that clearly enough. Other people were only important to him when they could give him what he wanted. He could contemplate rape. Why not then murder? He had obviously been attracted to Marcia Martindale at one time, since he had offered her a home at Rooks' Rest. And then there was the child. He had certainly been a little casual about her. But at least he had offered them a home.

I wondered about the child and the more I thought of it the more strongly I decided I must find out all I could and

256

that if I could see Mrs Gittings – who seemed to me a very reasonable and practical person – I might learn a good deal. If I did discover that this was all nonsense I would make sure that everyone in the neighbourhood knew and I would put a stop to this pernicious gossip.

The more I thought of it, the more possible it seemed. I had heard the name of the place where Mrs Gittings' sister lived. Perhaps something like this had been at the back of my mind for I had memorized the names. Mrs Gittings' sister was Ada Whalley and she lived at a place called Bristonleigh on Dartmoor. That was not very far from here, probably a matter of about fifteen miles.

Why not? The more I thought of it, the better the idea seemed.

I said to Daisy: 'On Sunday I should like to go and see a friend of mine who lives on Dartmoor, but I am not quite sure of the locality.'

'Sunday is a day, I suppose, when you could easily get away. I am sure you could arrange for one of the others to take over any duties you might have.'

'Yes, I am sure I could. I wonder if you have a map. I should like to see where it is exactly.'

'There are several. I'll show you.'

Bristonleigh was not marked on the first, but she had a map of Dartmoor and its environs – and there it was. It was clearly a small hamlet right on the edge of the moor. I made a note of the nearest town.

I should have to go there and take some sort of conveyance to this place, I supposed.

'There is one train which leaves here at ten thirty,' said Daisy. 'And the one which would bring you back doesn't pass through until four. That should give you a little time with your friends.'

'I'll try it. It will be an experiment.'

And so it was that I found myself speeding through the lush Devon countryside on that Sunday morning.

The journey was only half an hour and when I arrived at the station and asked the porter how I could get to Bristonleigh, he was a little dubious, but only for a moment. 'It's

257

three miles from here . . . uphill a bit. But I reckon Dick Cramm wouldn't mind earning a bit extra of a Sunday. He'd be just about up and about. He likes a bit of a lay-in on Sundays. But he be ready in case we gets calls, which we don't often.'

'Where can I find him?'

'Go through the yard. Turn to the right. You'll see his place. Crabtree Cottage with a great crab apple tree beside it. That's where it gets it name.'

I thanked him and went off in search of Dick Cramm who fortunately was up and fresh from his Sunday morning 'lay-in' and quite ready to take me to Bristonleigh.

'I want to see Miss Ada Whalley,' I said.

'Oh, she be a fine lady, Miss Ada Whalley.'

'You know her then?'

'Know her? Who don't know Miss Ada Whalley in these parts! She do grow the best vegetables round here. My wife has some . . . so does most. Some of 'em goes up to London for folks up there. I goes and gets them and puts them on the train for her. Oh yes, I know Miss Ada Whalley.'

This was great good fortune. I had imagined myself prowling the streets of Bristonleigh looking for Miss Ada Whalley.

'She do have her sister living with her now,' he went on. 'That be nice for her. She was saying so only the other day when I took down a load of greens. She said: " 'Tis nice having my sister with me." Poor soul. I reckon she were lonely before.'

We came to Bristonleigh. It was a beautiful village typical of England and especially of Devon where the vegetation seems to be more lush than anywhere else in the country. There was the old church, the village green, a few houses, mostly eighteenth century except the Elizabethan Manor House on the common. The church clock chimed twelve just as we entered the village.

'Miss Whalley, her's a bit apart from the rest. She's got bit of land for her growing things, you see. We'll be there in a few minutes.'

258

'I shall have to catch the train back. It's half past three isn't it?'

'That's so, Miss.'

'Will you come and pick me up and take me to the station?'

'That I will. Reckon I should be with you just before three. That all right for you, Miss?'

'It would suit me very well. Thank you so much. I am so glad I found you.'

He scratched his head and stared straight in front of him but I knew he was well pleased.

'Here's the house. I'd better wait. Make sure they're in like. Not that they're likely to go away without us knowing.'

I thought then how little there was country people did not know about each other. Of course in some cases they put the wrong construction on, but none could accuse them of indifference to their neighbours' lives.

I paid him and gave him a little extra which faintly embarrassed him but pleased him all the same.

'You have been especially helpful,' I said.

' 'Tweren't nothing. Oh, here be Mrs Gittings with the little 'un.'

And there, as though to make my venture smoother than I had dared hope was Mrs Gittings, emerging from the house holding Miranda by the hand.

'Miss Grant!' she cried.

I went hastily to her. I was aware of the driver watching intently so I turned to him and said 'Thank you. I'll see you just before three o'clock.'

He touched his cap with his whip and turned the horses.

'I must explain,' I said.

'Oh, Miss Grant. I *am* surprised to see you. Have you come all this way to see me and Miranda?'

'I heard you were here with your sister, and Mrs Baddicombe told me her name and where she lived. So this is where you always come with Miranda?'

'Yes. Did you want to . . . ?'

'To talk to you.'

259

Miranda was gazing at me with curiosity.

'She looks very well,' I said.

'It suits her. She's happy here.'

Mrs Gittings must have guessed that I was wary of talking before the child. She would be able to understand certain things and I did not want to say anything that would bewilder her.

'Come along in and meet my sister. We are having our midday meal early for Miranda. She sleeps for a couple of hours after. My sister will be pleased to see you. Then . . . we can talk.'

I guessed she meant when Miranda went to sleep, and was grateful for her tact.

Miss Ada Whalley had come out, hearing voices, to see who had arrived. She was a big-boned woman with muscular shoulders and her face was tanned by the weather.

'This is Miss Grant from the school, Ada,' said Mrs Gittings. 'You know . . . the school at the Abbey.'

'Oh, that's nice,' said Ada.

'She's come to have a talk . . .' She nodded towards Miranda and Ada nodded back.

'I reckon,' said Mrs Gittings, 'that Miss Grant could well do with a spot of dinner.'

'I'm sorry to have come unannounced,' I said. 'I didn't quite know what to do and I thought Mrs Gittings might help me.'

'That's all right,' said Ada. 'We're used to people dropping in from the village, you know. They like to sample my stuff, they say. I've no objection. All home-grown.'

'Even the pig,' said Mrs Gittings.

'He's little Piggy Porker,' announced Miranda.

'No, pet, little Piggy Porker is with his mam, gobbling away. He's the greediest one in the litter.'

Miranda grunted in imitation of a pig and looked shyly at me as though for admiration.

'Oh dear,' said Ada, 'it sounds to me as if little Piggy Porker has got in here somewhere.'

Miranda grunted and Ada pretended to look round in alarm. Miranda obviously thought it was a great joke. One

260

thing was immediately clear. With these two, she would not be missing her mother.

'I'll take Miss Grant to wash her hands,' said Ada.

I followed her up a wooden staircase to a room in which was a wash basin and ewer. Everything was so clean that it seemed to shine.

'You get a good view of the gardens from the back here,' said Ada, and I looked out over the rows of growing things. There were two greenhouses and a potting shed.

'And you do all this yourself?'

'I've got a man to help. I'll have to get another by the way business is growing. Now Jane's here it's a help. She does a lot in the house. And you've come to talk with Jane. I hope you're not going to tempt her away. It's such company to have her here and I've always wanted us to be together.'

'I haven't come to tempt her away. I just want to talk to her, to clear up a few mysteries.'

When I had washed my hands she took me down. Mrs Gittings was laying the table and Miranda was making a great show of helping her. There was a savoury smell of roasting pork coming from the oven and an air of supreme contentment in the little room in which we sat down to eat. The vegetables were delicious.

'Straight from the ground,' said Ada. 'That's the way to eat vegetables.'

'If you are fortunate enough to be able to do so,' I added.

'Now have some more of these potatoes, Miss Grant. It was a good crop this year, and I will say this for Jane, she knows how to cook. I used to be a bit slapdash myself. Jane will have none of that. She's a bit of an old tartar, ain't she, pet?'

She had a habit of seeking confirmation from Miranda to which the child responded with a wise nod.

Miranda was seated in a high chair enveloped in a huge bib and was feeding herself with results which were not too disastrous. When food failed to reach her mouth, Ada would laugh and shovel it in. 'This little bit lost its way. He didn't know he had to go down the red lane, did he, pet?'

'He didn't know, did he?' said Miranda with glee.

261

In due course the meal was over and Miranda was whisked off for her nap. Ada tactfully said she wanted to have a look at the greenhouses and that left me alone with Jane Gittings.

I said: 'I hope you don't mind my coming like this. It seems something of an imposition.'

'It's been a pleasure. Ada likes visitors. It's a treat for her to see people enjoy what she grows.'

'She is a wonderful person, I can see. Mrs Gittings, there is a great deal of gossip in Colby. People are saying the most extraordinary things.'

'It's that post woman.'

'I think she is at the heart of it. It was mysterious, wasn't it? I want to put a stop to the gossip, but I don't know how to. If I could discover what really happened . . . or where Mrs Martindale is and get her to come back and show herself or something . . .'

'It's difficult for me to say, Miss Grant, as I know no more than you do where she is.'

'But there is the child.'

'Sir Jason takes care of that.'

'Sir Jason then . . .'

'He always did. He asked if I would take the child to my sister and look after her. He'd pay me for looking after her and the child's keep . . . only he wanted us to go to my sister. Well, I knew what Ada would say to that. She's always wanted me to leave and go in with her and she loves Miranda. I said to Sir Jason that there'd be no troubles about that as far as Ada was concerned.'

'So he asked you to take her away. That would be a few days before Mrs Martindale left.'

'That would be it. When she went away I always took Miranda to Ada's. It was understood like. It was the day after Maisie went.'

'After Maisie went . . . ?' I repeated.

'Yes, she left. There was a terrible to-do . . . and the next day Maisie was off. She took most of Mrs Martindale's things with her, dresses and things like that. There wasn't much left when she went. I never knew the rights of it and

262

I'm not one to have my ears glued to keyholes. All I knew was that they were going on at each other. Then Maisie goes off and Sir Jason asked me to take Miranda to Ada's.'

I was filled with a horrible apprehension. 'So Maisie went . . . and then you left.'

'That's right. So you see I can't tell you what happened after that. I was right glad to get away. Mrs Martindale and that Maisie used to go for one another something shocking. I used to think Miranda would hear. Oh, I was glad to get away. Mrs Martindale never minded my going. She'd get a girl in from the village to do the rough. I never did none of that, anyway. It was the child who was my concern, though I did give a hand in the house, not being the sort to stand by and do nothing when there's things to be done.'

I wasn't listening. One thought was going round and round in my head. Maisie had gone, and after that he had asked Mrs Gittings to take the child away.

I heard myself say: 'The Coverdales . . . you remember them . . . they are living at Rooks' Rest, so it is obvious . . . she is not coming back.'

'Oh, I thought it might be something like that because Sir Jason said I was to take Miranda and the money would be paid to me here, and when she was five, which wouldn't be for some time yet, he'd make arrangements for her schooling. But she was to be in my sole care. Oh, I thought, so Madam is moving out. That means he'd done with her. Well, funny things always did go on there, and right glad I am to be out of it. Sir Jason said to me, "I know you're to be trusted, Mrs Gittings. There is no one who can look after the child as you do." A slap at her, if you ask me. Not that she cared. She never showed a blind bit of interest in the child. She didn't want her. Only wanted to show him that she could have them. There was all that talk about him not having an heir and all that. It's no way to bring children into the world, Miss Grant.'

'I'm not in the least concerned about Miranda's welfare,' I said. 'I agree that she is in good hands and I am sure Sir Jason is right. She is happiest with you and your sister loves her. I can see that.'

'I'm glad you think so, Miss Grant. I was afraid when I saw you that you had come with a message for me to take Miranda back. You'll tell Sir Jason how happy she is here, won't you?'

'If I see him, I certainly will. I really came to know if you had any idea why Mrs Martindale left so suddenly.'

'You could never tell with her . . . and after Maisie had gone off in a huff with all her fine dresses, I reckon she couldn't stand the country any more. She was always talking about London.'

I decided to be absolutely frank.

'There are rumours . . . hints. They aren't true, of course, but people do wonder why she went so suddenly. Did she say anything about leaving Rooks' Rest?'

'She was always talking about leaving. There was nothing more than usual.'

'Did she have any visitors?'

'Sir Jason came. Oh, I remember. There was a terrible scene. It was a few days before Maisie went off. Mrs Martindale was shouting and he was telling her to be quiet. Maisie was listening at the door. I caught her at it. I said, "You oughtn't by rights to be doing that." "Don't be silly," she said. "How am I going to know what's what, if I don't." She was laughing. Then she said, "I reckon this cosy little nook won't be ours much longer." I went away. It was soon after that I saw Sir Jason. He was riding by as if by chance and I was taking Miranda for her walk. He called to me and said, "Mrs Gittings, would you be prepared to take Miranda to your sister and stay there indefinitely." I was so shook up I couldn't take it in. And there he was seated on his horse looking down at me and making all those plans. I was to make my arrangements immediately; the money would be sent to me regularly every month and it would be paid in advance. If there was anything Miranda needed, I should tell him direct. Did I think my sister would be agreeable? I told him my sister would be jumping with joy. He looked very pleased and said, "I'm grateful to you, Mrs Gittings. You've solved a big problem."'

'What did Mrs Martindale say when you told her?'

'She shrugged her shoulders and made no objections. So I set about packing and we went. You should have seen Ada's face – because I hadn't had time to tell her. She kept saying, "Well, I never" over and over again. Then she hugged Miranda and said, "Wonders will never cease, will they, pet?" And she was half crying with joy. Ada did feel it, being on her own since our father died.'

'I think Miranda is very fortunate to have you both. I know. I myself have a beloved aunt who gave me the love a child needs when she is growing up. But what I really wanted to know is what happened to Mrs Martindale.'

'She must have gone away soon after we left.'

'Didn't she say she was going? Didn't she make arrangements?'

'She never told me she was going. She didn't say anything about plans.'

I began to feel sick with fear. My meeting with Mrs Gittings had only increased my suspicions.

'I can't tell you how happy I am to be here, Miss Grant,' she went on. 'It was no bed of roses with Mrs Martindale. She was a very wild sort of lady at some times. We were all rather nervous of her, even Maisie who could stand up to her. The times she told Maisie to get out! But Maisie seemed to have some hold over her. I'm surprised she went because, however much they quarrelled, they always made it up. I suppose that last time was just too much. Maisie always used to say they were on to a good thing. Sir Jason and all that . . .'

'It seems so strange that she should go so suddenly.'

'It is and then it isn't. You could never be sure with Mrs Martindale.'

We went on talking but I could discover nothing more. Dick Cramm came to collect me, and Ada came in from the greenhouses and said how pleased she was to have met me.

On the way back I thought of all that had been said and I was very uneasy.

*   *   *

265

I knew it would be impossible to go on avoiding Jason. He was determined to catch me and it was inevitable that he should eventually do so.

This happened four days after my visit to Bristonleigh.

I had two hours' break and I took out one of the horses. He caught up with me near the woods not far from Rooks' Rest. In fact I think he must have been coming from there.

'You've been avoiding me, Cordelia,' he said reproachfully.

His effrontery was amazing and I couldn't help laughing.

'Did you imagine I would do anything else?' I asked.

'No . . . after my appalling conduct the last time we were alone together. I've been trying to catch you to ask your forgiveness.'

'You surprise me.'

'Well then, am I forgiven?'

'I don't want to see you again. Don't you realize that you have insulted me?'

'Insulted you? On the contrary I have paid you the highest compliment a man can pay to a woman.'

'Don't talk nonsense,' I said and spurred on my horse.

But of course he was beside me.

'Please let me explain. I have come to ask you to marry me.'

I laughed again.

'Without my credentials,' I said. 'You are very rash.'

'By no means. I have given the matter great thought. I want you . . . and only you will do.'

'That's rather unfortunate for you. Goodbye.'

'I never take no for an answer.'

'You must remember it takes two to make a marriage. Perhaps your ancestors of whom you seem so proud used to drag their brides to the altar and force them at knife point to utter their vows . . . but that wouldn't work today.'

'We never did such things. Where did you get such an idea? We have always been the most eligible *partis* in the neighbourhood and females have schemed to inveigle us into matrimony.'

'This is all nonsense. I don't like you. I don't trust you.

266

You behaved to me in a barbarous manner and the only way in which you can earn my forgiveness is to get out of my sight and never let me see you again.'

'Alas, it appears I must do without your forgiveness.'

'I want nothing to do with you. I do not care to be thought of as having any connection with you. I shall be grateful if you will leave me alone.'

'That is not easy for two reasons. One the school pageant and the worthy Miss Hetherington. The other and even more insurmountable is that I am besotted about you.'

'Then find someone else quickly on whom to lavish your devotion. Where is Mrs Martindale?'

'In London, I think.'

'Are you completely insensitive? Do you know what is being said about her . . . and you?'

'I'll guess. I murdered her. Is that it?'

'That is the implication. Did you?'

He laughed at me. 'Good God! What a question. So you think I am a murderer, do you?'

'I saw a very ugly side of your nature not very long ago.'

'Dear Cordelia, I love you. I was trying to make you happy.'

'You are amused. I do not see what happened as a joke.'

'You would have been so happy. We would have sent that prim schoolmistress packing. We would have made plans. It would have been wonderful. I should have shown you a new Cordelia.'

'You have a great opinion of yourself. I do not share it. Nor I believe do others.'

'I wish you would give yourself a chance to know me.'

'I don't think from what I already know that it would be a pleasant experience.'

'Listen to me. I don't know where she is. She's gone. That's all that concerns me. You are too hard on me. You think the worst of me always. You have right from the start when I ordered your carriage to go back.'

'That was a typical gesture. It is how you treat people all the time.'

'Cordelia, let me try to make you understand. I know I

267

give the impression of being arrogant and selfish. I am. But I could be different with you. You could change me. We could be good together . . . because I'd change you too. I'd open your eyes, Cordelia. I feel alive just talking to you. I love the way you lash me with your tongue. They certainly taught you verbal sparring at Schaffenbrucken. I am what I am because of my environment. It was the way I was brought up. I want children to be heirs to my estate. That's natural isn't it? I don't want to go on as I have been doing. I want someone to help me become what I want to be. I know that is you. I have told you something of my child-hood. It was not a happy one. My brother and I were strictly brought up. You know he continued to live here under this roof when he married – and the girls are now my wards. My wife was a good woman, but I was never interested in her . . . even before the accident. Then she was immersed in her ailments. But it was not that so much as the fact that we had absolutely nothing in common . . . nothing to talk about. Can you imagine the dreariness of that. She was stoical and I was sometimes impatient. I had a grudge against fate which had saddled me with her. She could not live with me as a wife. I didn't care about that. Naturally there were others . . . many of them. There was no particular one . . . perhaps that was why there were so many. Have you understood so far?'

'Yes, of course.'

'And you are still sitting in judgement?'

'I am not. I just do not want to be involved with you.'

'She died . . . of an overdose of laudanum. She often said she would take her life if the pain became unendur-able. She was a religious woman and the pain must have been well nigh unbearable. She wouldn't have done it otherwise. We were good friends. She knew that I sought consolation elsewhere . . . and she died.'

'And you brought Marcia Martindale to Rooks' Rest. Why?'

He was silent for a few seconds. I asked myself why I stayed talking to him. I should have turned my horse and galloped away. Yet the urge to remain was irresistible.

268

He said: 'Marcia amused me. She could be so out-rageous. She was always playing a part . . . on and off stage. She became pregnant and in an impulsive moment I offered her Rooks' Rest so that she could get right away and have the child in peace. Then, she discovered the real state of affairs down here . . . invalid wife, estate with only two girls to inherit . . . the end of the name Verringer. It was like a play to her. She therefore decided that the child was mine, that she was showing me she was not infertile, and that if I were free I should marry her. It used to amuse me. Perhaps I wasn't serious enough. She made her fanta-sies, played them out, and if she liked them well enough, believed them.'

'And then your wife died.'

'Yes. That was when it became difficult.'

'I can see that.'

'She really believed then that I would marry her. I went away hoping that she would grow tired of the country and return to London.'

'But she joined you instead.'

'She did not join me. She might have, if she had known where I was, but I was determined that she should not know.'

'But she did go away, and it was said . . .'

'It was said! You have built up something against me on what was said!'

'Do you really think, after what I know of you, that I have to listen to other people's opinions. Haven't I had experience of my own?'

'You must realize that I acted as I did out of my desper-ate need of you. I know that had I succeeded I should have opened up a new way of life for you . . . for us. Oh, Cordelia, stop being the sanctimonious schoolmarm. You're not that. It's a façade you hide behind.'

I turned away, but he laid his hand on my bridle.

'You must listen to me. You must try to understand. I love you. I want you. I am asking you to marry me.'

'The ultimate honour,' I said with sarcasm.

'For me, yes,' he said earnestly. 'I love you, Cordelia.

269

Whatever you had done I would go on loving you. If you murdered Miss Hetherington and threw her to the fishes in the pond, I'd still love you. That's what real love is.'

'Very touching,' I said, and I felt a ridiculous pity for him. I could not understand why. He looked so strong, ruthless, arrogant, everything that I disliked most, and yet when he talked of his love for me, I could almost believe he was speaking the truth. He was like a boy groping in the darkness for someone to love and understand him as he had never been loved and understood before.

I said on impulse: 'Tell me what you know about Marcia Martindale's whereabouts.'

'I know nothing. I suspect she is in London with Jack Martindale.'

'Jack Martindale! Wasn't he her husband?'

'A sort of husband.'

'He died crossing the Atlantic.'

He laughed. 'Oh, you've heard that version. There is one in which he died in a duel, fighting for the honour of Marcia, of course. And another in a theatrical fire after he had saved the lives of many including Marcia. I believe he went back for her pet dog. That was the affecting one.'

'You mean it is all lies. You mean that this husband of hers is still alive?'

'I can't say that. I only said that she may have gone back to him.'

'Did she *say* she was going back? Wasn't it rather sudden?'

'Not by her standards. Listen to me, Cordelia. I was unwise to let her come here. But she was in difficulties . . . out of work because she was to have a baby. She had nowhere to go. Rooks' Rest was empty so I brought her here. I was in a low state. Sylvia, my wife, was suffering great pain. I scarcely saw her. I didn't think Fiona would be much use on the estate, and here was I getting older . . . and to tell the truth disgruntled with what life had done to me. I lived what you call wildly in London, and I thought it would be amusing . . . so on impulse I brought her here. I

270

was folly because she immediately began including me in her fantasies. And then when Sylvia took that overdose, I was pulled up sharp . . . and on the very day of her funeral I saw you. I knew at once that here was someone different from all the others . . . someone who excited me, not only physically but in every way, and I began to plan. It seemed to me that here was a new start. Everything else was behind me. And then there was that damned woman at Rooks' Rest.'

'Yes,' I said. 'Go on.'

'Do you understand? Do you accept my feelings for you?'

'No. Only that there have been many women in your life and that you think it would be rather amusing to add me to their number.'

'Are you being truthful with yourself, Cordelia? Your feelings are under control, I know, good schoolmistress that you are.'

'I wish you would stop sneering at schoolmistresses.'

'Sneer at them? They have my deepest admiration. A most honourable profession. But I have a different destiny marked out for you.'

'I am one who will make my own destiny. But I should like to know what happened to Marcia Martindale.'

'You can be sure she went to London. She was getting very smug. She told me to go to hell on more than one occasion, so I guessed she had plans. She realized that her little fantasy was at an end.'

'Yet you felt responsible for her child . . . although you seem sure that it is not yours.'

'I suppose there is a possibility that it might be.'

'I have been to Bristonleigh and seen Mrs Gittings.'

He stared at me in astonishment.

'I thought I would discover something about the mystery of which they were gossiping in the town.'

'The idea of your going to such lengths!' He smiled. 'Well, what did you discover?'

'Only that she had gone there on your instructions a few days before Marcia Martindale left Rooks' Rest, and

271

that you sent her there and have promised to look after Miranda.'

'And what inference do you draw from that?'

'That you knew Marcia was going . . . to disappear, and you decided to get the child safely out of the way.'

'Oh, I see. You have it all worked out. My dear, clever, little detective. What do I do now? Confess? I strangled her . . . no, I hit her on the head with a blunt instrument. I buried her body in the garden . . . No, I dragged her to the fishponds and threw her in.'

I faced him squarely. 'Her earring was found by the fishponds.'

He stared at me.

'Yes,' I went on, 'her earring. I knew it was hers. It was the one she dropped in your stables so I had seen it before. You might remember the occasion.'

He nodded. 'Why . . . should her earring have been there?'

'Because she was.'

'Where is the earring?'

'In the ponds. The girl who found it was Teresa Hurst. She showed it to me and she threw it into the water.'

'Why did she do that?'

'Because she was afraid . . . for me. She thought that you and I . . . Well, she had not a very good opinion of you, you see, and she warned me about you . . .'

He laughed. 'What a tangled web. I like Teresa. I should not like my enemies, of course, but she is a good girl and a smart one. I like her for her devotion to you.'

'Perhaps you understand why I do not want to have anything more to do with you than I have to through school business. When and if we meet, please do not attempt to single me out for attention. You owe me that.'

He continued to look aghast. He said: 'I must tell you that I sent Miranda away because, after the scene between us, I guessed Marcia was planning something. I thought she would go to London. She couldn't take Mrs Gittings with her to London. I knew that something had to be done about the child.'

I turned away. He had been shocked by my revelation about the earring, I could see.

When I galloped away he did not follow me.

*   *   *

At school there was talk of nothing but the pageant. Time was getting short, said Daisy. She had definitely decided on Midsummer's Eve. The evenings would be light. By great good fortune the moon would be full and she wanted to see what preparations we had made.

I had decided that we should have a commentary which should be read by three or four of the senior girls and, where it was possible, we should introduce little sketches. I would write these from the records beginning with the arrival of the emissary from Clairvaux with commands from St Bernard to choose a place far removed from towns and habitation and build an abbey.

We should have girls dressed as monks chanting as they walked through the ruins; and the commentary would explain how they worked at various tasks. Then we would come to the Dissolution and disaster.

The second part would be the Elizabethan age when the country was prospering and the Hall was built, using some of the stones from the Abbey ruins, and the Lay Brothers' Dorter restored. There would be girls in Tudor costumes singing madrigals and dancing.

The third act would be the present day with the girls showing what they did at school, singing, dancing, physical exercises, and ending with the singing of the school song.

Daisy thought it was an excellent plan and I must say that I quickly became caught up in it. It was the best possible way of taking my mind from all the doubts and fears which I had tried so hard to dispel and could not.

Daisy came into the calefactory where we were assembled, looking very pleased.

'There is to be a house party at the Hall,' she said. 'There always used to be at this time of the year – although it hasn't happened for some time. There was little entertaining when Lady Verringer was so ill. Well, a year has passed

273

since that sad event and now that Mrs Martindale has left, perhaps we can come back to normal. I have decided to invite the guests for the pageant. Parents like to hear of that sort of thing. There is to be a musical evening there. Some famous pianist or violinist will come, just like the old days. Sir Jason has extended invitations to the whole teaching staff, which I have accepted on your behalf. That will be the evening after the pageant. Naturally the whole school could not go, but Fiona and Eugenie will be there and they may take a few guests – their special friends . . . two or three each, Sir Jason and I decided. I think it will be a most interesting evening.'

I was ashamed of feeling exhilarated by the prospect, but I was.

Preparations went on. The costumes were examined and constantly commented on. There was a great deal of giggling as the girls dashed about in their white Cistercian robes. They were most effective on the tallest girls.

Fiona and Charlotte were to be in the chorus of the monks. They both had good singing voices. Mr Crowe wanted them to sing in the madrigals too, but Daisy said that all the girls must be given a chance to do something. 'We do not want certain girls taking *all* the kudos. If the performance were repeated at the end of term, parents want to see *their* children . . . so a part for everyone please.'

We rehearsed the Abbey scenes out of doors and it was very moving to perform among the ruins. Perhaps I was in love with words but when I heard Gwendoline Grey read her lines – she had a beautiful voice – I was deeply touched and I was sure the pageant was going to be a great success.

Mr Crowe was very excited about the singing, and I constantly heard the sound of voices trilling in the music room. Rehearsals were continuous and everyone was waiting for the day.

The weather was perfect, and although we had some three weeks before the performance, girls were already watching the skies anxiously and forecasting the weather.

As if it could not change in half an hour! However it was all part of the general excitement.

It was in the first week in June that we had a shock. During the break for riding Miss Barston had been the only one available to go with the girls and they had set off about two o'clock in the afternoon and would be expected back at four for tea.

At four o'clock they had not returned. The girls were so absorbed in their own affairs – mainly concerning the pageant – and the rest of us were too, that we did not notice they were missing until one of the juniors asked where Miss Barston was as she had to report to her immediately after tea.

'And where are Fiona and Charlotte?' asked Mr Crowe. 'I want to take the girls through the monks' chorus.'

We then discovered that the riding party was not yet back.

It was then half past four.

Then Miss Barston came bursting into the hall. She was very agitated and several of the girls were with her.

I said: 'What has happened?'

She said, 'We've lost the Verringer girls and Charlotte Mackay.'

'Lost them?'

'We suddenly discovered they weren't with us.'

'Do you mean . . . they just disappeared?'

'I don't know whether anyone knows where they are. They won't say.'

Discipline had never been one of Miss Barston's strong points, so I said: 'Someone must have seen them. Did any of you girls?'

'No, Miss Grant,' was the chorus.

I did not think they were all speaking the truth.

'If these girls have deliberately gone off, they should be punished,' I said. 'They know very well they are not allowed to leave the party. Are you sure nobody saw them go?'

There was still no answer. It was, of course, a point of honour not to tell tales; and I was sure this was one of the

275

occasions when that code was being put into practice.

I said: 'The three of them are together. They'll come to no harm.'

'I think perhaps I should report this to Miss Hetherington,' said Miss Barston.

Daisy however could not be found and the girls were not reported. It must have been five o'clock when they came riding in.

I went out to the stables with Miss Barston.

'Girls . . . girls . . .' she said hysterically. 'Where have you been?'

It was Charlotte who spoke. 'We went into the woods. We wanted to see if there were any bluebells still.'

'You had no right to leave the party,' I said.

'No, Miss Grant,' said Charlotte insolently.

'Yet you did,' I retorted.

'We were anxious to see the bluebells and forgot the time,' said Fiona apologetically.

I noticed something different about her. She looked flushed. She was one of the prettiest girls in the school but now she looked beautiful, and not in the least contrite, which was strange because she was a girl who, if left to herself, would have been peace-loving.

'It was very wrong of you,' said Miss Barston.

'It was inconsiderate and unkind,' I added. I turned away. It was Miss Barston's affair and I did not want to appear to be taking over.

I don't think Miss Barston reported the incident to Miss Hetherington, for I heard no more about it: and forgot it until it took on a special significance.

*   *   *

The great day arrived. We had had a hot dry spell for a week and it looked as though it would be with us for a few days longer. It was exactly what we needed and hopes were high. Rehearsals were over and all the performers should know by now what they had to do. There was an air of intense excitement everywhere. Miss Barston was putting

276

last minute stitches to gowns. We had had some Elizabethan costumes sent over from the Hall where they had a small collection and it was a matter of finding girls to fit them. Miss Barston, however, ran up costumes of her own and they were quite effective.

During the morning we set up the seating arrangements. Fortunately the ruins made a natural stage for there was a big open space in front of the nave, making a sort of grassy quadrangle; with the Lay Brothers' Frater and Dorter at right angles to the nave, and the open space being bordered by the guest houses and the infirmary on one side and the stables on the other, completing the square.

From this vantage point there was a superb view of the ruined church, the Norman central tower and the north transept; and it was possible to see, over the walls of the outer ward, the open country with the fish ponds and the river.

Jason came over in the morning. I was counting the seats which had been put out when he came from the stables where he had left his horse.

'Cordelia!' he said. 'What luck!'

I wanted to walk away and leave him, but we were in a very exposed spot and I did not know who was watching. I must try to behave as I would if there had never been anything between us more than casual acquaintanceship.

'I suppose, Sir Jason, you have come to see Miss Hetherington about the arrangements for tonight.'

'When I come here, it is to see you.'

'I understand you are bringing guests over tonight. We should like to know how many.'

'I shall be looking for you, and I have been full of expectation ever since dear Daisy invited me and my guests.'

'Parents with children approaching school age will be particularly welcome.'

'There are a few and I shall do my best to bring good business to Daisy tonight. Most of all I shall hope to be with you.'

'I have to be there naturally but –'

277

'There could be opportunities. Wouldn't it be dramatic to declare our intentions tonight? How about my standing there among all the monks and telling them that the school and Hall will be united more than ever because their own Miss Grant is to become my wife.'

'Dramatic indeed! Also ridiculously absurd. I will say good morning to you. I have a great deal of work to do, and here is Miss Hetherington. She must have seen your arrival. Miss Hetherington, Sir Jason has come to make sure we can accommodate all the guests he is bringing tonight.'

'We certainly shall,' said Daisy warmly. 'Isn't it a perfect day? And a full moon tonight. I wish we didn't have to start so late. I don't like the younger girls to stay up long past their normal bedtime.'

'Once won't hurt them,' said Sir Jason.

'No, I suppose not. Is everything in order, Miss Grant?'

'I think so. At the rehearsal yesterday there were one or two hitches.'

'Always the case in the most professional shows,' said Jason. 'A smooth dress rehearsal is said to be a bad first night.'

Daisy gave a little laugh. 'This is hardly to be compared with professional shows, Sir Jason. But I do hope we shall amuse your guests and it will be an unusual way for them to pass an evening.'

'They will thoroughly enjoy it.'

'And tomorrow you have your pianist from London.'

'Yes, Serge Polenski is going to perform for us, and I hope you and all your mistresses will join us. There will be a buffet supper after . . . and dancing.'

'I know they will most joyfully accept your invitation. One or two will have to stay behind, of course, because of the girls. I remember these occasions in the old days. There was usually some famous musician brought down to entertain the company.'

'A tradition from the days when we had the fiddlers playing in the minstrels' gallery.'

'Yes. The Verringers were always patrons of music.'

278

'We did our best, though we never succeeded in producing a genius ourselves.'

'Fiona sings very nicely and Eugenie has quite a talent for drawing. Miss Eccles says she is very good. Come into my study, Sir Jason, and we can discuss the seating there. Miss Barston was saying she wanted to see you, Miss Grant. Some muddle about the monks' robes. Something is missing I think.'

It was dismissal so I said: 'I'll go to see her at once.'

Jason gave me a rueful look and I went away leaving them together.

I found Miss Barston quite distressed.

'One of the monks' robes is missing.'

'It must be somewhere.'

'Well, I've searched. I've questioned the girls. Nobody knows anything about it.'

'You had twelve, didn't you?'

'I did and now there are only eleven. You count them.'

She was right. There were only eleven.

'I don't know what we're going to do. There'll only be eleven monks. At this late hour . . .'

'It must be somewhere,' I said. 'It can't just disappear.'

'But it has, Miss Grant. I cannot understand it.'

'Do you think someone's playing a trick?'

'A trick! At this late hour. If I cannot find that costume there'll only be eleven monks.'

'That won't make much difference.'

'It means one of the girls will have to stand down. Which one? Of course, Janet Mills hasn't much of a voice . . . I only put her in because she is tall and the costumes are man-size.'

'We'd better see if we can find that robe.'

'Miss Grant, if you can think of anywhere to look, please tell me. I've done everything.'

'If we can't find it, there'll just have to be eleven. We have to accept that.'

'Oh dear, it's so frustrating.'

'I daresay it will turn up during the day.'

279

I left Miss Barston to her frustration and went on with my duties.

Later that day Daisy summoned me to her study to discuss more arrangements.

'It's about this evening at the Hall. Fiona and Eugenie can select the friends they want to take. Miss Barston and Miss Parker will stay here and remain on duty. They don't care for socializing in any case. Cordelia, there are still unpleasant rumours. It is most unfortunate about this disappearing lady. I know there is no need to tell you to take special care with Sir Jason.'

'I understand.'

'It is a pity that he has this reputation. A good solid older squire would be so much better for the school. You don't seem to be quite so friendly with him now. I am pleased about that. I must say I did have some misgivings and then there was that matter of your breaking the window.'

'I'm sorry, Miss Hetherington.'

She waved her hand. She did not want to hear any revelations which might be unpleasant. All she wanted was for everything to run smoothly and in the best possible manner for the school.

'I promise you, Miss Hetherington, that nothing shall happen to give you concern – if I can help it,' I added.

*   *   *

We were lucky. The weather stayed perfect. Everything seemed to go smoothly, and that which would have been an ordinary amateur performance, by moonlight among the ruins had a special magic.

The girls' voices sounded young and innocently beautiful in the night air; they evoked the scene of the building, the rise of the Abbey and the rumblings of disaster; the King's break with Rome, his need for money, the tempting riches of the abbeys and then the Dissolution.

I looked round at the audience. An impressive one. The ladies from the Hall in their shimmering evening gowns, the men's black and white dignity, and Jason in their midst, more distinguished looking than any, I thought; and our

280

own mistresses in their gowns made for the occasion might seem less glorious than those of the Hall, but charming none the less; and in the centre of the front row – Jason on her right and Lady Sowerby on her left (Lady Sowerby had two girls who were coming up to the age when the Academy would be the best place for them) sat Daisy herself in a gown of pale grey satin with gold chains about her neck and a little pearl watch pinned to her bosom, looking magnificent and in complete control.

Seated cross-legged on the grass were the younger girls, for there had not been enough chairs to accommodate all the people and in any case they could see better and were young enough not to mind the discomfort. I was touched to see their wondering faces as they listened to the account of the monastery's beginnings and I saw how they caught their breath when the monks came walking from the ruined nave.

As I watched them slowly wending their way through the ruins, I remembered suddenly the drama of the lost robe and I counted them. Twelve. So Miss Barston must have found it.

This was indeed an impressive scene. It was so realistic. It was as though the past had really come to life. One forgot these were ruins. The Abbey was alive again and these were its inhabitants on the way to compline. Even the most blasé of Jason's guests were affected and the applause after the first act was genuine.

Then there was the Elizabethan scene with Mr Crowe playing a lute and the girls dancing Tudor dances and singing madrigals. We had the voices explaining how this was the age of revival. The Manor House had been built and some of the stones from the Abbey had been used in its construction. So the Hall and Abbey were united as they had been though the ages, and as tonight clearly showed.

There was more applause.

And then came the final scene. The reconstruction of the Lay Brothers' Frater and Dorter, the founding of the Academy. Then we had the dancing – Sir Roger de Coverley and Jenny Pluck Pears – in which all the girls who had

281

not taken the part of monks or Elizabethan courtiers could perform. Finally there was the school song . . .

During Sir Roger I had noticed Janet Mills seated on the grass. I stared at her. But the monks were still in their robes, waiting to come in at the end and take their bow. I had counted twelve. I must have been mistaken. No one else would have taken Janet's place at such short notice. She was only being left out because there was no costume for her. I must have made a mistake. There could only have been eleven.

The school song had ended. The applause rang out and all the performers came out to take their bows. First the Elizabethans – eight of them; and then the monks came out from the nave chanting as they had during the performance. They came and stood on the grass facing us. I counted them. Eleven. How strange! I had counted twelve when they were performing. It must have been an illusion.

There was no doubt of the success of the evening. Wine was served with light refreshments and the guests walked about the ruins mingling with the monks and the Elizabethans, all flushed and excited with their recent success, declaring to each other that there had never been such an evening.

I heard one bejewelled lady proclaim in audible tones that it was delightful, quite enchanting. She had never seen anything like it and wasn't Jason an angel to have arranged such an enchanting surprise for them all.

Daisy was in her element. The evening had been more successful than she had anticipated; she was delighted with the company and she was sure it would result in more pupils, for Jason had told her that he had made sure to invite several fond parents, and she must have seen by the appreciation and applause that they were delighted with what had taken place.

She came to congratulate me on the descriptive passages. 'So moving,' she said. 'So inspiring.' I glowed with pleasure. 'I'd like to get the girls in soon,' she went on. 'I don't like them running about among the guests. You never know. They are at such a difficult age . . . some of

282

them. I think it would be a good idea if you and some of the others rounded them up and let them know that I would like them to go to their rooms quietly. They will, I have no doubt, watch from their windows, but we have to turn a blind eye to that. I have already sent the younger ones to bed. It is the monks and the Elizabethans I want to get in.'

'I will do what I can.'

I found three of the Elizabethans who went off docilely. The monks were older girls and not so easy to find. I could see two of them talking to some of the guests from the Hall and decided to leave them for the time being. Then I saw one of the monks by herself making her way to the nave. I started after her but as soon as she was out of sight of the company, she started to run. She was making her way towards the sanctuary and the chapel of five altars.

I quickened my pace. Now she was stepping carefully across the flags; she was entering the chapel and as she did so, a tall figure in a monk's robe came out to meet her.

I called out: 'You two there. You are to go to your bedrooms. Miss Hetherington's orders.'

For a few seconds they stood as though petrified. They were so still that they might have been part of the stones around them. Then suddenly the taller of the two seized the other by the hand and dragged her away. They did not have to pass me because there were no walls to the chapel; all they had to do was pick their way over the stones.

'Come here,' I called.

But they were running as though their lives depended on it. The hood of one of them fell back and disclosed the flaxen hair of Fiona Verringer.

'Fiona,' I called. 'Come back. Come back, both of you.'

They ran on. They ran into the kitchens, and the tunnels, I believed, were very close.

I sighed. Fiona was changing. She used to be quite a good girl. Could the one with her be Charlotte Mackay? It looked to be someone taller, though Charlotte was tall and she might have been standing on a higher level.

I went back to the company to look for more performers who were to be sent to their beds.

283

It was after midnight before the company dispersed, and those who had devised the pageant stood with Miss Hetherington to receive the thanks and congratulations from the departing guests. Then the carriages took them back to the Hall.

Before I went to bed I must make my rounds of the bedrooms in my care. When I went to Fiona's room I remembered that she had run away when I called her . . . she and another.

She lay in her bed presumably asleep, her golden hair streaming over the pillow. She looked angelic.

'Are you asleep?' I asked.

There was no answer from Fiona.

Eugenie said: 'I'm not. Fiona is. She was very tired.'

I could wake her, of course, to reprimand her, but I decided to speak to her in the morning. It really was perverse of her to run away like that.

Well, they were all safe. Most of them were awake and whispering together about the evening.

What could one expect on such a night?

*   *   *

The next day everyone was talking about the visit to the Hall. Mademoiselle had a beautiful ball gown which she said came from Paris.

'We can't match that,' said Eileen Eccles. 'Plymouth is the nearest I can get to high fashion.'

'We should have had more warning,' said Fräulein.

'An invitation which comes unexpectedly is more exciting,' replied Mademoiselle.

Miss Parker and Miss Barston were greatly relieved that they had been selected to stay behind, so everyone was very satisfied with the arrangements.

I had debated what I would wear. Aunt Patty had advised me to take two evening dresses with me. She had said there were always the odd functions and I never knew what I should need. 'One subdued and one startling, my dear. You can't go wrong in that.'

I decided I had no wish to look subdued so I chose the

284

startling gown which was rather low cut and in a rather unusual bluish-green shade. It was made of chiffon and it had a closely fitted tucked bodice and a skirt which billowed out from the waist.

'There's an air of simplicity about it,' Aunt Patty had said, 'and oddly enough that makes it startling. You'd be the belle of the ball in that no matter where you were.'

A comforting remark on an occasion when I was going to be among the wealthy.

My gown was approved of by all in the calefactory and even Daisy – herself resplendent in mauve velvet – complimented me on its good taste.

Emmet was taking some of us to the Hall and Sir Jason was sending his carriage for the others; there might have to be two journeys for it seemed unlikely that we could all crowd into two carriages.

Fiona and Eugenie had gone over in the afternoon because as Daisy said it was their home and they were part hostesses. It would be good practice for the future. I was to go with Emmet and some of the mistresses.

About an hour before Emmet was due I was putting the last touches to my appearance when Elsa came in; she gave me that conspiratorial smile she always bestowed on me and which I think was meant to remind me of our days at Schaffenbrucken.

'You do look nice,' she said. 'I've got this for you.'

She produced a letter.

'At this time of day?' I said, surprised.

'The post came at the usual time but with all the fuss going on it was forgotten. I'm only just taking the letters round.'

I said: 'Everything's been topsyturvy today.'

I took the letter and she hovered. With anyone else I should have given a cool word of dismissal, but it was different with Elsa. It always had been because of memories of the past.

'Well, I hope you enjoy tonight.'

It was almost as though she were waiting for me to open the letter.

285

I put it down and turned to the mirror.

'Well . . . have a good time . . .'

As soon as she was gone I picked up the envelope. I looked hard at it because my name and address were in block capitals. The postmark was Colby. Who could have been writing to me from there? I slit the envelope. There was one piece of paper inside and the same block letters were used. The words sprang out and hit me like a blow:

WHERE IS MRS MARTINDALE?

DON'T THINK YOU CAN GET AWAY WITH MURDER.

YOU ARE BEING WATCHED.

I felt as though I were dreaming. I turned the paper over in my hands. Just an ordinary sheet of plain paper. I looked at the printing. Anyone could have done that. It was obviously written like that to disguise handwriting. I looked at the envelope again. The same printing. The Colby postmark. What did it mean? Some malicious person was suggesting that I had either killed Marcia Martindale or had had a hand in it.

How could they? What motive had I? Of course . . . in spite of my determination to remain aloof I was becoming involved. Jason's pursuit of me had scarcely been discreet and people had noticed. Thoughts raced round and round in my mind. The person who had written this letter believed that Marcia Martindale was a rival of mine and that we both wanted to marry Jason Verringer.

'You are being watched.' What horrible ominous words!

I looked over my shoulder. I could almost feel eyes peering at me, even in my own room.

I read the note again and again.

The evening was spoilt for me. I was being drawn farther and farther into this turmoil of deceit. Where was Marcia Martindale? If only she would come back and show herself! Nothing short of that would stop this gossip.

I looked again at the paper. Could it be Mrs Baddicombe? No. Surely she would not go so far as that. Hers was over-the-counter gossip. She was not the sort to write anonymous letters. Who was? One could never be sure.

286

That was at the root of the whole nasty procedure. One could never be sure.

I tucked the letter inside my bodice. I could hear the sounds of bustle below. The carriages were waiting.

I was hardly aware of driving to the Hall.

'You're dreaming,' said Eileen Eccles. 'Is it of delights to come?'

I roused myself and tried to smile.

Jason was receiving his guests. He took my hand and kissed it. Nothing very unusual about that as it seemed to be his mode of greeting to most of the ladies.

'Cordelia,' he whispered, 'it's wonderful to have you here.'

I wanted to cry out, I have a letter . . . a horrible . . . horrible letter and it is all due to you.

Instead I said nothing and heard myself being introduced to a gentleman whose name I was too bemused to catch. There was a great deal of talk about last evening's entertainment and the excellence of the production.

'I understand from Jason that you were responsible for that, Miss Grant,' said one young woman. 'How very clever you must be.'

I acknowledged the appreciation and the gentleman whose name I did not catch said that the most thrilling moment was when the monks suddenly appeared among the ruins chanting.

'I got quite a *frisson*,' said the lady.

'I suppose that was what was intended,' replied the man. 'In any case, you brought the atmosphere alive.'

'It was really quite creepy. Look, Serge Polenski has arrived. They say he is one of the greatest pianists of the time.'

'That is why Jason has him here. He's taking London by storm and I hear he has just come from Paris where he was a great success.'

'He's such a little man. I imagined him taller. But perhaps he looks small beside Jason.'

'When is he going to perform?' I asked, feeling it was time I said something.

287

'Very soon, I should imagine. Jason is taking him to the music room now. Shall we follow?'

I walked with them into a smaller room where there was a grand piano on a dais. The room was decorated in white and scarlet and there was a high bowl of red roses on a marble consul table. Their scent filled the room. The windows were wide open to the moonlit lawns. I could see a fountain and flower-beds and the trees of the shrubbery in the distance. There was an atmosphere of complete peace in great contrast to my state of mind.

I noticed a group of our girls together. There were eight of them. Fiona and Eugenie had been allowed to ask three each. I saw Charlotte Mackay, Patricia Cartwright and Gwendoline Grey among them.

Teresa had told me that she had not been invited but she didn't care.

Charlotte looked up and smiled at me. So did the other girls.

I went over to them and said: 'This is going to be wonderful.'

'Oh yes, Miss Grant. We are looking forward to it,' said Gwendoline, who longed to play the piano professionally, an ambition which Mr Crowe regarded with some scepticism.

'You'll be able to see how it should be done,' I said.

'Oh yes, Miss Grant.'

I left them and went back to my seat.

The concert was indeed wonderful and for a few moments I forgot the horrible implications of that letter as I listened to Serge Polenski playing some pieces of Chopin and Schumann.

Too soon it was over. He was taking his bow to rapturous applause and Jason was thanking him and leading him from the room.

Conversation broke out and everyone said: 'How marvellous!' And then we were all drifting into the ball-room. I was still with my unknown lady and gentleman and another man had joined us. He talked knowledgeably of the magnificent performance of Serge Polenski and we seated

288

ourselves close to a pot of palms. Flowers from the greenhouses had been brought in and because of the time of the year there was a spectacular display. Servants in livery of blue and silver flitted in and out, most of them making their way through a door which I presumed to be the supper room.

I could not see Jason and supposed he was still with the pianist. From the minstrels' gallery the music began and one of our party asked me to dance.

We talked as we danced. He came from Cornwall. 'Some fifteen miles away. Just over the border, you understand. My brother is with me. We have been visiting Colby all our lives. Of course, during the last years of poor Sylvia Verringer's life it was not easy. She was such an invalid.'

'Yes,' I said.

'Jason had rather a bad time. Perhaps now. Well, it's a year since Sylvia went. Poor soul.'

I wanted to tell Jason about the letter. I wanted him to know what harm he was doing me by his rash actions. It was almost supper time before he came my way.

'Cordelia,' he said. 'It's wonderful to have you here. I've been trying to get to you the whole evening. Let's dance.'

It was another waltz. At Schaffenbrucken there had been great emphasis on dancing, and I was quite good at it.

He said: 'What do you think of the Hall?'

'It's very grand. I have seen it before.'

'Not properly. I want to show it to you. Not tonight but come over tomorrow.'

'I've had a letter,' I cried.

'A letter?'

'It's horrible. It's accusing me . . .'

'Of what?'

'Of murdering Marcia Martindale.'

'Good God! There must be a madman here. Why . . . why *you*?'

'Isn't it obvious? People are thinking she was my rival. It's all so sordidly horrible.'

'Have you got the letter?'

289

'Yes, I brought it with me.'

'Have you any idea who sent it?'

'None. It's in block letters.'

'I want to see it.' He had whirled me to an alcove where we were slightly sheltered from the ball-room by tall potted greenery.

He looked at the letter.

'Malicious,' he said.

'I wondered if it was the postmistress. She says some scandalous things.'

'This printing could be anyone. It is obviously meant to disguise the handwriting. What about the girl who found the earring?'

'Teresa! She would never do anything to upset me. She sets herself out to protect me.'

'Nevertheless she has ideas.'

'Only because she is afraid for me. She would never deliberately upset me.'

'Girls can behave oddly. There is obviously talk about you and me. The best thing to stop it would be to announce our engagement.'

'Scandal doesn't stop with engagements. The only way to stop this is to produce Marcia Martindale.'

There was a cough behind us. I spun round. Charlotte Mackay was standing there.

'Charlotte!' I cried.

'I came to find you or one of the mistresses, Miss Grant.' She was looking from me to Jason with just a hint of amusement in her expression. I thought, surely they can't be talking at school, and yet they must be because Teresa had been disturbed by it.

'Well,' I said sharply, 'what is it, Charlotte?'

'It's Fiona,' she said. 'She's got a headache. She wants to go back.'

'She can lie down here,' said Jason. 'She has her room.'

'She said it was nothing and she would be all right in the morning, but she does want to leave now.'

'Emmet is waiting, I think. He can take her back.'

'I'll go with her, Miss Grant, and Eugenie will too.'

290

'Oh, but Miss Hetherington said you could stay to supper if you went immediately afterwards.'

'We don't really want any supper and Fiona says her head's getting worse with the music and everything.'

'Where is Fiona now?'

'She's sitting downstairs. Eugenie is with her.'

'Perhaps you'd better ask Miss Hetherington.' I went with her. I did not want her to go away and tell people that she had left me alone with Jason. It was bad enough that she had found us alone together.

We found Miss Hetherington seated with an elderly Colonel and they seemed to be getting on very well together. I told her that Fiona wanted to go back and why.

'Very well,' she said. 'Emmet is there. Who will go with her?'

'I will, Miss Hetherington,' said Charlotte promptly, 'and Eugenie wants to go too. We don't need anyone else. We don't want to spoil the evening for them.'

'H'm. Very well. But go quietly. After all Fiona and Eugenie are hostesses in a way. Never mind. You three girls slip away quietly.'

The girls went and I left Miss Hetherington with her Colonel.

Someone asked me to dance. It was the supper dance and after that we went to eat. Jason had reserved a place for me at his table. There were four other people besides us so there was no opportunity to talk privately. I was rather glad of that. I felt he was not taking the anonymous letter seriously enough.

The evening to which I had looked forward had been something of a nightmare.

I was glad when it was over. I suppose I was rather silent on the journey from the Hall to the school. The others were all talking brightly and it didn't matter very much. I hoped no one noticed.

The girls who had remained after Fiona, Eugenie and Charlotte went, left immediately after supper so they should all be in their beds by now. Before retiring I must take my last look round.

291

When I came to the room shared by Fiona and Eugenie I remembered Fiona's early departure and wondered if she was cured of her headache. I looked in. I saw at once that Eugenie was awake, although as I opened the door she shut her eyes quickly – but not quite quickly enough.

'So you're awake, Eugenie,' I said.

She opened her eyes then. 'Yes, Miss Grant.'

'How's Fiona?'

She looked over to the other bed. 'She was tired. She went to sleep at once. She'll be all right in the morning.'

'Well, good night,' I said.

The other girls were all sleeping. I envied them. I knew that I had to endure a sleepless night. Whatever I tried to think of I came back to the same question. 'Where is Marcia Martindale and does Jason know where she is?'

*   *   *

The next morning came the shock, and I doubt whether there had ever been a greater one in the whole history of the Academy.

I had risen earlier than usual after a sleepless night and I knew the girls were stirring because of the sounds of activity which came from their rooms.

Eugenie came to me and there was a sly look of triumph in her eyes.

She said: 'Fiona has gone.'

'Gone! Gone where?'

'Gone to get married.'

'What are you talking about?'

'She went last night . . . straight from the Hall. She never came back here.'

I dashed into her bedroom. I saw the heap of clothes under the covers on Fiona's bed which last night I had mistaken for her.

I said: 'You will come down to Miss Hetherington with me immediately.'

I had never before seen Daisy at a loss for words. Her face was grey and her lips twitched. She looked from

292

Eugenie to me as though imploring us to tell her that we were joking.

Then she spoke. 'Gone? Fiona! Eloped . . . ?'

'She's gone to get married, Miss Hetherington,' said Eugenie.

'It's some horrible mistake. Go and tell Fiona to come to me immediately.'

I said gently: 'I think it's true, Miss Hetherington. She's not in her room.'

'But she came back last night. She had a headache.'

'The headache was obviously a pretence. I gather she left the Hall. Her lover must have been waiting for her.'

'Her lover!' cried Daisy. 'One of my girls!'

I was sorry for her. She was really distressed and I could see her trying to reject the story and at the same time wondering what effect it was going to have on the school. But she would not have been Daisy if she had not quickly recovered from her shock.

'You had better tell me everything,' she said.

I spoke first and said that when I had made my rounds last night Fiona had appeared to be in her bed. This morning I had discovered that what I had thought was Fiona was in fact a bundle of clothes, and Eugenie had told me exactly what she had just told Miss Hetherington.

'You admit this, Eugenie?'

'Yes, Miss Hetherington.'

'You knew Fiona was going and you said nothing about it?'

'Yes, Miss Hetherington.'

'That was very wrong. You should have come to me or Miss Grant at once.'

Eugenie was silent.

'Who is this man?'

'He is very good looking and romantic.'

'What is his name?'

'Carl.'

'Carl What?'

'I don't know. He was just Carl.'

'Where did you meet him?'

'In the woods.'

'When?'

'When we went walking.'

'Walking alone in the woods!'

'There were others with us.'

'Who?'

'Charlotte Mackay and Jane Everton.'

'When was this?'

'On May Day.'

'Do you mean to say you talked to a stranger?'

'Well, it wasn't quite like that. He asked the way . . . and we got talking.'

'And then?'

'He asked about the school and the girls and all that and he seemed to like Fiona particularly. Then we saw him again. He was always in the woods. He was interested in the trees and the country. He had come here to study them.'

'You mean he wasn't English?'

'He seemed it. He'd come from somewhere . . . I don't know where.'

'You only knew him as Carl. You don't know where he came from, and Fiona goes off with him!'

'It was love at first sight,' said Eugenie. 'She was very happy.'

'And you conspired . . .'

'Well, she is my sister. We had to help her.'

'We? Who had to help her?'

'She means Charlotte did too, I daresay,' I said.

'Oh dear,' said Daisy, putting her hand to her head. 'Someone had better go over to the Hall and tell Sir Jason of this disaster. Perhaps it is not yet too late.'

It was obvious that we were not going to learn much from Eugenie. Perhaps Jason would be more successful. I could have slapped the girl. She stood facing us with a rather mocking expression, and the manner in which she pressed her lips together showed clearly that she was not going to give anything away.

Daisy sent her to her room with instructions to stay there

294

until sent for and she put Miss Barston in charge of her. She talked a little incoherently while we waited. 'They left last night . . . It was when they went from the Hall. A headache! Oh, the duplicity of girls! Have they learned nothing here? It was before supper . . . and that was at ten. Where could they have gone? Could they be married now, I wonder? One does not expect this sort of thing nowadays . . . And one of my girls! Sir Jason will know what to do. He'll bring her back, I daresay. I do hope there isn't talk . . .'

It was becoming a nightmare. Yesterday the letter. Today Fiona's elopement. What next? I wondered.

Jason came immediately and Daisy went off into explanations. He found it hard to believe.

He sent for Eugenie and questioned her. She began by being defiant and then broke down and said that Fiona was in love and had a right to get married if she wanted to. Carl was wonderful. He loved Fiona and Fiona loved him. They were happy. Yes, she had known Fiona was going. Charlotte had helped her. Fiona hadn't got into the carriage with them when they had gone back to the school but had gone to Carl who was waiting for her. Yes, she had made it appear that Fiona was in her bed so that I had been deceived when I looked in.

Charlotte was sent for. She was equally defiant. It was quite clear that there had been a conspiracy between them all and this lover . . . this Carl had taken advantage of it.

But in spite of the gruelling questions, the pleas and the threats, we could get nothing more from them than that they had met Carl in the woods, he had asked the way and they had talked; he had seen them again. Once they had ridden off to meet him because they were making arrangements for the elopement. I remembered that occasion well and how scared Miss Barston had been.

Jason said: 'Someone must have seen them leave. I'll get down to the station. If we can find out where they went it might give us a clue to start with.'

He went off.

There was little concentration on lessons that day.

Everyone was talking about Fiona's elopement. It was clear that the girls were very excited. They thought it was the most romantic thing that had ever happened at Colby Abbey Academy for Young Ladies.

I could not rest. I had half forgotten the letter in all the turmoil of Fiona's flight, but every now and then memory of it came back to sicken me. The entire picture seemed to have changed. I looked back at the peace of last term and could not believe so much disaster could have come about during such a short time.

Something occurred to me and I went in search of Eugenie. As it was the half hour after the midday meal and lessons did not start until two I guessed that she would be out of doors. I found her with Charlotte at the fish ponds.

'Eugenie,' I said. 'I want a word with you.'

'With me?' she said insolently.

'Perhaps both of you can help me.'

There was something in the manner of both girls which I found offensive. They had never forgiven me for separating them when I arrived. It had seemed like a victory for me then but I always felt uneasy with those two girls and when I considered how they had connived and probably schemed with Fiona and her lover, they worried me a good deal.

I said: 'I have been thinking about the pageant. Do you remember Miss Barston lost one of the costumes?'

'Yes,' said Charlotte with a laugh.

'Perhaps you will tell me why you find it so amusing?'

They were both silent.

'Come on,' I said. 'Lessons will be starting soon. Do you know anything about that costume?'

Eugenie looked at Charlotte who said defiantly: 'Fiona took it.'

'I see, and during the performance someone wore it. Could it by any chance have been the romantic Carl?'

They tittered.

'This is a very dangerous matter,' I said severely. 'Did Carl wear the costume?'

They still stood there suppressing their mirth.

'Did he?' I thundered.

296

'Yes, Miss Grant,' said Charlotte.

'And he had the temerity to appear with the monks?'

'He had to see Fiona. He had to tell her about the arrangements.'

'I see. And you were in the secret?'

They were silent again. I was thinking of that moment when I had almost caught Fiona and her lover. If only I had. If I could have unmasked this man I might have stopped this disastrous elopement.

'You have been very foolish,' I said.

'Why?' demanded Eugenie. 'Love is good and Fiona is happy.'

'Fiona is very young.'

'She is eighteen. Why should love be right for some and not for others?'

There was a direct challenge in their eyes.

'I said this is a dangerous matter. Go back to your classes now.'

They ran across the grass and I followed.

Jason called at the school that evening. Miss Hetherington invited the mistresses to her study to hear what he had to say.

He had discovered that two people had arrived at the station before the nine o'clock train for Exeter was about to depart. The man was a stranger and the station master did not recognize his companion. She was wearing a cloak which covered her head completely. There were two other passengers . . . both men. That was all he could remember.

'They could have gone to Exeter . . . or London . . . anywhere,' said Jason. 'It seems as though we are not going to get on their trail.'

There was gloom in the study. I think most of us conceded that Fiona had successfully escaped.

Jason went to Exeter next day. I believe he made extensive enquiries but he was of course working in the dark.

We tried to settle down to a normal existence but it wasn't easy. I had never seen Daisy so depressed. She was terribly concerned about what effect it would have on the school.

297

'In a way,' she said, 'it is a blessing that she is who she is. Sir Jason knows exactly how it happened and it was after all from the Hall that she escaped. He doesn't blame us for negligence. All the same, girls talk, and I don't know what parents' reactions will be to an elopement at the school.'

Four days after the elopement, Eugenie had a postcard from Fiona. There was a picture of Trafalgar Square and a London postmark.

'I'm having a wonderful time and am very happy. Fiona.'

The postcard was seized on, examined and Sir Jason was invited to come over. But in fact it gave us no information except that Fiona was happy and in London.

'And that,' said Eileen, 'is like looking for a particularly elusive needle in a rather more than usually large haystack. It's no use trying to find her. She's gone off. She may be married. I expect she will be as she has a nice fortune. Maybe that's the crux of the whole matter. Though Fiona is a charming child . . . quite the most pleasant of that unholy trinity which comprises her sister and the odious Charlotte. I'm sorry it wasn't Eugenie or Charlotte who went off.'

That was an indication of the way people were thinking. They were getting tired of the subject of Fiona's departure. It was evident that she had gone and would not come back to school. 'Let it rest there,' said Eileen. 'After all I doubt she is the first schoolgirl to elope. I think there was quite a crop of them last century . . . always heiresses, which I believe contributed to the main purpose of the exercise. So this runs to form.'

When I went into the post office I found Mrs Baddicombe round-eyed with curiosity.

'My word,' she said, 'we do see life. What do you think of that young lady running off like that! Well, what's the world coming to? They say he was such a handsome gentleman. Swept off her feet. Well, you know what young girls are. No stopping 'em. I reckon there was a bit of a to-do at the school and at the Hall.'

It seemed that the excitement aroused by Fiona's elopement had superseded that of Mrs Martindale's disappearance.

298

I registered a parcel to Aunt Patty. There was no need to. It was some artificial flowers which I had happened to see in Colby and I thought she would find them suitable for trimming a hat. She would be surprised that I registered them but I could explain to her when I saw her.

'Would you please write the receipt in block letters please?'

'Block letters!' cried Mrs Baddicombe. 'What's them?'

'Like printing.'

'Well, I never did before. I always write out my receipts natural like.'

'It would be easier to read.'

She looked at me suspiciously, and rather laboriously complied with my request. She handed me the receipt and said: 'I wonder if we'll have any news. She's got spirit. I will say that for her. Always thought she was a quiet one. But then, as I say to Baddicombe, you never do know and it's the quiet ones who turn out to be deep.'

She gave me a knowing wink.

I said good day and came out of the post office clutching my receipt. I could not see any resemblance to the printing on the envelope I had received.

*   *   *

The term went on uneasily. The hot weather had broken and it was raining most of the time. At Assembly, Miss Hetherington had spoken to the girls and told them that they were on no account to hold any conversation whatsoever with people whom they did not know; and if anyone spoke to them they were to report immediately either to her or to one of the mistresses.

The girls were suitably subdued, but I guessed they were all thinking what a marvellous thing had happened to Fiona and would have greatly enjoyed being the heroine of such an exciting romance.

I avoided Jason more than ever. My thoughts were in a turmoil. I could not forget the letter and I could not help feeling that it was more important to find Marcia Martin-

299

dale than Fiona. I was desperately longing to get away from school. I could not wait for the twentieth of July.

* * *

It was two days before the end of term and we were all preparing for departure. Jason came over. I was with Daisy when he was shown in. He had had a letter from Fiona. It was posted from a place called Werthenfeld in Switzerland.

'Do you know this place?' asked Daisy.

'I know it fairly well,' replied Jason. 'It is a few miles from Zürich. She says she is happy and there is no need to worry about her. She is married and enjoying life. Read it for yourselves.'

We read it. There was no doubt of her happiness. The exuberance came over in the writing. She was in love and married. Were we perhaps worrying too much about Fiona?

I saw the postscript. 'Carl has promised to teach me to ski.'

I looked at Jason. I said: 'Well, she seems to be happy.'

'Carl,' he said. 'She doesn't give us any other name. It could be foreign. I think I should go to Werthenfeld. She is my ward and a considerable heiress. If I could discover who he is, I would be satisfied perhaps. It might be the best thing that could happen to her. She was always retiring. Different from Eugenie . . . and I have thought of their future quite a lot, bringing them out and so on. If he is fairly presentable and she is happy, what are we worrying about?'

'I don't like his methods,' commented Daisy.

Jason shrugged his shoulders. 'He's probably young and thought it might be a bit of fun to elope, no doubt.'

'Why shouldn't they have come out into the open?' asked Daisy.

'There would have been all sorts of formalities with a girl like Fiona. Let's suppose he was carried away.'

'An heiress, yes . . .'

'That does raise a niggling doubt. It is one of the reasons why I think I ought to follow up this clue.'

300

'You are right,' said Daisy, 'and the best of luck go with you.'

The twentieth came . . . a hot and sultry day. I saw the girls off and then prepared to leave with Teresa.

Daisy stood in the courtyard to say goodbye.

'We all need a rest,' she said. 'Thank heaven this term has come to an end. In all my days I never knew one like this one. Next term it will be a new start.'

A Visitor in the Country

*

Aunt Patty was waiting for us at the station in a hat made almost entirely of violets. We were all laughing as we embraced.

'My goodness,' said Aunt Patty, 'this is a bit of a change from last time. Do you remember, Cordelia? No Teresa.'

'I'm glad I'm here now,' said Teresa.

'Not more glad than we are to have you. Violet's in quite a state wondering whether those cousins of yours were going to foil us right at the last minute. She'll be in a fever of excitement till we get back and couldn't make up her mind whether to come with me to meet you or stay at home and watch the lardy cakes. She says they're a special favourite of yours, Teresa, and she wanted to have them ready for you.'

'Let's get home quickly,' said Teresa.

We got into the dog cart and Aunt Patty took the reins.

'What's the term been like?' she asked as we rode along.

'Full of incident,' I said quickly. 'Too much to tell you now.'

'Well, we'll wait until we're sitting pretty,' said Aunt Patty. 'By the way, a gentleman came calling. He wanted to see you.'

'Who was it?'

'It was Violet who saw him. She was bowled over by him. Said he was the handsomest and most pleasant gentleman she had ever met.'

'But . . . what was his name?'

'She didn't get it. Trust Violet. Too busy trying to lure him in and give him some of that almond cake of hers which she is always showing off with. She said he wouldn't stop though. He's staying at the King's Arms.'

302

'How strange. I can't think who it could be.'

I had thought at first that Jason had decided not to go to Switzerland and had come here instead. But then he would know exactly when I should be arriving and would not have called yesterday. Moreover, Violet had already met him.

'Violet will tell you more. Nearly home now. Come on, Buttercup. He always gets excited when we turn in at the lane. You couldn't get him to go past the house if you tried.'

There was the house, set back from the road with its green lawns and the hedge of macrocarpas which Violet had planted. At first when they arrived they had been little feathery sticks, I remembered, and they were already growing fast. There was the lavender and the buddleia covered in white butterflies – and that air of perfect peace.

Violet had appeared hastily wiping her hands. She embraced Teresa and me.

'There you are. Welcome home. Cordelia, you look a bit pale. And you, Teresa, how are you? I was afraid those cousins of yours were going to put in their spoke again. Well, here you are and here you're going to stay. The lardy cakes are all ready and as soon as I heard the trap turn into the lane I put the kettle on.'

I said: 'It's good to be home.' And we went into the house.

Violet was saying: 'What do you think about tea outside? It's sultry. The wasps are a pest this year. Let's have it indoors. We can have all the windows wide open so that we can see the garden. Best of both worlds, eh? You can go to your rooms after. Tea first.'

'And Violet's word is law, as we all know,' said Aunt Patty, comfortably seating herself. 'Well, what's been happening?' she went on.

'The great news is that Fiona Verringer eloped after the pageant.'

'Eloped! Is that the girl from the big house?'

'Yes, one of the two sisters.'

'Someone called here once,' recollected Violet. 'Wasn't he from there?'

303

'Yes, he's the uncle. There was a terrible upheaval, wasn't there, Teresa?'

'Oh yes. Miss Hetherington was furious.'

'I should think so,' said Aunt Patty. 'Girls eloping!'

'It was very romantic,' put in Teresa wistfully.

'I think they are somewhere in Switzerland.'

'I wonder if they are anywhere near Schaffenbrucken?' said Violet. 'Here, have another of these lardy cakes, Teresa. They're done specially for you.'

'Oh Violet, I shouldn't. What's for supper?'

'Ask no questions and you'll hear no lies. You know very well I don't talk about my dishes till I serve them. Wait and see . . . and it's a long time off and I'd have another lardy if I were you.'

Teresa helped herself and I was amazed to see the moodiness which I had noticed last term drop from her. was wondering whether I should tell Aunt Patty about the anonymous letter. I'd wait and see. I did not want to disturb the peace of the place. While I was here I could forget.

'By the way, Violet,' I said. 'Aunt Patty says somebody called.'

'Oh yes. Yesterday. Such a nice gentleman. Well spoken, nice-mannered, tall and good-looking.'

'And you don't remember the name of this shining knight?'

'He did say. But bless me, if I can remember. He said he particularly wanted to see you . . . Something about the past.'

'What do you mean . . . the past?'

'Well, apparently, he knew you then.'

'And you don't remember his name. Oh, Violet . . .'

'Well, he did say it when he came and you know what one I am for names. You'll know tomorrow. He said he coming then. I know he will. He looks like a man of his word, and he was so anxious to see you.'

'Tall you say?'

'Tall and fair.'

I was transported back to the forest. I thought: This is the

304

time for strange things to happen. He has come back. He will explain.

A great excitement took possession of me. I thought how wonderful it would be to see him again.

I said: 'Was his name Edward Compton?'

Violet considered. 'It could have been. I wouldn't say it wasn't . . . and then I wouldn't say it was.'

'Oh Violet,' I said in exasperation.

'Well, what's all the fuss? You'll know tomorrow. Patience is a virtue . . . and I'm not talking about you, Patty.'

Aunt Patty smiled, not betraying that she had heard that so-called joke a hundred times before from Violet.

Tomorrow, I thought. It is not long to wait.

*　　　*　　　*

The familiar peace of Moldenbury descended on me. I unpacked my things and went for a walk with Teresa. After supper we sat in the garden and talked desultorily of village affairs. The usual 'Bring and Buy' and the church fête were looming. There was a controversy as to whether the proceeds should go to the tower or the bells. Aunt Patty was on the side of the tower. 'We don't want that toppling down on us,' she said. But Violet was for the bells. 'I do like to hear them. Specially on a Sunday morning,' she said.

'Bells wouldn't be much use if the tower collapsed,' pointed out Aunt Patty.

'Not much use having a tower if there's no bells to bring people to church.'

And so it went on.

When I retired for the night Aunt Patty came to my room.

'Is everything all right?' she said. 'I thought you seemed a bit . . . remote. Not worried about that girl eloping are you? They're not blaming you for letting her get away, I hope.'

'Oh no. Daisy is most fair. It wasn't the fault of anyone at the school. It was the girls more likely. They had been meeting this man, some of them. If it had been Eugenie Verringer I wouldn't have been so surprised, but that Fiona

305

should have been so bold . . . well, it was unlike her.'

'In love, I suppose. They say that changes people. Cordelia, do you want to tell me what's on your mind?'

I hesitated. Then I burst out: 'I had an anonymous letter. It was horrible. Accusing me of being involved in . . . murder.'

'Good gracious me!'

'It concerned a woman who disappeared suddenly. She had been Jason Verringer's mistress at some time and he . . .'

'He seemed rather interested in you when he came here. I remember that.'

'Yes,' I said.

'And how do you feel about him?'

'I try to avoid him all I can, but he is not the sort of man to respect anyone's wishes if they conflict with what he wants. He is arrogant and ruthless. He is very powerful. He seems to own everything in Colby . . . including the school. Even Daisy Hetherington is a little subservient.'

Aunt Patty nodded her head slowly. 'I daresay there is a lot you haven't told me.'

There was. I could not bring myself to speak of that scene when I had cut my hands at the window.

She went on gently: 'You could always leave. Come back here. You could do something else later if you wanted to. Daisy's is not the only school in the country, you know.'

'Leave the school? Leave Colby? I should hate that. Besides, I should have to give a term's notice, so in any case I should have to go back to all that gossip and rumour. Even Teresa is upset.'

'Where is she involved?'

'There must be a lot of chatter about Jason Verringer and me. She thinks he is involved with that woman's disappearance, and I believe she is afraid for me. I fancy she wants to warn me against him. As if I needed to be warned!'

Aunt Patty was looking at me quizzically.

I went on: 'The girls talk a great deal. They over

306

dramatize. She has a notion that he killed this woman. To girls of Teresa's age there are only the good and the bad . . . the saints and the devils.'

'And she has put him into the devil's category.'

'She certainly has.'

'You too?'

I was faintly embarrassed, remembering so much about him and that peculiar kind of pleasure which his proximity brought to me.

'I remember him well from the time he came here,' went on Aunt Patty. 'He did not strike me as a very happy person.'

'I don't think he has ever been really happy. His marriage was a failure and I imagine he has gone out in all the wrong directions.'

'It's strange,' said Aunt Patty, 'how so many who have worldly possessions lack real happiness. I suppose he is richly endowed.'

'Very much so.'

'I've always thought that the really successful people in life are those who know how to be happy. If you are not happy you're not a success. You may have all the kingdoms of the Earth and if you haven't found happiness you've failed. After all, that is what we are all striving for, isn't it?'

'You're right. You and Violet must be the most successful people in the world.'

'It makes you laugh, doesn't it? Here we are tucked away in our little house . . . of no importance to the world . . . except to those who are near us . . . yet we have reached the goal to which everyone is striving. Yes, we're happy. Dear child, I want that same happiness for you. Perhaps it was easier for me. I've always been single. I've made my own life. It's been a good one.'

'You have made it so.'

'We all make our lives what they are. Sometimes there is a partner to help you make it. Then it's not always easy to go the way one wants to. That's where the difficulties lie. That poor man! Interesting . . . but I sensed something

307

dark there. He's not a happy person. You are, Cordelia. You came to us . . . and everything was right . . . from the start. We gave you love and you took it and gave us love in return. It was easy . . . no complications. I'm not being clear, but I want you to be very careful if the time should come when you decide to choose someone to share your life.'

'I am not thinking of sharing my life with anyone, Aunt Patty, except you and Violet.'

'You think a great deal about that man.'

'Aunt Patty, I dislike him. I find him most . . .'

She held up her hand. 'You are so vehement.'

'So would you be if –'

She waited and I did not go on.

Then suddenly she bent forward and kissed me. 'My dear,' she said, 'you have chosen your profession and it suits you. You were meant to guide, counsel and protect. He is, as you imply, a man of the world and sometimes they are the ones who need most care. Well, we shall see. Now you are here and you are going to be lazy and rest, and we shall talk and talk. But it is time you were in bed. Good night, my dear.'

I threw myself into her arms and she kissed me. Then she released me and went to the door. Neither of us cared to show the depth of our emotion; but our love and trust in each other was known to us both and there was no need to talk of it.

I lay between the cool lavender-scented sheets and thought of Violet assiduously collecting the blooms and making them into sachets to scent the household linen as well as Aunt Patty's clothes. Peace . . . and yet how could I enjoy it?

Then I was thinking about the next day when the mysterious gentleman would call. I was convincing myself that it was the stranger of the forest who had at last come in search of me. I could remember his face clearly. Yes, he was undoubtedly handsome. His fair hair grew back from a high forehead and he had strong features and rather piercingly blue eyes; and there was something about him which made him different from other men, something not quite of this world. Or had I imagined that after I had had that eerie experience in the Suffolk graveyard?

How strange it would be if I really did see him again. I wondered what the explanation could be and how I should feel when I came face to face with him.

*   *   *

We had breakfasted and Teresa was helping Violet with the washing up. Aunt Patty was going to the Vicarage to discuss the 'Bring and Buy' and was wondering if I would like to go with her.

'You'll be roped in for a stall,' she said. 'For Heaven's sake don't take the white elephant if you can help it. They turn up year after year. Everybody's got to know them by now.'

'Elephants never forget,' called Violet from the kitchen. 'And people never forget white elephants.'

'Violet's in a spry mood this morning,' commented Aunt Patty. 'It's because she's going to get Teresa to help her in the potting shed.'

'I'll go and get my coat and come with you,' I said.

When I came down, a man was coming up the path. He was tall and fair and I had never seen him before.

Violet had glimpsed him through the kitchen window.

'He's here,' she cried. 'The gentleman who called.'

I went into the front garden.

He said: 'You must be Cordelia . . . Miss Grant.'

'Yes,' I replied. 'I'm afraid I don't know –'

'You wouldn't know me but I felt I had to come and see you. I'm John Markham, Lydia's brother. You remember Lydia?'

'Lydia Markham! But of course. Oh, how nice to meet you.'

'I hope you don't mind my coming like this.'

'I'm pleased you called.' Aunt Patty had come up. 'Aunt Patty,' I said, 'this is Mr Markham. You've heard me talk of Lydia who was with me at Schaffenbrucken. This is her brother.'

309

'It's nice to see you,' said Aunt Patty. 'Did you call the other day?'

'Yes, I did, and I was told I would find Miss Grant here today.'

'Do come in.'

'Weren't you just going out?'

'It doesn't matter.'

I took him into the small drawing room. Violet came in.

'You came back then,' she said. 'Now do sit down. I'm going to get you something. Would you like coffee or tea?'

'First,' he said. 'I would like to talk to Miss Grant.'

'I'll bring you something later,' said Violet. 'The parsnip wine was particularly good this year.'

'Thank you.'

'I shall get off to the vicarage,' said Aunt Patty. 'You two can have a talk and we'll all meet later.'

So they withdrew and left us.

He said: 'I hope I haven't come at an inconvenient time.'

'Certainly not. I'm so glad to meet you. I have wondered about Lydia quite a lot because I wrote to her and I never had a reply. How is she? I wish you had brought her with you.'

'Lydia is dead,' he said.

'Dead! But . . .'

'Yes. It was a great blow to us. We miss her very much.'

'But she was young . . . She was never ill. How did she die?'

'It was an accident . . . in the mountains . . . in Switzerland. She was skiing.'

'Lydia skiing! She always avoided outdoor sports when we were at school. She even used to dodge gym if she could.'

'She was with her husband.'

'Her husband! So Lydia married!'

'It's quite a long story. I wanted to see you because she had often talked of you. I think of all her school friends, you were the favourite. Then you wrote to her. I found your letter and I felt that I had either to write and tell you what happened or come and see you. So I came.'

'I'm sorry . . . I can't think clearly. This is such a shock. Lydia . . . dead!'

'It was very tragic. Her husband was heart-broken. They had not been married more than three months.'

'I can't believe this. I thought she was to have another year at Schaffenbrucken.'

'Yes, I know. She was only seventeen. But she met this man and fell in love with him. We wanted them to wait but Lydia wouldn't do that. She could be very headstrong. Our father was most uncertain but he doted on Lydia. My brother and I were several years older. He was devoted to us all but he just adored Lydia. He died soon after she did. He had a weak heart and the shock just finished him.'

'I can't tell you how upsetting this is.'

'It is good of you to care so much. I wanted you to know. I thought you might write to Lydia again.'

'Where did she meet this young man?'

'Mark Chessingham was staying near our farm in Epping. We're not farmers. The farm is run by a manager but it is a hobby for us. We live mainly in London and escape to the farm for weekends and when we can get away. He was there studying law. His family had their business in Basle and quarters in London, but he had come down to the forest to work. He had examinations to pass. Our farm is right on the edge of Epping Forest which is very convenient being so near to London. Actually that was why my father selected the spot in the first place.'

He paused for a short while and then went on: 'She met him one day. They fell in love and wanted to marry. My father would have preferred a long engagement but Lydia wouldn't hear of it and threatened to elope if consent was not given. In the end my father gave way . . . with misgivings, of course . . . But Mark was charming and it seemed quite a suitable match. As it was so quick there was a quiet wedding.'

'She didn't write and tell me.'

'Strange really, because she often mentioned you, and was so proud of him and of being married. He was a very pleasant fellow. Lydia had a little fortune which came to

311

her on marriage. At first I thought that might have had something to do with it, but he seemed to be so well-off himself and his family's business was known, even in England, and he never showed the slightest interest in her money. They left England almost immediately after the wedding and three months later . . . she was dead. We had such happy letters from her and even my father had come to the conclusion that after all he had been right to allow her to marry. The one day we got the news. Mark was heart-broken. He wrote a most pathetic letter to us. She was too reckless, he said. Many times he had warned her. But she took risks. She was so enthusiastic, so anxious to shine in his eyes and tried to undertake what the experts did. That was the end. They didn't recover her body until a week after the accident.'

I was silent and he said gently: 'I am sorry to distress you like this. Perhaps it would have been better if I hadn't come.'

'No, no. I'd rather know. But it is such a shock. When you have known someone as well as I knew Lydia . . . even though it is some time since I saw her . . .'

'I'm glad you were so fond of her.'

'Tell me,' I said, 'are you on holiday?'

'No. I am working in London but I thought I would take a few days off and come to see you. I just had the feeling that I wanted to. I have to confess that I read your last letter to Lydia and I felt then that I had to let you know. I didn't want you to think she hadn't bothered to answer.'

'Lydia used to talk about her family quite a lot. She was so fond of you all. I suppose you are the head of the family now.'

'You could say that. There has never been a patriarchal attitude in our family. We were all such good friends.'

'You're in banking, aren't you?'

'Yes.'

'In the City of London?'

He nodded. 'We have a house in Kensington, and then of course the farm. My mother died but we were always lucky in having good governesses for Lydia. There was always a

312

lot of fun at home. Our father was more like a brother to us. Perhaps he wasn't strict enough . . . with Lydia for instance. If she had waited . . . If she had not been so reckless . . .'

'She was such a happy girl. The way she talked about home . . . you could tell what it meant to her.'

'Then she went away with a man she scarcely knew.'

'That,' I said, 'is love.'

'I suppose you are right. If only . . . This is a morbid subject. Please tell me about yourself. Lydia used to say you were going into partnership with your aunt in some wonderful Elizabethan manor.'

'I think I must have exaggerated about the glories of that Elizabethan manor. Perhaps I tend to exaggerate when I'm proud of something.'

'It may be that we all do.'

'I seemed to give the girls an impression that we were fabulously rich and that we had this priceless manor with a very successful school as a kind of hobby. When I got home for the holidays I found that my aunt was in financial difficulties, was selling the house and that I was to have a post in another school.'

'Which you did.'

'Yes, in Devon – a rather marvellous old place in the midst of a ruined Abbey. The school is the old Lay Brothers' quarters.'

'It sounds fascinating.'

'Yes, it is.'

'And you enjoy it immensely.'

'It is exciting. I have the utmost admiration for my headmistress and the way the school is run and for holidays I escape to this place.'

'It's a lovely house. I don't know why . . .' He stopped short. 'I'm sorry that sounded . . .'

I laughed. 'That sounded like the truth. An ordinary little house . . . not much more than a cottage, but there is something about it, isn't there? You haven't been here half an hour and you feel it. It's my aunt. She does that to places.'

313

'I hope I have an opportunity of seeing her again.'

'When do you have to go back?'

'I thought of leaving tomorrow.'

'Well, I feel sure you'll be invited to stay to lunch if you play your cards right. At any moment Violet . . . my aunt's devoted friend and companion . . . will appear with a tray on which will be glasses and a bottle of her parsnip wine. If your drink it with relish and if you will go so far as to tell her that you have never tasted better parsnip wine, you will surely be asked to stay to luncheon.'

'Does it depend on that?'

'Of course not. My aunt will ask you, and I have already decided to do so. That is good enough. But it would please Violet. Don't be too effusive for she is shrewd. Just savour, put your head on one side and say Ah. She is such a dear, though people don't always realize it. We like to tease her and please her.'

'Thank you for the warning.'

'And here is Violet,' I said; 'and yes, she is bringing her parsnip wine.'

'It was a good year,' said Violet, 'and no one can make good wine without a good crop. You'd know that, Mr . . .'

'Mr Markham,' I said.

'Oh yes, I remember now. Mr Markham, now try that. Teresa, bring in those wine biscuits.'

'You are spoiling me,' said John Markham. He took the glass reverently and raising it to his lips sniffed the aroma as though he were testing wine in the cellars of some *château* vineyard. He sipped, there was a deep silence.

Then he raised his eyes to the ceiling and said: 'I knew before I tasted it. The bouquet is superb, and this must indeed be a vintage year.'

Violet flushed pink. 'Well, I can see you are one to know what you are talking about.'

'I was suggesting to Mr Markham that he might care to stay to lunch,' I said. 'He's at the King's Arms.'

Violet grimaced. 'I heard the food's not up to much there. Well, if I'd have known . . . but there's only shepherd's pie and apple tart.'

'I can think of nothing I should like better than shepherd's pie and apple tart.'

'Well,' said Violet, still pleased. 'It'll be a pleasure. I'll see about laying another place.'

Teresa had come in and was introduced.

By the time Aunt Patty returned John Markham had succeeded in making a remarkably good impression on both Violet and Teresa. For me he was Lydia's brother and hardly seemed like a stranger.

*   *   *

He stayed to lunch and went back to his hotel afterwards but not before he had received an invitation to dine with us.

I knew that he had been deeply saddened by Lydia's death, but he was not the sort to burden others with his grief. He was amusing and interesting. He talked about banking, his life in London and on the Epping farm. He said that his brother Charles was in London. It was always pleasant to get down to the farm when they had a chance.

'It is amazing,' he said, 'what pleasure there is in haymaking and bringing in the harvest . . . particularly after you have spent your days in an office juggling with figures and doing all that makes up a banker's life. Not that I'm averse to banking. I find it fascinating. It's just the change . . . the joy of rolling up one's sleeves and getting into my old farm clothes and throwing off the polish of the city for a bit of rural activity.'

Violet, who had been brought up on a farm, listened avidly. I had never seen her take to a newcomer so quickly. He had so many stories to tell of the farm and how in the old days he had not had the faintest notion of how to go on. He made it all sound very amusing.

Teresa listened to his anecdotes with great interest. 'I should like to live on a farm,' she said.

After dinner we sat in the garden.

'The cool of the evening is the best time of the day,' said Violet.

We all walked down to the gate to say goodbye to him, all very sorry that his visit was at an end.

But the next morning he called again.

Violet was in the garden peeling potatoes which she often did out of doors on fine days, and Teresa was beside her shelling peas. Aunt Patty was dressed for going out and I was going with her to the village to shop. And there he was. From my window I saw him coming up the path.

I called out: 'Hello. I thought you'd gone.'

'Couldn't tear myself away,' he said.

'Go into the garden,' I replied. 'I'll be down shortly.'

Violet said: 'My patience me!' And was pink with pleasure, and so was Teresa.

'As a matter of fact,' he said, 'I thought I'd stay another day.'

'We're all rather pleased about that,' I told him.

Aunt Patty came into the garden wearing her sunflower hat. 'This is a nice surprise.'

'It's a nice welcome,' he replied.

'He's staying another day,' said Violet. 'Teresa, pop in and get me three more potatoes. I think there'll be enough peas.'

'Thank you,' he said. 'I was rather hoping you'd ask me to stay.'

'When I think of what that King's Arms serves up in their dining room it wouldn't be right not to get you out of that,' commented Violet.

'I was hoping,' he said, 'that I might be asked for another reason.'

'What was that?' asked Teresa.

'That you found my company entertaining enough to want to put up with me for another day.'

'Oh, we do,' cried Teresa.

'And there's roast pork for dinner,' said Violet.

'Is that a statement or an invitation?'

'Knowing Violet,' put in Aunt Patty, 'it's both.'

'It seems as though I have arrived just as you are going out,' he said, looking at Aunt Patty and me in our outdoor clothes.

'Just down to the village shop. We were going in the dog cart. Would you like to come? Cordelia can show you the church while I'm in the shops and we can all come back together. The church is well worth looking at, though the tower is in danger of falling down at any moment.'

'And the bells are cracked,' put in Violet. 'You should hear them, Mr Markham, or rather you shouldn't. It's a shame.'

'I think we should be going before we get into the tower versus the bells controversy,' said Aunt Patty. 'Come on.'

It was a pleasant morning. John Markham and I went to the church and I showed him the stained glass which was renowned in the neighbourhood and the brass effigies of our most illustrious inhabitants and the names of the vicars dating from the twelfth century. We went through the graveyard stepping over ancient tombstones, the inscriptions on which were almost obliterated by time and weather; and by the time Aunt Patty joined us, I felt I knew John Markham very well.

Over dinner that night, he said: 'I shall have to go to London tomorrow and I shall be going to the farm the week after next. I shall be there for a whole week. I wish you would come and see it.'

'What!' cried Teresa. 'All of us?'

'There's plenty of room and we like visitors. The old farmhouse doesn't get used enough really. Simon Briggs, our manager, has his own place. He never uses the farmhouse at all . . . it's purely for the family and we're always saying it ought to be used more. So, what about it?'

Aunt Patty looked at Violet and Violet looked down at her plate. Normally I should have expected her to raise all sorts of objections. But she did not.

Aunt Patty, who liked unexpected things to happen, was smiling at me.

Teresa said: 'Oh, do let's . . .'

'Are you sure?' I said. 'There are four of us.'

'That's nothing for Forest Hill. The old place can take twenty without cramping. What do you say?'

I said: 'It sounds . . . inviting . . .'

Everybody laughed and then we were making excited

317

plans to go to the Markhams' place on the borders of the forest.

*   *   *

The week we spent at Forest Hill was one which would remain in our memories for a long time to come.

I thought often of Jason Verringer and wondered how he was faring on the Continent in his search for Fiona. But I did wonder what he would do if he found her. If she were married he could not very well bring her home. It did occur to me that when he returned he might come to Moldenbury and I did not want him to arrive when we were at Epping, so I wrote a brief note, saying that I hoped he had found satisfactory information about Fiona and that I should not be at Moldenbury as we were visiting friends.

There was a great deal of bustle getting ready for the visit. Violet insisted on doing a minor spring clean, 'Just in case anything should happen. I wouldn't want people coming in and finding the place all at sixes and sevens.'

'What do you mean . . . anything?' I asked.

Violet pressed her lips together and wouldn't say, but being Violet she had thought of accidents on the railway in which we were all killed or some such dire event. In any case the house must be as it would for a special visit.

We let her get on with it. Teresa and I packed our bags discussing interminably what to take for a week on a farm. Aunt Patty had three hat boxes each containing two hats. We did not comment on that, knowing that Aunt Patty and her hats were inseparable.

John Markham met us in London and all went down together, and from the moment we arrived we loved the place.

Because of the hot summer, harvest started early and we played our part in it. Anxiously we watched the sky for signs of rain; Teresa and I took out bottles of cold tea and bread and cheese to the workers. We sat down with them in the shade and listened to their talk.

Teresa and I went off for rides through the forest. Sometimes we walked. The forest was beautiful but the

318

trees were already beginning to show the tints of autumn and the beeches, elms, birches and sycamores were tinged with yellow; and the oaks were turning reddish brown. I remember the smell of the honeysuckle which grew profusely round the door of the farmhouse. Even now it brings back to me a memory of peace.

At night I would lie in my room and savour the pleasures of being physically tired and intoxicated with sunshine and fresh air. I slept better than I had since I had received the anonymous letter and I was amazed to realize that all through the day I had not thought of it and the rumours and scandals; so tired was I, so full of the impressions of the day that I could not feel the same apprehension and horror that I had known previously. I felt that I was being healed.

We ate the midday meal at the big wooden kitchen table with the windows wide open to the smell of new mown corn, and we listened and joined in the talk of the harvest.

'It's a pity you won't be here for the harvest home,' said John. He seemed so different from the immaculate gentleman who had called on us at Moldenbury. I felt – and I knew the others did too – that I had known him for a very long time.

'Perhaps we could be,' said Teresa hopefully.

'Teresa,' I said, 'we have to go back to school soon.'

'Don't talk of it,' replied Teresa gloomily.

John told us about the harvest home and the festival. 'It's the best time of year. The children make the corn dollies when it is all gathered in.'

' "Ere the winter storms begin," ' quoted Violet.

'And we hang them on the walls. They are talismans in the hope of getting a good harvest next year.'

'We used to do that in my home,' said Violet.

'It's a universal custom,' added John. 'And I think it goes back to the Middle Ages.'

'I like to see the old ways kept up,' said Violet.

I think she was the one who amazed us most. She was really enjoying being at Forest Hill. She had taken over the kitchen. The manager's wife, who usually looked after the

319

household when the family was there, was only too pleased to pass over the responsibilities, and Violet was in her element. She grew quite sentimental talking about her childhood.

In spite of the happy time we had I could not get Lydia out of my mind and when John told me: 'You have Lydia's bedroom!' I seemed to sense her there and I dreamed of her once or twice.

I thought I heard her voice in my dreams. 'You mustn't worry about *me*, Cordelia. I'm dead.'

I woke up with the words echoing in my ear. The light curtains were blowing outward, for the wind had arisen and the window was wide open. Startled from my sleep, I thought it was a ghost standing there.

'Lydia!' I cried and sat up in bed.

Then I saw what it was and, getting out of bed, half shut the window. It seemed quite chilly.

I went back to bed but not to sleep. I kept going over days long ago, remembering Lydia.

But in the morning I forgot her and was out in the fields laughing with the rest of them.

John came with us to London. He was going to Kensington which he did after putting us on the train to Moldenbury.

'It was a wonderful week,' said Teresa. 'Oh, I do like John.'

*   *   *

The holiday was coming to an end. The next day Teresa and I would leave for Colby.

On that last night, after everyone else had retired Aunt Patty came to my room for one of her chats.

'It was a very happy holiday after all,' she said. 'I like the Markhams.'

'Yes, what a happy family. I think they are all feeling the loss of Lydia.'

Aunt Patty was silent for a few seconds. Then she said: 'I think John Markham is half way to falling in love with you, Cordelia.'

320

'Oh, Aunt Patty, I've known him such a short time. You're very romantic.'

'I know you think I'm an ignoramus in these matters because I am an old spinster living in the country. But I do send to Mudies for my three-volume novels and the goings on in them is something of an eye-opener, even to a silly old spinster like me.'

I put my arms round her and kissed her. 'I don't allow disparaging remarks about you, even when you make them yourself.'

'It was such a lovely house.' She looked a little wistful. 'I often think of your being married and having babies. Do you know, I should love some babies.'

'Oh, dear Aunt Patty. I'm sorry I can't oblige.'

'You will one day, I don't doubt. I just thought what a lovely household that was . . . how friendly and easy to get on with. I think John Markham is such a *good* man. You could put your trust in him. You'd know that he would always be there when needed . . . to do what was best.'

'I'm sure he's all that.'

'I daresay we shall be seeing more of him.'

I laughed. 'You're weaving dreams of romance, Aunt Patty.'

'Do you think they are only dreams? I know the signs. You smile. That is because you are considering my lack of experience in such matters. I am not wholly ignorant. I might have married once . . . only it went wrong.'

'You never told me.'

'It was not worth telling. He met someone else.'

'What a fool he must have been.'

'He was very happy, I believe. Life is a matter of taking the right road at the right time. Time is the important thing . . . opportunity too . . . and they must come together. The important thing is to recognize the opportunity while there is time. Cordelia, when the time comes, you must make the right choice. Good night, my dearest child.'

She held me tightly against her.

'I was always comforted when you held me like that,' I said. 'You did, the first time we met. I remember the hat

321

and the smell of lavender . . . and it was just the same then.'

'It will always be, Cordelia,' she said.

Then she kissed me and went out.

The Alarming Discovery

*

The new term had begun. Daisy called her usual pre-school conference and we were all assembled in her study.

'We will do our best,' she said, 'to forget the events of last term. The girls should be under closer supervision when they are out . . . even riding. It was fortunate that the girl involved was Fiona Verringer and that it was from her own home that she finally escaped, and not the school. If it had been one of the others, there could have been unpleasant difficulties with the parents. However, we must guard against such eventualities. I gather from Sir Jason Verringer that he has no idea of the whereabouts of Fiona and her husband, though he actually visited the Continent in search of them. Well, we will hope for a more peaceful term. We don't want too much gossip among the girls. The incident should not be referred to. Girls are inclined to admire those who do foolish things. Another elopement would be a disaster for the school. So . . . that matter is closed.

'It would be a good idea to get them started on some entertainment for the Christmas festivities. It seems early to think of that, but it would keep the girls' minds occupied. Say scenes from Shakespeare . . . little extracts which they could act before the school. It makes for excitement and speculation and keeps their minds busy.

'Miss Grant, I am putting Charlotte Mackay back in Eugenie Verringer's room. They were together originally and have always been good friends. I thought it would help Eugenie. She must be missing her sister. She spent her holiday at the Mackay's place up north near Berwick. I don't want Eugenie brooding too much about her sister. It was a good idea to let her go to the Mackay's place rather than stay at the Hall to be reminded that her sister was no longer there. Eugenie's is not a very placid temperament to begin with and girls like that can be difficult in so many ways.

'There is a new girl. Margaret Keyes. She seems a pleasant creature. She can go into Charlotte's place with Patricia Cartwright.'

She went on to discuss other aspects of the term and finally we were dismissed to go to our rooms and 'settle in' as she called it.

That night I made my rounds. They were all safely in their beds and seemed demure enough, even Charlotte and Eugenie, though Charlotte did give me a somewhat triumphant look as though to remind me of that first night at school when there had been a contretemps over who should sleep in whose room.

The first few days passed uneventfully until one night when I was awakened from sleep by a figure standing by my bed and I heard a voice saying urgently: 'Miss Grant. Miss Grant.'

I started up. Charlotte was standing there.

'Charlotte!' I cried. 'What's wrong?'

'It's Eugenie,' she said. 'She's ill.'

I hastily put on my dressing gown and slippers and followed her to their bedroom. Eugenie was lying back looking very white; there were beads of perspiration on her forehead. It felt clammy.

I said: 'Go for Miss Hetherington at once.'

Charlotte, who seemed really frightened, quickly obeyed.

Daisy was soon at the bedside, her fine white hair in two plaits tied with pale blue ribbon, but she looked as much in command as ever.

'Eugenie is ill!' she said. She leaned over the girl.

'Do you think we should get the doctor?' I asked.

She shook her head. 'Not just yet. It's probably only a bilious attack. We don't want the girls to know. They exaggerate so. There is some sal volatile in my room. Will you go and get it, Charlotte. It is in the cupboard on the right hand side.'

Charlotte went.

'She has probably eaten something which doesn't agree with her,' said Daisy. 'It happens now and then. What did they have for supper?'

'It was fish. And then they had their milk and biscuits before retiring.'

'It must have been the fish. Give her half an hour. If she's no better then, I'll call the doctor.'

Charlotte returned with the sal volatile.

'There,' said Daisy. 'That's better.'

Eugenie opened her eyes.

'Do you feel better now, dear?' asked Daisy in that brisk voice which demanded an affirmative.

'Yes, Miss Hetherington.'

'Felt ill, did you?'

'Yes, Miss Hetherington . . . sick and dizzy.'

'Well, lie still. Miss Grant and I will stay here until you go to sleep and we know you are all right.'

'Thank you,' said Eugenie.

'Charlotte, you should get into bed. You can keep your eye on Eugenie, but we shall be here for a while. It is only a common bilious attack. The fish couldn't have agreed with her.'

How magnificent she was, our Daisy! No general could ever have given more confidence to his troops. One knew that with Daisy in command everything must work according to plan.

Yet . . . there had been the elopement. But then she had known nothing about that until it was a *fait accompli*.

Eugenie had closed her eyes. She was breathing more easily and looked much better.

'I think she's asleep,' said Daisy. 'She looks more like herself.' She touched Eugenie's forehead. 'No fever,' she whispered.

After five minutes of silence she rose and said: 'I think we can return to our beds now. Charlotte, if Eugenie needs

325

anything you'll wake Miss Grant. And if necessary come for me.'

'Yes, Miss Hetherington.'

'Good night, Charlotte. We look to you to keep an eye on Eugenie.'

'Yes, Miss Hetherington. Good night. Good night, Miss Grant.'

Outside my room Daisy paused. 'She'll be all right in the morning. As I thought, a touch of biliousness. Charlotte did well. Do you know, I think that girl would improve considerably if she had something to do. If she felt herself useful . . . What do you think?'

'I'm sure of it.'

'Well, we must watch them both,' said Daisy. 'I don't think we shall be troubled again tonight.'

I went to bed. I was tired and soon asleep.

In the morning Eugenie was better – almost herself, but I thought she should take a little rest. She didn't want to. She was rather ashamed of being ill.

'I'm all right really, Miss Grant. I don't know what it was but I just felt a bit funny.'

'I think you should have a rest this afternoon.'

'Oh no, Miss Grant.'

'Yes, Eugenie. That sort of attack does weaken you more than you realize. I insist that you have a rest this afternoon. You can read or perhaps Charlotte will be with you.'

She agreed rather ungraciously.

It must have been about three o'clock when I went to my room and remembering that Eugenie was resting, I thought I would look in and see if she had obeyed my orders.

The door was closed but I heard the sound of giggles coming from behind it. I guessed Charlotte was with her.

I hesitated, but decided to look in. I tapped at the door. There was a brief silence so I opened it and went in.

Eugenie was lying on her bed and Charlotte was stretched out on hers. On the chair sat Elsa.

'Oh,' I said.

'You told me to rest,' replied Eugenie.

326

'We came to cheer her up,' said Elsa grinning at me.

'You certainly seem to have done that. How are you feeling, Eugenie?'

'All right,' said Eugenie.

'Good. Very well, you can get up when you want to.'

'Thank you, Miss Grant.'

As I went out and shut the door the giggles continued.

I thought about Elsa. She certainly did not behave like a servant and I wondered, as I had on other occasions, whether I should reprimand her for consorting with the girls as though she were one of them rather than a house-maid. But she always contrived to remind me by a look of the old times at Schaffenbrucken when she had behaved with me and my friends rather in the same way as she was with Eugenie and Charlotte. It was one of the disadvantages of being in a position like mine, when someone who had known you as a schoolgirl was present. One could hardly reprimand others for what one had done oneself. Perhaps the most extraordinary aspect was that Charlotte, known to us all as something of a snob, should be so friendly with a servant.

However, I did not think very much more about the incident.

There was a letter for me from John Markham. He asked me what it felt like to be back at school after the holidays. 'That was an unforgettable week we all had together,' he wrote. 'I felt we had all known each other for years. Why ever didn't Lydia ask you for holidays? We might have known each other earlier. I do wish I could see you. Is it taboo to visit the school? I suppose it would not be considered quite *comme il faut*. Isn't there something called a half-term? Do you go home? Perhaps it is rather a long way for such a short time. It wouldn't be quite so far to come to London. I'd like you to meet my brother Charles. Perhaps you and Teresa could visit us? Do think about it.'

I did think about it and it was rather enticing. I did not mention it to Teresa because I felt it would raise her hopes and I was not sure whether I should go.

I was still suffering from the shock of my encounter with

327

Jason Verringer in the Devil's Den at Colby Hall. It had disturbed me even more than I had thought at the time. I could not stop thinking of him and my mind built up images of what might have happened if I had not made that dramatic gesture in thrusting my hands through the window. It had been a hopeless gesture in any case. I should never have been able to elude him if he was determined to catch me. And if I had managed to get through the window would I have jumped from the top of the tower? What I had implied was that I preferred death to submission to him. It was foolhardy. Yet it had sobered him. He had been really shocked to see the blood on my hands.

Stop thinking of him, I admonished myself. Forget him. It was just an unpleasant experience from which I had emerged unscathed. Even the scars on my hands had healed now. But at Colby I was surrounded by ruins of the past with all the grim legends and terrible sufferings that must have occurred and I was overwhelmed by an ambience of disaster and doom.

Here strange things happened. Jason Verringer seemed never far away. What had really happened to his wife? Where was Marcia Martindale? There would always be questions where Jason was. He was a man of dark secrets. One could almost believe that the Devil had been one of his forebears.

And how different it had been at Epping – the sunshine, the smell of corn, the *simplicity* of everything, the way of life, the people. It was clean and fresh and easy to understand. Peace . . . that was what it offered . . . and peace seemed very alluring just now. I had a desire to be there and yet . . . almost against my will I was drawn to the dark towers of Colby Hall and the ruins of the Abbey.

What finally decided me about taking up John's invitation was another letter I had. It was forwarded on to me by Aunt Patty and was from Monique Delorme.

'Dear Cordelia,' she wrote in French.

'I am no longer Mademoiselle Delorme but Madame de la Creseuse. Yes. I married Henri. Life is

328

wonderful. We are coming to London. We have been lent a house for two weeks by friends of Henri. So we shall be in your capital from the third of next month. It would be wonderful to see you. Write to me there. I will give you the address. I look forward to hearing your news. Do come.

Always your loving and faithful friend.

Monique.'

I told Daisy that I had received an invitation from some friends with whom we had stayed in the summer.

'Their home is in London, but we were with them in the country for a week. I could go in mid term. It is only for five days, including the week-end. I thought I might take advantage of it.'

Daisy was thoughtful. 'Few of the girls will go home. Of course there are no lessons. I don't think any of the other mistresses plan to go away. Yes, I do think you might manage it.'

'Teresa is invited too.'

'Oh, that will be nice for her.'

'Then it is quite all right for me to make my plans?'

'Yes. I think so. Go ahead.'

So I did. John wrote back that he was delighted. Teresa was wild with joy. I also wrote to Monique at the address she had enclosed in her letter and said that I would call on her when she was in London.

*   *   *

John was at Paddington station and in a short time we were trotting along in a cab to his home in Kensington. It was a small house in a square and guarded by two ferocious-looking stone lions; the white steps leading to a heavy oak door were gleaming and the brass shone like gold.

When he opened the door with his key, a tall young man was hovering in the hall.

'This is Charles,' said John. 'He's longing to meet you. He's heard all about your stay at the farm.'

329

It was the same open face and good looks. I liked Charles at once.

The maid appeared.

'Oh yes, Sarah,' said John. 'They'll want to go to their rooms. Teresa, you are next to Cordelia.'

We mounted a staircase richly carpeted in a warm scarlet and came to a landing. The maid opened a door and I was in a bright bedroom with a four-poster bed, not a bit like the ones they had at the Hall, heavily curtained in velvet. This one had lace curtains draped at either end and caught into bows of pale mauve satin ribbon. It had brass knobs and rails and seemed to glow with freshness. There was some light and elegant furniture which suggested eighteenth-century France. It was charming. I went to the window and looked out on a small paved garden in which were pots of greenery which must glow with colour in the spring and summer. Chrysanthemums and Michaelmas daisies were still in flower against a grey brick wall.

Teresa came in. She looked radiant. She had a lovely little room and there was a communicating door between it and mine. I went in and had a look. It had obviously been a dressing room.

'Isn't it wonderful?' she cried.

She was so happy. Not only to get away from school but because we were here with John. She was a girl who fixed her affections firmly when she found an object of admiration. She had turned to me in desperation and from our association had come all the people she cared for most. Myself. Aunt Patty. Violet. And now she had added John to that band. It was overwhelming for her who had had no one and then suddenly so many.

I feared she was a little dramatic. I should never forget how she had flung Marcia Martindale's earring into the ponds. She was so young and had little control over her emotions and, being inexperienced, saw everyone as very good or very bad. There were devils and angels . . . and nothing in between. She would have to learn, but for the next few days she would be with those whom she loved and admired and was happy.

330

Dinner that night was exciting. There was a gracious dining room with long windows onto the street. As we ate we heard the clop clop of passing horse-drawn carriages and occasionally the sound of a newsboy selling late night papers.

We talked of the week in the country, of school, of London and what we should do during our stay.

'There is so much to show you,' said John. 'Now what shall it be first?'

'I have an appointment with an old school friend,' I said. 'She has invited me to call. That is for the day after tomorrow.'

'Well then, what's for tomorrow. Teresa, have you any idea? The zoo is amusing.'

'I like animals,' cried Teresa.

'All right then. Tomorrow morning, zoo. How would you like to ride in the Row, Teresa?'

Teresa was slightly less enthusiastic. She had never fully recovered from her fall, although I had persuaded her to ride again. 'Yes,' she said hesitantly.

So it was agreed.

We had a wonderful morning. It was not only Teresa who was delighted by the animals. We watched the seals fed; we marvelled at the lions and tigers; and we laughed at the antics of the monkeys. We sipped lemonade on the terraces and I thought how happy I was. I did not want the visit to end.

Dinner was a hilarious affair with everyone – now that they had got used to us – trying to talk at once. We sat in the elegant drawing room, rather like the dining room only at the back of the house instead of the front, with French windows facing the little patio-like garden.

We talked until we were drowsy and rather reluctantly retired to our beds because this was the end of another happy day.

*   *   *

331

John had to go to his bank on the next morning, and on the way there took me to the address which Monique had given me.

It was an elegant house in Albemarle Street leading off Piccadilly. We had driven through Hyde Park, which I thought enchanting, then turned into Piccadilly, where fashionably attired people strolled, and the horses and carriages passed picturesquely down the main thoroughfare.

John took me in. A smart young maid said that Madame was waiting for me. I was ushered into a drawing room and there was Monique looking very pretty indeed in a frilly morning gown of turquoise blue.

I introduced John, and Monique begged him to take a little coffee or wine with us, but he said he had business in the City and would collect me in two hours' time.

'So soon?' said Monique in her attractive English.

'I shall have to go then,' I said, 'for we have arranged to take a trip on the river this afternoon.'

John left us and we settled down.

'What a charming man!' said Monique, when he had gone. 'Henri, too, is out on business. He hopes to meet you when he comes back. I have talked so much of you.'

I said: 'Marriage suits you, Monique.'

'Oh, Henri . . . he is so good.'

'It turned out very well then . . . You used to call it your *mariage de convenance*. Do you remember?'

'Oh yes, it was decided in our cradles. Oh, the papers and the lawyers . . . the settlement . . . the arguments.'

'And it worked!'

'And this Mr Markham . . . he is for you?'

'Oh no. He's just a friend. I should have told you. He is Lydia's brother.'

'Of course . . . Lydia Markham. Where is Lydia then?'

'Oh . . . you don't know . . . Lydia died.'

'But no!'

'It was a skiing accident.'

'Lydia . . . skiing! I am surprised. But how terrible. I never knew.'

332

'Well, I suppose I shouldn't have heard if I hadn't written to her. Her brother opened my letter and then came to see me. That was when I was with my aunt.'

'Oh, the aunt, yes. How you used to talk about the Aunt! Who was it?'

'Aunt Patty.'

'The good Aunt Patty.'

The maid came in bringing coffee. When she had gone Monique poured.

'I cannot stop thinking about Lydia . . . To die like that. It is hard to believe.'

'Yes, a terrible shock. I was astonished when her brother told me she had married.'

'Oh, I knew that. Lydia wrote and told me so. She was wildly happy.'

'She didn't write to me.'

Monique was silent and I looked at her sharply. Her lips were pressed together. I remembered that it was an old habit of hers. It meant that she knew something which she should not tell.

'I wondered why she didn't write to me,' I said. 'When I wrote to you I wrote to her also. I had replies from you and Frieda but nothing from Lydia.'

'Well, she didn't write to you because . . .'

'Because what?'

'Oh . . . I don't suppose it matters now. She thought you might be a little upset.'

'Upset? Why should I be?'

'About her being the one to get married, you see.'

'Why should I be upset?'

'Well, because we thought, didn't we, that you were the one.'

I looked blank.

'I'm sure it doesn't matter now. It might have been you who had the skiing accident. But I don't suppose you would have. You would have been better at it.'

'I don't really follow all this, Monique.'

'Cast your mind back. Do you remember Elsa?'

'Yes, and it's a funny thing. She's at my school now.'

333

'Elsa . . . at your school? Well, that is very strange. What they call a coincidence, of course.'

'She said she got tired of Schaffenbrucken and came to England. She had one job which she didn't like and ended up at my school.'

'Very odd. But then life is.'

'You were telling me about Lydia.'

'I was saying, do you remember how Elsa told us that if we went into the forest at the time of Hunter's Moon we might meet our future husbands?'

'Yes. We were a silly lot. We believed it.'

'Well, there was something in it. Do you remember the man we called the Stranger?'

'Yes, yes, I do remember.'

'We thought he liked you. He seemed to. That was why Lydia didn't want you to know she was married. She thought you'd be upset because you would know it wasn't you he had liked after all. It was Lydia.'

The room was swinging round me. I could not believe I was hearing correctly.

I said: 'His name was Edward Compton.'

'No, it wasn't that. It was er . . . let me think . . . Mark somebody. Mark Chessingham . . . or ton . . . or something.'

'It couldn't have been.'

'Yes, it was. She was ever so excited. She said it was true about meeting your future husband. Elsa was right about that. But she said she wasn't telling you because she thought you might be hurt. What's the matter?'

'Nothing. It seemed so odd . . .'

'You do mind, Cordelia. You did think that he . . .'

'I'd almost forgotten him. I'd told myself he didn't exist.'

'Oh, he existed all right. He was Lydia's husband. Poor Lydia! He was very good-looking, wasn't he? I only saw him once but he really was . . . fascinating. Do have some more coffee.'

She went on talking but I was not listening to what she said. I could only think. So he went away and married

334

Lydia. But why had he said his name was that of a man who had been dead for twenty years?

I don't think Monique found my visit as exciting as she had thought it was going to be. John called for me as we had arranged and I was immensely relieved when we said goodbye to Monique and her husband who had returned just before our departure.

As we drove to Kensington, I said: 'I have made an alarming discovery.'

Then I told him about the man in the forest and how I had seen him on the boat and again at Grantley, how he had disappeared suddenly and that when I had gone to the village in Suffolk where he had told me his home was, I had found that the manor house which he had said was his home was burned out and the name he had given me was on the tombstone of a man who had died twenty years before. And this, according to Monique, was Lydia's husband.

He listened intently. He said it was an incredible story and he wondered what it meant.

'I'll tell you what we'll do,' he went on. 'We'll go down to that Suffolk village where you saw the tombstone and we'll see what we can find out.'

*   *   *

There was a train to Bury St Edmunds at eight thirty next morning and John and I decided to catch it. Charles was taking Teresa on the river from Westminster Stairs to Hampton Court so they were safely disposed of.

It was a relief to be able to talk to John about this strange affair, because I did feel now that it not only concerned me but Lydia.

He asked me to describe the man. It wasn't easy because the description could fit so many. Not that he was ordinary by any means. But fair curling hair, blue eyes, chiselled features . . . many had those, and it was not easy to explain that quality of other worldliness.

I told myself there must have been a mistake. Lydia could have imagined that her lover was the romantic

335

stranger she had met in the wood at the time of the Hunter's Moon.

'I can't believe that she would do that. Lydia wasn't a dreamer. She was very practical really.'

'That's true. How are we going to start looking?'

'Well, his name is Edward Compton or Mark Chessingham.'

'But why should he give two names?'

'I don't know. That's what we have to find out. He mentioned this place Croston in Suffolk and the name of Edward Compton. You went there and saw the name on a tombstone. There must be some connection.'

'Yet he was really Mark Chessingham.'

'Very odd. The thing is, how are we going to start our enquiries?'

'There were some houses. Perhaps we could ask there.'

'We'll see how it goes.'

We left the train and took the small branch line to Croston. Memories came back to me. We walked first to the graveyard and I showed John the tombstone with Edward Compton's name on it.

'What next?' I asked.

'I noticed quite a large house on the common. What if we told them we were trying to trace someone. They might be able to help.'

We went to the house, which was obviously the most important in the village. A maid admitted us and John asked if he could see the master or mistress of the house. It says a great deal for his business-like manner and air of respectability that we were granted an interview.

Mrs Carstairs was a comfortable looking middle-aged woman who was clearly a little intrigued to find her callers were strangers. She graciously bade us sit down and state our business. She was clearly impressed by John's urbane manner. He gave her his card with the name of his bank on it.

'We are making enquiries about a man who, we think, may have lived here at some time. Unfortunately we are not sure of his name. It could be Mark Chessingham.'

336

He waited. She gave no sign that she had heard that name. 'Or Edward Compton,' he added.

'Oh, that must be the family who were at the Manor. There is not a Manor now. It was burned to the ground. There's been talk of rebuilding but they never seem to get round to it. But the Comptons lived there. It was a tragedy. I think that several members of the family were burned to death. There aren't any Comptons now.'

'Oh dear,' said John. 'The trail seems to end. Perhaps there is some branch of the family . . .?'

'I've never heard of them. I don't think I can help you. You seem to be talking about people who have been dead long ago.'

'You've been most helpful. We knew we had a difficult task.'

'You have to live here for centuries to be recognized by the people here. We're looked on as foreigners almost, though it's nearly fifteen years since we came. Oh, wait a minute. There's old Mrs Clint. She's a know-all. She's lived here all her life and must be about ninety. She'd remember the fire. If you want to know anything about the people who lived here she'd be the one to tell you.'

'It's most kind of you to be so helpful. Where could we find her?'

'I'll take you to the door and show you. Her cottage is just across the Green. She's bound to be in. She can't get about much now. Her daughter goes in and does what is necessary.'

'Well, thank you very much.'

'I'm only sorry I can't be of more help.'

She stood at her door and pointed out the cottage across the Green.

'Knock,' she said. 'She'll call for you to go in. She likes visitors. The trouble is that when she starts to talk she doesn't know when to stop. I hope you've got plenty of time!'

'The whole day,' said John.

We walked across the Green.

'Well,' he said, 'we didn't draw entirely a blank.'

337

It was as the lady of the house had said. We knocked and were bidden to enter.

Mrs Clint was in bed, a bright old lady in a white cap from which fine grey hairs straggled; she wore woollen mittens over her claw-like hands.

'I thought it was my daughter dropping in with the broth she's bringing for my dinner,' she said. 'Who are you?'

'We have to apologize for disturbing you,' said John. 'But the lady from the big house across the common told us that you might be able to help us.'

'That's Mrs Carstairs from London. They don't belong here. What do you want from me? Give a seat to the young lady and you have that rush chair. Mind, it's a bit weak. Old Bob hasn't been round mending this year. I don't know . . . people nowadays. Used to come regular as clockwork. He'd do the chairs and sharpen the scissors. You could rely on him once. What are you looking for?'

'Mark Chessingham or Edward Compton.'

'Mark Whatsisname . . . no. And if it's Edward Compton you're looking for, the graveyard's the place for you.'

'We might have the wrong name,' said John. 'The man we are looking for is tall and fair. He has a slight accent . . . Might have been German. Very faint . . . almost unnoticeable.'

'Oh yes,' I said excitedly. 'I remember that. He had. So you noticed.'

Mrs Clint scratched her head through her cap.

'Twenty years or more, the whole house burned down. The children . . . It was a blow to the village. But not many remembers now . . . only us old ones.' She paused. 'A bit of an accent you say and he lived here . . . I only ever heard a German accent once. My son Jimmy he had an ear for that sort of thing. He was a builder and he went abroad with his master on some big job. When he came back he said the Dowlings had German accents. The mother was German you see. Dowling he wasn't much good. Worked up at the big house at one time. Drink, it was . . . His downfall. Never had a job after the Manor went.'

'Who had the German accent?' asked John.

338

'She did. Well, she couldn't speak much English. Couldn't always grasp what she was trying to say. My Jimmy used to say you could understand that with her, but the young ones, born over here . . . brought up over here . . . you'd think they'd be different.'

'And what was their name, did you say?'

'Dowling.'

'Could we see them?'

'If you know where they've gone to you could.' She gave a hoarse chuckle. 'What'll stop you is, you don't know where they are. They went away . . . all of them. There was a boy and a girl . . . very handsome both of them. Some said they went to Germany. Old Dowling had gone by then. So had she. He took more than the usual and one night fell down the stairs. He lingered for a few months. Then that was the end. That was years ago. Always together they was . . . the brother and sister. They were what you might call a devoted family.'

'You have been a great help to us, Mrs Clint.'

'Have I now? I'm glad of that.'

'Thank you very much and now we have to be getting on. Good day to you.'

'A good morning's work,' said John as we came out onto the green.

'So you think we've discovered something?'

'Only that the Dowlings were half German and although Lydia's husband never said that he was, it is in my mind that he must be.'

It had been an interesting time and I had enjoyed being with John as I had done before; we had found out very little in Suffolk and we did not even know if that was relevant; the mystery remained as deep as ever; but at least I knew that my stranger had gone from me to Lydia and I constantly asked myself why he had come first to me and then given a false name; and why should it have been that of someone long dead?

It was baffling and somehow alarming to think that he had gone straight to Lydia and disappeared as far as I was concerned without even saying he was going.

339

It was certainly mysterious and I still had a niggling feeling that he might not have been human, that he was some spirit of doom, the ghost perhaps of that boy – or man – whose life had been cut short and now lay in Croston churchyard. Fanciful thinking, but then the matter was fanciful.

Daisy had welcomed me back and implied, with only the slightest trace of reproach, that I had been missed. After all, it was the half-term holiday and if one could get away one was entitled to do so.

'Eugenie had another bad turn while you were away,' she told me. 'Charlotte came and wakened me.'

'That's rather alarming,' I said. 'I hope she is not sickening for something.'

'It was the same sort of thing . . . sickness and giddiness. It was a little worse than last time. I got the doctor in to have a look at her.'

'What did he say?'

'Just what I thought. Something she had eaten did not agree with her.'

'But that's the second time it's happened.'

'She may have some weakness internally. There may be something which she cannot digest.'

'Was it fish again?'

'No. Oddly enough. It was stew. All the others were all right. I had some myself. It was very good.'

'You don't think she's in a nervous state, do you? That could have this effect.'

'That's what I mentioned to the doctor. She must miss her sister.'

'Although she was always more friendly with Charlotte than she was with Fiona.'

'Well, blood is thicker than water. I think she may feel restless. It's a pity Fiona doesn't bring that husband of hers to the Hall and make it all normal. I think that would be a help.'

'I am sure it would and perhaps she will in time.'

'We'll watch Eugenie and see if we can find out what is upsetting her.'

340

'Yes, we'll do that.'

When I took my afternoon ride I met Jason Verringer. He had evidently been waiting to catch me.

I said: 'Good day,' and galloped on. But he was beside me.

'Slow down,' he said. 'I want to talk to you.'

'I have no wish to talk to you,' I flung over my shoulder.

He brought his horse directly in front of mine so that I had to slow down.

'I've had enough of this,' he said angrily. 'How long is it since I've seen you?'

I felt an excitement grip me and realized afresh how much I enjoyed my battles with him. He might subdue me through his greater physical strength but never mentally. I was a match for him and I couldn't help revelling in making that clear.

'Did you expect me to call? Leave my card with grateful thanks.'

'My dearest Cordelia, how wonderful it is to be with you again! I have been so bored . . . so wretched . . .'

'I have always believed that you are prone to self pity. I have to get back to school now.'

'You have just come out.'

'It is such a short break.'

'I hear you have some new and very charming friends. The Markhams. I know the name. City bankers. A very respectable family.'

'How knowledgeable you are!'

'I make a point of knowing what you are doing.'

'You waste your time for it can be of no importance to you.'

'Stop it. You know it is of the utmost importance. Let us go into the woods. We can tie up our horses and we can talk comfortably.'

'You must think me very gullible if you think I would ever put myself in a vulnerable position with you around.'

'Are you never going to forget?'

'Never.'

'If you had not been so unadventurous it could have been

341

the turning point. I could have shown you what you are missing.'

'You showed me very clearly. That is why I am asking you not to try to see me again alone. I know that, because of the school, a certain amount of contact is necessary and unavoidable. But I want no more than that.'

'Of course you had a wonderful summer holiday, didn't you?'

'I did.'

'I heard through Eugenie.'

'Teresa has been talking, has she?'

'I understand this banking fellow has all the virtues. I heard he is something of a paragon.'

'That would be Teresa's version. Teresa is inclined to glorify the people whom she likes.'

'And vilify those she doesn't.'

'It's a habit of the young.'

'Cordelia, do stop this. We must talk. It is no use your trying to pretend you are indifferent to me. Do you think I don't know how you feel? If you'd stop being so restrained and were natural, you'd come to me right away. It's what you want. But you are so under control . . . so much the schoolmistress. But we're not in the classroom. We're two living creatures . . . a man and a woman, and the most natural thing in the world is for us to be together.'

'You don't understand me in the least.'

'But I do. You want me . . . *me*. I am the one for you, and you are fighting against it all the time. Why? Because respectability is standing beside you, urging you not to become involved with a man who may have helped one woman to her death and murdered another because he found her a nuisance. You listen to gossip. You accuse me . . . when all the time you want me. I could show you that you want me as much as . . . or almost . . . as I want you.'

I was afraid of him when he talked like that. Why did I stay here with him? Why did he excite me as he did? Was there something in what he said?

He went on: 'You believe I killed my wife . . . an overdose of laudanum . . . so easy to administer. And then

342

the other . . . strangulation . . . a blow on the head . . . and then I buried her body in the woods . . . no, I threw it into the fish ponds. That was the better idea. It was done by a member of my family before. In spite of this . . . the gossip, the scandal and your lack of faith, you want me. What could be a stronger indication than that? You turn away from me, but you can't hide the truth. You wanted me in the Devil's Den. You were longing for me. You wanted me to force you. Then you could have come to terms with your conscience. But old Respectability was standing by your side. "Escape", he said. "Break the window. Leap out." Anything that dear old Respectability should be satisfied. Do you think that would have stopped me?'

'Yes. It did.' I laughed because I couldn't help it and he laughed with me.

He went on: 'Oh, Cordelia, you are throwing away what you want most. If you reject me you will regret it all your life. This knight in shining armour . . . this Galahad, this symbol of purity, this miserable banker who always adds his figures correctly and has never had a single mistress and is without sin and stain . . . do you think he is your sort?'

I was laughing again. 'You are quite ridiculous,' I said. 'I am sure he would be amused to hear himself so described. Surely there is nothing to be despised in adding up figures correctly, and I should imagine there is a certain amount of that involved in running an estate. You seem very anxious to marry me off. I might tell you that it has not been suggested, and I am surprised that you listen to schoolgirls' tattle.'

'The proposal will come. Bankers always know exactly how long to wait and how to get the right answer.'

'Admirable people,' I said.

'Oh, I am tired of your schoolmistress attitude to life. You are afraid to live . . . afraid of scandal.'

'Which you never were. You see how different we are. We should never match.'

'Not like you and your banker. Precise, conventional, the household accounts always in order, making love every Wednesday night, having four children, that being the

343

correct number. You're laughing. You're laughing all the time at me. You're happy with me, aren't you?'

'Goodbye,' I said, and galloped away in the direction of the school.

It was true in a way. If I was not entirely happy with him, I was exhilarated as with no one else. No, I was not happy with him; but on the other hand I was not happy away from him.

It would be better if I never saw him alone. I would shut him right out of my mind. I would remember those peaceful days on the farm.

I went straight to my room to change for my class.

Elsa was standing on the stairs, a duster in her hand, outside my room.

'Good afternoon, Miss Grant,' she said with her familiar smile.

'Good afternoon, Elsa.'

I was about to walk past when she said: 'Miss Grant, is Eugenie Verringer all right?'

'Eugenie? Why?'

'Well, she's been ill, hasn't she? She's been ill twice. I was worried about her.'

'She's all right. It was only bilious attacks.'

'Oh, I'm glad. You get fond of some of the girls . . . like I did at Schaffenbrucken. There was you and the French girl and that German one and that other English girl.'

'Lydia,' I said. 'Lydia Markham. You'll be sorry to hear she was killed in a skiing accident.'

She clutched the door and looked really disturbed. 'Not that Lydia . . .'

'Yes. I discovered it only the other day. Her brother came to see me and told me all about it. She was married.'

'She was only a young girl.'

'Old enough to be married. By the way, Elsa, do you remember when we went into the forest? You told us about Hunter's Moon and all that.'

'That was a bit of rubbish just to amuse you girls.'

'Well, you were right that time. We met a man and he got to know Lydia afterwards. He married her.'

344

'You don't say!'

'Rather strange, wasn't it?'

'And then her to die like that. Skiing did you say? I shouldn't have thought she was a one for that sort of thing.'

'No, her husband must have changed her.'

'Oh, Miss Grant, this is a bit of a shock for me. Of course it's a long time since I saw her . . . Fancy you meeting her brother like that. It must have been a shock for you.'

'A terrible shock. I saw Monique . . . you remember her? She told me about Lydia. Lydia hadn't written to me.'

'Oh dear, it's all come about in a funny sort of way . . . You not knowing and all that. But what I really wanted to ask you about was Eugenie. I heard they had the doctor to her. What did he say?'

'Nothing serious. It seems she's prone to biliousness.'

'Oh. I'm glad. It was her having it before made me wonder. Weakening, that sort of thing.'

'Yes, but Eugenie's young. It's just that something must be upsetting her. We'll find out what it is and put an end to these distressing attacks. It happens now and then.'

'I'm sure it does. I'm glad it's nothing serious. I began to wonder . . . And it's a terrible shock about that Lydia.'

'Yes,' I said, and went into my room.

*   *   *

November had come, dank, dark and gloomy. Aunt Patty wrote that the Markhams had asked us to spend Christmas with them. She thought it would be a lovely idea. 'A sort of Dingley Dell Christmas, dear. Can't you imagine it? Teresa, of course, is included in the invitation.'

I thought of it. It would be pleasant. When I told Teresa she clasped her hands in ecstasy.

'Oh do let's go. Do let's.'

I was still smarting from my encounter with Jason and I thought how peaceful it would be on the Essex farm, and impulsively I wrote back to Aunt Patty and said we must accept.

I felt I was being drawn closer and closer to John Markham. It was true what Jason had said – he would not

345

be impulsive. His life would be orderly, lived on an even keel; and after the events of the last months, that was a state of affairs which seemed very inviting.

We were busy at school. There was what Eileen called the usual Christmas fever. All the anguish about who was to play in the pieces we were doing: *Romeo and Juliet* and *The Merchant of Venice*. Eileen said she wished Miss Hetherington would show a little of the quality of mercy and instead of giving us two extracts concentrate on one.

'The Merchant would have been ample,' she said. 'And I am surprised that dear Daisy thinks that the sight of Juliet quaffing the draught which is to send her into a trance is suitable for impressionable girls.'

It seemed that rehearsals were going on all the time and it was more like a theatre than a school.

'It pleases the parents and we'll do it the day before break-up,' said Daisy. 'However, we'll have a show two weeks earlier to make sure it is all right for Parents' Day.'

Eugenie had another attack in the middle of the night. We didn't take much notice. We were used to those attacks now. It was just something that did not agree with her.

'We must find out what it is,' said Daisy. 'It seems the poor child has a weak stomach . . . nothing serious. When we discover what is causing these upsets we shall be able to stop them.'

Eugenie seemed to take the attacks lightly, for two days later she was playing Juliet with great verve.

There was an atmosphere of Christmas in the town. The shop windows displayed goods and invited people to shop early for Christmas. Mrs Baddicombe had a special window full of cards and had white cotton wool on strings like beads hanging down to give an impression of falling snow.

When I went in, she said: 'Do you like my window? Christmassy, don't 'ee think? And how is it up at the school now? Getting ready for the break. Mind you there's a whole month to go yet.'

I said we were all well and I hoped it was the same with her.

'We're that busy,' she said, 'and likely to get more.

346

How's that Miss Verringer? I heard she was very poorly. That maid up there . . . she said the poor girl was very ill, and she wouldn't be surprised if she were sickening for something.'

'That's nonsense. She just has a weak stomach, that's all.'

'Weak stomachs can be a sign of something worse . . . according to that maid of yours . . .'

'What maid?'

'The foreign-looking one. Oh, she's not really foreign but there's something different about her. Elsa . . . is it?'

'Oh I know. She talked about Miss Verringer, did she?'

Mrs Baddicombe nodded. 'If you want my opinion, she's upset about her sister going off like that. Nobody's ever heard where she be to, have they?'

'I daresay she'll be bringing her husband home in due course,' I said.

'It's to be hoped she's got one.'

'Mrs Baddicombe, you shouldn't . . .'

'But you know what men are. Or perhaps you don't. But you'll find out.' Her eyes twinkled. 'Soon, I shouldn't wonder.'

I found all my resentment rising against her. I did not want her inventing illnesses for Eugenie so I hesitated and said: 'Miss Verringer is quite well. We haven't any anxiety about her health.'

'Well nobody could be more glad than me to hear that. If you ask me that girl . . . what's her name . . . Elsa? . . . I reckon she's a bit of a gossip.'

I couldn't help smiling and Mrs Baddicombe went on: 'She's not a bad-looking girl. I think she's got someone tucked away . . . in foreign parts, I reckon.'

'What do you mean . . . tucked away?'

'I reckon she's over here saving up to get married. She's always writing to someone . . . and it's a man. I've seen the name on the envelope when she's sticking on the stamp. A Mr Somebody . . . I couldn't quite see the name. Well, it's not easy upside-down. I said to her I said in fun like, "Oh,

347

another love letter eh?'' and she just smiled and wouldn't say a thing. When you think how she'll come in here and talk . . . But some can be close about themselves though ready enough to talk of others. But I know there's somebody. She's always writing to him. And he seems to be on the move a bit . . . sometimes it's one country, sometimes another. I have to look up the cost of the stamp. France . . . Germany . . . Austria . . . Switzerland . . . all of them places. Last time it was Austria.'

'Perhaps she has lovers in all those places,' I said.

'No, it's the same one . . . as far as I can see. Sometimes she'll get the stamps and don't put them on at the counter. Then I am in the dark.'

'How perverse of her.'

'Well, that's life, ain't it? You'll be going home soon I expect. Nice for you.'

I bought my stamps and came out.

I always felt there was something sinister about that abnormal curiosity of hers. The idea of checking up on the stamps people bought and not only speculating about the recipients of the mail but discussing it with anyone who came into the shop!

Towards the end of November it started to snow.

'They boast in this part of the world that they only see snow once in seventeen years,' commented Eileen. 'This is two years running. We must be approaching another ice age.'

The girls enjoyed it. It was fun for them to be cut off for several days. From our windows the ruins looked like something out of another world – ethereal and delicately beautiful.

'I wish the wind would drop,' I said. 'When it blows from the north it makes queer whining noises like souls in distress.'

Eileen said: 'It must be all those monks rising up in protest against old Henry who destroyed their Abbey.'

'That's no reason why they should complain to us,' I pointed out.

'They're complaining about the injustices of the world,'

348

retorted Eileen. 'Mind you, we all feel like that some-times.'

'Oh, Eileen, you're contented enough.'

'I shall be when we break up for Christmas. Just imagine the bliss. No more trying to make Constables out of people who can't draw a straight line. The only one here who has a modicum of talent is Eugenie Verringer, though Teresa Hurst is coming on nicely. No more lovers of Verona and that wretched pound of flesh. Clare Simpson sounds more like a pork butcher than a brilliant young lawyer. It was a great mistake to cast her as Portia.'

'She has two young sisters, candidates for the Academy,' I pointed out. 'Don't forget parents will be coming to the perfected performance.'

'Who knows, it might be enough to put them off forever. I must say Charlotte makes a fair Romeo. She's quite a good actress, that girl. I don't think Eugenie is right for Juliet, but then the poor girl lost her sister. I wonder how Sir Henry Irving would like to choose his actors for Daisy's reasons?'

'Oh, Eileen, it is only the school play!'

Eileen put on an air of mock despair. 'How can I be ex-pected to produce a masterpiece when you, my fellow con-spirator in this impossible task, see it only as the school play!'

So it went on. The sessions in the calefactory were a great relief and Eileen was always amusing. There wasn't one who was not looking forward with anticipation to the Christmas holidays.

It was the beginning of December. The cold persisted although we were able to get out. Miss Hetherington allowed tobogganing down the gentle slope and the girls were enjoying it immensely. The gardeners had made extra toboggans so that several of the girls should indulge at the same time.

Then one night I was awakened. This time by Eugenie.

'Miss Grant. Miss Grant.' She was shaking me. 'Wake up. Charlotte. She's ill . . . just as I was.'

I hastily put on my dressing gown and slippers and went to their room.

349

This was worse than Eugenie's attacks. Charlotte was writhing in pain; she was very sick and her face was the same colour as the sheets.

I said: 'Get Miss Hetherington at once.'

Daisy came and I could see that even she was alarmed. This was a different aspect of the case. Eugenie might have had a weakness, but when another girl was taken ill that was a serious matter.

'We'll get the doctor at once,' she said. 'Go down to the stables and see if you can find Tom Rolt. Send him off immediately. Better put something warm on first. We don't want you down with pneumonia.'

I hastily put on boots and a cloak and dashed out, my steps crunching on the snow, the wind blowing my hair about my face. I found Tom Rolt, who lived over the stables. He was disgruntled at being called out and it took him a little time to get the trap ready. He took it because he said he would be able to bring the doctor back with him.

This he did, but it was an hour and a half after Eugenie had awakened me before he came and by that time Charlotte was a little better. The pain seemed to have disappeared and she lay white and still in her bed.

The doctor was a little peevish to have been brought from his bed for what he considered to be another bilious attack. He had thought at first that it was Eugenie he was coming to see and was surprised to find it was another girl.

'It's the same complaint,' he said. 'There must be something here which is upsetting the girls.'

'I can assure you, Doctor,' said Daisy with a hint of righteous wrath, 'that there is nothing in this school to harm my girls.'

'It is something they are taking. You see, Miss Hetherington, the symptoms are the same. There is something which is poisoning them and naturally they are rejecting it.'

'Poisoning them! I never heard of such a thing! Everything we eat here is of the best. We grow our own food. You can question the gardeners.'

'There are lots of new ideas now, Miss Hetherington.

350

There are things that poison some and not others. It seems these two girls are rejecting something which they are eating.'

'Charlotte's attack is worse than Eugenie's.'

'It may be that she has not got the same resistance to it. This girl is very weak. She will have to rest for a week, I should say.'

'Oh dear, how distressing. We shall have to find a new Romeo.'

I couldn't help smiling although I was upset to see Charlotte so ill. Heaven knew she had been a trial to me but she was pathetic now, a shadow of her former arrogant self.

'She should be carefully fed while she is recovering,' said the doctor. 'Just a light diet. Boiled fish, milk puddings . . .'

'Of course,' said Daisy. 'She should stay in bed, you say.'

'Yes, until she feels strong enough to get up. This will have weakened her considerably. The main thing is to be careful of what you give her to eat. There must be something which is not agreeing with the girls.'

'It is strange,' I commented, 'that it should have happened to two in the same room.'

The doctor looked round the room as though searching for some evil there in those four walls.

'A coincidence most likely,' he said. He looked at Eugenie who was sitting on her bed looking frightened. 'She should have absolute rest. She'll sleep tonight for I am going to give her a sedative, and I should like her to sleep through tomorrow. It would be better if she could be in a room on her own.'

Miss Hetherington looked perplexed. 'All the rooms are fully occupied at the moment . . .'

I said: 'Eugenie's bed could be moved into my room.'

'That's an excellent idea, Miss Grant. We'll get that done tomorrow. For a few nights, Eugenie, you will sleep in Miss Grant's room. In the morning take what you need as quietly as you can.' She turned to me. 'It would only be for a few nights. Then we'll be back to normal.'

'Good,' said the doctor. 'She's sleeping now. She'll be

351

better in the morning . . . but rest and then very careful diet.'

'We need have no fears,' said Daisy. 'Miss Grant is in charge of this section and she will see that everything is as you say it should be.'

'Yes, indeed I will, Miss Hetherington.'

'Well, I'm sorry we had to call you out, Doctor,' went on Daisy.

'Oh, that can't be helped, Miss Hetherington.'

'I think you had better take a little brandy before Rolt drives you back.'

'Thank you. That would be pleasant.'

They went off leaving me in the room with the two girls.

'I should try to get some sleep now, Eugenie,' I said.

'I was so frightened, Miss Grant. She looked so ill. I thought she was going to die. Did I look as ill as all that?'

'Yes, you looked quite ill . . . and see how you recovered. Now go to sleep and in the morning your bed will be taken into my room.'

'Yes, Miss Grant.'

She was very subdued and unlike the Eugenie I had known.

On a sudden impulse I tucked her in and kissed her as I might a child. As soon as I had done it I reproached myself. But oddly enough, Eugenie seemed pleased. She smiled and said gently: 'Good night, Miss Grant.'

*   *   *

In the morning Charlotte was still very weak and tired. Daisy brought up two men from the stables to move the bed and this was done quietly and with speed. The doctor came again and I could see that he was more concerned than he had been on the previous night. Then I supposed he had been a little irritated at being called out and been inclined to dismiss Charlotte's indisposition as trivial.

He said: 'It's a case of rather virulent food poisoning.'

Daisy was horrified. She was quite fond of the girls though Charlotte's nature had never been an endearing one, but her real concern was for the school. An elopement

352

last term. A death by poisoning this! That could be fatal for the Academy.

During that first day Charlotte was very ill and Eugenie was very upset indeed. I was surprised that she could show such depth of feeling, even for her greatest friend, for she had never struck me as a particularly affectionate girl.

In a way it made her more vulnerable, more amenable, and oddly enough she seemed to cling to me for comfort. When we were in bed – she in hers under the crucifix which was carved into the wall and I on the other side of the room – she would lie sleepless and I sensed she desperately wanted to talk.

'Miss Grant,' she said on our first night. 'Are you going to marry my uncle?'

I was taken completely by surprise. I stammered: 'My dear Eugenie, what gave you such an idea?'

'Well, he wants to, I know. And he was always trying to be with you . . . though not so much now. I wouldn't mind if you did. You'd be a sort of aunt, wouldn't you? You mightn't like it though. He's not very nice. And Teresa says you are going to marry that other man John Somebody. She says he is lovely . . .'

'Well,' I said, trying to speak lightly, 'you girls seem to have settled my fate.'

'Miss Grant, is Charlotte going to die?'

'Of course not. She'll be better in a few days.'

'Suppose she did. She'd want to confess . . . about that letter.'

'What letter?'

'The one about Mrs Martindale.'

'You sent that. You . . . and Charlotte!'

'Yes. We were so angry with you because you parted us when you first came. Charlotte said we'd have revenge. We'd bide our time, she said. That's what we did and when it seemed as if it might be true, it didn't seem so bad.'

'It was a wicked thing to do.'

'I know. That's why I have to confess . . . in case Charlotte dies with it on her conscience. She wouldn't want that.'

353

'First of all stop talking about Charlotte's dying. You'll laugh at yourself in a few days' time. And as for that letter. It was silly and unkind, and only mean people send anonymous letters. Your accusations are quite untrue. Your uncle says that Mrs Martindale went to London. If she wants to do that it is no one's concern. Never do such a thing again.'

'But you forgive us?'

'Yes, I do, but remember . . . it was mean and cruel and wicked.'

'All right. I'll tell Charlotte if she's well enough.'

'Yes do, and tell her that I think you were two silly and immature girls . . . and that's an end to the matter.'

'Oh, thank you, Miss Grant.'

After that she seemed to get quite fond of me and I liked her better too. She had been worried about that letter and that did show some finer feelings. I forgot how it had upset me and had really changed my feelings towards Jason; but it was a relief to know that at least that unsavoury matter was cleared up.

During the next day Charlotte seemed a little better, but still very weak, and she hardly noticed that Eugenie was not in her room.

It was Eugenie's second night in my room when I made the shattering discovery which was to open my eyes and make me realize that I was in the midst of some sinister and dangerous conspiracy.

Eugenie lay in her bed, ready for what seemed to be becoming a bedtime chat – a mark of our new relationship.

'Charlotte was all right during the day before she was so ill, and she was laughing and joking. She said she was going to see if she could jigjag the toboggan down the slopes the next day and to see if we could skate on the fish ponds. They were frozen then.'

'I hardly think Miss Hetherington would allow that.'

'We were sure she wouldn't.'

'And you wouldn't be so foolish as to attempt such a thing without first asking permission.'

'Oh no, Miss Grant, we shouldn't have done that.'

354

'You do realize it could be very dangerous.'

'I think that was why Charlotte liked the idea. She was laughing about it. She was so well. She had a second helping of soup. She said it was too salty and it made her thirsty, so later on she drank my milk as well as her own. I didn't want mine. So it didn't matter.'

I had been thinking of the girls' attempting to skate on the fish ponds and was pulled up sharp.

'What did you say? She drank your milk?'

'Yes. She was so thirsty. The soup was too salty.'

I felt myself turn cold. Charlotte had drunk the milk intended for Eugenie and she had been ill as Eugenie had previously . . . when presumably Eugenie had drunk her own milk.

'Are you asleep, Miss Grant?'

'No . . . no,' I said faintly.

I was thinking of the milk which was served to the girls. Milk and two plain biscuits . . . the last thing before they retired to their rooms. I visualized the maids going round the tables and the tin of biscuits. The maids took it in turn to do this duty.

I heard myself say: 'So . . . Charlotte drank your milk?'

'Yes. It shows she was all right because she drank her own as well.'

'Who gave you the milk? Do you remember?'

'No . . . It was one of the maids. I wasn't noticing because Charlotte had this idea about skating on the ponds.'

'I wish you could remember.'

'Well, you don't always notice the maids, do you? They all look alike in their black dresses and white caps.'

I was thinking: Am I dreaming this? Eugenie sick three times . . . and when Charlotte drinks the milk intended for Eugenie she is ill. I wished Eugenie would stop chattering inconsequentially and would concentrate on this.

'She's good fun and she's clever. It did come out all right though we thought of it as a joke at first.'

'What?' I said absently.

'Oh, she knows a lot about old legends.' I realized then

355

that she was talking about Elsa. 'Do you believe in them, Miss Grant? She said if we went into the wood at full moon time one of us would meet our future husband . . . and it happened to Fiona.'

'What?' I cried, sitting up.

'What's wrong, Miss Grant?' asked Eugenie.

I must be careful, I thought. This is becoming frightening.

'Tell me more about that,' I said.

'It was May Day. That's a special night for the old religions. Druids and all that, I think. Elsa said all sorts of things could happen on certain days and if we waited till the moon was full and went into the forest even in daytime, which was the only time we could go anyway, we'd meet a man . . . We laughed and didn't believe it and we said we'd go into the woods and when we got back tell Elsa we had met a man, but when we went into the woods, there he was . . .'

My mouth was dry and I found it difficult to speak.

I said at last, 'So you met this man and Fiona ran away with him.'

'Yes. It was so romantic.'

'Eugenie,' I said, 'what was the name of the man you met in the woods.'

'It was Carl.'

'Carl What?'

'I never heard his other name. Fiona talked about him as Carl.'

'And you and Charlotte helped her to elope.'

'Yes, we did. On that night when we went to the Hall.'

'And you found a monk's robe so that he could come to the pageant?'

'It was so exciting. He had to see her that night to tell her what time she was to meet him. They were going to London first. We thought it was the most fantastic thing.'

'Eugenie,' I said quietly. 'Miss Eccles says you have a real talent for drawing.'

'Oh does she? I love it. It's my favourite subject. I wish I could do it all the time.'

356

'Could you draw me a picture of Fiona's husband?'

'Oh . . . I could try. I'll do it in the morning.'

'I want you to do it now.'

'Now, Miss Grant? When I'm in bed?'

'Yes,' I said. 'Now. I want to see it now.'

I got out of bed and found a pencil and paper. She sat up in bed and using a book as a prop, started to draw, screwing up her face in concentration.

'He's very good-looking. It's hard to do. It's a bit like him though. Yes, he's very good looking. His hair is fair. It curls a bit . . . like that. His face . . . well, it's different from other people's faces. There's a look in his eyes . . . I can't get that.'

'Go on,' I said. 'It's coming.'

And so it was. The face that looked back at me bore a strong resemblance to that of the stranger in the forest.

I took it from her and put it carefully in a drawer. I was not sure what I was going to do now. I had made a discovery so startling that it numbed me.

I could not think what it meant.

'It's funny you should want it now,' began Eugenie.

'It's getting late,' I said. 'I think we ought to go to sleep.'

She lay back and closed her eyes. 'Good night, Miss Grant.'

'Good night, Eugenie.'

I was saying to myself, Fiona's husband was Lydia's husband. Lydia died skiing and he is teaching Fiona to ski. I was sure now that someone was trying to poison Eugenie, and that someone must be Elsa who was deeply involved in this macabre affair.

I must act quickly. But how?

357

The Meeting in the Mountains

*

I did not sleep at all that night, and the first thing in the morning I went to see Daisy. I had decided that I must lay the whole matter before her and I began by my account of my meeting with the stranger in the forest. She listened in silence.

Then she said: 'I think that you and I should go immediately to the Hall and tell Sir Jason this fantastic story. It seems that Eugenie may be in danger.'

I agreed and felt considerably better than I had during the night.

Early as it was, we rode over to the Hall. Sir Jason was out riding, which he apparently did before breakfast, and when he returned was astonished to see us.

Miss Hetherington said: 'You had better tell the story, Cordelia, just as you told it to me.'

So I did.

'It seems clear,' said Daisy, 'that this maid of ours is connected in some way with the man who makes a practice of meeting girls in the forest and presumably sweeping them off their feet.'

'Clear enough,' said Jason. 'It is obvious that he intended the same fate for you, Cordelia.'

'I think I know now why he disappeared so suddenly. It was when he learned that my aunt was selling up the Manor. He then went to Lydia and now Fiona. Is there any reason why there should be this attack on Eugenie?'

'I can think of one,' said Jason. 'Fiona inherits the entire fortune which was left to the girls if her sister dies.'

'So Elsa is trying to dispose of Eugenie. How diabolical!'

'It will be Fiona's turn next.'

358

'The man is a mass murderer!' said Daisy turning pale.

'I believe that is what is emerging,' I said. 'His accomplice works at fashionable schools where wealthy young ladies will be. She selects the most desirable, tells them of legends and gets them to a spot where the man can emerge, sets out to charm and decide who shall be his next victim. Lydia had a small fortune. She died on the ski slopes. Do you realize he is teaching Fiona to ski?'

'My God!' said Jason. 'We've got to find her.'

'How?' I asked. And we were all silent.

'He told me that he lived in a place in Suffolk,' I said. 'I went to this place and discovered that a family named Dowling had lived there. There was a son and a daughter and this man might have been the son. He told me his name was Compton, but the Comptons had been dead for twenty years. I imagine he gave me the name at random, but the fact that he chose that name and place shows he must have had a connection with it at some time. I think we ought to find out more about that family. In the meantime what are we going to do?'

'We've got to find Fiona,' repeated Jason.

'You went looking for her without success. There is one thing that occurs to me. Fiona appears to be safe while Eugenie lives. He wants the whole of the fortune . . . not merely half. That is Fiona's safeguard.'

'I think Eugenie should be taken away,' said Daisy.

'I agree,' I said. 'Elsa . . . if it is Elsa . . . has tried to poison her. I can see it now. She was trying to do it gradually so that when the final dose was administered it would appear that Eugenie had had a more virulent attack than those from which she had been suffering. Perhaps the dose taken by Charlotte was meant to be the final one. Charlotte has been very ill and it may well be that Eugenie, weakened as she was, would have succumbed.'

'It would be incredible if there was not so much evidence to make it plausible,' said Jason. 'We've got to act promptly.'

'I wish I knew how,' I said.

'Let's think. Let's try to see all the implications. That

359

man has Fiona. He has married her. We don't know in what name. We don't know where his is.'

'He was Mark Chessingham for Lydia Markham.'

'He wouldn't use the same name again.'

'No. Eugenie says he was Carl Someone. She had never heard his surname.'

'What are we going to do, go raging round Europe again looking for a man named Carl with a wife named Fiona? Not very helpful, I'm afraid. I think we have to go to the police. This man has to be found quickly.'

'There is something that has occurred to me,' I said.

They looked at me expectantly. 'Yes,' I said slowly, 'Mrs Baddicombe has her uses. I thought she was a silly old scandalmonger but I'm feeling quite fond of her just now. Elsa writes letters to someone abroad . . . She writes fairly regularly. He isn't always in the same place because Elsa has to ask Mrs Baddicombe the price of stamps, so our postmistress knows that she has been writing to Switzerland, France, Germany and Austria. She also knows the gender of the recipient of these letters. A man. Now if Elsa is writing letters to her accomplice, and I assume that that is who it is, it must be very likely that he is writing back to her.'

'I see,' said Daisy, looking at me with approval.

'If we could get hold of one of those letters it will tell us something.'

'It should be fairly easy to do that,' said Daisy. 'As you know one of the men from the stables goes and collects the mail every day because it's too far for the postman to come right out here. He usually leaves it with one of the maids. I can give instructions that he brings it straight to me.'

'I daresay Elsa is on the lookout for the return of the man with the post.'

'That can easily be dealt with,' said Daisy. 'I will vary the man's time of calling so that she suspects nothing. What do you think?' She was looking at Jason.

He said: 'Yes, do that. But we can't wait for posts. I shall go to London today and in the meantime I think Eugenie should come to the Hall.'

360

'We should have to have a good excuse for her doing so and a plausible tale to give the girls,' said Daisy.

'We could say that you have special guests you want her to meet and that she is breaking up a week or so before the rest of the school,' I added.

'We'll manage something,' said Daisy. 'What about Charlotte? I'm a little uneasy about her.'

'Let her be moved to the Hall. She is fit to travel now and she can keep Eugenie company. I think we shall have to explain to the girls . . . I mean Charlotte and Eugenie.'

Daisy looked at me. 'You know them well.'

'I am not sure of that. But in Eugenie's present mood I think I might be able to talk to her. As for Charlotte, she is too weak to argue. We could say we are taking them for a drive, get them to the Hall, and tell them they are to stay there.'

'I'll leave that to you, Cordelia,' said Daisy, dismissing the matter with that air of breezy finality which she used when assigning difficult tasks to her employees.

'Bring her over this morning then,' said Jason. 'I'm going to make arrangements to go to London to put something in motion. There is so little to go on.'

'I pin my faith on a letter,' I said. 'I think there must be a fairly frequent correspondence.'

I went up to my room. Charlotte was sitting in a chair looking pale and listless. I asked how she was and she said she was feeling tired of being in her room all day.

'Would you like to go for a drive?' I asked.

She brightened and said she would.

'Then I'll get Eugenie to come along with us.'

So far so good. I felt a great deal better now I was taking some action.

Eugenie was delighted to miss lessons and take a ride with Charlotte.

'Where are we going?' asked Eugenie.

'We're going to the Hall.'

'To see Uncle Jason?'

'I don't know whether he's there.'

'He was yesterday,' said Eugenie.

361

'We'll see,' I replied.

When we arrived at the Hall I went in with the two girls. Charlotte was clearly exhausted and I asked one of the servants to take us to a room which had been prepared for her.

'Am I going to lie down?' she asked.

'You feel like it, don't you?'

'Just for a little while.'

'You can lie down, and Eugenie and I will sit with you. I want to tell you both something.'

When she was lying down, I opened the connecting door between that and the next room which was also a bedroom.

I said: 'Now I want you to listen to me carefully. You're going to stay here for a while.'

'Stay here?' cried Eugenie. 'What about school?'

'Well, you have both been very ill . . . mysteriously ill. We thought it would be better if you stayed here until break-up. Then I don't know what Charlotte's plans are but you'd be coming here in any case, Eugenie.'

'What will Miss Hetherington say?'

'She knows. In fact it is her idea and mine and your uncle's. We want you to stay here because there may be something at school which is not good for you.'

They were silent, looking at each other, and I could see that neither of them was displeased to have the term cut short.

'I know what it is,' said Eugenie. 'It's drains.'

'Drains?'

'Yes, they make you ill sometimes. I was ill and so was Charlotte and they think we ought to get away. It's something in our room, I expect. Below the window.'

I thought that was an easy way out as I did not want to tell them that we feared an attempt was being made on Eugenie's life.

'Well, you'll have a good time here together, and, Eugenie, you'll look after Charlotte won't you? You'll find plenty to do.'

They looked at each other and laughed.

'What about *Romeo and Juliet*?' asked Charlotte.

362

'Alas poor Romeo,' said Eugenie. 'You were quite good, Charlotte. I could never get my lines right. Who'll take our places.'

'I think it is being eliminated,' I said. 'They'll just have to do with *The Merchant of Venice.*'

Charlotte looked regretful.

'You wouldn't be well enough,' I said. 'Think how you would have hated to see someone else do it.'

Realizing that, Charlotte could accept the decision. If Romeo was not Charlotte Mackay, then no one else should be.

I said: 'I shall go back now. Your uncle will be here in a day or so, I believe, Eugenie.'

I left them and went back to school. When I told Daisy what had happened she was at first outraged by any question of the drains at her school being imperfect; but she soon recovered from that and realized that it was better than telling them the truth.

She said: 'I feel very uneasy about that girl Elsa.'

'Yes, but I think it is imperative that she does not know we suspect anything. She need not find out for some little time that Eugenie and Charlotte have gone.'

'And when she does?'

'I think she may begin to wonder. We must be very watchful of her.'

'I should like to put her in custody right away.'

'On what evidence? It is mostly supposition. We must have proof. Let us hope we get that soon. In the meantime let us keep watch on Elsa.'

*   *   *

By the next day the girls were talking about the departure of Eugenie and Charlotte. I had explained that Charlotte needed recuperation and that Eugenie, who was her greatest friend, was with her. Elsa would quickly learn that, and I wondered what she would make of it. She might not be suspicious. On the other hand she would not be able to carry out her plan of murder . . . if we were right in supposing that was what she was doing.

363

Jason returned from London in two days. He had little hope of Fiona and her husband being found. It had been pointed out to him that they could be anywhere in Europe, and that all the information we had was that he called himself Carl and his wife was Fiona.

I waylaid Elsa and tried to discover what she was thinking. She betrayed nothing and I could not help wondering whether I was mistaken about her. She had been at Schaffenbrucken and she was here. But certainly she would never have come to Colby if she had known I was here. She had told the story of meeting a man in the woods. Was it possible that that could be a coincidence? Oh no . . . it was too neat. She was involved. I was sure of that.

I asked if she was looking forward to going home at Christmas.

'Oh yes, to my sister's place. It's a long way from here. Up north.'

'Oh, where?'

'Newcastle.'

'That *is* a long way.'

'Yes, but she's my only sister. Families have to stick together, don't they? I'm lucky to have somewhere to go. You want to be with your family at Christmas time, don't you? Teresa tells me she is going with you.'

'Oh yes . . .'

'I hope Miss Charlotte's getting on all right.'

'I believe so.'

'Poor girl. She was bad. And Miss Eugenie's with her. I'm glad of that. Thick as thieves, those two.'

She went on flicking her duster in the aimless way she had. It was difficult to suspect her.

It was the beginning of the Christmas week and we were breaking up on Wednesday. Rehearsals were over and the great day had come. It was just to be *The Merchant of Venice* which, Eileen said, was a blessing. Nobody seemed to think it was very strange that Charlotte had gone off to convalesce and that Eugenie had gone with her, and Eileen was delighted to be relieved of *Romeo and Juliet*.

Daisy sent for me and when I went to her study she was

364

holding a letter in her hand. It was addressed to Miss Elsa Kracken and the postmark was Austria.

'I think,' she said, 'that this may be what we have been waiting for. I haven't opened it. I think we should be careful about that as it may well be necessary for her to have it and in that case she must not know that we have seen it. I therefore intend to steam it open very carefully and then if necessary we can reseal it.'

We sat down side by side and read the letter:

'Dear Sister,

'What disaster! But you must not blame yourself. These things will happen, and I have told you many times that if we do our best and things go wrong we are not to be blamed. But it was most unfortunate and I am a little alarmed. I sensed danger as soon as I learned that woman was there. Perhaps you should have left after we completed the first part of the plan. If you had we should have finished the project by now. That is what we are going to do. Give your notice at once and tell them that you will not be returning after Christmas. Say it is for family reasons. Make it all very natural. You understand that.

'I know when to say Enough. We will be content with what we have. Our little bird is well endowed and we will accept half because to attempt the rest is clearly dangerous. I shall settle this project once and for all. Perhaps it shall be the last and we shall buy our little mansion somewhere . . . anywhere. It will be a mansion as grand as Compton just like we used to dream about. But we shall be masters of it. It will not be for us as it was for our father. We shall not be the slaves of the rich. They shall be ours . . .

'Most of all, dear sister, I would not have you blame yourself. Circumstances were against us in this instance. I should have been more wary when I heard that woman was there. She has been our evil genius. I was deceived in her in the beginning, and if it makes you feel less guilty, sister, let me remind you that I, too,

365

made my mistakes. I made grave errors. It is so easily done when one is off one's guard. Carelessly I gave her that name which meant so much to us in the past . . . and not only the name but the place as well. I realized immediately what a grave error I had made, but as I said we are all careless at times. That worried me a great deal, I can tell you. But I tell you now to remind you of the mistakes we can make when we are taken off our guard for a moment.

'It was no fault of yours. Your method was right. How did you guess that girl would drink the milk? If you had attempted to stop her as you suggest you should have done that might have been even more disastrous.

'No, stop blaming yourself. Get away and I will finish this project and then we'll be free.

'We have had great success with our plans and if this one is a half success, that is good enough for us.

'You will soon be with me. As soon as you can leave without arousing suspicion come to this hotel. I shall be here for some little time. Until I can say finis.

'In deepest affection, dearest sister,

Your ever loving

Brother

'PS It will be good to have my sister with me. You will be able to comfort me in my "bereavement." '

Daisy and I looked at each other.

'It's true,' cried Daisy. 'The wickedness! And Fiona . . .'

'Fiona is in the gravest danger,' I said. 'But look, we have the address.'

'But not the name.'

'The address is what is important. I think I should take the letter at once to Sir Jason.'

She nodded and within ten minutes I was riding to the Hall.

When Jason read the letter he was deeply shocked.

'What will you do?' I asked.

366

'I shall go to London. There I shall see the police, and then I shall myself go to this place. There must be no delay. Who knows what will be happening to Fiona.'

'Oh Jason,' I said, 'God go with you.'

He paused for just a second; then he put his arms round me and kissed me.

'I must go at once,' he said; and I left him.

Two days later a man called at the school and asked to see Miss Hetherington. He was closeted with her for a short time and when he left Elsa went with him.

'They have been most kind,' said Daisy. 'They did what had to be done with as little fuss as possible.'

'Is it an arrest?' I asked.

She nodded. 'She is arrested on suspicion of being an accomplice to murder.'

We went to her room. In her cupboard we found an array of bottles and some dried herbs.

Daisy smelt them and said: 'She must have made her own poisons. She was a clever girl. It's a pity her talents were so misguided.'

*   *   *

The Merchant of Venice was quite a success and those parents who had come to see it were very impressed.

We waved the girls off for the Christmas vacation. Teresa and I were going to Moldenbury the next day.

'I thought last term was the most extraordinary I have ever known,' said Daisy, 'but this one goes even further than that. I wonder how Sir Jason is faring. Oh dear, I do wish this dreadful business was over. So far, fortunately, the school remains unscathed. I hope there is not going to be too much publicity about that girl working here. When I come to think of that I can't look forward to next term with much comfort.'

Teresa was in high spirits speculating as to which hat Aunt Patty would be wearing and what cake Violet would have baked for tea.

In the train which was taking us to Paddington, as we had

367

a compartment to ourselves, I talked to Teresa. I thought she looked a little uneasy and I asked her if she was worried about something.

'Not now,' she said, 'I think it's going to be all right now. It is wonderful that we are going to Epping for Christmas.'

'I am sure we shall enjoy it.'

'Aunt Patty, Violet, you and I . . . John and Charles. It's going to be lovely.'

'I can't think why, with such a prospect before you, you were looking quite sad a moment ago.'

She was silent for a few seconds, biting her lips and looking out on the fields speeding by. 'There is something I ought to tell you. It won't matter now. It's over. Perhaps . . .'

'You'd better get it off your conscience,' I said.

'Yes,' she said, 'it's safe now. There are Epping and John . . . and I think he's lovely. He's just right.'

'Please tell me, Teresa.'

'I didn't find that earring by the ponds.'

'What?'

'No. It was in Eugenie's room. She had found it in the stables at the Hall and was going to give it back to Mrs Martindale but forgot. It was in the drawer in her room for a long time. So I took it.'

'Oh Teresa . . . you lied.'

'Yes,' she said, 'but I think it was a good lie really. He's a wicked man, Cordelia, and we all knew that he wanted you.'

'Teresa. How could you?'

'Well, people said he'd got rid of her. And they didn't know about the earring. That was only for you. To stop you, to show you . . .'

I was silent.

'Are you very angry with me?' Teresa watched me anxiously. 'I did think that you liked him rather . . . and he is wicked. There's the devil in him. Eugenie said so. She said that you and he . . . That was why I threw my shoe at her. You don't want anything to do with him, Miss Grant. And there are Epping and John . . . and Violet says she

368

wouldn't be surprised if he popped the question pretty soon.'

I said: 'We shall be in Paddington shortly.'

'Are you very angry with me?'

'No Teresa,' I said. 'What you did you did for love. I suppose that excuses most things.'

'Oh good. Shall I get the bags down?'

Aunt Patty embraced us with affectionate delight.

'We're going to Epping the day after tomorrow,' she said. 'I thought you'd want a little time at Moldenbury to get things ready.'

'It'll be such fun,' said Teresa. 'I wish the snow had stayed.'

'Not so easy for getting about, my dear. It might have been so bad that we couldn't have travelled,' Aunt Patty reminded her.

'Well, I'm glad it's gone.'

'Mind you,' went on Aunt Patty, 'the forest would have looked very pretty.'

Violet greeted us with gruff affection and the statement that we must all be gasping for tea.

'There's hot toast over a basin of water so that the butter soaks well in, and keeps it hot at the same time,' she explained. 'And there's lardy cakes to follow because a little bird whispered to me that they were Teresa's favourites.'

The same cosy homeliness. It was hard to believe that it could exist side by side with horrible death.

The next day the letter came. As soon as I saw the Austrian stamp I began to tremble and for a few seconds I was afraid to open it.

It was in a strange hand and it informed me that there had been an accident. Sir Jason Verringer was unable to travel and he was asking for me. His condition was such that I should lose no time.

It was signed with a name I could not decipher but it had the word Doctor underneath it.

Aunt Patty came in. She stared at me and then took the letter from my hand.

369

I said: 'Something terrible has happened. I know it.'

She understood at once because the previous night I had told her everything. Now she looked at me steadily.

'You'll go,' she said.

I nodded.

'You can't go alone.'

'I must go,' I insisted.

'All right,' she replied. 'I'll come with you.'

*   *   *

It was a long and tedious journey across Europe and seemed longer than it actually was, because I was impatient to arrive.

It had not been easy getting away from Moldenbury. Violet was nonplussed and said we were mad – and on the eve of Christmas too! Teresa was angry and sullen.

We tried to explain but it was not easy until Violet grudgingly said that she supposed if Patty thought it was right then it must be. Aunt Patty said that Teresa and Violet should go to Epping without us. There was a great deal of argument, but finally it was agreed that that was what they should do.

Aunt Patty was wonderful during that journey. She said little because that was how she knew I wanted it. She left me with my thoughts and they were all for Jason Verringer.

I learned a great deal during that journey, for all the time I was thinking that I might arrive too late and never see him alive again. I knew that he was in danger: the wording of the doctor's letter had told me that, and while I was looking out of the train windows at hills, rivers and majestic mountains I was trying to imagine what life would be like without him. I had avoided him, but what would it be like if he were not there to avoid?

If he were not there I should never want to go back to the Abbey. There would be a deep sadness in my life and memories which I should strive to forget and never be able to.

'I don't think,' said Aunt Patty suddenly, 'that the doctor

370

would have suggested you make this long journey if there had not been some hope.'

She knew how to comfort me. I could not have borne probing questions, condolences, expressions of sympathy. I might have known that Aunt Patty would understand what was going on in my mind and not attempt to divert my thoughts to subjects which I had no wish to think of.

And so at length we came to Trentnitz.

It was a small hotel, halfway up a mountain – one of the lesser-known resorts for winter sports. We were taken from the station halt to the Gasthof in a kind of sleigh. As soon as we entered the wooden chalet-like building and said who we were, we were told that the doctor was with Sir Jason now and he would certainly see us at once. He had taken the precaution of reserving a room for us, which Aunt Patty and I could share.

The doctor came to us. He spoke fair English and there was no doubt that he was pleased to see us.

'This is what our patient needs,' he said. 'He wants you with him. You are his fiancée, I believe. I am sure that will help.'

'How bad is he?'

'Very bad. The crash was . . .' He lifted his shoulder searching for words. 'It was a great mercy he was not killed with the other. The police will be here. They will wish to see you. But first . . . the patient.'

I went to him immediately. He was in a room with a window open to the mountain. Everything was very white and clean looking. He himself seemed drained of colour and for a few seconds I hardly recognized him.

'Cordelia,' he said.

I went to the bed and knelt down.

'You came,' he whispered.

'As soon as I heard. Aunt Patty is with me.'

'It must be Christmas,' he said.

'Yes.'

'You ought to be at Epping.'

'I think I ought to be here.'

'I'm pretty well smashed up.'

371

'I haven't talked much to the doctor. We've just arrived and he brought me straight to you.'

He nodded. 'I have to learn to walk again.'

'You will.'

'I got *him* though. Fiona's here. You'll have to look after her. She's in a bad state. She's in bed here. We've turned the place into a regular hospital between us.'

'What happened?'

'I found him. It wasn't difficult when I knew where. I just came here. Carl and Fiona . . . That was all I needed. I saw them together. It made me feel I wanted to strangle him with my bare hands. You see, it was the way he behaved to her, so loving and tender and she . . . she was looking at him as though he were some god. I saw them well before they saw me. They were going out skiing and the thought hit me. He could be going to do it then. He might be going to take her out there and stage an accident. The other girl died that way . . . now it was Fiona's turn. So I went after them. When Fiona saw me she cried out in dismay. Then he swung round. It was amazing to see his face. She had called out Uncle Jason . . . and he knew. I said "You murdering swine . . ." and I went for him. We grappled there. I knew what he was after. He was going to send me hurtling down the slope. He knew the place. He was experienced in the snow. He had the advantage. But I was determined to get him. He had me on the edge . . . and I thought, if I'm going over I'm taking him with me. He'll not have a chance to go on with his game of murder. And . . . together we went . . .'

'You should have waited,' I said. 'The police would have got him. They were on the trail. They've arrested Elsa.'

'When would they have got him? After he had murdered Fiona? No. We were dealing with a practised murderer, a man whose business was murder. I knew they would have come in time, but I had to be there . . . right away . . . as soon as I knew. I couldn't let it be too late.'

'What happened to him?'

'The best thing. He was lucky. He broke his neck. I

372

broke lots of things but my neck was intact. I landed in a heap of snow . . . I was buried in it. He went onto hard rock.'

'Does it upset you to talk of it?' I asked.

'No. It does me good. It's Fiona who worries me.'

'I'll see what I can do.'

'Try to explain to her. She won't believe you, but you have to make her. I know it's hard but she can't go on shutting her eyes to the truth. Cordelia . . . it was wonderful of you to come. I suppose I kept asking for you when I didn't know what I was saying.'

'Would you have only asked for me when you didn't know you were?'

'I knew about Epping. Eugenie has kept me well informed. I guessed the rest.'

'Well, I came here instead.'

'Foolish of you.'

'I think it was rather wise. Do you remember you once asked me to marry you?'

He smiled faintly. 'A bit of a braggart, wasn't I?'

'Is the offer still open?'

He did not answer and I went on: 'Because, if it is, I've decided to accept.'

'You're carried away by the emotion of the moment. Pity for the man who will never again be what he was. That is not how it should be between us. There's that paragon awaiting you. He will give you all that a woman could want.'

I laughed.

'What's amusing?' he asked.

'I have been telling you for a long time that I never wanted to see you again and you were insisting that I must. Now, I'm saying I will and you are pointing out the reasons why I should marry someone else.'

'What a perverse pair we are. We've changed. It's been a complete turnabout. You have left the practical schoolmistress in England and I have left the swaggering scoundrel halfway down a mountain. How can people change so much?'

373

'They don't. It is just little facets of their characters being revealed. Do you really love me?'

'Do I have to answer?'

'I want a clear answer.'

'Oh? The schoolmistress is not far away. If it isn't the right answer, take a hundred lines. Of course I love you.'

'Then the matter is settled. You may be the wicked villain with a trace of the devil in him, but haven't I always known how to cope with him?'

'Even in the Devil's Den.'

We were silent. We dared not look at each other for fear of betraying the depth of our emotion. I took his hand and laid it against my cheek.

I said: 'Ever since this happened I have been doing a lot of thinking about you and myself, and coming here in the train when I did not know what I was going to find, I understood myself . . . my feelings . . . and what I wanted. If I had found you dead, I shouldn't have cared very much about living myself. I realized that I had never felt so alive, so much in love with life, as when I was fighting with you. I mean our verbal contests. To whip up my defiance of you, that was the most exciting thing that had ever happened to me. I learned how dull and meaningless life would be without that. I suppose antagonism sometimes conceals attraction.'

'You are talking nonsense,' he said. 'You are carried away by sentimentality. My dear little schoolmistress is doing what she considers the Right Thing.'

'If you don't want to hear any more I'll go.'

'Stay.'

'That sounded like a command.'

'You don't like commands. You make your own decisions.'

'Yes, and I have decided that I am going to stay as long as I like. You're going to get well. I'm going to see to that, and the only way I can do it efficiently is by marrying you. There is only one thing which will stop me and that is if you tell me you don't want me.'

374

'Listen to me,' he said. 'You must wait, Cordelia. You must see what has been done to me.'

'You've saved Fiona's life. Remember that.'

'She won't thank me.'

'She will in time. Now what do you say?'

'You'd be better off with the banker.'

'Shall I go back then?'

'No,' he said. 'Stay. Suppose you married me. How do you know I wouldn't give you a dose of laudanum?'

'I'll take the risk.'

'And suppose I murdered you and put you in the fishponds, or buried your carcass in the Abbey grounds?'

'I'll take that risk too.'

'Imagine the scandal! Mrs Baddicombe will have a field day.'

'I'm feeling rather grateful to Mrs Baddicombe at the moment. I'd be quite happy to provide her with a few items for her repertoire.'

'You won't be serious.'

'I'm deadly serious. I'm going to see the doctor. I want to know exactly what state you're in. I'm going to stay here until I take you back with me.'

I hid my face because I was afraid he would see my tears, and when I looked at him there was a kind of wonder and immeasurable joy in his face.

Revelation

---*---

It was not until the spring that I married Jason. By that time he was able to walk with the aid of a stick. I had been with him for three months in Austria. Aunt Patty had gone home after three weeks. She said that she thought I could manage without her and she wanted to see what Violet was up to.

She had been a great help with Fiona who would not believe that she had been married to anyone other than the romantic hero whom she had always known. He had been tender and loving. I thought how strange that was and I wondered afresh at the complexities of human nature. I supposed that when he was with her he was all she said he was – and yet all the time he was waiting for the opportunity to kill her. I wondered what sort of man he could be to play two such parts with conviction.

There had been a great deal in the papers about the case which was called that of the Satanic Bridegroom. It was revealed that Hans Dowling was the son of a German mother and an English father; he had murdered two women. There was one before Lydia. Evidently it was a method of amassing wealth, for each of the murdered women had left money to him. His big killing was to be that of Fiona and her sister, through which he would get not only Fiona's fortune but that of her sister – which would pass to Fiona on Eugenie's death. It was the prospect of getting Eugenie's money as well as Fiona's which had kept Fiona alive. But for that she would have been despatched long ago.

Jason was my main preoccupation. Together we concentrated on getting him well. There were hours of exercising in which I helped; I was with him all through the days and we often engaged in those stimulating verbal battles which had been a feature of our relationship.

I was happier than I had ever been, once I knew that he was going to recover; and I often marvelled that so much happiness could come out of so much that was evil.

Daisy was grieved that I had not returned to school and that a little of the glory of Schaffenbrucken influence was removed from the school's prospectus; but she made it clear to parents that the young lady who had brought in the Schaffenbrucken influence was to become Lady Verringer, wife of the largest landowner in Devon. And I think she took some comfort from that.

Elsa was extradited and stood on trial in Austria. She had not actually killed, though she was accused of attempted murder and of complicity in murder. She confessed all, which helped Fiona to accept the truth, and she was given a long prison sentence.

There must have been a great deal of talk in Colby and I could imagine what took place in those across-the-counter-parleys in the post office. Daisy wrote to me, most gratified, because no parents had seen fit to remove their daughters.

So we came home and were married in Colby church and the bells rang out on a very different note from that which had heralded my arrival.

Elsa turned out to be an exemplary prisoner and was eventually allowed privileges which enabled her to write a book about her life. It was very revealing.

She explained how she and her family had lived in poverty in the village of Croston in Suffolk. Their mother was thrifty; their father a drunken spendthrift. Before the fire he had worked for the squire, Edward Compton, and after the manor had been burned down he had worked only intermittently and eventually had drunk himself to death. At home the children had spoken German and at the village school English, so they were proficient in both languages. Elsa and her brother Hans were very close; they used to play together in the burned-out ruins and imagine that they owned such a mansion and lived there in splen-

377

dour. Hans vowed that when he grew up he would find a way to own such a place and he and Elsa should live there together. It was the constant dream through the hard years of poverty. Hans had become resentful of the rich. He used to go to the cemetery and look at the grave of Edward Compton. 'You were burned to death,' he would say. 'Serve you right. You had everything. We have nothing. But one day I shall have everything I want . . . Elsa and I together.' They used to go into the church and stand before the plaques and monuments to the Compton family . . . It was a vow. He told Elsa that it was a battle between such as they were and the rich. If the rich had to die to give them what they wanted, then die they must.

Elsa remembered the night she had gone with Hans to the ruins and he had looked at the moon and made a very solemn vow. It was the full moon . . . the Hunter's Moon. He had said, 'I am the hunter. I am hunting for that which I intend to have and when I have it, dear sister, I shall share it with you.' Then he had gone into the church and there solemnly announced his intentions. It was a saying between them: 'Remember the night of the Hunter's Moon.'

Elsa had been pledged to help him. She had been frightened after the first killing, which had been in Norway, but it had been carried out without a hitch. The marriage, an accident in the mountains, a grieving bridegroom who collected the wife's money and passed on. The first had brought small rewards and he had decided to look higher. Then he had heard of Schaffenbrucken – one of the most exclusive and expensive schools in Switzerland. All the young ladies there would be in their mid teens . . . marriageable. And they devised their plan.

It was interesting to read about it, and something of Elsa's character came through in the book. She was fond of people; she liked gaiety and laughter; it was incredible that such a person could light-heartedly contemplate murder.

She made it clear that they had both made damning mistakes. Her brother had made his when he had not found out enough about my expectations and had in a moment of thoughtlessness given me the name of Edward Compton.

He had an almost mystic belief that he was going to succeed in my case because we had met at the time of the Hunter's Moon. It seemed to him a significant time; and that had made him over-confident and so . . . careless. She had made her mistake in staying at the school when she discovered that by an odd quirk of fate I was there.

'It was one of fate's mischievous tricks,' she wrote, 'that we should have chosen a school in which one of our intended victims was working.'

She and her brother used to pick the wild flowers which grew among the ruins of Compton Manor. They read of the properties of these plants both healing and otherwise. They discovered that many of those which people regarded as ordinary flowers could produce deadly poisons. They had embarked on a career of murder and they might need poison. They learned that foxglove contained digitoxin and, though it could be used medicinally, in large doses it could be fatal; the leaves and seeds of the yew contained a deadly toxin; the various fungi growing in woods could produce death. Elsa became expert and distilled the juices, and tried them on animals to test their effectiveness.

'Strangely enough,' she wrote, 'I liked Eugenie. She was one of my favourites among the girls, but when I had to get rid of her I didn't think of her as Eugenie. She was just an object who was stopping our getting the mansion we had dreamed about. Hans said he felt the same. He didn't dislike his victims. He was quite fond of them and even when he committed the act of killing he did it in a cold-blooded aloof sort of way. There was no malice in him towards his victim; it was just part of his grand scheme that they should be removed.'

It was a revealing document. It explained so much about which we had hitherto wondered. I could not, of course, understand Elsa. But then who does fully understand another human being?

Two years after my flight to Austria, Teresa married John Markham. She was then nineteen. She was married from Moldenbury for her parents were still in Rhodesia. She adored him and was supremely happy. I was sure it was

379

a perfect marriage, for if John had ever thought of marriage with me – which I believe he had – and if he had been disappointed when I married Jason, he would accept what had happened and find happiness elsewhere. He was the sort of man who would be successful in anything that came his way and that would include his emotional life. He would be the same good-humoured, loving and tender husband to Teresa as he would have been to me. He was just what Teresa needed.

But all this was some time ahead.

For the time there was my own marriage and the joyous realization that Jason and I were the sort of people who could never have been really happy with anyone but each other.

How we laughed at the excitement in the town. The marriage had completely superseded the great murder mystery which had touched the school.

Memories were revived.

'What about his first wife? Does that schoolmistress *know*? And then there was that Mrs Martindale. He's a one, he is. Well, didn't they say the Verringers had the devil in them?'

We laughed at the gossip. I was rather glad of it. It showed me and Jason without a doubt that I was ready to accept anything for his sake. I wanted him to know that, and to go on remembering it.

It was round about Christmas time, two years after our marriage. We were the proud parents of a son by that time.

Jason was very anxious that we should go to London.

'You can shop,' he said. 'There must be lots of things you want.'

I was not averse. I had an excellent nanny for young Jason and I had no qualms about leaving him.

When we arrived at the London house, Jason said he wanted to take me to the theatre, for there was a play he particularly wanted to see. I was amused when we arrived to see that it was *East Lynne* and when I glanced at the programme the names seemed to rush up at me. 'Marcia

380

and Jack Martindale. Together again in their original roles.'

The curtain went up and there she was. The Lady Isabel.

I don't know how I sat through the play, and afterwards we went backstage to see her and Jack.

'Miraculously risen from his watery grave,' I said.

'Oh, he's a survivor,' replied Marcia dramatically.

We told her about the speculation in Colby about her departure, which she thought was highly diverting. So did the hardy Jack.

'I tell you what we'll do,' she said. 'We'll pay a call this Christmas. Won't that be fun, Jack? We'll ride through the streets and show all those dear old gossips that we are still on Earth.'

They did. Marcia insisted on showing Rooks' Rest to Jack and going to visit her dear little baby on the moor.

We were delighted to see their departure and we laughed a great deal about them.

'They'll act their way through life,' said Jason.

'I'm wondering what Mrs Baddicombe will have to talk about now.'

'I'm rather sorry in a way,' he said. 'I always used to say to myself. She must love me a great deal to marry me when there's this cloud of suspicion hanging over me.'

'Well, now you can tell yourself that there was never any reason to doubt it.'

'No. And yet it never ceases to amaze me. There's a great deal you don't know about me.'

'I'm glad,' I said. 'I shall look forward to improving my education.'

381